MW01126704

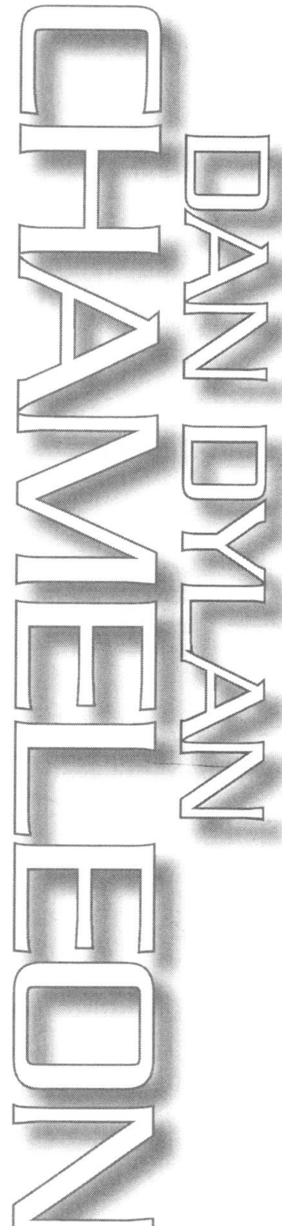
DAN DYLAN
CHAMELEON

CHAMELEON

ISBN: 1439234140
ISBN-13: 9781439234143
Library of Congress Control Number: 2009902658

ACKNOWLEDGEMENT

Seldom is a book the product of one individual's efforts. A work of fiction by a first-time author requires the encouragement and support of caring family, friends, and colleagues. So it is with heartfelt thanks that I acknowledge the following individuals for reading—sometimes more than once—and offering valuable critiques: Katy, Cheryl, Nicole, Ellen, Matt, and Marty, my intrepid typist who began this adventure with me more than ten years ago.

To my editor/wife, who told me "just to write," you knew there was, within me, a story with a purpose, and you never doubted.

Dan

To Brenda

Glad you enjoyed

CHAMELEON

Dan Dylan

Chameleon (**ka·mē′lē·ən**) **n. 1. A tropical lizard (genus *Chameleon*) with a long protrusible tongue, prehensile limbs and tail, and the power of changing its color. 2. A person of changeable character or habits like a chameleon.**
[<L *chamaeleon*; <Gk. *chamailleōn*; < *chamai*, on the ground + *leōn*, lion]

(Webster's Dictionary of the English Language, Deluxe Edition, Copyright 1992)

It's easy to come and go when you're able to change at will...to blend in, to hide, unseen and unknown

Eddie Vinson

CHAPTER ONE
MARCH 2000

Eddie Vinson lit a second cigarette from the butt of the first, which he smashed in the muddy dregs of a Styrofoam cup. He exhaled and smoke coiled toward the ceiling. In the stillness, two other paramedics slept restively. Eddie focused momentarily on the muted infomercial for cheap gym equipment that repeated hourly. There had been no calls since 11:30 p.m. when he came on duty; some nights were like that, but not many. Just as he was nodding off, an incoming call fractured the silence.

"First Alert Emergency Services," Eddie answered, controlled and professional.

A frantic woman babbled something about a motor vehicle accident. "Hurry, please!" she begged. "There are people trapped...in a turned-over van. We tried to get 'em out, but we can't."

"What's the address, ma'am?" Eddie asked calmly.

"Central Avenue, a block south of Roosevelt Road!"

"Get your rears in gear!" Eddie prodded a groggy Rizzo who emerged from the supply room, and Jenny who was also shrugging off sleep. He grabbed a duffel bag and his hat. "Sounds like we've got a bad one on Central." He snagged the keys off the board, and pushed through the swinging glass door to the covered portico where the life support vehicle was parked. He felt the predictable jolt of adrenaline as he slid behind the wheel. Tony Rizzo pulled shotgun, and Jenny Fox entered through the back of the van to prep equipment they would probably need once they arrived on the scene.

Driving fast was a definite job perk for Eddie. He could break speed limits, run red lights, force people over. In more frivolous moments, he imagined ramming vehicles that showed the audacity to get in his way. Eddie hit the siren and stomped his foot to the floor. "Don't ya just love this?" he yelled over the wail because he knew Tony hated these high-speed trips; as usual, Rizzo held the bar above the door in a death grip, and his eyes darted side-to-side.

As the speedometer cruised past seventy miles per hour, Eddie wove in and out among the few late-night travelers on Central. He was focused, pumped. Mayhem was out there; death could be waiting. He felt like this on every call. The worse the accident, the greater the thrill, and he pitied Tony for not being able to feel it.

The night was clear, cold, and dry; though it was already March, winter was hanging on tenaciously. Seven minutes had passed since the incoming alert. A block up and over, Eddie could see dust swirling in the air, or maybe it was smoke. As he wheeled to the right, Tony tensed and muttered, "Looks like fire."

Stellar! *Blood, guts, and terror, in spades*. They did for Eddie now what drugs had done for him in his twenties. He pulled in beside two police cars. Their blue and white lights pulsed into the cloudless night, creating a surrealistic scene with images he filed in memory for later use—privately.

Jenny was first out of the vehicle. She ran to a young girl, maybe six years old, who lay twisted and bleeding against a wire fence. Most of her clothing had been peeled from her body by the impact of the wreck. The child looked dead.

Not for the first time, Eddie imagined how death must feel...natural forces converging at a single time and place. He had sensed that focus in his work with the dying. He jolted back to the present as Tony shoved him roughly and urged, "Let's get going!"

"All right, all right...just do what you do, and I'll take care of me," snapped Eddie. "I'll take the van. You see to the guy in the bushes."

An obese white male lay curled in a fetal position beneath a spiky hedgerow. A cop was already kneeling beside the victim, holding his head, talking to him softly, probably encouraging him to hold on, or some such crap for which the police are famous. It was obvious the man was critical, and the policeman was afraid to move him. Tony sat on the frigid ground to check the victim's vitals.

Eddie shouldered a fire extinguisher and sprinted toward the front of the overturned van. One wheel continued to spin lazily. He slowed, glided through the kaleidoscope of flashing red, blue, and white lights, and surprised the shit out of a cop who was standing by the vehicle.

"Damn!" said the cop, "Where the hell did you come from?" Eddie ignored him and circled the van, looking for leaking fuel or other hazards. He blanketed a small mound of smoldering brush with foam, but the gas tank appeared to be undamaged.

Completing his inspection, Eddie returned to the front of the vehicle. Acknowledging the policeman with a nod, he knelt to examine the remaining occupants of the upside-down van. Two women were suspended by their seatbelt harnesses and tangled in the deflated pillows of the airbags; both were unconscious. Eddie flashed back to childhood days when he would capture beetles and ladybugs; he'd flip them onto their backs so they struggled frantically, unable to right themselves without his help, which he could give, or not. *Hell,* he thought, *this isn't any different. I'm still in control.*

"What are you going to do?" questioned the cop, his breath visible as he spoke.

Eddie dropped to his belly and reached in the passenger-side window to check vital signs of the nearest victim. The woman appeared to be in her forties, thin, well dressed. Blood soaked her slacks and blouse, dribbled onto her chin and into her left nostril. She had lost a lot of blood, and Eddie couldn't find a pulse. "She's gone," he said.

"Shit," shuddered the cop. "How 'bout the other one?"

Eddie edged around to the front of the van. The windshield had popped out on impact so he was able to slither through the opening to gain access to the driver. She looked to be in her early twenties, medium build, full breasts. One breast was partially exposed, and he admired its pale curve and pink nipple. He could hear the rasps of her breathing as he inched his way over the dashboard. The steering wheel had pinned the woman in such a way that she was pressed into her seat.

"Miss, can you hear me? Miss?"

Seconds passed. Then, slowly, the victim opened her eyes and looked directly at Eddie. Her anguish was palpable. As had happened before, he was suddenly ablaze in heat, a flash-fire of arousal which peaked, not in ejaculation, but in a powerful orgasmic sensation nevertheless.

"Where am I?" the woman asked.

"You've been in an accident. I'm here to help you," said Eddie, infusing his voice with a soothing gentleness. "I've got to check you over before I dare move you." He liked this part best. He could toy with the victim, in this case, the woman, touch her anywhere, and she would accept, no, appreciate, every gesture from an EMT who was there to rescue her. Eddie leisurely fondled the woman. Lovemaking with his wife couldn't come close to the exhilaration he felt in such moments...total illicit control of another individual, and the assurance that he could get away with it.

Eddie continued to maintain eye contact with the woman as he caressed her most intimate places. She gasped with shock when his fingers stroked firmly between her legs on his way to the ragged gash on her thigh, but he smiled reassuringly and her breathing calmed.

"You're fine," Eddie smirked. *Mighty fine!*

Miraculously, the young woman had not sustained any serious breaks or lacerations, and she could be extricated from the vehicle without apparent risk of additional injury. Eddie cut the seatbelt with a snick of the illegal stiletto he carried in his back pocket. He eased the woman onto her side, then onto her back, and used the deflated airbag to wrap and protect her from broken glass. Then, beckoning to the cop for assistance, he began to slide her out through the windshield opening. Together, they placed her on a stretcher, and as a precaution, Eddie secured a neck brace. He scanned the scene as they rolled the stretcher to a second ambulance that had just arrived. They loaded the stretcher, and then assisted Jenny with the loading of her child victim who had been stabilized. It appeared that the child would make it, as well. The ambulance departed immediately.

Tony's male victim was dead at the scene, so he assisted Eddie in removing the woman DOA from the van. They loaded the two casualties into their vehicle, and followed their colleagues to the nearest hospital, in this case, Berwyn's McNeal Memorial.

Eddie never stuck around the hospitals if he could help it. More often than not, the EMTs would be pressed into service by overwhelmed ER staff. When he spotted another First Alert ambulance ready to leave, Eddie gave Tony a thumbs-up, and, with no further explanation, he shagged a ride back to base. Ignoring the time clock, he cut out twenty minutes early. *Let 'em prove it*, he thought as he pulled his keys from beneath the car seat.

Heading home, Eddie fought to douse the adrenaline as he drove. He opened his window and inhaled the fresh air of a luminescent dawn. It was the only time he could breathe freely—that brief period when the toxins of the city had been cleansed by night, and before they began to accumulate again, as they always did.

Eddie didn't want a long, drawn-out exchange with his wife and niece who would just be getting up. Maybe they were still in the shower, or whatever. He entered the house quietly from the garage. Sonya was standing by the coffeepot at the kitchen counter; she wore her ratty yellow robe. God! He hated that thing. She held out a steaming mug to him. He nodded his thanks, touched her shoulder briefly, and kept going. "Rough night...shower and bed," he mumbled through a jaw-wrenching yawn.

As the stinging shower sluiced down his scalp and back, Eddie thought about the night's one emergency run. For the two dead, he felt no sorrow; they were the lucky ones...worthy of his respect. They had crossed over. The younger woman, she had been good for a hard-on and a pleasurable rush; she and the kid would survive. Better luck next time.

Eddie slid between the sheets and covered his nakedness. No sense giving Sonya ideas. He shut his eyes and drifted. *The peace of the innocent,* he smiled...and slept.

With another night shift ahead of him, the last of this rotation, Eddie surveyed the Chicago west-side headquarters of First Alert Emergency Services. The place was large, surgically clean, almost sterile; the corners of the white room were blurred, indistinct in the icy glare of the florescent overheads. There were no windows to relieve the starkness, no pictures on the walls, only a tasteful grouping of plaques and framed certificates attesting to the qualifications and good works of the paramedics. His name wasn't among them; it never would be. He would move on long before his name was engraved on any plaque.

Eddie wore jeans and a T-shirt, battered Nikes, and a blue windbreaker with the First Alert logo. He stood five feet, ten inches. He had a muscular frame, probably due, at least in part, to his teen-age obsession with weightlifting. He had sandy blond hair, gray eyes flecked with black, like granite, a dominant chin, and an aquiline nose that divided his face cleanly. The years had been good to him, thirty-five in all, despite the drug and alcohol abuse of his twenties. He still struggled to keep a grip on these compulsions, not all that successfully in recent months, because, under the influence, he had learned the hard way, he was less adept at keeping straight all the cons he had going at any one time. *Mustn't be sloppy,* he chided himself.

Eddie had been a Chicago paramedic for seven years although he was new to First Alert. The company afforded him a leg up and a ten-thousand-dollar per year raise. The money was nice, Eddie thought, but not crucial; he'd accepted the position because it was time to move on, and because First Alert was a bigger, more prestigious firm that conferred greater stature among his colleagues.

Technically, as a new FA employee, Eddie was supposed to be gaining additional training. *As if these yo-yo's could teach me anything...as if I need to learn any more. I know my shit.*

Of the First Alert staff Eddie had already worked with, Jenny Fox was the most likeable. She was genuine, earnest, and hard-working. She had the longest service record with FA. She was thirty-two years old and plain; however, she had piercing blue eyes that sometimes made him uncomfortable as he sensed she saw more of him than he wished to reveal. Jenny had fine sable-brown hair that she tamed in an unflattering ponytail while she worked. He had seen her on other occasions when her hair flowed like silk around a body too slight and angular for his taste. At the moment, Jenny was trying to sleep; he'd seen her drop off between one breath and the next. Because she was on her back, Eddie could watch the rhythmic rise and fall of her supple breasts, the best feature of her slender frame. As he studied her, he lit up an unfiltered Camel. He enjoyed these quiet moments; he knew that they were usually precursors to havoc, as had happened last night.

In emergency situations, he and Jenny sometimes shared eye contact over a broken body ejected from a vehicle, or the bloodied victim of a drive-by. In that eye contact, Eddie had been aware of a threatening intimacy. He shied from such thoughts and dragged deeply on the cigarette. As he exhaled, Jenny rolled onto her side, and the smoke seemed to caress the contours of her body.

Eddie's mind often took him places; sometimes to quirky or frivolous places; sometimes to black, unspeakable places. For the moment, he considered what it might be like to tend to Jenny if she were an accident victim. In her pain...perhaps, at her last breath...he wondered if they would share that same connection. Eddie imagined it would be a safe intimacy for him then, because she would die, and her knowledge of him would die with her. No one would know. *No one can know.*

Again, Jenny stirred, and her sigh broke Eddie's concentration. Fear arrowed through him. Could his thoughts have communicated themselves to her? Could she be that attuned to him? He flushed at such foolishness. Of course, Jenny was unaware of his preoccupation with her, although she had once hinted that she might be interested in a relationship with him. He had purposely missed the hint, and she never mentioned it again. He wasn't interested in sex with a co-worker; an affair was out of the question, too intrusive, too confining. *Mustn't mix roles*, he thought. *Each one played must be pure*.

Eddie's other co-worker was Tony Rizzo. Although he and Eddie had never been particularly simpatico, they worked well together. Tony was about six feet, rugged, and strong as an ox. More than once, his brute strength had saved a life. Just in the short time he'd been with First Alert, Eddie had seen Tony pull out a jammed car door and remove debris from a wreck that no two people could have lifted.

Rizzo was black-haired, olive-complexioned, and Italian-handsome, at least women seemed to think so. He had the square, chiseled jaw of a B-movie leading man. He must have had a few fights in his day, however, because his nose was flattened unnaturally, and that alone kept him from being beautiful. His eyes revealed a gentleness that belied Tony's size and strength, and gave away his soft heart and sensitivity.

Eddie had seen Rizzo become tearful while working over a woman or child victim. A few weeks back, as they had stowed their gear after a particularly gruesome fatal accident involving a mother and two small children, he had asked Tony why he was crying.

"Don't you feel their pain?" Tony asked.

"Yeah, man," Eddie responded, not because it was true, but to keep Tony talking.

"It's like I can feel the pain deep in my gut, actually... deep in my groin. It's the damnedest thing." Tony wiped his streaming eyes and nose. "I've had this thing since I was a kid."

Maudlin schmuck! thought Eddie, and rolled his eyes.

Turning back to Tony, he said, "Yeah, sometimes it happens, but I've found a way to channel the feelings that works for me."

Tony stilled and focused on him. "What do you mean?" he queried, "What do you do?"

Eddie felt a rush. He paused, drawing out the moment, watching Tony's eyes; he lowered his voice and said, "I jerk off, you know...." *That oughta screw him up real good.*

Eddie enjoyed confusing people, combining violence and sex in subtle ways. His jaw clenched as he clamped down on the smile that threatened his con.

Tony looked baffled and his tears spilled over again.

Eddie said nothing more and let time spin out.

Tony turned away, clearly taken aback. He fished for his handkerchief, which carried the blood of the infant boy they had been unable to save. He focused on the rusty stain, and a sob tore from his throat.

CHAPTER TWO

Eddie Vinson's childhood had been punctuated by a string of dysfunctional moments that eventually shaped his personality, and not for the better.

Eddie was a deceptively skinny kid, but sinewy and strong, and he garnered a grudging respect from peers who'd learned the hard way not to mess with him. He was soft-spoken, although he had a deep voice that could mesmerize and command attention, if and when he chose. He looked pretty much like any other kid in his neighborhood. He was fair-skinned with a generous crop of freckles splattered across his cheeks, which made him look young and innocent. Eddie had massive hands, however, and his grasp of a football was the stuff of neighborhood legends. He moved effortlessly, gracefully, a natural athlete; yet he knew how ordinary he appeared to others, and, early on, he learned to use his nondescript features to advantage.

Eddie thought of himself as superior, and he honed his natural abilities. He liked to confound his "friends" by creating subtle changes in his appearance or demeanor. He could change his behavior at will, barely noticeable differences that, nevertheless, unnerved his peers, his teachers, and even his parents, and gave him his leverage. It could be as simple as parting his hair on the left instead of the right, or rolling his Levis up one turn too many, exposing his ankles as though he'd shot up over night. He might walk with a subtle limp and then abandon it mid-stride.

His social style emerged from such subterfuge. Eddie called it, "Keep 'em guessing." He thought of "them" as fools, living for the next breath, the next meal; keeping to the familiar; avoiding danger, and fearing risk. He, on the other hand, relished risk and courted danger. He embraced change, found it thrilling. By age ten, Eddie had begun to think of himself as a chameleon. Controlling others by means of manipulation and deception became his credo, his modus operandi. How else could he escape the insanity his parents had forced upon him?

At eleven, Eddie moved with his parents to yet another trailer park, this one on the outskirts of the southwest Chicago industrial park where his father worked, as did most of the neighborhood residents. The dome of sky over their huddled tin-can community was often weird, polluted orange or gaseous lime. The air stunk; morning, noon, and night, its cloying odor, like burnt fish, smothered the unfortunates who lived there, and Eddie was, sadly, one of them.

When not in school, Eddie was usually alone, bored out of his skull, while his parents worked. He hated the pinched, crammed-in feeling he got from the sardine can in which they lived, and he resented like hell that his mother and father had relegated him to a do-nothing life under the inversion of toxic air, seemingly without a thought for his wants or needs.

Looming above and beyond the trailer tops were gigantic white petroleum tanks, seemingly benign marshmallow look-alikes, which dotted the fields for as far as Eddie could see. Marshmallows, ha! With near-nuclear capabilities! He envisioned the tanks exploding. Better still, he imagined himself blowing them!

Eddie wondered how his busy ant-like neighbors would feel if the petroleum bombs exploded. He conjured up hundreds, maybe thousands, of silently screaming, writhing souls drenched in liquid fire, flesh charring, curling and peeling like so much barbecued pork that was always served at the pathetic company-sponsored family picnics. From bosses to janitors, they would fry while he watched from the safety of a well-chosen hiding place.

CHAPTER THREE

Chicago has more psychologists per capita than necessary. Nevertheless, John Foster, Ph.D. enjoyed a solid professional reputation. He had opened a west-side practice as a clinical psychologist several years ago, after putting in his twenty with the FBI. At retirement, he had served nine years as a profiler for the Behavioral Sciences Unit. He had worked cases for serial killers, murderers and rapists, and, more recently, terrorists wanted by various state and federal agencies. He had been challenged by the work at the time, but grew weary, and, by his own assessment, had lost his drive, his edge. Eventually, one case struck too close to home, and he could admit that fear became the deciding factor that pushed him into early retirement.

Foster and his wife had returned to Chicago to be near aging parents. They had chosen a spacious upscale townhouse in a well-maintained section of Oak Park. Ostensibly, they shared a leafy jungle of a courtyard with three families, but because the other residents never availed themselves of it, the courtyard had become Foster's private oasis for unwinding and reflecting at day's end.

The alarm clock blared and the CD feature, for which Foster had paid handsomely so he could enjoy a non-confrontational start to his work days, played the pre-programmed track. *The William Tell Overture*? Oh, he was gonna *kill* Joyce! His eyes flew open to a blurred, Monet-like vision of their bedroom's tranquil, muted colors. He rolled to the edge of the bed. The damned alarm clock was just beyond his fingers. "Where the hell is the off button?"

"First on the right," came a pillow-muffled taunt. "Same place it was yesterday at this time."

"What happened to the *Bolero* I distinctly remember programming yesterday morning?"

No response. He hadn't expected one. Foster stretched and swung his legs to the side of the bed; his feet hit the cool satin finish of hardwood floor. He had wanted thick, cushy carpet, but Joyce pressed for bamboo, and because she so seldom asked for anything, he had agreed. Joyce lay still, buried beneath the down comforter. Rather than short-circuit the rousing overture she had chosen—he was already aroused—he let it continue. *Sauce for the goose!*

He headed for the bathroom, and gave a grudging nod to his reflection as he passed the mirror to get to the john. "Putting on a few pounds, hey, man?"

"You still got it, Babe." Joyce peeked around the corner, catching him mid-stream and in his moment of personal insecurity. She offered a wink and her quirky smile, grabbed her robe, and headed for the kitchen to start the brew.

Actually, Foster thought, he did still have it. He retained his muscular build, for someone who didn't work out any more as he should. He had always enjoyed good health, and, now in his mid-fifties, time had been forgiving. He could pass for five years younger, ten, if you believed his wife.

As he returned to the mirror to examine his prickly morning face, Foster conceded that his hair now had more than the proverbial "hint" of gray, and his jaw line was sagging. He liked to think his sense of humor accounted for the laugh lines radiating from the corners of his eyes, which, according to Joyce, were the color of sinful melted dark chocolate. He had shaggy, untamed eyebrows that children found amusing, and adults, comforting. *Go figure!*

The smell of strong Columbian interrupted his perusal and drew him to the mug on his bedside table. Joyce, sans robe, lay on her side, her elegant back to him. Mug in hand, moving carefully, Foster curled himself around her spoon-fashion. Thirty-four years of marriage, through college years, FBI years, and now, semi-retirement, had layered friendship with humor and unwavering support, and over all, with a passion that was as breathtaking now as the day they met.

"Do you have a full schedule today, John?"

"Kinda...a forensic exam with an accused murderer, and two counseling sessions. The accused is pleading not guilty by reason of insanity, and his attorney has probably prepped him to act crazy. I hate it when they play crazy. Goddamn lawyers, they know just enough to create an image of insanity, but not enough to get their clients through a comprehensive evaluation, thank God. Makes my job harder, though, when they try to fake it."

"I thought you enjoyed the hunt, John." She pulled the covers up and over their heads, for the moment, shutting out the world.

"I do, but these shysters don't have any regard for mental health professionals, and think they can fool us with their bullshit schemes. It just pisses me royal!" He drew the quilt down over their faces, and Joyce rolled her eyes at him. He knew that she understood his frustration; she was adept at grasping his viewpoint, however subtle. She lay quietly, watching him sip his coffee; when he'd drained the mug, she rolled to her side and nudged him with her delectable derriere toward the edge of the bed. It was time for him to get crackin'. In an hour, he was out the door.

Foster enjoyed the short drive to the office in his vintage '68 Targa with its lordotic back end that, somehow, reminded him of his wife. As a kid growing up in Pensacola, he'd always envied the Naval flyboys who sported around in their fast cars. He had promised himself he would have one someday, and about two years into private practice, he'd been fortunate to pick up a cherry '68 Porsche, with embracing leather bucket seats and a custom walnut dash.

Foster needlessly took the Interstate so he could put his baby through her paces on the way to the clinic. Sliding smoothly into second gear, he summoned a growl from the engine like the threat of an angry panther. The drive took under ten minutes.

Foster parked behind his clinic, and locked the car. He noticed Louise had already opened the French doors; the coffee would be brewing. His secretary was a creature of habit, reliable and wonderfully predictable. She would be scurrying around, turning on lamps, straightening magazines, and choosing CD's for the day. As he stepped through the doors, a mug of freshly brewed Kona blend slid into his palm.

"Morning, Dr. John."

"What's happenin', Kid?"

Louise launched into his daily appointments. "You've got a nine o'clock that I scheduled for the entire morning. It's a court-ordered sanity. Your favorite. Sullivan is the attorney, and he asked to speak with you by phone before you began interviewing his client."

"Get him on the line. I'd just as soon get this over with."

Louise went to her desk; delicate fingers leafed through the Rolodex with unerring accuracy. "I'm dialing," she said unnecessarily.

Foster went into his office and slouched into the brown leather swivel chair that had cradled his ass for more hours than he cared to contemplate. His desk was an antique piece that he'd acquired while still at Quantico. It had been a bitch to move, but he enjoyed having it with him, a connection with his past and a testament to much hard-earned experience. He held on to things he liked. He put his feet up, and noted the wearing away of the desk's patina that came from years of foot-propping.

"Mr. Sullivan's on the line, Dr. John."

"John. How you doing?"

Foster could hear Sullivan's good-ole-boy greeting before the receiver even reached his ear. "I'm fine, thank you; how are you?"

Sullivan was unaware that Foster had long ago figured out how he and his fellow attorneys thought they manipulated their *expert* witnesses into reaching opinions that would be favorable to their cases. They withheld information; disclosed half-truths; imparted subtle emphasis to meaningless details. At the core of all the rhetoric might be a kernel of truth, a white-on-black image of the client as his lawyer wanted him portrayed. Clever, but once the methods were clear, it was easy to filter out disinformation and avoid misdirection.

"Listen, you're gonna see my guy this morning, and I thought I'd give you a little background."

"OK." A weary resignation settled on Foster's shoulders; it was a physical feeling.

"Look, he's a good kid, a really good kid. Really. He was brought into this crime by a girl who manipulated him...drove him crazy. You know how girls are."

There it is, 'crazy,' thought Foster. *That's the operative.*

"He fell for this girl and she used him, right down to killing her mother and grandmother for her. You must have read about it in the paper."

"Uh huh."

"She hated her mother, but couldn't do anything about it. So, she brings my guy in to do the dirty deed."

"I see."

"He wasn't responsible, didn't know what was coming down until it was too late. She had him so twisted up." There was a long pause as Sullivan waited for Foster to respond. He didn't. "I got all this from the DA, John. The girl spilled that whole story—her way. She's innocent of course! My guy says he can't remember anything.

"John?"

"Yes?"

"Do you want any more about this guy?"

"No," said Foster matter-of-factly.

Sullivan seemed uneasy. Of course he did; he wasn't getting the desired responses. Foster could hear him breathing heavily into the phone.

"Well, thanks Pete. I'll send my report to the judge. It's not likely you'll need me in court if it's as cut and dried a case as you say, but I'm always available if you need me." Foster disconnected and permitted himself a smug grin.

Foster sat quietly for ten minutes, clearing his brain. Then, he reviewed the factual background data and police record of arrest provided by the Court. As Foster read, he found no evidence of the poor misguided victim who had been led around by his dick as reported by Peter Sullivan, Esquire. Instead, he learned that Frank Davis, age nineteen, was accused of brutally murdering Gerry Fisher and Janice Wright on the night of September 17, 1999. Their bodies were found in their beds, their heads bashed in by an andiron, a weapon of opportunity that was found by a small gas fireplace, and later thrown in the front shrubs. The autopsies confirmed that each victim was probably asleep at the time of assault.

Arlene Fisher, age twenty, was missing from the family home where she had lived with her mother and grandmother. Subsequent lab studies confirmed that only Davis's fingerprints and Arlene's mother's were on the andiron. Davis also could not be located by authorities in the days after the murders.

A break in the case came about three weeks later when a credit card belonging to Janice Wright was used at a Jackson, Mississippi motel by someone who signed her name. It wasn't long before the police were able to trace Davis and Fisher; they were arrested and returned to Illinois where they were both charged with first-degree murder.

Arlene immediately made a deal with the prosecutor. She claimed she was abducted by Davis after he killed her mother and grandmother. Davis acknowledged he might have killed the two women, but said he didn't actually remember doing so. His lawyer subsequently entered a plea of not guilty by reason of insanity.

"Dr. John, your nine o'clock just arrived," Louise's voice floated over his shoulder from the intercom.

"Thanks. I'll come out for Mr. Davis in a moment."

The waiting room was an L-shaped space of sun-washed, soothing colors and inviting, deep-cushioned chairs and couches. Foster hated overhead lighting, so there were table lamps to read by, and calming classical music, which was probably wasted on the young man who sat awkwardly on the edge of a chair, handcuffed and shackled, and flanked by two sizable, armed deputies. The kid gulped audibly as Foster entered the room.

"Good morning. I'm Dr. Foster." He spoke in what Louise dubbed his "reassuring voice."

One of the deputies, Morton, had done this sanity gig before, and he hefted his bulk from the chair to shake Foster's hand. He introduced his partner, and then the prisoner. The young man did not raise his eyes to acknowledge the courtesy. He bobbed his head, and continued to stare at his shoes. He was dressed in the standard-issue orange jumpsuit. His cuffed wrists were chained to a wide leather belt, further restricting his movements.

Davis was short in stature, and slender, almost delicate. He seemed younger than his nineteen years. Acne-pitted skin molded prominent cheekbones and a girlish turned-up nose. He had already acquired the typical jailhouse pallor of a frog's underbelly. His head was shaven, and looked bluish-black, like an aggressive five o'clock shadow. His fingernails were bitten, almost to the point of mutilation. When Davis cast a furtive glance at the deputy who was jangling the keys to his cuffs, Foster could see he had a black eye.

"How long's it gonna take, Doc?" asked Deputy Morton.

Foster studied Davis, and replied, "It depends, but probably all day. I've scheduled my entire morning with him. The afternoon will be for testing"

The deputies exchanged resigned looks. Babysitting was not choice duty. "OK, Doc, you're the boss," said the new guy. He settled into his chair, and reached for the current issue of *Field and Stream.*

"Mr. Morton, please bring Mr. Davis to my office, and release his hands," Foster requested, leading the way. The younger deputy looked at him as if to ask, "Are you crazy?" but Morton unlocked the cuffs. He left them dangling from the ring on the wide leather belt around Davis's waist.

"In a moment will you please join my secretary in witnessing Mr. Davis's signature on the consent and release forms, Deputy? Then you can make yourself comfortable in the waiting room. I'm sure you remember that there are no exits directly from my office that you need to worry about."

Foster seated himself at his desk. "Do you know why you are here today, Mr. Davis?"

"Uh, to see if I'm crazy, I think," said Davis, still refusing to establish eye contact.

"Well, not exactly...see, you're here to talk to me about the crimes you've been accused of. It is my job to assist the Court in determining whether you understood right from wrong at the time you allegedly committed the crime. Also, the Court wants to know if you can go to trial now to face the charges against you, and whether you can help your attorney as he prepares to defend you. I have a form here that allows me to do this on your behalf. You need to read it carefully and sign at the bottom. I'll be glad to answer any questions you may have before you sign it."

Davis leaned forward to read the consent form. His lips moved as he read each word slowly. Nevertheless, he nodded his understanding of the information, and without any questions, signed his name at the bottom. Foster noted that Davis had written his name legibly despite a fine tremor of his right hand. He seemed to be very nervous.

Louise and Morton witnessed his signature and left the office.

Foster folded his hands on his desk and sat quietly. Surprised by the silence, Davis looked at him for the first time, and Foster held the contact. Then he proceeded with a routine Mental Status Examination.

In responses to standard questions, Davis showed himself to be oriented to time, place, person, and circumstance. His immediate, recent, and remote memory were intact; his attention and concentration, adequately focused. His fund of information suggested probable average intelligence, and he demonstrated adequate verbal abstraction skills. He used good vocabulary, although he spoke only in short, declarative sentences.

Davis was clearly apprehensive, and although his affect was blunted, he did not show any signs of clinical depression that often emerged from protracted jail time while awaiting trial. His decision-making and social judgment appeared to be in keeping with estimated intelligence. There was no evidence of cognitive or perceptual distortions, and Davis denied suicidal or homicidal thoughts.

Because Davis was pleading NGBRI upon the advice of counsel, Foster interspersed very simple questions among more difficult ones throughout the Mental Status Exam to assess for malingering. The questions elicited no obvious dissimulation during the MSE, and Davis seemed to give a genuine effort.

Foster led Davis through a comprehensive social history. Davis reported that he was a high school graduate. He had worked summers for his father as a carpenter's helper. He denied any significant medical or psychiatric history, although he admitted to regular use of marijuana during his early teen years, and to getting busted one time for possession.

Until the time of the alleged crime, Davis had been living at home with his biological parents and three younger siblings. He denied any physical or sexual abuse during childhood. His descriptions of family interactions and experiences suggested a socially and economically stable middle class environment with supportive parents. There was nothing to suggest that this young man would be capable of murder. If there was something missing from the details that Davis provided, it was a conspicuous absence of any substantive references to his mother who he described only as a "wonderful parent." Given Davis's clear reticence to say more about his relationship with his mother, Foster probed further. Davis's head sunk to his chest and his shoulders became rigid. Body language alone suggested that there was much he was not saying, but the tears that began to fall were clear evidence of hidden pain. Gently, Foster led him through the disclosure of chronic and severe emotional abuse by his mother that had always been hidden from his father. There had also been carefully concealed blows to the head where long hair had hidden the evidence of his mother's fury. Intense fear had rendered him incapable of informing his father of the abuse, and the absence of a nurturing mother had left him with unmet dependency needs.

After an hour of standardized interview, Foster asked Davis if he would like to take a break. He declined, and stated that he would prefer to continue.

"Tell me about the night Ms. Fisher and Ms. Wright were killed."

Davis blanched; he was visibly surprised at the direct question. Foster had learned from experience that such non-emotional, open-ended questions phrased as subtle commands would give him the edge when interviewing a defendant, and the element of surprise sometimes elicited the unexpected, the kind of unguarded responses that made defense attorneys foam at the mouth.

After a few moments of frantic thought, Davis said, "I don't know what you mean." He was clearly rattled, and all the coaching by Sullivan had not prepared him for a frontal assault, however politely it was rendered. The tremor of his hands became more pronounced; beads of sweat popped out on his upper lip, and his ears turned scarlet.

"Well, what I mean is, where were you when your girlfriend's mother and grandmother were killed?" asked Foster. "Where might you have been?" he rephrased, throwing out a hypothet to see if Davis would bite.

Davis looked directly into Foster's eyes. "They say I was at Arlene's house."

"Been there before?"

"No, never," answered Davis.

"Where is this place?"

"It's in Lyons, on Skyline Drive."

"What's the house look like?" queried Foster, encouraging the boy to give more information.

"Oh...uh, a brownstone, two stories, nice place," said Davis. Foster sensed he had established a rhythm of questions and answers, and pushed for more details.

"These brownstones...usually the living rooms are where you enter from the front door. Right?"

"Yeah," Davis agreed, "The kitchen was straight back, two bedrooms and a bathroom on the right."

"Was Arlene home?"

"Yeah, she was really pissed at her mom because she didn't want her going out with me. I had been in some trouble before, like I said, the drug stuff, but nothin' serious. Her mother knew about it.

"Arlene and I were planning to run away that night."

"Why do they think you killed those two women?" asked Foster.

"I don't know; I can't remember," said Davis. His eyes became glassy and fixed on Foster. "Is everything I say here today going to be reported?"

Foster suspected that Davis was on the verge of saying more. Nevertheless, he answered without any hesitation or inflection in his voice, "Yes, nothing you say to me is confidential."

"Oh," said Davis, and he began to sob.

"Why so sad, now, Frank?" Foster used his first name to offer comfort.

"I've had dreams," muttered Davis.

"Tell me about them." Foster spoke softly, reassuring and knowing, while he considered that the young man might be describing memory caused by mild stress-induced dissociation.

"There's blood all over, and I can see my hands hitting those women in the head. You know...with the iron." Tears were flowing freely now, but Foster let him continue.

"Shit, shit!" Davis squealed and lunged forward suddenly, but because of the shackles, he landed awkwardly on his knees.

Morton appeared at Foster's door, and his hand was on his weapon. Foster shook his head and gestured for the deputy to withdraw. He moved from behind his desk, extended a hand to Davis and helped him back into the chair. For a brief moment, Foster touched the back of the young man's hand, and then he returned to his seat.

Davis continued as though the outburst had not occurred. "I don't know how it could have happened. I just wanted to go away; I love Arlene, but she kept saying we had to do more than just run. I didn't want to." Davis's voice trailed off. He lapsed into silence and seemed to fold in on himself.

Foster respected Davis's silence. He had heard enough. Davis had clearly shown that he knew right from wrong at the time of the crime, that he felt remorse, and that the murders had not been planned, at least not by him. He also showed that he could give a coherent account of his actions, and, thus, could assist his attorney in providing an adequate defense. All that remained to complete the sanity evaluation were routine intelligence and achievement tests, along with some standard personality instruments to confirm Foster's clinical impressions.

"Frank, that's all the questions. You did just fine. I'm going to give you a few minutes to pull yourself together, and then we'll wrap this up with some psych testing and questionnaires for you to complete."

"All right, Doc," he said, "I'm sorry. I didn't mean to fall apart."

Foster simply nodded in acknowledgement. At his desk, he reviewed his notes until he observed that Davis was beginning to get antsy. When he rose, Davis did too. Foster escorted him across the hall, deputies in tow, and introduced the young man to his technician, Katy. Foster did not have the time to do the labor-intensive psychological tests, so he hired a psychometrician to free him for the conceptual work. His tech was efficient and compulsive about details; he trusted her observations, impressions, and insights. By 1:45, she was finished with the testing.

Louise subsequently settled Davis down with a half dozen White Castle hamburgers and a large steaming coffee to fortify him. Two lengthy personality questionnaires would take him the better part of the afternoon to finish, and the deputies just might earn some overtime before returning Davis to his cell.

Foster smiled as the smell of "Whitie Castillies" permeated the office and intruded into his awareness. Louise always dipped into petty cash to feed the prisoners whatever junk food would fulfill their cravings. She might be twenty-six and single, but Louise was a born mother hen. She would keep Davis working, even when he tired and his eyes began to cross from all the true and false circles on the various tests. The demands of testing could be overwhelming, especially to a prisoner who had been subjected to months of enforced boredom and the lack of intellectual stimulation that is the way of jail life.

At 4:00 p.m., Foster met again with Davis, grasping his hand warmly before the deputy replaced his cuffs and attached them to the leather belt in preparation for transport back to jail.

"Good luck, Frank," Foster smiled.

There was an eloquent plea in Davis's eyes. "Am I crazy, Doc?" he whispered.

"No, Frank, I don't think so."

Davis looked genuinely relieved, then disappointed. Foster suspected that he was thinking he had not done what his lawyer instructed. Davis nodded, dropped his shoulders in defeat, and followed the deputies from the clinic.

Foster's final impression was that of leg chains clanking rhythmically to the boy's shuffling gait as he negotiated the steps. *What a waste,* he thought grimly, returning to his office. He paced once around the room before grabbing his tape recorder and launching into the sanity report. It was easiest to give a detailed accounting of the background information while all the data was still in his working memory. The test results, summary, and conclusions would come later. The one thing he already knew, however, was that the severity of Davis's abuse by his mother had initiated a cycle of violence that came full circle the night he killed the two women. His girlfriend's ability to tap into his dependency and foment his rage at his mother made him the tool she needed to accomplish murders she could not commit. *Victim becomes perpetrator...perpetrator becomes his own victim. It's classic.*

Foster lowered his recorder to the desk. He realized that the intercom had cleared its throat several times in succession. "Yes? Louise?"

"Sorry to interrupt, Dr. John; your four o'clock canceled. It was a...wait a minute, a new client. Her name is...a Mrs. Vincent. She rescheduled."

"Did she say what the problem was?"

Louise hummed, "Oh, something about her husband that was worrying her; she wants some advice about what to do."

"Nothing 'til five, then?"

"Nope, no five o'clock either. You're a free man," quipped Louise.

"How about a very late lunch, or an early supper? Did you even have lunch? I have a taste for Italian. We could go to Fascottis. I could call Joyce to join us—that is, as long as you two let me express an opinion every now and then."

Louise didn't hesitate. She really enjoyed her job, but most of all, she anticipated meals shared with her boss and his wife. They loved to eat; she loved to eat! What could be better?

"You make the call to Joyce. I'll lock up."

As he patted his pockets for his cell phone and found his car keys instead, Foster heard the office phone ring, followed by Louise's groan. Their get-away hadn't been fast enough! Because he was closer, he reached over and punched phone buttons until he hit the right line. Before he could even say hello....

"Hey, Doc. How'd my man do?" It was the irrepressible Sullivan.

"He did fine, just fine. You know I'm under court order, Pete. Can't talk to you about my findings...just can't. I'll get my report to the judge by the end of the week. Check with His Honor after Friday."

CHAPTER FOUR

"Eddie, you up yet?" Sonya Vinson yelled up the stairs. It was three fifteen, and he was usually awake by now.

Groggy, irritated by Sonya's lack of consideration, and by having to pull an extra night shift tonight to cover staff shortages, Eddie stretched, only to find his legs ensnared in damp, twisted sheets. Hastily, he fought the tangle and covered his groin; he lay back just as Sonya entered the bedroom. He yawned and scratched his chest.

"Mornin'."

Sonya grinned. "It's after three, Sleeping Beauty."

Eddie set aside his irritation. It paled in the shadow of his raw attraction to Sonya. He seldom showed her that facet of himself. He watched her from under the screen of his lashes. His wife was a sultry and statuesque woman, two inches taller than he was and, at thirty-eight, three years older. She had a clear ivory complexion, a cap of glossy blond hair, and unusual, oval whiskey-colored eyes. Golden brows and lashes accentuated the refined Scandinavian features of her mother's family. Sonya was a knockout when she was "on," although, lately, she seemed to have lost the spark that had drawn him to her. She seemed to be struggling; she looked older, more somber, drained. Even her occasional laughter, like now, seemed forced. There was a brittleness about her, and a pervasive tension that was totally out of character for the woman he thought he knew.

He and Sonya had been married seven months. They had known each other for three months before they moved in together, and then another month before they tied the knot. He recalled what first attracted him to Sonya when they met at an AA meeting...a great place to meet women! Sonya was a self-professed co-dependent from a previous abusive relationship. He learned that Sonya's substance abuse had been her way of coping. With sobriety, however, she seemed so calm and in touch with herself. Fascinated, he had watched her throughout that first evening as she moved freely from one group to another.

She radiated a natural beauty, a calm assurance and composure that attracted him from the moment he laid eyes on her. Slowly, he made his way into her orbit. When, at last, she joined the group to which he had attached himself, he turned toward her and introduced himself, "Hey, I'm Eddie, and I'm an alcoholic," he said matter-of-factly.

Sonya smiled and extended her hand. Her fragrance, subtle and floral, enticed him. "This is my first time with this group, but I've been to others. So far, I feel at home here." It wasn't the truth, but it was the right thing to say. He knew the drill.

Sonya turned to him with quiet assessing eyes. She didn't rush to fill silence with superficial chatter. She simply studied him. Eddie wanted to shuffle his feet or crack his knuckles like some gawky youth with his first girl. She threw him off balance in that way.

"Welcome, Eddie. I'm Sonya. Would you like some refreshments?" Her voice was low, liquid, with a cadence that ebbed and flowed. She drew him in, warmed him, and before the evening was over, they had a date for dinner the following Saturday. From that night on, he courted Sonya; he romanced her relentlessly and took her by storm. She never stood a chance.

Eddie was well aware that he needed more than any one woman could possibly give. He had been with scores of women before he met Sonya, but he had promised her that he would be faithful, and in his way, he was. His fidelity was freely given, not because of any sacramental drivel or Biblical dogma, but because she suited him; she was his safe haven. She was also perfect camouflage, and he wasn't going to blow a good thing. Or was it possible that he had already done so? The errant thought caused a nasty riff up his spine.

Sonya's niece, Dottie, on the other hand, was a whole 'nother ball game. At fifteen, she was all nubile temptation—with a capital T. Ripe and ready for plucking was the way he thought of her. With Dottie down the hall, Eddie's commitment to fidelity was challenged daily. To his way of thinking, she was "long overdue."

Dottie reminded him of his first piece of ass when he was thirteen. Lola had been a leggy, fourteen-year-old wannabe dancer with a penchant for nude performances before the living room window while her pig of a father slept off his nightly drunk. Dottie had more class, of course. Like Sonya, she was artless and natural. He watched her when she was unaware. He watched, and he wanted, but he didn't touch. Once, she had innocently plopped herself on his lap as they whispered about a birthday present for Sonya. His immediate physical reaction went seemingly unnoticed by Dottie, but, taking no chances, Eddie tipped her off his lap and scooted his chair closer to the table to hide his erection. The moment passed and he filed it away for later consideration.

Eddie catalogued his secrets the way he catalogued his fantasies. Lola and sex; Dottie and sex; Sonya and sex.... If the average male thought of sex at least once every fifteen minutes, well, Eddie figured he was a shoe-in for *Believe It or Not* fame.

Sex was never far from his thoughts, and even though Lola had been his first fuck, she hadn't given him his introduction to sex. No, that honor went to a pervert babysitter when he was five, followed by an encore with the lard-ass father of his friend, Phillip Prychek, when Eddie was twelve.

Phillip and Eddie played sandlot baseball together, and their friendship grew out of proximity and boredom. Although they were often together, Eddie had never been to Phillip's home, so he had been surprised by a rainy afternoon invitation to play cards and "mess around." Phillip wasn't cool like some guys, like Eddie himself, but it turned out he lived in a nice house about twenty minutes away by bike, which was a pleasant change from the trailer park.

Much to Eddie's surprise, Phillip's father was home when he arrived. Not only that, the old fart seemed to think he was gonna play gin with them. Eddie's repeated looks at Phillip got him nothing. *What was goin' on here?*

Reality struck when his father sent Phillip to the store for a pack of Luckies, and Phillip left without a squawk. He was already on the sidewalk, when Eddie dashed to the door, mumbling that he would go too. He was floored when Prychek blocked the door; he laid a restraining arm about Eddie's shoulders. There was no force to his gesture, and he didn't say a word, but the threat was real nonetheless.

Old Man Prychek was a large man, flamboyant and flabby. He was dressed in worn black, sharkskin pants, a wrinkled, starched shirt with the first few buttons undone, and a loosened tie of black and white checks below the wattles of his chin. He wore black and white shoes, too, that Eddie thought belonged on a golf course. The man's taste was all in his mouth.

"What?" asked Eddie, eyes flashing in sudden anger.

"What?" mocked the old man, a slob if ever there was one. His fingers, fat like stunted pork sausages, moved deftly from one shirt button to the next. Eddie watched in fascinated disbelief as Prychek's bloated belly covered with sparse gray and black hairs emerged from the shirt's opening. The stink of beer and cigars, sweat, and unwashed flesh enveloped him. Epithets and insults threatened to spill from Eddie's lips. Jesus, but the guy looked like an aging hippo. Eddie had seen naked old men at a distance before, when he went to the Y sometimes to exercise, but he'd never seen ***gross*** up close like this!

"What are you doing?"

"Just getting comfortable, my boy. Ya want I should show you my French playing cards?"

Eddie had been twelve and naïve, but not stupid, about adult sex. To this day he wondered if Phillip had known, had purposely offered him up in his place to be his father's new boy toy, but at the time, he'd been intrigued so he followed Prychek across the hall. When the door closed behind them, Eddie's eyes scanned the sagging bed covered with a mangy, fake-fur throw, and the framed girly pictures on the walls.

"Nice decor," he said, hiding his smirk by rubbing his nose. The room's fragrance was definitely eau de cum. *That* smell he recognized.

"Guess you've never seen anything like these before," Prychek said, patting the mattress beside him. Eddie sat gingerly, leaving space between them. The old man ruffled the deck, and Eddie saw anatomical bits and pieces of naked broads flicker past.

Phil's dad was breathing heavier, and Eddie knew from experience that such a physical response could portend trouble. Many a fight or a fuck started with heavy breathing. His unease ratcheted up a notch.

Prychek fanned the cards again, and with a flourish, he drew out the Ace of Spades to reveal a black and white photograph of a naked woman straddling a man's hips, a coy smile on her face. Eddie felt warm; he knew what that meant, too.

With no less drama, Prychek held up one grimy card after another to reveal what Eddie's mother would call "all manner of perversion." One card, however, held his attention. It was the Ten of Diamonds which showed a young girl seated on a wooden chair, legs spread, her most private parts captured in intricate detail by the photo. As he studied the card, Eddie felt Prychek's hand come to rest on his shoulder and slide slowly down his back…to his crack.

Eddie didn't need a slap 'side the head to know what Prychek wanted. He had never forgotten the male babysitter who touched him in that way…. He'd finally escaped to his closet, and held the jerk off *(snicker)* with his baseball bat until his parents got home. Oh yeah, he knew all about what Old Man Prychek wanted. The question was...did he wanna go along? He was curious, sure, and a little excited. He knew how it felt to touch himself. Hell, he did that all the time, but to respond to the old fart's overtures…?

What the hell! He held his breath as Prychek leaned into him, reaching for another card. He turned over the Six of Spades.

"Um…that's a good one."

"What?" Prychek yelped. His eyes bugged and glazed over when Eddie casually dropped his hand onto the old man's thigh, his eyes fixed on the obvious tenting of Prychek's trousers. He smiled, the picture of innocence; the locus of control was now in his hands.

"This one?" prodded Eddie. "What's this?"

"Uh, oh, that's oral sex." Prychek speared him with porcine eyes that suddenly clicked into focus. His hand moved haltingly toward Eddie's crotch, and when he made no complaint, Prychek pressed gently against his dick. Eddie could feel the damp heat of Prychek's sweaty paw through his pants, and his reaction was immediate, inevitable. The old man seemed to take his hard-on as the consent he was waiting for. He stumbled to his feet, and the rasp of his zipper scraped the silence. Prychek opened his pants.

"C'mon. Before the kid gets back." When Eddie failed to move, Phil's father pulled him roughly to his feet. He tucked Eddie's ass right into his exposed crotch and rubbed against him while reaching around and fumbling with Eddie's fly. A drop of Prychek's rancid sweat ran down Eddie's neck and under his shirt; he tracked it as it rolled down his shoulder, over his nipple, and on down his belly to be caught by the waistband of his briefs. His jeans parted like the damned Red Sea and dropped to his knees in one un-denim-like fluid motion. His underpants followed. Prychek bent him forward over his arm.

Just a little pain and the rest is easy. All I gotta do is go to my special place. No one can hurt me there. I'm invisible. I'm invincible.

When the pervert was finished, he was gasping like a beached whale. "Vinson? Vinson? You're a good boy, Vinson." Prychek adjusted his clothes and stepped back.

"Thank you, Sir." Vinson straightened slowly and locked his knees. He turned and looked Prychek right in the eye as he leisurely pulled up his jeans and tucked in his shirt. "I gotta go now. Please tell Phil for me. Will you, Sir?" *And tell him for me, too, I'm gonna kill you, you motherfucker.*

The following night, Vinson roused himself from a doze, and reached for the phone beside the couch. He dialed Phil's number. Prychek answered.

"Mr. Prychek. Hey, it's Eddie Vinson. I was just thinkin' about yesterday afternoon."

"Yeah? It was great, Eddie."

"Great," he echoed. *You bastard!*

"Would you...uh, meet me at Wilson Park, Mr. Prychek? You know, where the coaches have us meet for practice?"

"Sure, Eddie, any time...when?"

Was he already panting? "Now, Mr. Prychek? I'd like to meet you now," he said softly.

"Sure, Son, I'm on my way."

To Hell! Straight to hell, you asshole.

Vinson found a place near the burned out street light closest to the bathrooms for the ball field. Thick bushes grew behind the chain link backstop. A railroad track ran parallel to the first base line, and Vinson knew a rapid freight usually came through around 1:45 a.m. *My timing's perfect,* he thought as he hefted his favorite baseball bat, a Louisville Slugger, onto his shoulder and crouched down behind the shrubs to wait.

In his peripheral vision, Vinson caught the lumbering bulk of old man Prychek as he came around the corner of the fence and started across the infield. In the blue-black silence, Vinson could hear the slap-slap of the poor turd's bedroom slippers, and he strangled on silent laughter. His eyes watered and snot bubbled from his nose as he held in the hilarity so he didn't give himself away. He wiped his face against his forearm, and fought for control.

"Eddie? Eddie?"

Vinson was suddenly mirthless and intent.

"Eddie, you here?" Prychek stood on home plate. He scanned the outfield, then searched again more carefully; his back was to Vinson who stepped around the bushes and into the open. Soundlessly he approached Prychek.

As if in slow motion, Prychek turned to face Vinson. He did not seem alarmed by the bat resting, non-threatening, on Eddie's shoulder. Vinson walked right up to him and smiled. "I want to thank you for what you did for me yesterday, Mr. Prychek. You gave me a reason to do something I've thought about for a long time."

Vinson inhaled and his lungs expanded. *I could grant him life..., but I won't.*

In one fluid motion, his hands dropped to batting position, and he swung. *Payback!*

Each time he replayed that first murder in his head, Vinson could hear the blunt thwack of the bat striking Prychek's pulpy forehead. The motion of the bat became almost surrealistic as it seemed to wrap itself around the poor sod's skull and the blood arced into the dead of night. Prychek dropped to his knees and bounced once before he sprawled on the chalk line toward first base. Vinson stepped around to see his face, and the old man's eyes rolled up to meet his. Understanding passed between them. He took aim and ended Prychek's life with a single blow to the forehead.

How long he sat on the pitcher's mound listening to the silence, Vinson could not remember, but when he heard the whistle of the distant freight, he realized that he was cold and stiff. His crotch was wet, sticky. He stood and approached Prychek. Grabbing hairy wrists, Vinson grunted and exhaled hard as he began to drag the body's dead weight toward the outfield and the small overgrown gate that gave access to the railroad tracks. He would go back later and erase the scuffs created by the dragging and scatter sand and debris to cover the blood spatters.

An adrenaline rush gave him greater strength, and a chorus of farts escaping the body kept him amused as Vinson made his way across the scrub grass and weeds ringing the ball field. Although he was winded by the time he reached the railroad tracks, he had never felt more alive. He placed the body face down, lengthwise along one rail where the freight's steel wheels would do the most damage.

Vinson retreated to the shadows of a stunted oak on the fence line to wait. He could feel the shaking of the ground as the train approached. Its giant wheels cleaved the body in half, shredding flesh, bones, and organs. The smell of shit filled the air.

"Eddie? Eddie?" Dottie's voice claimed his attention and brought him back to the moment, "Why are you so quiet?"

"Sorry…I was remembering something from a long time ago. Just a memory; no big deal." *Except for this boner I'm hiding under the table, and the fact that they never solved Old Man Prychek's death.*

CHAPTER FIVE

Sonya Vinson was becoming increasingly worried about her husband. For the past several weeks, she had noticed that Eddie sometimes drifted off in the middle of conversations. For no apparent reason, he would tune out, become oblivious to those around him. His lapses left others feeling awkward and uncomfortable. Even Dottie had mentioned the change in him. Out of the blue, Eddie had also begun to speak of himself in the third person, as Vinson, which was, in Dottie's words, "really weird." Sonya agreed.

Did the changes in Eddie's' behavior coincide with his sudden preoccupation with the Internet and chat rooms? Sometimes, in the night, Sonya would reach for him, and he had not come to bed. She'd find him at the computer. Because the old wooden stairs creaked at unpredictable intervals, her approach came as no surprise. She would find Eddie playing the sophisticated combat or martial arts games that seemed to hold his attention for hours. But the other night, it struck her that he was always at the beginning of a game when she entered the room. That night, he was sitting in his underwear, his scrub pants in a heap beneath the desk. She had leaned over his shoulder and nuzzled him; Eddie had tensed, and his rebuff was obvious. Equally obvious had been his erection, and it definitely was not the result of her caress. She said nothing, and left the room feeling cold, so very cold, and confused.

Sonya's emerging distrust of Eddie had its roots in her childhood. Together, her father and mother, until they were caught, had run a successful cocaine distributing operation. Because they partook of their product, Sonya was one of many responsibilities they chose to ignore. She was sixteen when her parents were convicted and sent to their respective penitentiaries.

Sonya was placed in a foster home where she felt confined and out of place. She never formed an emotional attachment to her foster parents, and waited impatiently for her eighteenth birthday, and freedom. She refused to visit or write to her parents in prison, and when they were released, she ignored their attempts to contact her. By then, she was self-supporting—barely—and living on her own. She had secured a position as a researcher in a small law firm. Her duties were challenging, and she acquired more and more responsibilities along the way. The independence was heady stuff, and she learned to be frugal, to count on only herself, and to guard her privacy. She was considering law school when, at twenty-five, she fell in love and married Mark, a new associate attorney who joined the firm.

Sonya's marriage was stable for two years, although wedded bliss had faded quickly. Then, the pressures of Mark's growing practice and a miscarriage late in their fourth year caught them off guard, and their relationship began to unravel. With hindsight, she realized that she had failed to support the one thing that was important to Mark, his career; in moments of absolute honesty, she also acknowledged that she had neglected his needs for intimacy in the months after she lost their child. Eventually the cold estrangement between them became anger. Mark's temper grew more volatile, and a couple times, he beat the tar out of her. She doused the flames of her own anger in bottle after bottle of crystal clear spirits.

Sonya's salvation finally came from the smart mouth of her niece, Dottie, her brother's only child. Family Services foolishly placed Dottie with her after the auto accident that killed her brother and sister-in-law. She accepted Dottie's custody against her husband's wishes, and found she had acquired a bitter and defiant ten-year-old who quickly and accurately assessed the sorry state of her marriage. Dottie used the tension between Sonya and Mark for her own ends, and became adept at manipulating them. She grew bolder and more oppositional, until the night when she found herself caught between Sonya and an enraged Mark who took his fists to both of them.

On their seventh anniversary, Sonya turned tail and ran. Mark soothed his conscience by agreeing to pay child support for Dottie; he used the money as his justification for walking away and never looking back.

Dottie's defiance did not survive the dose of reality delivered by Mark's fists or the ever-present reminder of the small scar in her hairline, which he inflicted. As she and Sonya settled into a new apartment and worked together to establish a routine, Dottie began to buckle down and contribute. Her efforts made Sonya feel guilty that she was still retreating nightly into a gin bottle once Dottie was in bed. She drank rapidly and deliberately to quell the pain. As the months passed, Sonya let the guilt have free reign. Finally, when she could stand it no more, she sought a 12-step program, and began to attend regularly. She devoted herself to Dottie, and the relationship they nurtured together was rewarding beyond belief. It was Dottie who cajoled, pleaded, and pushed, and finally contacted her grandparents on her own so that Sonya was forced to confront her feelings and begin to rebuild burned bridges.

When Dottie discovered the opposite sex, she deduced, incorrectly, that her aunt must be lonely. Sonya could find no way to knock her off that particular bandwagon. Then, just to prove that Dottie's assessment may have been more accurate than she would care to admit, Sonya met Eddie.

Dottie took to Eddie immediately, and he seemed to accept her affection for what it was—the unfamiliar devotion of an insecure young woman who did not know quite how their relationship should play. Dottie accepted Eddie's moving in, and threw herself into the wedding that was to be a no-frills civil ceremony. Eddie's forbearance with Dottie put Sonya to shame. He seemed to understand, and when Sonya's exasperation with her ebullient niece approached some critical threshold, he would spirit Dottie away to go shopping or to the zoo or the museum, and give Sonya time to decompress.

If alcoholism and gratitude to Eddie for his willingness to assume a father's role and responsibilities with Dottie were the basis of Sonya's allegiance to her new husband, she was astute enough to know it. Still, the other aspects of her marriage were more than satisfactory. *And the sex ain't bad either!* Rather, it hadn't been, until recently.

Eddie was clearly distancing himself from her; he was not cold exactly, more restrained, preoccupied. He was also withdrawing from Dottie, acting strange, almost shy, with her. Dottie seemed hurt and confused, and over-compensated by clinging to him. Several times his annoyance had been apparent, even to Dottie.

Because she, too, was bewildered by the inexplicable changes in Eddie, Sonya had scheduled an appointment with a psychologist who was recommended to her by her pastor, but she had panicked and called to cancel only three hours before the appointment. Sonya reasoned that to talk to someone about her husband without his permission would be a betrayal that Eddie would not forgive; yet the moment she hung up the telephone, she knew that canceling was the wrong decision. She needed an unbiased and unemotional assessment of her husband's behavior, so she called back and accepted the earliest available appointment.

CHAPTER SIX

John Foster was well respected in the field of forensic psychology. His FBI training and years of experience evaluating and treating accused felons and a random mix of sociopaths, narcissists, and other character disorders, had afforded him a solid reputation. He was able to pick and choose among the highest profile cases in the state, in the nation, too, if he wished to cast his professional net wider, which he usually did not. Every day, he met both the perpetrators of violence and their victims. He was known for his ability to come at a case from either perspective, violator or victim, and render a fair and impartial assessment.

In quiet moments, Foster had pondered what set him on this particular career pathway. With hindsight, the only conclusion that made any sense to him was his upbringing.

As a child, Foster had grown up in a 1950 blue-collar Pensacola neighborhood where he had become attuned to the sounds of abuse. He was never abused, but the evidence of abuse was all around him. Through open windows or thin apartment walls, it was common to hear fathers or mothers yelling and the sounds of flesh against flesh as corporal punishment was dispensed. Children in his neighborhood routinely wore the cuts and bruises of harsh physical discipline, and there were few child protective agencies like today to challenge the brutality. He never knew other parents to intervene or come to the rescue of a child not their own.

Foster was always aware of his father's acute discomfort when they would hear his friend, Teddy, who lived downstairs, catching hell from his raging father. Teddy's cries when the belt slapped his buttocks floated up the cold air duct, as did his father's obscenities and his mother's ineffectual pleadings. At those times, Foster's father would not look him in the eye; he would turn up the radio and retreat behind the daily paper. His reaction was always the same. As Foster got older, he realized that he was angry at his father for not standing up to Teddy's brute of a parent. Surely he could have done something to protect the boy.

Just when he first promised himself that he would not cower in the face of brutality, especially against children, Foster couldn't say for sure, but by the time he was a junior in high school, he was already aware that he would accept the challenge to protect and defend. As he grew older, he assumed that law enforcement would be his career, that is, until he realized that once law enforcement became involved, it was already too late.

In college, Foster pursued a pre-law curriculum with heavy emphasis on criminal justice, but he was unmotivated and drifting, and he knew it. It was an Abnormal Psychology course that finally lit a fire under him. Before he stopped to catch his breath, he had a Ph.D. in clinical psychology in hand, and an interview with the FBI three weeks after graduation. Hell of a way to develop a career path, but one, he reasoned, that was as valid as any other.

Spring and summer in Chicago usually caused a spurt of referrals for mental health services. This year was no exception, and it was only March. On this day, Foster had a full pull. "What's on the docket, Louise?" he asked.

"Oh, let's see, you've got that Ms. Vincent...again. You remember, the lady who cancelled last week? She called back and seemed really upset, so I worked her in first for a half hour this morning."

The remainder of the day's schedule included two marriage-counseling cases, and three state referrals of kids who had been mistreated by their parents. Foster was at the back door when a woman pulled into the clinic parking lot. Before getting out of her car, a late model Toyota, she checked the vanity mirror to apply lipstick and run a brush through her hair. She opened the car door, stepped out, and briskly approached the clinic. As she came into the waiting room, Ms. Vincent was greeted by Louise who presented her with the required information about clinic policies, patient privacy, and the legal parameters of a counseling relationship.

When Ms. Vincent had completed the paperwork, Foster approached to introduce himself. He nodded to her and smiled. "Good morning. I'm John Foster. How are you this morning?"

"Hello. I wish I could say I was doing alright, but then, I wouldn't be here. Would I?"

Foster accepted her response for the ambivalence it showed because her tone was soft-spoken and her demeanor, polite. "Then let's begin," he suggested, and led her to his office.

"Care for a cup of coffee, Ms. Vincent? I have no need for formality, so please feel free to call me John."

"OK, and my last name is Vinson, not Vincent."

"Ms. Vinson, forgive me," corrected Foster. He would have to remember to speak with Louise again about asking for the spelling of patients' names, which she invariably failed to do. He gave himself a moment to curtail mild annoyance by scanning the demographics provided by Ms. Vinson, and reviewing Louise's documentation of her two telephone calls to the office in which she had outlined briefly the reasons for seeking an appointment.

"Please make yourself comfortable, and when you're ready, tell me why you are here."

Ms. Vinson exhaled forcefully, blowing up at wispy bangs that concealed a high forehead. "Dr. Foster, I mean John, I'm afraid I don't know where or how to begin." Her words were the refrain uttered most often by new patients, yet such lead-ins could be followed by revelations of the most mundane personal problems, or the most tragic.

"Start where you feel most comfortable, Ms. Vinson."

She swallowed audibly and clasped her hands. Raising her glance to Foster for a moment only, she said softly, "It's very difficult for me to be here today." Her eyes filled with tears. Rather than have them fall, she widened her eyes and tipped her head back, careful not to blink.

Foster remained silent, relaxed, and still, but waiting, giving her time to secure the composure she would not surrender. "I don't know how to begin, but I know I've got to tell someone about Eddie."

"Your husband?"

"Yes, Eddie, my husband of seven months."

"Go on."

Ms. Vinson's face contorted in pain. She raised a delicate hand to cover her face, but caught herself and lowered it. For the first time, she looked Foster in the eyes and held the contact. *There's strength here*, he concluded.

"Look, Ms. Vinson...may I call you Sonya?" asked Foster. "What you have to tell me is confidential. Unless you or your husband have abused a child, or are a danger to others...what you say will remain between us. There are no law suits or legal matters pending, are there?"

She shook her head. "No, nothing like that."

"OK, then, relax and tell me why you're afraid of Eddie."

Surprise, and then resignation, flickered across her expressive face. "I didn't say...

"Yes, I'm afraid." She dropped her chin, and the tears finally overflowed to dot the lapels of her silk blouse. After several moments of deep breathing, she continued, "One month ago, give or take, we were broken into. I mean, someone broke into our house. It was terrifying. Nothing like that had ever happened. It's so personal."

"Tell me."

"There's so much to tell, but...because the bottom line is, my marriage...."

"Sonya, don't censor. I know that your husband is the crux of your concerns, and if I'm to be able to understand your circumstances, you have to give me details."

"This *is* confidential, for sure? I mean, if Eddie isn't going to hurt anybody, you can't tell?"

"That's right. You know, the best thing, not the easiest, but the most beneficial thing you can do right now is to trust me. You've taken the biggest step already; you're here. Consider that while I ask my secretary to rearrange my schedule for this morning so we can have more time together to address your concerns."

When he returned, Ms. Vinson greeted him with a wobbly smile. "You offer trust for my consideration," she said, "knowing full well that, from where I sit, I don't have any choice."

"Well...yes," Foster grinned, "but then, you're smarter than most, and it did earn me a lovely smile."

Sonya squared her shoulders. "As I said, about one month ago, someone broke into our house. Dottie, that's my niece, she's fifteen.... We returned home in the late afternoon from a long weekend with my parents to find the back of the house completely trashed, and the window was broken in the guest room which doubles as a computer room. Eddie wasn't home; he had to work a swing shift, but I noticed an empty bottle of his favorite liquor, Old Charter, on its side by the computer monitor. Later, when I looked more carefully, I noticed that there was more glass on the grass outside than on the floor. The window had been broken out from the *inside*, not broken in."

"What did you make of this?"

"Well, initially, I passed right over it because...uh...it was such a shock."

"Did you call the police?"

"Yes, I did. Apparently there was little usable evidence, no substantive leads, and nothing has come from their investigation.

"I think it was Eddie," she whispered, seemingly in response to the question Foster had not asked.

"Say again, please."

"Eddie. I think Eddie did it. He wasn't upset by the damage; by all rights he should have gone ballistic. That would be what he should have done, given his personality. It was like he didn't care, or he wasn't surprised. I don't know, and, as I said, he didn't even mention calling the police. I called them. Several days later, two or three, I think, I found a pair of Dottie's panties in the back pocket of Eddie's jeans in the bottom of the washing machine. The crotch part of the panties had been cut out. The laundry had been a load of Eddie's jeans and dark flannel shirts." Ms. Vinson closed her eyes, seemingly drained. There were no more tears. Her breathing returned to near normal as she sat quietly.

Foster respected her silence, and almost five minutes elapsed before she asked the one question that needed to be addressed. "Do you think, if Eddie did it, that Dottie and I are in danger?"

There was no room for equivocation. "Yes," Foster said gently, "You should consider taking Dottie and leaving until we can sort this out. Go somewhere safe, where he won't come after you. I'll need to see him as soon as possible, and if he won't come in voluntarily, well...we'll cross that bridge if we need to. He could be picked up by the police for questioning, but that wouldn't necessarily give me access to him unless he agreed.

"Do you have someone you can go to who will protect your confidence...and not be intimidated if Eddie gets angry?"

Sonya smiled for the first time. "My Dad," she said, "He takes 'nothin' from nobody.' Just ask him; he'll tell you!"

"Good. Good. Then, when you leave, tell Eddie, leave him a note; tell him that you made an appointment for him with me. Make it clear that you have talked to me, and until he sees me, too, you're not coming home. You and Dottie need to leave immediately. Don't overreact and alarm her, but Dottie needs to understand that the situation could be serious, that Eddie may need help. She should be mature enough to understand, with your support."

Giving her elbow a reassuring pat, Foster escorted Sonya Vinson to Louise where she scheduled an appointment for her husband for Thursday morning. "Call me each day, during the lunch hour, if possible, but call, regardless. Here are the numbers that will reach me anywhere, at any time, and don't hesitate to use them. I stay on a short leash; Louise or my paging service can always find me."

Foster returned to his desk to dictate a detailed record of his session with Ms. Vinson. Then he sat quietly considering, sifting through the things she had said, and the things she had not. In summary, he wrote, "Provisional diagnosis for husband: rule out Alcohol Abuse; rule out Personality Disorder versus Impulse Control Disorder. Information provided by wife suggests need for security; advised her of same. Plan: Interview Mr. Vinson."

CHAPTER SEVEN

Sonya drove directly home, even though her intuition told her to leave immediately and not go back to the house. She would quickly gather some essentials and personal items for herself and for Dottie who was still at school. She decided she would pick Dottie up at school, and not warn her parents that they were coming because it would only cause them to worry until she could explain everything fully.

Eddie would guess where they were, but it was doubtful that he would confront her father. He had met her parents only a few times. Shortly after their wedding, Eddie had described her father as a "grizzled old alpha male," and the portrayal had stuck in her mind, both because it was an astute assessment, and because it carried a grudging respect. About her mother, Eddie had said nothing.

Despite his sixty-two years, Sonya's father was still a powerful man. He owed his physique to twelve years of bodybuilding during his incarceration on drug charges. He owed his keen intellect to those same twelve years, which he had devoted to educating himself about any subject that snared his interest. He expected to be the dominant player in any situation, and few would challenge his right. If he had a weakness, and he did, he kept it well hidden behind his forceful persona. That weakness was "his harem," his wife, his daughter, and granddaughter. No one messed with his girls!

Sonya knew, because she had been a shy child given to listening, that her father had served in the Marines before he married. He had maintained ties with a number of Marine buddies, and when she was old enough to understand, she realized that the missions about which they reminisced were no ordinary military maneuvers. Over drinks, their conversations returned, time and again, to "the black ops." Although their discussions were couched in military jargon and oblique references to people and places, she understood enough to know that they spoke of infiltrating drug organizations and assassinating key players. She could not reconcile her gruff and loving father with the commander whose buddies held him in such high esteem.

What made even less sense to Sonya was that her father had followed his military service with a short-lived "career" in cocaine distribution, and had even involved her mother on the periphery of the operations. It was so out-of-character, so aberrant a behavior, as to be incomprehensible to her. Twelve years behind bars had been a steep price to pay. Right now, though, she needed her father's protection and his strength until she was sure that she and Dottie were in no danger. If her father had once been the "bad ass motherfucker" she'd heard him called affectionately by his men, so much the better.

"We'll be all right," she whispered to herself as she pushed two small suitcases toward the front door. Sonya then selected a sheet of her favorite stationery with the irises on it. She knew Eddie would recognize it as hers because she collected anything with irises. She wrote quickly, "Eddie, I have to leave for a few days. Dottie is with me. Please don't come for us. I'll call you soon. I love you, Eddie, but I don't feel safe with you right now. You've been acting strange for a while. I talked with a doctor today, and he suggested you come in to speak with him. His name is John Foster, and you can find his address in the phone book. He's a psychologist. I scheduled an appointment for you on Thursday at 9:00 a.m. Please go see him, Eddie, for me. I love you, Sonya."

CHAPTER EIGHT

Eddie entered the quiet house a little after 9:00 p.m. He was working days this rotation, but he'd covered his own shift and half a swing shift for Rizzo whose wife was sick; he was beat. Sonya hadn't been home when he called to let her know he was staying late.

Eddie sensed change immediately. The light on the answering machine was still blinking, which meant Sonya hadn't retrieved his message. There was no light on over the stove, and it was too still. Small things were out of place. He couldn't smell Sonya, and, although his senses told him she was gone, he could not think why.

He saw the folded paper on the Martha Washington table, and picked it up as he went into the living room. He looked at it without opening it, ran his thumb over the indentations of the wrong side of the embossed iris. He should get a drink, sit down, relax. Whatever was on the paper would wait. Instead, he surrendered to the couch and closed his eyes.

Eddie woke to the sodden gray of rain at dawn. He was chilled; his clothes were damp with sweat and clinging to him. He turned on his side, and saw Sonya's note on the floor. He picked it up, scanned it, and felt his gut coil.

Discomfort prodded him from the couch. Holding his thoughts at bay, he trailed a cold draft to the kitchen, and found the back door standing wide open, his key still dangling in the lock. *Boy, was I ever out of it!*

As he veered toward the counter for the coffeepot, Eddie stumbled mid-stride. Fear detonated in his vitals, and the lethargy of sleep was deep-sixed by a few words on a pretty piece of paper. Sonya was gone. She had gone, and taken Dottie with her. What's more, she had talked to someone about him...a goddamn psychologist.

Eddie's skin flushed and his vision narrowed as nausea roiled through him. He swallowed convulsively, sank to the floor, and dropped his head between his knees. His nostrils flared and his chest heaved as he fought to suck in enough air to keep the waves of blackness from swamping him. *Get a grip! Think. No harm done…been careful. She couldn't know…just scared; went to her parents…feels safe there. Needs reassurance. Left me no cover; gotta get her back. Think! Can't know…been careful. She left a note…a friggin' note.*

Eddie rolled to one hip and put his feet under him. He stood and leaned against the counter; he waited for his vision to clear and his stomach to settle. He pulled the note to him; Sonya's fragrance, faint, wafted from the paper as he reread it. Her words caused him another nasty jolt. *She's guessed. She knows, and she talked. Danger. Any shrink with half a brain…. Won't protect me now…scared. Exposed; hafta get to her. Hafta leave. No other way.*

"Sonya." Eddie wondered at the sorrow in his voice. *Could it be that he loved her? Had she become more than his cover? Was he capable of love? Can't think of that now.* The note slid from his fingers and fluttered to the floor. He palmed his wallet from the counter, and moved toward the back door where he removed his keys. The gravel drive was a painful reminder that he was barefoot.

Look like a wild man. Fuck!

Eddie returned to the kitchen. He started coffee on his way to the shower. Then, he stood under the needle-sharp spray, hot as he could take it, until his mind emptied. He imagined rage bleeding from him in molten torrents. When the water began to cool, he wrenched the handle to cold and concentrated on regaining his equilibrium. An icy calm settled over him. *Nothing more dangerous than going off half-cocked…that's how mistakes are made.*

Eddie burrowed into the recesses of his closet for the Perry Ellis slacks and shirts Sonya had added to his wardrobe. He knew she had been disappointed when he found no reason to wear them. For the time being, however, he needed an image, to give the right impression, do some damage control. He retrieved his black loafers and dusted a spider web from them, then went in search of shoe polish. He snickered. When, in the last twenty years, had he spit shined shoes? Too bad Sonya would miss the transformation.

For the second time, Eddie left the house, not bothering to lock the door. There was nothing to hide now. He slid behind the wheel, let the glove-soft leather seat embrace him, and closed his eyes. He was out in the open once more, exposed; he might as well use it to his advantage. Twenty-four hours was enough time to plan an attack. Sonya's good doctor, the shrink, wouldn't expect him to be on the offensive.

Eddie cranked the Vette engine. He shifted into first, and internalized the raw power. He popped the clutch and headed down the alley, scattering gravel and laying a strip of rubber as he hit pavement. He smiled. Sophisticated veneer, be damned, he was a brawler, and now he had only himself to rely on. So be it.

Second gear...tires squealed. Without slowing, Eddie pulled out onto a little-used back street that led to the interstate. A left here, a right there.... The engine and drive train screamed for freedom; he reached seventy in seconds. In third gear, at 97 mph, a flick of his wrist and he glided onto the access ramp. He muscled his way into the traffic flow, and instead of backing off, put his foot to the floor and shifted into fourth. The greater acceleration forced him back into his seat. He hooted as cars jockeyed to get out of his way. The tach read 6200-rpm, the speedometer, 127 mph, and it seemed that the faster he went, the slower the landscape passed. Just a leisurely scenic ride.

With another flick of the wrist, Eddie downshifted and cut a hard right, took a long straightaway exit. At the last moment, he stomped on the brake and came to a halt at an intersection; with the jolt of sudden deceleration, all of his senses were challenged to defy the forward motion. The mechanical protests were momentarily deafening. Then there was silence. *Now, the fury is gone.*

Eddie glanced at the fuel gauge; he needed gas. *Shit!* He was on the outskirts of the city; traffic in-bound was picking up. He turned left and eased into the far right lane. A whirly-bird traffic cop swooped low overhead. Eddie extended his middle finger out of habit. When he saw a gas station coming up, he took the exit onto an old state highway. *Out of harm's way…just to be on the safe side.*

The gas station had the old-fashioned rounded pumps, and boasted an "oasis." A neon palm tree pulsed anemically in the daylight. It looked like one of those old Petro Plazas from his childhood that had been dying for decades since the Interstate system stole the life-blood of main-street America. Simply crossing the pot-holed parking lot would take him back a good twenty years! The patrons were few, a couple semis, and a custom van tackied up the wazoo!

This is my kinda place.

The sign in front read, "**Jean ette's**."

Jean ette's? Probably "Jeannette's."

The restaurant smelled like a bakery, and fresh coffee was dripping into a sparkling glass carafe. Eddie's saliva began to flow immediately. The counter, bar stools and booths were well worn, but everything was clean, as in spotless. Every table wore a fresh bud, blossom, or branch of green leaves that showed pride of ownership, and sunshine from windows high above painted the walls a warm glow.

That same warmth was reflected in the smile of the woman behind the counter. Her hair in a bun, flour on one cheek, a bib-apron…someone's grandmother, to be sure. Jeannette? As Eddie watched, the woman whisked away some dirty cups; served fresh coffee and a glistening slice of chocolate cake; pinched the cheek of a gnarly old trucker; slipped a tip into her apron pocket, and patted the hand of a young man who got up to leave. He turned and blew her a kiss as he reached the door. "See ya next run, Jeannette," and he was gone.

Eddie slipped onto a stool at the end of the counter.

"What'll you have, son?" Jeannette's smile warmed her entire visage, but her glance missed nothing.

Better get your shit together. "Hello." He smiled, and found he really meant it.

"I'll have a sirloin steak, medium rare, three eggs over easy, hash browns, coffee, lots of it, and a piece of that," pointing to the chocolate cake.

"Coming up, Sweetie." Jeannette grabbed the steaming carafe and poured coffee into a real china cup.

"Starbucks," she whispered, and grinned. She hooked a small black and white cow cream pitcher with her index finger and sent it along the counter so that it stopped right in front of him. "Moooo!" she giggled, and disappeared into the kitchen in back.

Over a shoulder-high divider, Eddie could see Jeannette's silver bun in constant motion. He turned his head to the lone trucker who was mangling one toothpick with his teeth while cleaning his nails with another. Their eyes met; each man nodded, and turned away.

"Having a rough day, son?" Jeannette materialized, startling Eddie who had been...well, he didn't know where he'd been. He'd been staring at the old-time Lucky Strike poster on the wall, but he hadn't *seen* it. He'd been thinking of Prychek.

"Huh?"

"Rough one?"

"Yeah, rough," Eddie allowed himself the luxury of a sigh.

"Here, Sweetie. Drink up. Maybe this will clear your head."

Eddie sipped and burned his tongue. "Incredible!"

"What?" asked Jeannette.

"Hot."

"Yeah, real hot...never could abide cold coffee. You remember that awful crap? Iced coffee? Hot is the only way."

Eddie held Jeannette's eyes. He could see she'd been a place or two, and was better for it. "Are you the owner, Jeannette?"

"Yeah, it's my place. Me and Arnold, that's my husband, were on vacation, to Biloxi, wanted to see the Gulf of Mexico. We stopped here for a meal, chicken fried steak and fries, on our way south. That was thirty years ago," she grinned.

"Arnold and I spent a week on the Gulf, and Bam! He dropped dead. I drove back alone, stopped here just to feel close to him. Got into a discussion with the lady who owned it, and lo and behold, she offered me a great deal. After I buried Arnold, we closed the sale with his life insurance proceeds, and I've been here ever since. Life… that's just how it happens."

And how! "I know exactly what you mean." Impulsively, Eddie reached out his hand, palm up on the counter. Jeannette took it, squeezed and released. He could smell lemons.

"You're a good boy. What's your name?"

"Eddie."

"Eddie. That's a nice name. A nice name for a nice boy. You from around here, Eddie?"

"Yeah, now. But—coincidence—I was born in Biloxi. Small world."

Jeannette didn't say anything, but put her hand back in his.

She thinks I'm nice. Huh.

"My wife left me…I think." *Where the hell did that come from?* Eddie's swallow was audible. His voice cracked.

"That's tough, son. What are you going to do?"

"Do?"

"Do? Yeah, do?"

"Survive, make it through, get up and over....

"Or maybe not. Maybe I'll die. I could die. You know, it's not hard to die. I see it all the time. I'm an EMT and I live with it. It's funny…to live with death. Maybe it's to… to die from living."

"You've got to pull yourself together, Eddie." Jeannette turned stern, no nonsense. "Life's too precious. You touch lives. That's what you do every day. That's a good thing."

"Yeah. I guess I do." Eddie sat, pensive, while Jeannette served his steak and eggs. He wasn't really that hungry any longer, but he could eat, and after all, it was delicious.

When his plate was empty, another cup of coffee appeared at Eddie's place. He smiled. "That was a fine meal, Jeannette."

"Glad you liked her."

"Her?"

"Yeah. All things delicious are female. Didn't you know?"

Eddie smiled at the twinkle in her eye as their connection solidified. His thoughts raced ahead, and he imagined Jeannette as a twenty-five year old woman, "I'll bet you were…."

"What, Eddie?"

"You know, hot."

"I was OK, Sweetie, married young; never got to strut my stuff." Jeannette turned and walked down the counter to the trucker who was still sipping his coffee, "Anything else?"

"No. I'm good."

"OK, Hon, drive safe this haul." She gathered the dirty dishes and disappeared into the kitchen.

"Jeannette?" Eddie called over the partition. He was alone in the café. She bustled to the counter, and grabbed the coffee on her way by.

"No, thanks, Jeannette; I have to be on my way." He placed a $20 on the counter and placed his hand over his empty coffee cup. "Just want to tell you how glad I am to have met you. I needed someone to pull me up by my bootstraps, and that's just what you've done, reminded me how much I hate complainers!

"I don't get out this way much, but when I do, you can bet I'll be in. Your cooking is a powerful draw! Take care, Jeannette."

CHAPTER NINE

It was 9:15 a.m. and Foster was waiting for his first appointment, Eddie Vinson. He was pacing, and if he was honest, uneasy.

"Must be a no-show, Dr. John," offered the all-knowing Louise.

"A blooming no-show! Why do you bother to confirm appointments? Even disturbed people are capable of common courtesy."

Louise ignored him as he ranted; he usually did when someone didn't keep a scheduled appointment.

The phone on her desk rang and Louise answered, "Dr. Foster's office. May I help you? He's right here, Mr. Vinson," Louise placed her hand over the phone, "He wants to talk to you."

"I'll take it."

Louise handed over the phone. "Foster, here. May I help you?"

"Dr. Foster?"

"Yes?"

"I'm Eddie Vinson. I had an appointment at nine. Sorry, but I'm unable to make it."

"Uh, huh. I guess that's obvious, Eddie? Can I call you Eddie?"

"Right. Anyway, I'd still like to come in. Maybe tomorrow, maybe early next week?"

"OK, alright," Foster stuttered as unease slithered up his spine and constricted his throat. "Are you all right?" Foster asked, sensing his caller's distress and remembering Sonya Vinson's concerns.

"Alright? No, I'm not alright, but I will be," Vinson snorted, "Will I be?"

A riddler, Foster thought, ignoring Vinson's cryptic comments. "OK, I'll give you back to Louise to reschedule your appointment. I'll look forward to our meeting." He handed the phone back, "Soon," he mouthed to Louise.

Louise leafed through the appointment book, looking for an open spot. She backtracked through the pages. "How about tomorrow at two?" she asked.

Foster wasn't truly annoyed, but his instinctive response to his conversation with Eddie Vinson had to be construed as defensive. *This one will be interesting. I hope he's not a borderline. They scare the shit outta ya...get into your head before you even know they're there!*

Many psychologists tend to think of the Borderline Personality Disorder as the most complex of diagnoses and the most troublesome of all clients to serve. Foster paced the waiting room and launched into a muttered recitation of borderline characteristics as Louise concluded the phone call. She listened and smiled. She'd heard it all before!

Suddenly, "I'm going out for a few minutes, Louise. I will be back for my ten-thirty, OK?"

"OK, see ya. Tell Joyce hi for me."

"Who said I was going home?"

"Lucy, I'm home."

"Desi?"

"Nope, the milkman. Want a quart of chocolate milk?"

"Very funny." Joyce's laughter floated from the back bedroom. "You just left. What are you doing home?"

"I had a damn no-show."

"Say what?"

"What?" Foster broke out laughing.

Silence. Joyce knew his moods, and laughter or no, something was wrong. She came into the kitchen, and whether by accident or design, she stood in a ray of sunshine. She was dressed in cut-offs and sweatshirt with no bra. He loved that look.

"You're definitely a good bad girl.

"Careful there! You might get something you're not expecting."

Joyce hooked her arms around his waist and dropped her head to his shoulder. She was well aware that the seemingly amorous banter was a cover for something. Her even-keel husband was uncomfortable, off balance.

"You're so sexy, Lucy."

"What's wrong, John." He was asking her to put things in perspective for him; she knew that. The question was, *"Why?"*

"Nothing, really, just a mild case of red-ass. I hate no-shows."

"Oh, that," Joyce murmured. She hooked a chair with her bare foot and pushed him down. She began to massage his shoulders. Foster relaxed, slumping forward; he could smell her warmth, and he buried his head in her abdomen. "Much better, Lucy." He sighed and nuzzled.

"I have an abuse case at 10:30. From the social summary provided by the child protection worker, this child was reportedly sold by her crackhead mother for sex. I suppose, to buy more crack. Shit. Can you imagine giving over your kid to a couple of lowlifes in exchange for a drug rush? Unfrigginbelievable. Eight years old."

Joyce didn't say anything. No response was needed. She began to rub more gently now, trying to ease John's distress with her touch. What he needed was some time away. "Think 'beach,'" she whispered. It was time for rest. Their sanctuary was a homey and unpretentious Gulf-front condo in Perdido Key, Florida. They stole away three or four times a year, usually once each season, for the symbolic cleansing that enabled John to return to the harsh realities of his profession. When he lifted his eyes to her face, Joyce could see tenderness warring with frustration.

"Remember me telling you about that guy whose wife made an appointment, canceled it, and then came in. She had grave concerns about him? He was the no-show this morning. I'm not psychic, we both know, omniscient, but not psychic.... I've got a bad feeling about this guy."

Foster dropped his head again and drifted on the fringes of sleep. Joyce's hands continued to stroke rhythmically, working their soothing magic. He thought of the cherished flying dreams of his childhood, so real that he would wake, certain that he could lift off as effortlessly as in his dreams. It was like that with Joyce; her love for him was always there to sustain him.

CHAPTER TEN

On the way back to his office, relaxed and refreshed, John's nostalgic mood lingered. He often shared childhood experiences with colleagues and friends, sometimes even with patients when it was appropriate. His stories about sandlot baseball games were always favorites.

John could hit "lefty" when there were too few players to cover all positions; this was often the case during summer months when family vacations decimated their ranks. If there weren't enough players to field a regulation team, he and his friends modified their games accordingly to defend play based on the ability of each batter and what could reasonably be caught on a fair play. As an adult, in a moment of enlightenment, John came to understand that the kids had not followed any *rules* for such accommodations. They had simply accepted the rightness of making these changes based on a simple logic and sense of fairness.

John recalled one game when he hit a ball as cleanly as he was capable of doing. He **connected** with that ball, and watched it sail away. "Going, going, gone," he shouted, gloriously giddy.

Wumph! His perfectly hit ball smacked leather, and when John looked, disbelieving, there it was, nestled—impossibly—in the cradle of Denny Adamson's glove. Goofy Denny, who'd never before caught a ball in his life, looked at that battered baseball in his glove, and a silly-assed grin spread from ear to ear.

John eventually understood that it had been purely accidental, a fluke, that the ball was caught at all. Still, in that moment, the chills chasing up and down his spine were no less thrilling because fate intervened on Denny's behalf. To John's way of thinking, Denny was due. He deserved his moment of glory. Denny's father died when he was an infant; his mother worked long hours to support them, and relied on her dull-witted sister and brother to care for him. Consequently, Denny had all but raised himself, and never had the comfort of one loving parent, much less two.

Jimmy Goodell was another of John's many childhood friends. As is often the way with children, allegiances were fleeting and fragile...best friends one day, bitter enemies the next, usually as a function of jealousy, rivalry, or territory, and later, girls. So it was that on a perfect summer afternoon, John and his rowdy friends decided to throw hard balls at each other. Given the outcome, no one ever claimed to be the genius who thought up the competition.

When John and Jimmy, his best friend at that moment, drew matching short straws, John magnanimously let his friend go first. He knew Jimmy couldn't hit the broad side of a barn, and besides, Jimmy promised he wouldn't hit him even if he could. John believed him; he'd been raised that way, to accept people at their word and give them benefit of the doubt. It wouldn't be until graduate school that he learned to spot the obfuscations that people routinely use to hide their intentions. That long-ago afternoon, John turned sideways to reduce himself as a target. Jimmy threw the ball, and John would always remember the deep, penetrating sting on the back of his thigh where the lucky shot struck. In all his years, even when he had been shot, John could not recall any more intense pain than that he experienced from one wild pitch on a summer afternoon that ended a stupid game and a friendship. He and his cronies never spoke of the incident again; neither did they forget.

Over the years, John learned to value the memories that intruded from time to time. In his more contemplative moments, he could accept them for their ability to ground him in his past, give clarity to the present, and though he wouldn't admit it, sometimes, point the way. Thus, he could only surmise that, when all the pieces clicked into place, his recollections of Denny's lucky catch and Jimmy's wild pitch might have some bearing on his current concerns, whether personal or professional, only time would tell.

CHAPTER ELEVEN

Eddie Vinson never, *ever* ventured into conflict without getting up close and personal with his adversary. His upcoming appointment with the shrink, which had been mandated by his wife, was no exception. Corvette keys in hand, Eddie intended to check out one John Foster, Ph.D. The air was heavy with moisture and the humidity made him feel sluggish; the beer and pastrami sandwich sitting in his stomach didn't help. He wasn't at his best, but he was up to some covert observations of the good doctor on his professional turf. If it came to that, he'd check out his home and family another day.

After circling a several block area, Vinson chose the corner of an apartment building parking lot across the street from Foster's office. He parked between two brightly painted cars so he wouldn't stand out. His leather seat felt like butter warmed in the sun. If he weren't careful, he'd be fighting sleep in no time. As he settled in to wait and watch, he flashed back on other stakeouts when he prowled mall parking lots for pick-ups. He had this enduring fantasy about stalking and abducting a woman of his choice, and setting her up as his plaything. He had never acted on the fantasy, but he could.

The front of Foster's office had been remodeled to resemble a New Orleans courtyard. There was no sign to indicate the building's occupant, only a discreet wrought iron plaque with the address hanging to the left of the gated entry. An iron fence enclosed the courtyard of old bricks, stone benches, and urns overflowing with blossoms. Arching tree limbs provided dappled shade, and a stone fountain completed the landscaped oasis.

Handsome beveled glass doors graced the entrance. An arrangement of three mullioned floor-to-ceiling windows was located on the right front corner of the building, probably Foster's office. An old brick drive lined with adolescent willows disappeared behind the building, presumably to private parking. *The doc must have some kind of dough or one helluva green thumb if he spent that much time and money on the outside of his office.*

Vinson glanced at his watch as a well-dressed couple entered the courtyard. It was 1:50 p.m. Marriage therapy, perhaps, just to pay a few bills? Surely all Foster's cases weren't of the high profile and headline variety. As Vinson watched, a rusting sedan pulled into the parking lot behind Foster's office. A harried woman shepherded three children under six into the office. So, Vinson thought, Foster was an equal-opportunity shrink. Interesting.

In the waiting room, Foster greeted the young couple whose fairy-tale society marriage of eighteen months tanked when the bride discovered a Cartier charge for a sapphire tennis bracelet that she did not receive. She had studiously ignored lesser bits of incriminating evidence, but the Cartier expenditure was simply too blatant to let pass. She accused, and her husband admitted. Where did that leave them? The one thing they agreed upon was that they wanted John Foster, Ph.D. to fix their problems.

Foster had bet Joyce that the couple would not return for this, their second appointment. He would pay up gladly; it was a small price for the information he gained by learning that his stern confrontation of the couple at the conclusion of their first meeting had not run them off. Maybe their relationship was salvageable after all. Today he would split up husband and wife and let them each sling all the mud they could in a half-hour. In fact, he wouldn't put them together in therapy until the tantrums, grudges, and accusations had run their course.

Foster's concentration was highly developed; from years of therapy, he had learned to relax his body and focus his attention on details so that the stresses of emotionally charged sessions took a lesser toll on him. Thus, he let the wife's petulance and pettiness and her wandering spouse's intense anger flow past him. He sifted out the relevant data while his gaze drifted over the red sports car across the street in the sunshine. His focus narrowed to the vehicle and its occupant; they seemed out of place, though Foster couldn't say why. Too flashy, maybe, for the middle-class working residents of the apartment building.

Foster concluded the therapy session and escorted the wayward young husband to the reception area. "Thanks for coming in. Have Louise make your next appointment for two weeks, and be careful with one another. Do not go into any detail about the issues we've discussed here today until you each have a better handle on your feelings. You're both still too sensitive to address these matters without an arbiter present. That's me." He smiled and then turned away, ignoring the wife's attempt to catch his eye. He suspected she had dredged up more dirt during the half hour he was with her husband, and wanted to have the proverbial last word, in private.

"So sad," Foster said to himself, as he stood alone at his office window. The young couple had every advantage that money could buy, and yet, for the moment, they had nothing. He'd counseled countless couples where an affair seemed to the straying partner to be a harmless excursion outside the boundaries of the marital contract. How wrong they were. The emotional repercussions penetrated all layers of a relationship, and could never be excised without scars. Foster had seen otherwise stable partners crippled by self-doubts and recriminations. It took an exceptionally strong couple to find their way back from infidelity and rebuild trust. He didn't believe his young society maven and her narcissist spouse had what it would take. The only positive was that they had no children to use as weapons against one another. *Cynic*.

Again, Foster glanced through his office window. The Corvette was still there; it had been about an hour since he first noticed it. He moved to the rear entrance to his office and opened the French doors. As he stepped outside onto the steps, Foster's change of location put him about twenty feet closer to car and driver. Given that the man's sudden postural change indicated he had observed the strategic shift, Foster considered that he must be the object of the man's scrutiny. He stared fixedly at the driver, and altered his stance, an aggressive maneuver that should be obvious even at that distance. Foster recognized a pissing contest when he saw one, even at fifty yards. Sure enough, the driver slid down in his seat, and keyed the 'Vette to life. As soon as traffic allowed, he exited the parking lot and was gone.

CHAPTER TWELVE

John was beginning to anticipate his much-needed time in Florida...his retreat from the detritus of other people's private lives. Stretched out on the living room sofa, he called to Joyce, "Baby, can you hear me?" No response, not unusual for his Joyce. She was the most singular-minded person John had ever known. When she tackled a project, an issue, or challenge, she was in for the duration. Quitting wasn't part of her make-up.

John first confronted this aspect of his wife's personality in the early months of their marriage. A cranky garbage disposal in their first home was the means to his education. More than once, he had tackled the disposal, but his handyman skills were limited, at best, and he finally judged the dang machine to be terminal. He admitted defeat, and was washing up when he felt Joyce's breath on his neck.

"What are you doing, John?"

"Well, it's time to call a plumber and replace the stupid thing," he grumbled in anger.

"Can I look?" she asked sweetly.

Despite his grumpy pronouncements of futility and wasted effort, Joyce had the machine running within thirty minutes, and the repair lasted for the three years they lived in that first apartment. Such were their roles. Foster was well aware that his fix-it skills were nil, and Joyce had more mechanical acumen than most men. She let him try his hand; she always let him try, and when he'd reached maximum frustration, she would soothe him with words of praise for his effort, and fix whatever it was herself.

Joyce emerged from the kitchen where she'd been preparing lunch. Foster came home at noon as often as time allowed. He could smell the aroma of homemade vegetable soup heating on the stove and freshly baked bread. Joyce's homemade soups were the stuff of family legends. She made them by the gallons and froze them so there was always soup when comfort food was needed.

His Joyce was a meticulous cook. Her vegetable soup, for example, started with selection of the perfect beef bone. She had charmed more than one butcher into saving meaty knuckle bones for her and cutting the joints in half so that the marrow was exposed to give the deepest flavor. Then, she'd select a lean sirloin to add with the freshest of organic vegetables: tomatoes, skinned and seeded; celery, onion, zucchini, okra, if she could find it, mushrooms, carrots, potatoes, not too many; beans of all kinds, barley, parsley, garlic, bay leaves, pinches of thyme and oregano, and salt and pepper. The ingredients were covered with water, and God did the rest. Eight to ten hours later, the soup was pure heaven.

"Joyce, are you getting us ready for Florida, yet?"

"Not yet; lunch is ready. C'mon while it's hot.

"I'll start packing tomorrow. I did get the tickets, though; we can leave here about 9:00 a.m., depart O'Hare at 11:30, and be in Pensacola by 3:00. I also called the rental agency, and they'll have a car waiting."

John and Joyce loved their Gulf-side home in Perdido Key. Perdido was Spanish for "lost," and so the community remained, even now, when compared to Destin, for example, which no longer resembled the sleepy fishing village it once had been. As a boy, John's family would travel through Perdido Key on their way to visit relatives in New Orleans. They usually took old Highway 98 because of its scenic Gulf views. When he and Joyce eventually considered buying a place on the coast, they looked at places along the panhandle from Pensacola to Panama City, but found them to be pricey and the communities, overpopulated. Furthermore, vacationers in the Southeast flocked to the "Redneck Riviera" during the summers, and snowbirds fleeing northern winters had discovered that the area was more affordable than Florida's East Coast. He and Joyce had a more private retreat in mind, however, and so it was that he recalled the remote beauty of the Key.

Foster had been disappointed to see that growth was evident from the high-rise condos being built along the narrow strip of the sandy key; however, development was not as rampant or as tasteless as in other areas. Additionally, because several large stretches of beach and dunes had been designated as national seashores, the area was afforded vital protection from the destruction of fragile wildlife habitats caused by the overbuilding of multinational corporations who gobbled up beaches by paying inflated prices to greedy landowners.

Foster often wound down at the end of a day by visualizing white sand beach, a tidal pool warming in the hazy sun, and gentle waves. If he really got into the imagery, he could hear the waves lapping the shore – or crashing, if that was his mood. Industrious sandpipers searched for food, and gulls circled lazily overhead. He thought of the aging blue heron who had been his fishing companion for three years now. The scoundrel was a relentless beggar, and if the fish weren't biting, he'd been known to help himself to the shrimp bait when Foster wasn't looking.

"Joyce, the soup is delicious, as always. Comfort by the spoonful! You were generous with the beans; I see some I don't recognize, and you found fresh okra.

"While, I'm thinking of it, will you dig out my Joseph Campbell tapes and pack them. I think they're in my bedside table. I need a dose of his inspiration, and I have a patient with whom I want to use Campbell's discussions of the Hero. His metaphor may be effective in this man's therapy. He has the knowledge and the abilities to overcome his problem, but he lacks the courage to use the tools at his disposal. Maybe Campbell's intellect will inspire him."

Foster sat back in his chair, looked down at the empty bowl, and whispered, "Thanks." He lingered over a kiss, inhaling Joyce's fragrance to fortify him for the afternoon. Another kiss of good-bye, and he headed for the door. "See you about six if my schedule holds up. Love you."

"Love you, too," Joyce trailed off. He was gone.

Louise was fielding calls left and right as Foster sauntered through her office. She looked harried. "Thank the Lord we don't have three telephone lines! I didn't even get lunch; it's been crazy," she pouted.

"Crazy gives you job security, Girl," Foster shot at her. "When I'm with my 1:00, put the answering machine on and scoot. Use some of that authority the kids all think you have as *my boss!*"

"Oh, your 2:00, Mr. Vinson, he was a no-show for his first appointment?"

"Yeah?"

"Well, he'll be late for this one."

"Figures," was all Foster said.

Judith Radovitch, his 1:00, was a first-time appointment. *Where are all the new clients coming from? Is it a full moon?*

Louise's notes of Ms. Radovitch's initial telephone contact indicated only that she wanted to discuss some "very personal issues." Foster seated her in the overstuffed chair adjacent to his desk. He did not believe in putting distance between himself and his patients, and he didn't use his desk to establish his authority or create a barrier.

Ms. Radovitch was attractive, probably late twenties, with a slender, but curvy, build. She had short, brown hair, sleekly styled, and strikingly blue eyes, unusual for a brunette. Her nails were perfectly manicured, and her open leather sandals, easily recognizable for their Italian workmanship, showed that fingers, toes, and lips were all the same glossy deep red. Her cosmetics provided a stark contrast to her casual gray cotton sweater and white slacks.

"Ms. Radovitch? Did I say your name correctly?"

"Yes...but please call me Judy." Her voice had a demure, childlike quality.

Foster smiled and told her she could call him John.

"John, I've got a problem, I think."

"OK, tell me how I can help you." Foster assumed what his wife and his secretary called his "listening posture." Some of his lawyer friends kidded him about his habit of putting his right hand to the corner of his mouth, and then ever so slowly, rubbing his thumb and forefinger together as though he were twirling a toothpick or the tip of a handlebar mustache. They claimed it had a hypnotic influence if you watched him too long.

Ms. Radovitch began by telling him about her live-in boyfriend. She met him at work...well, school, actually. She taught sixth grade; he taught seventh. They had been living together for about four months, discreetly because of their jobs. She was beginning to worry about her boyfriend's relationship with her seven-year-old son. Ms. Radovitch faltered, "You see...in the past few weeks I've been noticing some changes in Devon's behavior.

"How so?"

Ms. Radovitch began to hyperventilate, and Foster surmised his simple request that she put her suspicions into words, thereby acknowledging her fear to another individual, was pushing her anxiety to some critical threshold. Before she could answer, Ms. Radovitch slid from the chair to the floor. She tucked her legs beneath her and seemed to fold in on herself as though in self-protection.

When she continued to breathe rapidly and erratically, he moved quickly from his chair to kneel before her. "Stop!" he said with authority, hoping to short-circuit her anxiety reaction. "Now, take a deep breath, slow and easy."

Judy struggled to regulate her breathing. When she had calmed and could maintain eye contact with him, John placed a firm hand beneath her elbow, and guided her back into her seat. He asked if she was ready to continue, and she nodded.

Because Judy had been unable to respond to an open-ended question that allowed her to discuss her concerns, he changed tactics and began with specific questions to which, for the moment, she could answer only yes or no.

"Have you noticed any suspicious behaviors, any problems between Devon and your live-in...what's his name?"

"Brian...no, I haven't seen anything specific."

"Has he developed any physical symptoms?"

"No physical symptoms exactly, but bedwetting and two instances of loss of bowel control. He's not sleeping through the night, and his appetite is way off.

"His daily homework grades are falling all of a sudden, and he got into a fight on the playground last week. None of these behaviors are typical for him." Judy's eyes were shuttered, and her hands in her lap showed white knuckles. "Do you think Brian could be abusing him? I know the statistics in situations like this..."

Ah! The real reason for being here. "Let me answer you this way, Judy.... There is little doubt that Devon is showing signs of an Adjustment Disorder of Childhood. However, to attribute his symptoms to Brian's entry into your lives or to possible sexual abuse, which is your fear, is a big stretch at this point in time. There could be any number of possible explanations for the changes in Devon that you are seeing. Could be a bully at school. Devon might be unsure about his relationship with you as you grow closer to Brian.

"Has anyone in your family died in the past few months? A grandparent, perhaps?

"Actually, my sister passed away in early February." Judy's eyes filled with tears, and her gaze traveled to the unusual mullioned windows which were the only decorative aspect of Foster's simple but elegant office. "I hadn't thought of that...and now that you've asked, we had to leave her memorial service because Devon had diarrhea."

"Was Devon close to your sister...and was this his first experience with death?"

"Yes, and yes."

"Hmmm," was Foster's knowing response.

"Hmmm?" asked Judy, her eyebrow raised.

"Yes, hmmm. It can be a very effective therapeutic response. I learned it in graduate school," said Foster lightening the moment.

His words caused a visible easing of tension. He went on to ask Judy Radovitch to provide a comprehensive developmental, academic, and social history. He asked her to think back to any other similar episodes of behavioral decompensation such as her son was currently experiencing. Once he had documented the necessary background details, Foster suggested that Judy make an appointment later in the week to bring Devon in for a talk, and he offered suggestions for how she should prepare her son for the meeting so that it would not cause additional anxiety.

Following Judy Radovitch's departure, Foster considered briefly whether there was sufficient concern to warrant a report to Child Protection based on her fears about possible sexual abuse of her son. Given that the likely cause of Devon's symptoms would prove to be the death of his aunt, he decided that such a report would be premature. He would reconsider after his meeting with Devon.

"Your two o'clock, Mr. Vinson, is here."

Foster braced himself against the unease that flowed through him. Despite Mr. Vinson's warning that he would be late, he was early. Foster returned to his office to review the notes of his interview with Sonya Vinson; then he went to greet her husband.

"Mr. Vinson, I presume?"

"That's right, Doc."

Eddie Vinson stood and extended his hand. His grasp was harder than necessary, just short of painful. He looked directly into Foster's eyes, immediately challenging.

The hairs on Foster's neck registered his physical response. His greeting did not. "Nice to meet you, Mr. Vinson. Please come back. First door on your right."

Foster purposely directed a too familiar Vinson to an upright upholstered chair in front of his desk. The chair was not particularly comfortable, and this time, he felt he might need the authority that such an arrangement conferred. Similarly, he dispensed with the usual banter that he used to put new patients at ease. Echoing Vinson's earlier inappropriate familiarity, Foster addressed him by his first name without asking permission, something he never did with new patients.

"Eddie? You know, we should be straight with each other from the start. Do you think?"

"Right."

"Sonya came to see me several days ago; I know she told you that. She reported concerns about you and about some things that happened in your home that have really worried her. Perhaps we could begin by addressing her concerns."

Vinson was dressed in ambulance greens, typical hospital garb that withstood repeated washings and the harsh detergents used to remove bodily fluids. Foster noticed what were probably spurts of blood on his battered Nikes. About twenty seconds passed before Vinson launched into a recounting of his drug history rather than addressing his wife's concerns as Foster had asked.

"Drugs?" Foster wondered aloud, when Vinson paused to take a deep breath. *Where is he going with this?*

"Drugs, yes." Vinson continued. "So many drugs... marijuana, LSD, alcohol, and oh, yes, speed. I loved crystal meth. I haven't used for about seven years, but I remember those old demons, and they often taunt me." Eddie was speaking freely; throwing out negatives first, before Foster could flush them out. He appeared outwardly confident, but there was a sadness, maybe fear, in his eyes that belied his self-assurance.

"Two years ago, I began to question my chemical dependency diagnosis. So, I started to experiment with controlled drinking."

Foster had heard this one before. The last rendition was from a boat skipper who operated along the shores of Lake Michigan. He was determined to show his employers he could drink safely while shouldering the responsibilities of his job. He couldn't, and two men died for his foolishness.

Eddie went on to say that his drinking had escalated about five months ago. It coincided with a change of employment, but he wasn't sure the new job was the trigger for the increase. He believed he had been able to hide his drinking from Sonya, his wife of seven months, who was a recovering alcoholic.

Then.... "I think I had a blackout one night. I was drinking pretty heavy, and I was losing track of time. My wife and her niece were spending a long weekend with her parents. While I was out of it, somebody broke into our house. They trashed the back of our house, mostly the computer room. I didn't hear a thing, and didn't even find the damage before I left for work. When Sonya and Dottie returned that next afternoon, they discovered the mess. It was a shocker, I tell ya. Dottie handled it pretty well, but my wife felt really threatened."

Without warning, Eddie appeared to sob. His behavior seemed extreme for the situation he was describing, and as Foster watched, he noted an absence of tears. *Manipulation, plain and simple, and often, an indication of guilt.*

"Go on, Eddie," Foster said softly, not acknowledging the man's phony distress. He shifted in his chair, a behavioral gesture that often encouraged further information from a client as Foster remained silent.

When a minute or two passed in silence, Foster prodded, "Tell me more about what happened at your home?"

"Sonya seems to think that I did it."

"Did what?"

"Killed the chicks."

"Chicks? I thought we were talking about vandalism?"

"I was, but let me tell you about the chicks. I had a couple dozen. They're so cute when they're tiny. I just love 'em. Dottie does too. I sell them to local farmers when they get big.

"Have you ever smelled chicken shit?"

Foster belted out a single harsh laugh. "No, but I've put up with a lot of it."

Vinson nodded solemnly, and seemed to miss Foster's quip altogether, but then, he smiled coyly.

"What about the chicks?"

"They smelled to high heaven, I admit, and with my new job, I wasn't tending to them. Sonya...," he paused. "Sonya had had enough. She said, 'No more chicks.'"

"You know, she's older than I am, smarter, too, and we live in her house. She used to be so soft and giving, but in the last few months, she's become such a bitch; always happens when you marry 'em." Vinson sat back and resumed his casual pose.

Foster let the outburst pass without comment, but Vinson's response had registered. *You're giving me clues, Eddie.*

"So, I had to get rid of them. I grabbed a black plastic garbage bag and placed each bird inside, each in their place, making sure not to hurt any of them. They never did anything to warrant what Sonya was asking me to do. One after the other, I put them in their places, but they didn't stay. They got real active and scared. I tied up the top of the bag with...shit...what do you call those things?"

"Twist-ties?" Foster offered.

"Yeah, twist-ties. And that was it."

"It?"

"Well, I threw the bag on the passenger seat and drove out to the Chicago River. I figured to throw 'em off the bridge, but I just couldn't do it. They're such helpless little things. I was s'posed to care for 'em, and I was betraying their trust. Ya know?"

"Hmmm."

Vinson was beginning to wonder if he was giving too much information, but Lord, this was fun! He was throwing out red herrings left and right, pure garbage, chaff on radar! Give 'em more shit than they can handle, and they won't believe the truth when they hear it. Furthermore, as he had prepared for his meeting with a psychologist, he had realized that anything he told the shrink within the confines of the doctor-patient relationship would remain confidential.

"What then, Eddie?"

"I headed home, but stopped and parked in the Forest Preserve instead. It was quiet.

"I took each chick out of the bag. How many did I say?"

"Two dozen or so," Foster supplied. *He's checking to see if I'm paying attention.*

"I rubbed each chick where they like to be petted. Each one looked into my eyes as I twisted its neck between my thumb and first finger. There was a cracking sound, like when you crack your knuckles. I could tell they thanked me when I did it. They had been frightened in the bag. Snapping their necks showed me that death is noisy. Have you ever noticed, Doc, how noisy death can be?"

Foster blinked, "Noisy?"

"Yeah, you know, screaming, yelling, cursing, moaning, whimpering, begging...whatever...noisy. Get it?"

"I think I understand what you mean, Eddie. Birth and death can be some of the noisiest events in our lives."

Foster disengaged from the conversation by making brief notes in Vinson's file. *How do you document bullshit? All that, and Vinson hasn't answered my original question. It doesn't matter, though; everything he says provides clues.*

Realizing that Vinson was not going to continue, Foster steepled his fingers and said calmly, "Look, Eddie, what I want you to do is make an appointment for early next week. In the interim, I'm asking you to begin a journal in which you record some of the most important memories in your life, going back to childhood. Bring these recollections to our next meeting, and we'll examine them from your current perspective, who you are today, and see how they have impacted your relationship with Sonya."

Foster noted Eddie's bewildered reaction; he'd seen it in other patients. It came from the sudden fear of having to look at yourself, even in private, and sharing who you are and how you perceive your *self* with another person.

There was a trace of anger as Eddie asked, "Significant memories, huh? Well, we'll see." He stood abruptly and then devoted an inordinate amount of time to aligning the creases of his faded scrubs. Just as Foster stepped past him on his way to the door, Eddie stuck out his hand. Awkwardly, Foster moved his arm across his body to shake Eddie's hand.

Who's pulling whose strings here? Foster wondered as he prolonged the contact of their hands, and this time, he used more force than necessary.

"Thanks, Doc, that wasn't as bad as I thought it would be." Eddie's grin seemed contrived, disingenuous.

Foster noted the icy dampness of Vinson's palm. *Not as cool as you want me to believe, are you Vinson?* "I'll look forward to our next meeting, Eddie. Just talk to Louise, and she'll set up your next appointment."

"Right. Bye."

Foster strode slowly to the back door and glanced out to the parking lot. Only his car and Louise's were there. Then, a sliver of red fender pulled his attention to the Corvette in the far corner of the next-door printing company's parking lot. He'd almost missed it.

Foster returned to his desk, shaking his head wearily. The *pas de deux* with Eddie Vinson had been damn tiring, physically draining 'though all he'd done was sit on his ass. Was there sense to be made of their first encounter? Sure there was. He grabbed a pencil.

"Eddie Vinson: Slippery, clever about deflecting questions and resetting points of reference. Assumes he's in control. Methods of disclosure: confuses/confounds with meaningless details; throws out bull to disguise the few grains of truth. His agenda: Deception. Best to let it play out on his terms. Don't spook him. Assessment: Wants to tell me...more. Wants recognition within confidential setting."

Foster left his desk and sat in Vinson's chair to write more therapy notes. Maybe proximity would provide some illumination. He could still feel Vinson's body heat. He flipped his pencil from lead to eraser to lead. *Lead balloons. What am I missing?*

Eureka! The red Corvette. The pissing contest. Foster returned swiftly to the back door and opened it just enough to see Vinson ease himself into the striking red Corvette.

"Well I'll be.... Son of a buck, that was you!"

Foster returned to his desk. He wrote decisively: "Initial impressions: clever, offensively defensive, a riddler. Chemically dependent. Rule out sociopathy. Probably not an Impulse Control Disorder—more likely alcohol disinhibition. Impression from Sonya Vinson's interview confirmed.

Plan: review journal entries and take social history, but don't press for information. Allow him to reveal what he is willing. Psychological testing if he agrees."

Putting the case notes in Vinson's file, Foster carried it to the front desk. "Louise?"

"Yes, sir?"

"Sir? Sir? Who? Where? Are you my Louise?

"What do you think of our Mr. Vinson?"

"Well," she paused, "he was kind of strange. He looked at me funny." She pulled a face.

"He paid by check, and he held the check too long, like he didn't want to give it up. When I looked up at him, he let it go. Then, he said something weird."

"What?"

"He said, 'Have a good life.' Then he turned and left, and I thought I heard him chuckle."

Foster took a second to absorb the implications of Louise's interaction with Vinson and his off-putting statement which had been heavy on the sarcasm.

"Don't worry. He's all right, just a little confused, maybe, torn." *Don't want to scare her.*

"Is it all right? Dr. John, really?"

"Yes, really, it's OK, kid.

"What's next?"

"Uh, Dr. V's coming at three-thirty. He had an emergency surgery this afternoon, so he'll be late for his regular three o'clock. His nurse called to explain the circumstances, and your schedule could accommodate the half-hour change."

Dr. Erik von Kovska was a long-standing therapy client. He had been a resident physician in Warsaw, Poland in 1985. He was one of the region's most accomplished surgeons. Because of his intrinsic value to the Soviet Union, not just for his life-saving skills, but for the publicity his good works generated, he was closely watched. In 1985, the Chicago Medical Association held an international convention for trauma specialists. Von Kovska was the invited speaker. Following his presentation, he begged a bathroom break, excused himself from inquisitive colleagues, and slipped from the building into the crowded Chicago streets. He made his way to the U. S. Embassy and requested asylum.

Von Kovska was now a U.S. citizen and on staff at Northwestern University's Feinberg School of Medicine. He also served as a Professor Emeritus at the University of Chicago, where his primary involvement was with the Comer Children's Hospital. It was there that Foster first met Erik at a fundraiser for children with life-altering physical injuries, some due to physical abuse. Their connection had been immediate. Because Foster sometimes received referrals from university hospitals for children who also suffered psychological trauma resulting from their physical injuries, he was aware that Erik performed medical miracles with great regularity. Thus, when the daunting Dr. von Kovska turned up in his waiting room, appointment card in hand, Foster was honored, intimidated, and intrigued. He would have chosen a friendship over a therapeutic relationship, but the choice had not been his to make.

Erik was now in his early sixties. His bearing was formal, confident, sometimes arrogant. He seemed to have stepped from the frames of an old black and white movie, and he even looked like Charles Boyer. It was his warmth and caring, however, that drew his child patients to him and comforted their parents.

During their first therapy session, Foster soon realized that the very somber von Kovska had had a drink or two to fortify him. He made no reference to prior professional or social meetings between them or their shared interests in the treatment of children. Erik's presentation showed clearly that his need was for a therapist, and that he was placing himself in Foster's hands. Having made the decision to do so, he proceeded to confront the terrors of his years under Soviet domination. His reasons for needing some liquid courage so that he could confront his demons were soon apparent.

In halting and broken English and a foreign accent that Foster had never heard from the gifted physician who spoke perfectly the language of his adopted country, Erik spoke of the brutality he had witnessed and experienced himself in his native Poland. His innate intelligence, his medical genius, and his humanity all set him at odds with those in authority at every level of his profession and his Soviet-controlled country. Conflict was the price Erik had paid daily to heal those he could, and to ease the suffering of those he could not. Yet he was not a rebel; by nature and nurture, he was a pacifist.

As a twenty-year-old student at the university in Budapest where he went to study medicine on a Soviet-sponsored scholarship, Erik had been aware that university intellectuals planned a peaceful protest against the Soviet government. Like his native Poles, the Hungarian people yearned for the liberation that had been paid for with the blood of men, women, and children. Although he admired the spirit of those who would tweak the nose of the Russian giant, Erik was not a participant. He remained singularly dedicated to completing his medical training.

When peaceful demonstration became brutal conflict, and Soviet tanks dispatched idealistic students and faculty, von Kovska was drawn to the conflict by cries of the wounded on the steps of the library where he had been preparing for exams. His medical knowledge was supplemented in those next frantic hours by hands-on treatment of flesh torn from muscle; muscles torn from limbs; limbs torn from…and everywhere, death, needless, pointless death.

The path of von Kovska's life was altered forever by those bloody hours in Budapest where he first *practiced* medicine. He continued his medical education, and sought specialized training in trauma and reconstructive surgery. As the years passed, Erik's caseload in Poland, and then the United States, became more and more those trauma victims who had exhausted all other resources. They were the individuals, particularly children, for whom he was the last resort.

Foster diagnosed Erik von Kovska with a Posttraumatic Stress Disorder - Delayed. Many of their sessions were spent guiding Erik through confrontations with his own emotional trauma, trying to make sense of the paradox that his life had become.

"Dr. John? Dr. V. is here," Louise still shied from pronouncing von Kovska's name, so he was reduced to an initial.

"Have Dr. von Kovska come back." Foster enunciated clearly for Louise's benefit.

"John, my friend and colleague," Erik's voice rumbled, deep and throaty, soothing in its own way.

"Erik, have a seat. Relax," he responded in kind. "How have you been since our last session?"

"I'm usually OK, but last week, I had a trauma case referred to me that brought it all back, you know…the crap."

"Your command of our American malapropisms continues to improve, my friend!"

As Foster listened to von Kovska, he couldn't escape the man's anguish. They had these talks, sometimes as long as three hours at a time, to desensitize, hopefully to extinguish the trauma component of Erik's disorder. Despite the excruciating psychic pain, with Foster's guidance, Erik courageously immersed himself in the imagery of his trauma.

Over the course of two years, since his initial appointment, von Kovska had made significant improvements. Before his therapy, Erik had coped with his trauma as most PTSD victims do, by dissociation, denial, fantasy, and defensive avoidance. To Erik's credit, with Foster's support, he stayed in the reliving of his trauma until the emotional components of horror ceased to overwhelm him, except in increasingly rare instances. Despite the injury, disfigurement, and death of his countrymen...and the depths of his personal grief, Erik had survived. In thanksgiving, he dedicated his medical knowledge and technical skills, and his compassion to those in need. Foster knew that Erik turned no patient away, and that, more often than not, he didn't even charge for his services.

CHAPTER THIRTEEN

By the time John and Joyce arrived at the coast, Chicago had been long forgotten. On the flight to Pensacola, they dined on Chicken Parmesan and a less than memorable white wine. After their meal, Joyce listened to music, and John dozed to a Clint Eastwood movie he'd already seen. Their clasped hands were warm and comforting in his lap. They so seldom shared such moments of inactivity. Having Joyce still and quiet was a gift—for as long as it lasted.

The touchdown in Pensacola was rough, three jarring bounces and the squeal of tires. "You can breathe, now, Luv," John whispered, nuzzling her ear.

Their rental car was waiting, and the drive to Perdido Key was uneventful. Crossing Pensacola from northeast to southwest at rush hour was not an especially enjoyable drive, but it beat all hell out of the bumper-to-bumper traffic they left behind. No spoken words were required to communicate their growing anticipation. The pines along Gulf Beach Highway began to replace businesses and homes. The heron's nest atop a platformed pole had survived a minimal tropical storm, and shared smiles of relief indicated that each had feared its loss. Up and over the Theo Barr Bridge...a setting sun on the blue-green sea.... They were home.

According to some long-ago agreement, they would not unpack tonight. They opened a favorite wine and strolled the beach—to Lillian's Pizza—shedding cares along the way. Après pizza, they would walk off their overindulgence and eventually find their way home.

In the distance, thunder rolled half-heartedly, threatening to curtail their first day on the beach. Joyce refused to look up from her book, but John pushed his sunglasses up and calculated the likelihood that they would get wet. Storms to their north usually stayed away from the coast, so odds were in their favor. Closing his eyes, John surrendered to the rhythmic lap of the waves and the warmth radiating from the sand.

"Wrong again," he grimaced as the first raindrops ended his snooze abruptly. A quick glance revealed that Joyce had abandoned him. *The rat!*

John found Joyce as she emerged from a steamy shower, wrapping herself in a towel. "You could have woken me," he grumbled. She shrugged, and an ominous intake of breath heralded who knows what. He waited—not for long.

"Do you like me, John?"

"*Like*? No." Not sure where she was headed, but certain he didn't want to go there, he let her hang. He should never have had that nap. He needed his wits about him when Joyce wanted to wallow in existential misery. *And damn the rain anyway!*

Into the pregnant silence, John sighed. "You gotta understand, Joyce. When a man *likes* a woman, he doesn't want to do the things we do together." Joyce hunched her shoulders and wouldn't look at him, so she didn't see the Ernie Kovac eyebrows. *Why the sudden insecurity…and where was it coming from?*

"When a good man likes a woman, he enjoys her company, and for him, there's a kind of relaxation…a feeling of safety in friendship that isn't complicated by sexual attraction.

"We began with friendship, remember? For about three minutes…then I knew I wanted you." He smiled and ducked his head so she couldn't read intent in his eyes. His hand snaked out and relieved her of the towel she was wearing. "So, when you're asking if I like you…the answer is 'no.' I don't like you; I love you, and I need you...now."

CHAPTER FOURTEEN

Eddie Vinson finally slept, thanks to the contents of an old bottle of Xanax he found in the medicine cabinet. Sonya's absence was taking its toll. He had come to realize the extent to which he had let her fill his empty spaces. The Xanax fogged his dreams and distorted the sound of his pager. As sleep receded, Eddie made a grab for his battered beeper just as the phone on his bedside table also began to ring. *What the hell?*

"What?" he mumbled, rubbing the grit from eyes that refused to stay open. Instinctively, however, he knew what was coming.

"It's Tony. I'm three minutes from your door. Got a bloody mess downtown. Multiple shootings, probably gangs, they're callin' everyone in. I'll be there in two."

Eddie was already moving.

The call had come in to First Alert at 2:07 a.m. Lieutenant Tom Hajec of the Chicago PD, desk-bound with a broken leg, had been contacting EMT services to help the police deal with the carnage. The radio transmissions from those already on the scene were graphic and grisly. Just this once Hajec was thankful for the bum leg.

South of downtown, a cloying darkness muffled the movements of several hooded and gloved figures slipping through an alley toward Cottage Grove and 71st. They were scouts and point guards for the several dozen cold, but hyped, gang members ranging in age from fifteen to twenty-five, who were hell bent on acquiring new territory. Knives, bats, and the occasional pistol were no longer the tools of choice. Every would-be warrior was now armed and well trained in the use of shotguns or automatic weapons.

Drive-bys were a familiar tactic of gang rivalries, but their brutality factor was limited by the hit-and-run method. Therefore, when tensions exceeded some ill-defined threshold, violence erupted, and all-out war was often the result. So it was that ambitious factions of the two largest gangs were making their bids for new territory. When the night was over, they would have blasted each other into oblivion. The final toll, as it would be noted in a two-inch single column at the bottom of Page Two of the Tribune, indicated that sixteen gang members died and fourteen were seriously wounded. Only the police and paramedics knew that the dead and injured were all under age eighteen, and that their fearless leaders were not among the casualties. Not one fatal shot was fired by police.

Lieutenant Hajec advised the responding medical services that the carnage covered several blocks, and that the danger to their EMTs had not yet been assessed because police were still pinned down in several areas. Cook County Hospital was to be the staging area although other hospitals and trauma teams were on stand-by.

Eddie reached the curb as Tony pulled to a stop in front of his house. Because they lived in the same apartment complex, Jenny was already with Tony; she reported that the latest radio transmissions indicated police were taking sporadic fire. She looked pale and was biting her lip.

"Great…just friggin' great," Eddie whispered.

At 2:30 a.m., there was no traffic on the Stevenson, so Tony made good time with lights and sirens. As they approached downtown, he slowed and cut the special effects so they wouldn't draw unwelcome attention. All three hunkered down in their seats and began to scan streets, alleys, doorways, and rooftops. Tony tucked the ambulance in behind a lone police car whose occupants were crouched behind the driver's open door. From the anemic wash of the street light, it appeared that nothing was moving, although there were three bodies on the pavement about fifty feet beyond the PD vehicle.

"What do you think, Eddie? Do we try to get to them?"

"What do I think? I think some people don't deserve our help. Accident victims and medical emergencies, sure, but this? Shit. They brought this on themselves!"

"Yeah, but we shouldn't judge; that's not what we do."

"Really?" Eddie smirked. "You wanna risk your neck? The assholes we transport tonight will be back on the streets and doing the same thing in a matter of weeks.

Why don't we just let 'em do themselves in, and everyone will be better off?"

Tony was staring at Eddie in disbelief, when one of the policemen scuttled up to tap on his window. Tony jumped a foot, and Eddie bit the inside of his cheek to keep from laughing. The cop passed on a radio message directing them toward 79th Street to transport wounded.

As they approached Halstead on 79th, they passed a logjam of police vehicles, and then nothing. Agreeing that they were exposed and would backtrack, Tony made a U-turn. A crackling sound, like distant firecrackers, accompanied the shattering of the windshield. In slow motion, the fractured sheet of glass rolled onto the dashboard.

Eddie was distracted by the broken windshield and its implications. Jenny, however, had reached across the center console and clapped her hand against Tony's neck. As Eddie's focus narrowed, he watched a jet of arterial blood spray Jenny's left cheek. He reached behind him to grab a pile of gauze pads, sliding them under Jenny's hand as she applied pressure to the wound.

"Help me slide him back here; we'll put him on the floor. It's fastest. You'll have to drive. Can you do it, Jenny? Don't fall apart on me."

There was icy fury in Jenny's eyes. "I'm alright," she hissed as she maneuvered Tony into a reclining position across the console so Eddie could hook his arms under Tony's shoulders and slide him onto the floor of the ambulance treatment area. She removed her hand from the gauze pads as Eddie's much larger hand applied pressure. Like a nimble sprite, she was up and over the console and into the driver's seat; the ambulance was moving before her bottom hit the plastic. Several bullets hit the back doors of the van, and one window fissured with a direct hit.

They had traveled a block and a half, when they came up on another ambulance. Its back tires were both flat, and it was a sitting duck. Jenny pulled alongside and tapped the horn; the two EMTs inside looked at her vehicle with relief. She pulled forward so that the back of the ambulance was even with their passenger door. They moved quickly from their van into the back of the ambulance. One moved forward to take the passenger seat beside Jenny, and the other knelt beside Eddie, quickly assessing Tony's status.

"Take over, will you?" Eddie asked, taking the EMT's hand and restoring pressure to the wound. With economical movements, he started an IV. Just as Jenny completed a transmission to report that she had picked up the two stranded EMTs and was taking a wounded Tony to Cook County, Eddie made his move.

"I'm gonna find the bastard who did this." He pulled the gun from his pocket, nodded to the EMT whose name he didn't know, and stepped from the ambulance as Jenny pulled away.

Standing in the silent shadows of the now-deserted street, Vinson scanned the abandoned buildings along both sides. Nothing moved. As he stepped toward the curb, he heard the guttural burp of a rifle, and concrete flew—too close for comfort. He looked up and caught a rooftop muzzle flash as a second bullet split the distance from the first.

Vinson turned and sprinted toward the fire escape of the building where the shots were being fired. There were 55-gallon drums beneath the fire escape, which he used to give himself a leg up. The bottom segment of the iron ladder dangled drunkenly; it shuddered and screeched when he tested it with his weight, but it held, and he scrambled to the first landing. He would be approaching the roof from the shooter's right side; hopefully the scope of the rifle would block his arrival and allow him to get close before he was seen.

As he reached the roof, Vinson stopped long enough to scan the distance to the shooter. The flat, composite rooftop was littered with broken booze bottles, discarded hypodermics, and ghostly condoms glistening in the light of a waning moon. There was also an overpowering stench of urine and shit. It appeared that he would be arriving by way of the "bathroom."

There were no safety rails around the perimeter of the rooftop. The sniper knelt beyond a tumbledown chimney and only his hooded head and the barrel of the rifle were visible. Vinson would have the advantage. He remained hidden and still until his breathing slowed.

He gathered his feet under him, ready to move, when the whop-whop-whop of a helicopter caused him to freeze. The chopper flew directly overhead, and if he'd been moving, the searchlight on its underbelly would have illuminated him, sure as shit. As it was, he closed his eyes momentarily so he wouldn't lose his night vision. Then, as he watched, the beam freeze-framed the shooter who threw up an arm to shield from the light. *It's a girl!*

Her profile was fine-boned and delicate. When she looked up, startled by the overhead chopper, the hood of her jacket slipped to her shoulders, and black braids tumbled free. Recovering quickly, she raised the rifle, which seemed to be a natural extension of her body. She fired two quick rounds at the helicopter and the searchlight winked out.

While her back was to him and the noise of the chopper masked his movement, Vinson stepped on to the roof and spurted to the skeleton of the chimney. He held his breath; he was only three feet from her. Then, inhaling and exhaling deeply, he moved around and behind the shooter, putting his gun muzzle to her spine. She stiffened and began to swing the rifle toward him. He nudged her just hard enough to hurt, and her movement halted.

"Lay the rifle down…slowly."

"Guess you got me." Her words seemed resigned, but she lifted her chin defiantly as she spoke.

"You could say that." When she failed to set the rifle down, he repeated, "Drop your fucking weapon, easy like."

"You can't hurt me." Suddenly, she sounded like the girl she was. Slowly she placed her weapon on the roof, and he noted that she managed to have the rifle butt closest to her.

"Why not?"

"Because, you're the man."

"Right about that, my little friend; I'm the man, and now I've got the only gun. You shot my EMT down there, and you'll pay." He kicked the rifle stock so it skittered out of her reach.

"All right, do what you gotta do, man. Let's get this over." She leaned forward and braced her hands on the broken chimney; her movement revealed drops of blood tattooed on the small of her back.

Vinson was put off by the girl's resignation. He'd expected arrogance, and he wanted her clawin' and spittin'. He slapped the back of her head. "Where's your fight, girl? You handled that rifle like it was part of you. Don't give up on me now. You're a warrior; act like one!"

At his admonition, she kicked back and caught him on the shin; he dodged an elbow, and caught her mid-turn as she aimed her knee for his balls. "That's more like it." He moved her away from the broken chimney, tucked her rounded ass into his crotch, and rubbed against her. Bending his knees to accommodate her smaller frame, he bent her over his arm so that she reached for the retaining wall to steady herself. He placed his gun to her temple. "A bullet's too good for you," he whispered at her ear.

Vinson slid the pistol into his belt, and placed both hands on the girl's taut buttocks. In one seamless move, he straightened his knees and lifted, propelling the girl up and over the ledge. He watched as she made a graceful turn in the air, and for only a moment, he saw the disbelief in her eyes as she rushed to pavement thirty feet below. He was rocked by powerful contractions that shook him to his knees.

How long he remained kneeling on the rooftop, Vinson had no idea. Eventually he registered that his ass was cold. Only then did he stand and pull himself together. He wobbled as he started toward the stairwell, but his steps firmed as he moved down the concrete stairs. By the time he reached ground level, two cops were examining the girl's body.

"Do you know what happened here, sir?"

"Shit happened. Shit happened here tonight."

The cops looked at each other and shrugged. "Well, we have two more dead in the next block. We'll call for an ambulance."

"I'm an EMT. My vehicle is around here somewhere. I'm turned around. Got the rear tires shot out, and one of my men took a bullet. Another ambulance took him to Cook. I stayed with the van, but I heard shooting, like it was coming from that roof, maybe. I gotta get to the hospital."

"OK, sir. We'll stay with you 'til the ambulance comes. Why don't you have a seat in the car? You look a little shaky"

When Eddie arrived at the hospital, Jenny was sitting alone in the ER waiting room. Tears spilled down her cheeks, and her shoulders were heaving, but she sobbed without making any sound.

"How's Tony doing?"

"He's gone."

CHAPTER FIFTEEN

It was 3:33 on the digital clock when Foster opened his eyes. Surf sounds filled the bedroom as he turned slightly to look at Joyce. Her back was to him, her breathing slow and even, in rhythm with the waves.

3:34 flashed in his eyes, and he realized that what woke him was thirst. A cold glass of orange juice would hit the spot. Moving quietly from the bed, Foster closed the bedroom door so Joyce would not be disturbed. The large living and dining area took on a silvery glow thanks to the moon glade on the Gulf waters. After pouring the juice into a tall, sea green plastic glass, he settled into an oversize oak rocking chair and turned on the television. He passed through five or six channels before stopping on WGN where he saw "Breaking News" flashing across the screen. An affiliate reporter was standing in front of an abandoned building.

"I'm standing in a now empty South Chicago street where, tonight, dozens of people have been killed or injured in what appears to be the largest gang-related disturbance in recent history. Early reports indicate that as many as twenty people have been killed or wounded in a clash between rivals. Officials say the outbreak of violence appears to have been spurred by a dispute over territorial use of this area which is populated only by the carcasses of decaying factories and industrial refuse. Both gangs have been linked to drug trafficking and other criminal enterprises. Several precincts were called in to restore order, but sporadic fighting has now broken out between remaining gang members and police. There have been reports that police, ambulances, and TV crews have been fired on."

When automatic gunfire burst nearby, the young reporter ducked for cover, but the cameraman continued to pan across the surreal scene, capturing, too, his newsman throwing up in the gutter.

Foster was stunned. Sitting in the embracing darkness of the coastal night, he wondered if he knew anyone who might have been caught up in the horror. Certainly, von Kovska and his triage unit and ER staff at Comer Children's would be one of the closest hospitals, and likely to receive some of the younger casualties.

As Foster watched, the seemingly fearless cameraman continued to move along the shadowed street. He left his fair-weather reporter far behind; his live footage spoke for itself, and seemed more gripping in the absence of narration. The only sounds were the occasional stutters of gunshots. Turning the corner, he came upon a police van waiting to transport uninjured gang members and ambulance personnel who were treating those with superficial injuries. One EMT stepped into the rear of an ambulance, and turned to accept the stretcher that was to be loaded for transport. The cameraman caught the EMT both in profile, and then head-on. The EMT was Eddie Vinson. *Eddie Vinson, how about that? Bet this is a night he won't soon forget!*

Knowing that he was too keyed up to go back to sleep, Foster went out onto the deck and pulled his favorite chaise to face East and the coming dawn. He allowed thoughts to drift and dissipate while the horizon adorned itself in veils of deep blue, then lavender, then pink, before the sun arose to cast its golden countenance upon the sea.

Foster closed his eyes to capture the image for safekeeping. Eventually he stood to follow the siren call of Joyce's fragrant warmth. They would return that afternoon to a fermenting Chicago that had focused world attention on its violent streets.

CHAPTER SIXTEEN

Eddie Vinson was having second thoughts about his upcoming session with Foster. Sonya and Dottie were still with her parents, and his only contacts with them had been brief telephone calls. Sonya had not volunteered to come home, and he hadn't asked her. She was sticking to her demand that he seek counseling.

"The sooner I get this over with, the sooner I get her back," he mumbled to himself as he approached Foster's office.

As Vinson entered the clinic, Eric von Kovska was just leaving after a one-hour session. Foster was right behind Erik as they walked to the front doors. Vinson looked stunned momentarily as von Kovska and Foster stepped aside for him to enter.

"Dr. von Kovska? Eddie Vinson. We met last week in the ER during the gang conflict downtown."

"Mr. Vinson. Oh, yes, the EMT. You were there with your friend. Terrible thing; I am sorry. How are you doing?"

"Oh, I'm alright. Everyone at the agency is subdued; we're s'posed to be the good guys, after all."

"I didn't realize you two knew each other." Foster interjected, wondering if either man was embarrassed to be seen in his office.

"Oh, no. We don't really know each other. We just happened to meet last week during the gang war or whatever it's been called in the headlines."

"Well, John. I'll see you in two weeks."

"Right, Erik. I'll see you then." Foster turned to Vinson and invited him to his office.

After settling in with informalities, Foster asked about Eddie's experiences during the shootings and about the death of his colleague.

"It was pretty rough, Doc, but you know, I don't need to talk about it now. I've handled it, and I'm OK. What I really want is to go right into some of the things you asked me to do. You know, writing in my diary."

"OK, Eddie. Where did you want to start?"

"Well, when I began writing these things down, what happened was unexpected. At least, it wasn't what I expected, but it seemed that the more I wrote, the more I remembered. To be honest, I had been dreading it since you told me what you wanted me to do. I hadn't thought about many of these experiences in years, but there they were, flowing out of me. So many details, like they were just waiting for me to scratch the surface."

"Why don't you go ahead then, and read what you have, Eddie."

"OK," Eddie reached into his inside jacket pocket and pulled out folded loose-leaf pages. He scanned the first few paragraphs, and then began to read:

"In first grade, I used to chase girls in my class and try to kiss them. My teacher caught me twice and tried to persuade me to stop. Of course, I didn't stop. After the third time, I guess, she tried to cure me by embarrassing me. She made me kiss every girl in the class. I remember feeling a little embarrassed, but mostly it was great because I got to kiss the prettiest girl in the class. It seemed that I was always in trouble in school for fighting, swearing, and refusing to do my work. I also spent a lot of time in the nurse's office pretending to be sick.

"I used to get so mad when I was sent to detention at school, or when my parents put me in time out. I'd go to the top of my bunk bed and deliberately push myself off; I'd land in a belly flop on the floor. I would keep it up until my parents let me out of my room. Once, I broke my wrist when I landed.

"When I was five or six, maybe seven, I was sexually abused by a neighbor, a man. I'd been abused before... by my babysitter's brother. Later, he and I began to have sex together, mutual oral sex. As we got older, we formed a kind of partnership. We set up scenarios to bring in other kids our age, both boys and girls, and have sex with them. We'd have sometimes as many as ten or eleven at one time. Some of the older kids brought porno mags, and we'd look at them and masturbate or perform oral sex on each other. Sometimes, the whole group would get together in an abandoned trailer near where I lived and have sex all day long. This went on until I was eleven. Then, one day, we got caught; the group disbanded and that was the end of it."

Foster listened to what sounded like exaggeration and made no comment as Eddie paused and looked up from his journal. He looked Foster squarely in the eye. "What do you think, Doc?"

"Did you find it difficult to recall such abuse, Eddie?"

"Answering a question with a question. Pretty slick. A shrink trick so you don't have to respond when you don't want to.

"Two can play the game." Eddie resumed reading without addressing Foster's question. "I don't know why this next memory came to me, but I remembered when I was about eight, I got a toy hammer and broke out several windows of my parents' trailer. I must have been punished for it, but I can't remember. I do recall that I was an angry kid, even when I was quite young.

"Once, I flushed my mom's fish down the toilet to get back at her for spanking me. She used to make me take off all my clothes and she spanked my butt with her hand. Sometimes, she undressed too, and she would lay me across her lap. The spankings hurt, but I could smell her, and that was nice. I didn't mind the spankings so much. Was that weird, or what?"

"What kind of relationship did you have with your mother as you got older? Where is she now?"

"Oh, she's dead."

"How did she die?"

"My father shot her...while she slept."

"How old were you when that happened, Eddie?"

"I was fourteen. That night, I was sleeping in her bed. Dad was a bad alcoholic, and he came home plastered as usual. He accused mom of touching me, and when she denied it, he beat her senseless. When I told him nothing happened, he said he'd be sure nothin' happened ever again. He got his shotgun from his truck, and just blew her away. I'd never seen so much blood, you know." *That's a lie!*

"Afterward, my father sat down beside her and cried, but when I fell asleep, he left. Didn't take anything with him; just walked out. I never saw him again. As far as I know, he was never caught.

"I was on my own, and when I was caught filching food at the grocery store, Social Services got their hooks in me. What a bitch that was, I tell ya! The next four years were a nightmare of asshole foster parents and group homes. In the end, the state was as glad to be rid of me as I was to get out of the system."

While he read what he had written, it became clear that Eddie was filling in details as he went along. Despite the horror of the childhood experiences he was relating, his mood never wavered, and he showed no emotional distress. One would have thought he was relating what he had for breakfast. For Foster, it was the absence of affect that was most telling.

Foster interrupted Vinson's reading, "Eddie."

"Yeah, Doc?"

"Eddie, what do you feel as you look back at your childhood, what you've read so far?"

"Well…I guess I don't *think* much of nothing about it."

Foster always trod lightly when it came to a patient's traumatic history, even if it was embellished, as he suspected Vinson's was. In his experience, abused children typically become so desensitized to the compounding of repeated traumas that any expression of horror by a therapist could damage rapport and interfere with the therapeutic process.

"Well, from what you've told me thus far, it appears, Eddie, that you were mistreated by a lot of different people,"

"Mistreated? Hell, I thought I was the one doing the mistreating. I remember taunting my father, for example. I knew what he thought, so I would sneak into my mother's bed and cuddle up to her and pretend to be asleep when dad came home. For a long time, I blamed myself for her death because I only intended to yank my Dad's chain, to torment him like I'd done before."

"OK, Eddie, I understand what you're saying. I just want you to consider the possibility that you were the victim here, and reread what you've written with that in mind. We'll pick up our discussion at our next session."

Within minutes of leaving Foster's office, Vinson felt a sense of foreboding wash over him. From his first meeting with the psychologist, Vinson had learned that Foster was no lightweight therapist who concentrated on warm and fuzzy feelings. No, Foster was made of sterner stuff, and was probably his intellectual equal. Last evening at work, while others slept, Vinson had pulled up Foster's website. It was polished, professional, and informative.

As Vinson followed links to the National Register of Health Service Providers and a legal database for forensic providers and expert witnesses, he was shaken to read that, not only had Foster served with the FBI as a profiler, but he was also a much-sought-after expert in his field. So, Vinson realized, his adversary was no piss ant suburban shrink with a high-tone clientele of addicted teens, bored matrons and their philandering husbands. What remained to be seen was whether or not the learned Doc would crash and burn under the barrage of psychobabble that Vinson was prepared to let fly.

CHAPTER SEVENTEEN

After accompanying Vinson to the front office, Foster returned to his desk to chart a summary of the session: "4/4/00 - E.V. Reading from his journal, appeared to fill in details as he was going along. No way of verifying the truth of his account; however, probable victim of repeated sexual abuse with more than one perpetrator; also, incest with his mother is suggested; physical and emotional abuse by both parents. Began acting out to vent rage as early as preadolescence. Antisocial behaviors emerged. Desensitization to traumatic events, with likely dissociation. Sexual and aggressive impulses clearly intertwined from early childhood. Diagnosis: Antisocial Personality Disorder."

"Mostly routine," was John's response to Joyce's "How was your day?"

"Mostly?"

"Except for Vinson." After a pause, "I'm beginning to suspect that he may be a sociopath. Like most, he'll be hard to pin down. You've heard me rant and rave enough to know that sociopaths are elusive as hell...and dangerous.

"Remember my first, during the Georgia internship? Evans...Tom Evans. Just thinking about him still gives me the willies. That guy had such a soft smile and gentle way about him. At first, he confused the heck out of me. He was arrested for allegedly promoting prostitution and the presiding judge determined he was unable to stand trial. Just goes to show that Evans was better at deception than the judge was at detection. Of course, he was the same guy who, five years after he was discharged from the hospital as "cured," was sentenced to death for the murder of an LSU coed. Anyway, this guy was a true chameleon. Now, I think maybe Vinson is another. Please let me be wrong."

Joyce was trying to hold in her laughter at his attempted levity, but John could see diaphragmatic spasms that gave her away.

"I sure wasn't laughin' back then. Evans was a harsh teacher for a novice Ph.D. He drew me in with his seemingly sincere desire to help his fellow patients. Before any of the staff knew it, me included, Evans turned thirty patients into a cadre of rebels, all bent on overthrowing the authority of the unit."

Foster recalled those days as if they had happened only yesterday. He could visualize clearly the patients selected by Evans to further his agenda. One was an older woman who had been admitted to a state psychiatric facility for the first time while in her teens following an attempted suicide. When Foster interviewed her, she was sixty-six. She had described for him her treatment in that first public psychiatric hospital. "It was horrid. They wrapped me in wet sheets and shocked me with electricity. Then, they locked me away and forgot me."

Another of Evans' *chosen* was a lovely, platinum blond waif of nineteen. She'd been hospitalized for abusing alcohol and Valium, a common cocktail of the 1970's. The pairing of booze and Valium in her blood stream caused the strangest detachment from reality and allowed uninhibited behaviors free reign. When her family could no longer cope with her substance-abusing free spirit, she was committed. She would have had a chance at "normal" life once she was detoxed and stabilized, but until then, her anger at her family for hospitalizing her made her a willing tool in Evans' skilled hands.

Imperceptibly, patients were maneuvered by Evans. As a neophyte, Foster had failed to discern the end toward which the unwitting patients were being manipulated, yet he knew what was required. He would need to wrest control of the patients from Evans if the staff was to reassert its authority. Foster understood power and control of groups from an academic perspective; however, in his position as a psych intern, he had neither. Therefore, the only weapons at his disposal would be his intellect and his academic training, and, if he were lucky, a measure of cunning that would not be obvious to Evans until it was too late.

When the moment of his choosing was at hand, Foster, at his obsequious best, asked Evans. "Do you understand how you upset the milieu of this unit?"

"What do you mean?" Evans returned. He was chubby and innocuous in appearance, Mr. Common Man. Nothing about him grabbed attention. He looked like an affable vacuum cleaner salesman. His head was shaved so that his light hair looked almost like peach fuzz, and his baby-pink complexion flushed readily. He wore the same muted plaid shirt and khaki pants over and over so that you could often smell him coming.

"Why do you think I've asked you to come in today, Tom? You're upsetting the other patients and it has to stop." Foster's voice was louder and more stern than usual. He struck a nerve.

"Let me tell you something, *Doctor.*" Evans enunciated the title, knowing full well that the conferring of Foster's doctorate was still months away. His rank at the bottom of the professional pecking order was made clear by his "office," a space too small and too dingy for a janitor's closet. Foster had had to requisition and beg help moving a battered gunmetal desk from the equipment graveyard. He didn't even merit his own telephone in the eyes of the hospital administration.

"Something you may have not have heard yet, in your young career...." Evans twisted his mouth in derision. "Try to understand. I'm a man with an urge. No, not an urge... a drive. You'd probably label it a compulsion. Whatever the fuck ya call it, I'm here on this earth to do something that other people can't, or won't, or are too afraid to do.

"You've probably noticed that some people are terrified by the prospect of change, yes? Not me. I thrive on it. I suck it up. I love it. It loves me. I'm the guy who stirs the soup of life round and round. Status quo be damned. That's the way it is here, *Doc,* Eva and the old lady, the others...they're drawn to my fearlessness because they don't have it. They think I can save them from their fear-filled lives. I don't give a shit about them as you know. They're a means to an end, just tools in my very talented hands."

Foster pursed his lips to halt a grimace as Evans spewed out his thoughts. *Well, at least I'm on his wavelength.*

"And what end is that, Tom?"

"Oh, come on, Doc, same as everyone else, peace of mind, comfort, thrill, ecstasy, whatever."

"While manipulating, confusing, and disrupting this unit?"

"Fuck, yes. I can't believe you're too dense to get it. It's the same for you, ya know. I'm just the evil side of the coin. You seek organization and feel fulfilled. Organization to me is boring; no, it's repulsive, anathema, an abomination. Now, I've got the unit and you got shit. I'm the guy with my finger on their emotional buttons. Hell, these people are happier with me than they ever were with your pious Dr. Feelgood therapies."

"I see, Tom. Well, what will happen to these patients tomorrow when you are escorted from the unit by the Sheriff who will be taking you back to jail to await trial?"

"What are you talking about? Don't you know I'm mentally incompetent? I'm unable to stand trial, Doc. It's a matter of public record. It's right there in my hospital records, too."

"Oh, you may have been incompetent once, Tom, but you've shown me that your thinking is clear and decisive, not to mention conniving, manipulative, exploitive, choose any adjective you like. So, how do you feel, now that you're cured?"

"I'm not cured. I haven't changed."

"You're right; your personality disorder will probably never change. From a legal standpoint, however, you've demonstrated that you're capable of proceeding to trial, and that is the hospital's recommendation to the court. Sheriff's deputies will be here tomorrow morning at nine sharp, so get your things together"

"Mother fucker," Evans spit, "Mother fucker."

"When Evans left my office, it was like the fight had drained out of him. It was only temporary, of course. He caused an awful ruckus on the unit that night, but I was told he was put in seclusion until the deputies arrived to take him away. Within two days of Evans' departure, the unit was back to normal, although I use the term loosely. The impact of a sociopath like Evans is powerful, but only so long as it remains undetected, behind the scenes. It was years later when I heard his name in passing. Evans had been arrested again, this time for the murder of an LSU student. I believe he was sentenced to life at Angola."

"Was Evans not insane, John?"

"How do you separate frank insanity from evil? They often seem to run the same course; each can masquerade as the other and, thus, be present in our daily lives. What's the phrase? 'Hidden in plain sight?' Bottom line, however, to the trained eye, sociopathy is glaring, and I'm sorely afraid this Vinson fellow *could* prove himself to be among the ranks."

Joyce counted the beats of her heart. After sixty, she looked at John, and smiled. His eyes were closed; a whisper of air sighed from him as he surrendered the cares of his day. She pulled off his shoes and gently maneuvered the ottoman under his outstretched legs. She collected their wine glasses and went to stir the soup. It would keep for the duration of a nap.

CHAPTER EIGHTEEN

Vinson sat quietly in his favorite neighborhood tavern. Chicago did not have to excuse Herself on that score. Every community boasted one or more comfortable bars or taverns, usually within walking distance of home. Although he hated routine and felt vulnerable with the predictability that routine conferred, he had been unable to resist the relaxing anonymity of O'Hearn's Pub. Sipping a Meisterbrau and contemplating the shot of Charter before him, he tried to place a familiar face, a dead ringer for a long-ago foster father. The man had been better than most, if he recalled correctly. Kindly caretakers were few and far between, and memorable for that very reason. "Foster parents," he muttered into the frosted stein.

"What Eddie?"

"Nuthin', Mick. Just muttering in my brew."

Michael O'Hearn was owner and bartender of the tavern which was 703 steps from Sonya's brownstone. The count was a nightly routine when he wasn't working swing shifts. He occupied the stool at the far end of the bar and furthest from the door. Occasionally he watched and listened to what was going on around him; often as not, he spoke to no one, and sought only liquid solace.

"Want another?"

"No...well, OK. Sure. Why not? Gimme a Guinness this time."

An Irish tune came with the building of the Guinness. Vinson had heard the plaintive song before, but couldn't remember its name.

"What's that you're humming, Mick?"

"Huh?" as the melody paused.

"The song, what's the song?" Eddie's voice had risen, and several pairs of tired, bleary eyes swung his way.

"Shit, man. I don't remember." O'Hearn placed the Guinness in front of Vinson, but didn't remove his hand from the glass.

Dropping his voice, Eddie shrugged. "You stand there humming the same fuckin' song day after day, you cocksucker, and you don't remember the name?"

O'Hearn's Irish temper erupted. He slammed both fists down on the bar. "Get out! Go on, get out, and don't come back if you can't keep a civil tongue in your head. I don't need your dirty money. A shot and two beers don't pay for the aggravation."

"Yeah...I...yeah, I know, Mick, I'm sorry. It's been a long damn day. I shouldn't a...."

"*Leave!*" O'Hearn growled, low and ugly, not backing down.

"Get out?" Vinson seethed, looking down the smooth walnut of the bar. Speaking only loud enough to carry to his sudden adversary, Vinson narrowed his eyes. "Who do you think you're talking to, Asshole?" There was no emotion in his voice.

"I'm talking to you, and you're not welcome here. Get your ass out of my tavern."

"No."

"*What?*"

"No," more subdued, but Vinson didn't move. As if he had all day, he raised the Guinness and took several long swallows.

One by one, nervous patrons drifted from their stools and booths. Trouble, if it was coming, was trouble they didn't need. When the last man had gone, O'Hearn spoke again, "Well, now you've cost me. You want something out of me, Eddie?"

"Maybe."

"Well, come and get it then." O'Hearn walked the length of the bar and came around to stand in the middle of the floor. He took a deep breath and flexed his hands, waiting.

"Maybe some other time." Vinson said, pursing his lips to avoid the added insult of a grin that threatened. He walked a straight line to the door, brushing past O'Hearn as he did so. At the door, he turned and saluted. "See you again, Mick. Soon."

When local papers hit the pavement the following morning, Michael O'Hearn's picture was under the headline, "LOCAL TAVERN OWNER SLAIN." The gory details were omitted, but those in the know would say that O'Hearn's brains had been splattered far and wide across the bedroom where he had been asleep. Despite an exhaustive search, an unknown blunt instrument, possibly a baseball bat, had not been recovered at the crime scene or in the neighborhood.

Vinson was tending to the broken arm of a plucky ten-year-old redhead who had fallen about twelve feet from up in a mulberry tree. He was kneeling beside her, and last season's decaying mulberries stained the legs of his scrubs. "You picked a messy place to land, Red."

Looking up to the crook of the tree where the child had been perched, Eddie noticed a pack of Parliaments wedged between two smaller branches within arm's reach.

"Sneakin' cigarettes, huh?"

"Yeah. What of it?"

What's your name, kid?"

"Sissy. I'm Sissy." Her head came up and her chin jutted out like some elfin pugilist.

"I bet your mom would be pissed if she knew you were smoking.... Don't worry; it'll be our secret." Without warning, Eddie popped the child's dislocated left shoulder into place. Sissy's eyes rolled back in her head, and while she was out, he set to work stabilizing the fractured lower right arm. He pulled Sissy into the V between his legs and braced her with his upper body. *Mulberries on my ass now, too*, he thought, as he buried his nose in the tumbling fire-red curls, filling himself with her child's smell.

When Sissy began to struggle, he held her still and spoke softly. "Shhhh...no, no; stay still, Red. I've got you. Just relax; let me finish with the bandage." He nuzzled her, pushed his nose again into her hair. "You're a good girl." On impulse, he used his bandage scissors to snip a curl from behind her ear, which he put into his shirt pocket. Again and again he inhaled, and finally, he laid his cheek against her hair.

"That's it, Red; you were real brave. Jen, bring the gurney; the kid's kinda woozy." Jenny had talked to some kids playing in the next yard over to learn where the girl lived, and sent two older children to find the girl's mother.

Vinson gathered his weight under him, and then stood, easily lifting the child in his arms. He could see a frantic mama running along the fence line. *A cow, a gone-to-shit fat cow! How could such a piece of piss-poor protoplasm spawn such a beautiful child?*

"Jenny, help with Mom, please. She's not making things any better."

"Have to take you and your mom to the hospital, Red, get you a cast for that arm. Shall we use the lights and sirens and impress all your friends?" He spoke directly into her ear so she could hear him over her mother's wailing. Sissy burrowed into his shoulder as he hugged her; he lowered her to the stretcher. He braced her upper torso with blankets and strapped her down, then openly kissed the top of her head.

"You might live to grow up if you quit climbing trees… and smoking," he added, dropping his voice to a whisper. "Friends?" he asked.

Despite the pain, Sissy favored him with a toothy smile, which made her green eyes crinkle. "Friends!"

"Lights and sirens, coming up! Hold on tight." Eddie laughed.

I'm ready for another round with Foster.

CHAPTER NINETEEN

Foster meditated while waiting for Eddie Vinson to arrive for his third session. He had devoted considerable time to thinking about this particular client. As he reviewed his notes from Vinson's first and second sessions, Foster became more certain that Vinson met the criteria for diagnosis of an Antisocial Personality Disorder and was capable of harm. He would have to be wary not to be sucked into Vinson's world. Of necessity, his therapeutic approach would have to be subtle and passive; direct confrontation would only drive Vinson away, and, perhaps, turn him loose on unsuspecting family or colleagues. Once he got a fix on his client's agenda, however, and Foster was certain Vinson had one, he would try to leverage his way into Vinson's world. From then on, it would be a case of one-upsmanship. *The sixty-four dollar question is whether Vinson is better at his sociopathy than I am at psychotherapy.*

The intercom chimed. "Dr. John? Mr. Vinson is here. Shall I send him back?"

"Ask him to wait one moment. I'll be right out." Foster scanned his last notation of the week before, and then closed the file, slipping it into his lower desk drawer. When he opened his office door, Vinson was already standing there, leaning nonchalantly against the frame. Foster could see a chagrined Louise at her desk; her body language communicated clearly that Vinson had ignored her request to wait.

The gauntlet is thrown, and we haven't exchanged one word. Foster relaxed his stance and offered Vinson a handshake, which Vinson ignored as he strode past.

"Eddie, how are you? Your day off? You're casual today." Foster withdrew his outstretched hand and transferred his pen to his right hand.

Vinson was dressing his part for today's session, faded jeans with a laddered left knee and a White Sox sweatshirt, same blood spattered Nikes. Gone were the Perry Ellis threads. He ignored Foster's inquiry and seated himself beside the desk, pulling his chair as close as it would go. *In your face, Doc!*

Without waiting for Foster to seat himself, Vinson opened, "You think I could have vandalized our house, Doc?" His question picked up seamlessly from their first session, and was the one obvious question that hadn't been answered by the conclusion of that meeting.

Damn, there it is! Foster moved casually to his desk and sat down. He focused on the whorled beauty of the patterned oak. "How do you mean, Eddie?"

"You know, like, a blackout, maybe?

"I think I did it, Doc."

"Hmmm...tell me why, Eddie." Foster looked at him, considering, but not showing the interest that Vinson had expected.

Vinson wondered if he was gonna lose the control he had seized at the outset. Foster seemed lethargic, apathetic, not the worthy opponent he had anticipated as he prepared for today's session. Abruptly, Vinson stood and walked to the window. "I remember a lot from that night, but you probably figured that out already, didn't you?"

"Tell me what you remember."

"Are you going to tell Sonya?"

"No. What you say is between us. Just us."

Still facing away from Foster, Vinson began speaking. "I'd been up more than twenty-four hours...pulled a second shift that day because of absences...several serious accidents back-to-back, and then, remember the three alarm fire in that hi-rise? It was that same day. I was really wiped out. I stopped for a couple beers to decompress, then went home.

"I expected Sonya and Dottie to be back from her parents by then, but they weren't, and she hadn't called or left a message on the squawk box. I was worried... and pissed. It was inconsiderate, and I was just too tired to leash my anger. I left long enough to go down to the corner and buy a fifth of Crown Royal. I drank a good bit on the way home, and was getting a pretty good buzz to drown out my mad. Do you ever get on the Internet, Doc?"

To Foster, a *mouse* was still a furry little rodent. He snorted and shook his head. "Seldom," was his only response.

"It's really cool; the world's at your fingertips. Anyway, I logged on to some of my favorite websites, and polished off more of the Crown. Do you masturbate, John?"

"Most everyone does at some time or another. Why do you ask?"

Vinson was gauging how far he should push. Foster's apparent passivity was new, out of character, and it was throwing him off his game. "Well, I do. Sonya's needs aren't as intense as mine, and besides she wasn't there. One website was a racy one, triple X. I began to masturbate. I'll admit I do it whenever I can get away with it.

"I was thirsty and wanted a beer; went to get one, but there wasn't any. I went back to the computer and logged on to another porn site; I sat there, jerking off, but I couldn't get an edge. You know how it is. Nothin' was going right, and I couldn't get off. I don't know; it doesn't happen very often; probably the Crown fucked me up Royal," he sniggered.

"Next thing I know, I'm in Dottie's room, and I got a pair of her panties...not clean ones, you know, from the hamper...dirty ones."

Vinson's body language indicated a growing agitation. He had begun to pace, and his eyes were like pinballs, bouncing off everything in the office, ceiling to floor, wall to wall. "You sure Sonya won't find out about this?"

Foster stood and walked slowly toward Vinson, being certain that his approach was seen and that his face showed appropriate concern. "I'm sure, Eddie. What you say is confidential; that is, unless you pose a danger to yourself or others. Could that be the case here?"

"No, it's alright, Doc, shit...telling you this stuff; it's good to get it off my chest." Vinson gave a gusty sigh. *Come into my web, said the spider to the fly. C'mon in, Doc.*

Foster allowed Vinson to see his concern, and it was genuine, but not for the reasons Vinson believed. Rather, Foster feared that Vinson was giving up too much information, too quickly, and even though Vinson still believed he was in the driver's seat, Foster perceived that his client's control was slipping precipitously.

"OK, Doc, so I put on this pair of Dottie's panties; had to cut a hole for my dick. It was so cool! They were real tight on me, gave a caressing, silky feeling. I dug out another pair so I could...could smell her, and damn if I didn't come all over everywhere.

"Things get a little fuzzy after that. The release was so friggin' powerful, I musta lost brain cells!"

Vinson paced and was silent. *Where to next?*

"Ya know, Doc. Someone once told me that rage is the ultimate helplessness. Not for me. For me, rage means control. I find, in those moments, I'm more connected, more alive than at any other time.

"Anyway, I lost it after that, just tore the place apart. I could see myself doing it…like I was watching from the corner of the room. I felt this incredible rush, euphoria really. Then, the energy was just gone, and I folded. The panic set in…I felt exposed, thought I'd really fucked up, and I had, of course.

"So," Vinson paused deliberately, "when I got my shit together, I made it look like an intruder: overturned tables and lamps, broke pictures; put the computer monitor on its face on the floor, took a leak in the corner. Then I broke out the window so it would look like the point of entry. It was about three a.m. by then, I think, and dark as the womb. After that, I went to bed, slept like a baby." Vinson returned to the chair and plopped down, but did not look at Foster.

"What do you think, Doc? Weird, huh?"

Foster only response was, "You did all that to cover up the fact that you masturbated using Dottie's panties." He made it a statement of fact, not a question.

"Well, sure. I couldn't have Sonya thinking I'm a pervert."

Curious. He'd rather be thought of as a violent maniac than as a guy with quirky sexual vices. Foster let the silence spin out, and, for the first time, Vinson squirmed.

Into the silence, Vinson blurted, "I remember having a real vivid dream when I was about fourteen; dreamed I was becoming a cat. Every morning I checked my body compulsively, each time dreading I would discover it was happening for real. I was especially worried about my genitals.

"About that same time, I started having other nightmares. I'd wake up sucking air, sure I was gonna die. I fought those damn dreams; they were awful. Then, I began to pray that I *would* have the dreams. Fuck, I'd been praying that they'd stop, and that didn't work, so I thought I'd ask God to give them to me instead. Kinda reverse psychology with the Big Guy.

"You might know, the dreams continued, but I started really getting into them. Actually came to enjoy them... started getting upset when I didn't have them. That was when I began to learn self-control.

"I had been keeping secrets for a long time by then. The power of secrets gave me a real high! Living in that world of nightmares taught me about parallel lives. I cultivated one for myself, and, for the most part, I remained undetected...until now. Shit has hit the proverbial fan, now. Sonya knows. You know."

Foster dropped his eyes, passive. "No problem, Eddie. We'll work this out."

"Don't think so, Doc, don't want to. Not my style to live by the rules. Why would I wanna fix what ain't broke? It's my nature, and I like it."

Foster nodded, did his best to push away his fear. "Tell you what. Why don't you ask Louise to put you in tomorrow at noon? I'll get us some sandwiches and sodas. We'll spend some time together over lunch, and process what you've told me today."

"OK, Doc, I'll be here, but that's enough for today."

They stood at the same time. Vinson extended his hand, and there was aggression in the forcefulness of his action. Purposely awkward and off balance, Foster extended his hand, managing to miss Vinson's palm and grasp only the tips of his fingers. A feral grin distorted Vinson's visage as he turned to go, leaving Foster's door ajar. He didn't stop at Louise's desk to make the appointment, and he wouldn't show at noon tomorrow. Foster was certain.

Reflecting on their third appointment, Foster was now convinced that Eddie Vinson was dangerous. He had described schizotypal tendencies in addition to a sociopathic orientation, especially the adolescent body distortions and magical thinking. His dreams about becoming a cat couldn't have been more appropriate metaphorically; cats are consummate stalkers, seemingly gentle one moment, ferocious the next. Vinson might be mind-fucking him, but the very details he chose to share were instructive; red herrings or not, they were indicative of Vinson's twisted thought processes.

CHAPTER TWENTY

One week passed with no contact from Vinson, and the silence was increasingly troubling to Foster. He'd begun to wonder whether Vinson might be experiencing a phase of decompensation or, perhaps, that he had missed something important—diagnostically. Thus, Foster was relieved when Louise interrupted his dictation time to tell him that Sonya Vinson was on the phone to speak with him. She was no longer calling in daily, only on an as-needed basis.

He hooked the telephone receiver from its cradle. "John Foster."

"Yes, Dr. Foster?"

"Ms. Vinson, how are you?"

"About the same. I'm still at my parents' home. Dottie's doing alright, I guess. Have you made any progress with Eddie? Is he keeping appointments?"

"Well, yes and no. I can't really tell you much, you know, due to confidentiality."

"I understand. I was just hoping you could give me some guidance. I don't know what to do at this point."

Foster paused a moment. He lowered his voice, and tried to infuse his words with meaning for her, to communicate on an emotional level, "You're doing the right thing, Ms. Vinson."

"You mean I should continue to stay away from Eddie?"

"You're doing what *you need* to do," Foster repeated, this time with more emphasis. "Eddie has a lot of issues to work out, and he'll do that better without you to distract him right now?"

"Where is he? Do you know?"

"No.... He missed an appointment last week, and he hasn't called to reschedule yet, so I don't know where he is, exactly. I am concerned; I can say that."

"I was in town yesterday and drove by our house; his car wasn't there. I went by the two places he hangs out. No luck, and his car hasn't been at work. I don't think I should call there about him, but I'm worried, you know? In spite of all this mess, I still love him."

"I know, but you've got to remain firm, and stay where you are until we get a better handle on several things."

"OK, Doctor Foster. Can I call you again?"

"Of course. Good-bye, Ms. Vinson," Foster listened for her phone to disconnect. He wished he had more information, more answers. He really wished he knew where Vinson was.

CHAPTER TWENTY-ONE

Vinson had not been to work since his third appointment with Dr. Foster, but he'd been busy nevertheless. His thoughts often focused on Foster. In the hours he'd spent with the shrink thus far, Foster had managed to learn more about him than anyone ever had, even if the doc was left wondering what was true and what was not.

Vinson vowed it would go no further. He could admit to feeling vulnerable, and the discomfort was a physical feeling. Soon, it would all be over. Vinson had toyed with the notion of killing Foster, but, eventually, he discarded the idea as unnecessary, at least for now. *Foster is no threat. Fuck him.*

Vinson was drinking more, especially after his calls to Sonya had been met repeatedly by her father's stonewalling. "She's not here; can't you get it, Eddie?" Her father had actually shouted at him the last time he'd called. He knew, of course, that Sonya and Dottie were with her parents, and since she had not called him, he could only assume that her father was doing what she asked.

Vinson simmered and fumed; if he let it, his anger would erupt full force. It was becoming harder and harder to reign it in, but he knew the time for rage was not yet at hand. In the wake of the nightmares that were again a nightly occurrence, he wanted to let the rage loose, to steep himself in the chaos to which he'd become accustomed.

Vinson finished the last swig of Charter, and pitched the bottle in the general direction of the slimy pink wastebasket. He'd not left the dank motel room for three days, but he was running low on libations, and he smelled. Sitting on the single bed which was at a right angle to the only window in the room, Vinson's attention focused on the rusty mattress stains that were clearly visible through the dingy, threadbare sheet... stains of unknown origins. *Better off not knowing! This fleabag joint is getting tiresome. Time for an upgrade,* he thought, as sleep ambushed him.

"Daddy?" he called out.

"No, son, look carefully; it's you, not me."

Eddie looked closer, and still he saw his father sitting at the window, watching and calling out to all the assholes who passed by.

"Daddy? Daddy?"

"Shut up, Shitface."

"Why, Daddy?" He began to blubber.

"Because you look like your mother." Those words had been hurled at him, times without number. The vitriolic tone never altered, even now, in his Charter-soaked dream.

"Fuck you and die," Eddie whimpered as he woke abruptly.

His first lucid thought was to break and run, to disappear, hide. The problem was...he wasn't willing to leave town. He had studied the greater Chicago area, charted its recesses and warrens. With a little planning and preparation, a man could vanish without leaving the city limits. He'd done it before.

Vinson had already hidden his car in a police impound lot on the southeast side. He'd been in the yard numerous times delivering wrecks from accident scenes and impounded vehicles from drug busts. It was a sideline he had picked up a couple years ago through a contact with the police department. It paid well, and he could do it when his schedule permitted.

During one drop-off, Vinson had lifted a key to the front gate, and held on to it for a "just in case." That day had come, and his beloved Vette was under wraps for the time being. He had driven the Corvette right into the yard under the bleary yellow eyes of the night watchman... about two hours after he'd delivered a vehicle from an early evening accident.

To Ryerson, the security guard who was known to nip a few, Vinson had brought a fifth of Jameson. He shared a snort with the lonely old guy, and told him he'd be back later with another junker. He left the bottle while he went to retrieve the second vehicle, his own. He took the EL back to pick up his car, and made a return trip to the impound lot. He'd leave his Vette for a couple weeks, and then he would move it elsewhere when he had the time. It was too distinctive to leave in one place for very long.

Sure enough, ole man Ryerson hadn't been able to resist the proximity of the whiskey. He hadn't a clue that Vinson had just dropped off his own car; Eddie signed the form Rye pushed at him, and then balled it up and stuck it in his pocket when Ryerson stooped to retrieve the half-empty bottle from the bottom drawer of his desk.

"Gotta go, Rye. The Jameson? Keep it."

"Come anytime, Eddie. God bless"

Vinson had many keys he'd gathered over the years; each was neatly tagged with information about its acquisition. Now that he'd stashed his car, one other key, in particular, was going to be very useful. It would grant him access to the Cook County Hospital Morgue, the repository for lost souls.

The ink hadn't even been dry on his EMT certification the first time he entered the bowels of Cook County's morgue. His team brought in a female drowning victim; they'd fished her out of Lake Michigan near Oak Street. She was about seventeen years old, brown hair, obese, and bloated to boot, with the pallor of dead fish. The girl had clearly been a floater for at least several days. When the victim was finally zipped into a body bag, Vinson and his partner each lifted on an unspoken three, and began the long trek across the gritty brown sand and rock to the grassy plateau where the ambulance was parked. They would deliver the body to the morgue.

Cook County's morgue handled thousands of guests each year. Its walls were an appropriate puke green. The floors were covered with once-white tiles, now cracked and stained with the effluvia of death. The slightest sounds created a rolling percussion down seemingly endless hallways, yet the refrigerated stainless steel chambers and their sliding trays, temporary housing in purgatory, opened and closed without making any sound. It was downright eerie. A curious Vinson looked around, taking it all in while his partner traded insults and gallows humor with the pathologists and technical staff. They released the body of the young woman to a distracted elderly pathologist named Russo, who never even looked at Eddie when he was introduced.

Dr. Russo had brittle gray hair that wreathed his head like a woolly Brillo pad. He was as pale as some of his *guests*. His teeth were tarred from decades of cigarettes, coffee, and neglect. His white lab coat was at least two sizes too big and dragged the floor behind him. He hunched forward as if his back was killing him, which it probably was, a hazard of his trade. When Russo spoke, it was all Vinson could do not to howl. Despite his mad scientist appearance, the good doctor spoke with a spitty lisp, and his mannerisms were one feminine affectation after another.

"Whatcha got?" Russo asked as his focus suddenly snapped to the body on the gurney. He flipped back the sheet, and smacked his lips.

"A stiff we pulled from the lake."

"Big mother, isn't she?"

"Doubt she was a mother, Doc; can't be more than seventeen or so," was Vinson's blunt assessment. He finally had to turn away to hide the grin he couldn't contain. Russo obviously didn't have much call to impress with his presentation or his attire. After all, his patients were dead, but good lord, the man was one weird son of a bitch!

Over the years, Vinson's relationship with Russo warmed. As an EMT, he made "deliveries" once or twice a month, on average. He never learned Russo's first name, but he did find out that the eccentric old man was without peer in the Midwest when it came to piecing together the clues left by Death. He was also an avid classical cellist.

It was during one of his visits that Eddie lifted Russo's key to the main door of the morgue to add to his collection. Russo never mentioned the missing key, and Vinson figured that when he reported the loss, hospital administrators simply assumed he had misplaced it. Hell, rumor had it that he'd once misplaced a body! Why not a key?

Sitting quietly in his darkened hotel room, Vinson reached into his duffel and pulled out a blue cotton drawstring bag. Slowly working the knot, he loosened the strings and poured the contents out onto the bed. There were twenty or so keys, and rooting among them, he found the one he was searching for.

"There you are, my beauty. Come to me." Vinson selected an oversized copper-colored key with an oval grip. He held it up in the orange glow of a flashing neon sign outside his window, and the key seemed to pulsate.

"Open Sesame." Vinson began to laugh hysterically and rolled from the bed with a thump. He scrubbed at the tears that coursed down his cheeks. He wanted a drink.

CHAPTER TWENTY-TWO

Many area residents who were lucky enough to live in the suburbs, but unfortunate enough to work in the city, made the daily trek to and from downtown on Chicago's famous "EL." There had been a time when kids from the "burbs" could safely ride the EL. A few coins dropped in the meter, and thirty minutes later, they would be gawking at tall buildings on State Street, shopping at Marshall Fields, or enjoying popcorn and a double feature from the ornate splendor of a dark theatre balcony.

Earl Johnson was one of the principal movers of Chicagoans to and from the city he loved. He had been conductor on the westbound EL for thirty-three years. After graduating from an inner city high school in 1967, his uncle secured him a job with the CTA. Earl had moved quietly, but steadily, up through the ranks, simply by being reliable and courteous, and doing his job well.

After five years as an apprentice, his uncle surprised him one day by dropping keys to an engine in his hand. Earl still remembered it as one of life's proudest moments, and he had always followed his uncle's only words of guidance, "Keep 'em safe."

Today was the day before Johnson's thirty-third anniversary as a conductor. Nobody would remember this day but him, of course. He had been given his twentieth, twenty-fifth, and thirtieth year recognition awards, and he needed no further acknowledgements. His work and the passengers themselves provided all that he required. The CTA had allowed him to make a good life for his wife and two children. He had kept his promise to his uncle, and had never caused any harm in his daily travels.

Earl's ancestors had lived in Louisiana as slaves and then sharecroppers. He often told the kids who asked to "drive the train" how his great, great grandmother had been the favorite servant of a plantation master and had borne him three children. Earl's great-grandmother was one of the children of that union. Before the plantation owner died, he gave his servants their freedom, and to his favorite, he gave ten thousand dollars so that she would be able to provide for their children. The stories of her accomplishments, and those of her children, had been passed down from generation to generation.

Earl readily shared his family stories with children, especially those who rode his train regularly. He was prone to embellishing, too, to hold their interest because, to him, children seemed to lack a sense of history. One favorite story was about the summer he was eight years old, a "city" boy from Chicago, who went to spend his first of many school vacations with his grandmother in rural south Louisiana. Once he'd learned his way around, he and a new friend took off for an entire day of exploring a nearby watering hole. The bayou seemed so still, and Earl could not see any movement other than the occasional ripples stirred by a turtle or fish, but the water was cooler than the steamy afternoon, and for that reason, it beckoned to him.

To the children Earl would say, "So, I shucked my britches and jumped in so quickly," he quipped with a Cajun accent he saved just for the telling of his stories, "that my friend didn't have time to tell this city boy to stop or to be careful. I hit the water and fell like a stone into the muck. Couldn't see my hand in front of my face; couldn't tell up from down! I finally just let myself relax and float toward the surface, but when I gasped for air, all I could see and smell around me was the strange muddy place in which I found myself."

Instinctively Earl knew that he'd come up into a small cave-like hollow on the side of the bank among the tangled roots of an old oak tree. He was standing knee deep in centuries of decayed bayou vegetation that sucked and squished between his toes. "It was almost pitch black, smelly, but dry," he said, "and I wondered if I was dead. I whispered and could hear my voice; I reached out into the dark, and my fingertips ran along something rough and bumpy. I pulled away so fast! Looking over my shoulder, I saw a shaft of sunlight rippling on the water, so I swam up and toward the light. When I broke the surface, there was my friend, mouth gaping, like he was seeing a ghost."

"What? You been in the gator hole, Earl?"

"Huh?"

"The gator hole. The ole alligator that lives under the bank."

"Yessiree! I learned a valuable lesson that day, always to look where I'm going!" Earl would conclude, seeing that the attention of his listener was waning. *Kids can only stand so much reality.*

Earl had driven Engine 49 for much of his career. It didn't take much to maintain the engine, although it required periodic safety inspections and occasional overhauls. The passenger cars, however, required constant maintenance. Earl tried to be philosophical about the disrespect shown to his beloved EL; however, over the past ten years, it seemed that riders had become more disrespectful, thoughtless of their fellow riders, and the trains themselves that ran day and night. Kids, uncertain of their identity, carved their names into the sides of the seats; an occasional drunk harassed other riders or vomited in the aisle. Cigarettes were outlawed in the cars, but that didn't stop the addicts from snuffing out butts and burning dime-sized pox on the floors.

It was the midnight shift, and Earl glanced to his left wrist; 4:31 a.m., the time flashed on the digital readout of his watch. He scanned the instrument panel in front of him; the train was moving swiftly, 72 mph. The forward compartment from which he monitored the progress and wellbeing of the 49 was designed with little concern for his comfort. As he looked down to the track flowing beneath him, he could see his reflection on the windshield. His eyes lifted toward his receding hairline, his expression quizzical. He still thought of himself as having a full head of hair. Nevertheless, he wasn't looking too bad for late middle age, a black Paul Newman with a receding hairline. The clear blue eyes, for which Newman was well known, were startling in Johnson's visage, a testament to the strength of the genes of his plantation owner ancestor.

Johnson's CTA badge with "49" on it glinted in his glass reflection. The cracked leather which was supposed to cushion his posterior in the hard metal cradle of his seat had worn thin over the years, and the end of each shift usually found him standing in self-defense. Johnson had stuffed a piece of foam rubber into an inconspicuous four-inch split at the back of the seat. He reasoned that it was best to take care of such things himself without foisting such a minor complaint on the powers that be.

The 49 moved toward darker corners of the city. Every trip to and from downtown was different, especially if you were watchful. The city was lit day and night, but pockets of darkness shielded the proverbial multitude of sins. From the EL, Johnson could see the denizens of night on rooftops and in alleys; the more brazen conducted their commerce openly on street corners. In thirty-three years, from his hard leather seat, he'd acquired hundreds of blurred mental snapshots of a side of life, down and dirty *real* life, and the perversity of his fellow man. Somehow, these shadow people, as Johnson thought of them, had become desensitized to the passing of the EL, day after day, year after year. They seldom even raised their ravaged faces as the 49 sped through the tenuous calm of their nights.

4:33 flashed in the corner of his eye. Johnson checked all systems then sat back in his seat. His eyes closed momentarily, and his body relaxed to the rhythm of the EL's familiar vibrations. "Mmmmn. Good vibrations," he hummed. Night sounds seemed softer, though he didn't know why. Maybe the humidity. The portside window was open about an inch and crisp spring air circulated though the cabin. It was intoxicating.

Johnson glanced at the posted route above the control panel. The 49's schedule was in his head, of course, but he checked it anyway. Next stop would be in four minutes. Earl reached behind him for the thermos of coffee; "black, as usual," he told his wife every night with a smile and a kiss. He liked his java with the hint of chicory, not too strong, that reminded him of the South. "Damn good coffee. My compliments, Annie," he toasted his wife.

Ahead, a man sat silently between the tracks, his legs stretched out in front of him. His eyes were closed to the glinting parallel steel rails that appeared to run straight to infinity, or was it eternity? An errant north wind caused him to tilt to the side a bit, but he made no effort to correct his posture. Night sounds filled the air: dogs barking, a gunshot, an approaching siren, shrill wailing and cursing from a tenement balcony with the best view of the tracks in the entire city. The metallic clatter of the EL was added to the soundtrack, and still the man sat, waiting for the 49.

One mile away, Earl Johnson was checking his instruments in accordance with CTA policy. He figured that smarter men than he had set down such directives for his protection and that of his passengers, for their own protection too, but he had no quarrel with regulations. Sure, he knew the rumors about whiskey flasks and pot and all, but he had no need to befuddle his senses to get through the workday. That was the benefit of having a job he loved.

"All checks out," he announced. "Easy does it." He smiled at his foolishness. Even Annie didn't know he talked to his train. He noted his speed had passed 75 mph on the straightaway. As Earl looked ahead, something caught his eye. His first thought was that he was seeing things. He rubbed his tired eyes and looked again. It was barely perceptible, but he thought it might be the engine's beam illuminating a black and white dog in the middle of the tracks and moving toward the train. He began to reduce the 49's speed.

"What the...? Can't be...!" he shouted. Yet there it was. Adrenaline shot through his system.

"Wha...shit! What is that?" His grab for the emergency brake was instinctive, although Earl knew it was futile. Forty tons of steel didn't stop on command, even his command. The lights of the train clearly delineated the figure of a man sitting with his back to its approach. Despite the shrill of brakes and the wrenching vibrations of Earl's beloved 49 as it fought its own forward momentum, the man made no attempt to move.

"Come on! Stop! Dammit!" Johnson screamed. "Stop!" The compulsion to close his eyes, to turn away from the inevitable, was overwhelming. *A suicide*, he thought as tears overflowed. *The man isn't going to move*.

The EL was slowing, but not enough. Johnson sighed. It was as though someone pulled a plug and the adrenaline drained suddenly from his system; a weary resignation settled over him, and he dropped his head forward. The words of the Lord's Prayer floated into consciousness, and he spoke them aloud.

In the final moments before the 49 struck the man on the tracks, Earl Johnson registered only broad shoulders and blond or light brown hair. There were no last-moment evasive maneuvers. *The man has courage*, Johnson thought. The sound upon impact was a single muffled whump, like a stick of soft butter landing on the kitchen floor.

The 49 came to a stop about forty yards down the track from the point of contact. *Body may still be under the cars*, Johnson reasoned. *They'll want me to pull forward so they can get to it. I'll wait; do what I'm told.*

As the black silence surrounded him in those first moments, Johnson, detached, began to catalogue his reactions: Cold enveloped him, and his limbs trembled. When his legs would not hold him upright, he propped himself in his seat and managed to grasp a bar overhead. Nausea roiled though him in waves. Yet it was the onslaught of guilt, not the physical reactions, which threatened Johnson's equilibrium.

Into the night came the queries of distressed passengers. Johnson focused on movements in his rearview mirror. Riders were getting off the EL, and standing along the tracks. Immediately aware of the danger to them from the electrified third rail, Johnson bolted to the first car. His directions to the passengers milling about were calm, clear, and concise. There was a malfunction; the CTA had been notified; no one was to leave the train. Would the tall gentleman nearest the rear door ask passengers who had left the train to reboard immediately, and would the man in the red jacket, a man in his early twenties, a student from the looks of him, convey these same instructions to passengers in the adjacent cars?

In the minutes that followed, conversations resumed and rap music could be heard from the rear of the first coach. Johnson saw no signs of panic, and passengers appeared to be returning to the cars and their seats. No one seemed to be aware that there had been an accident.

No sooner did he have that thought than a shout of alarm came from outside. Leaning out of the car, Johnson saw a man vomiting onto the tracks. He jumped from the car and approached the young man who was probably no more than sixteen or seventeen. Before Johnson could reach him, the man's hysteria had communicated itself to several passengers watching from the windows, and curiosity spread like a firestorm.

The bold among the passengers converged around the young man who was sobbing and pointing to the severed arm that teetered on the rail. Hoots and cheers and high fives erupted. It took only a minute before one greasy young ghoul reached down and grabbed the limb; he grasped it at the elbow and held out the hand for his buddy to shake. More handshaking and whooping and hollering followed.

Sickened by the disrespect and the circus atmosphere, Johnson turned to go back to his compartment. At the front of the train, he dropped his hands to his knees and relinquished the chicory coffee that had warmed him so pleasantly only minutes before. When the shudders passed, he mounted the steps and hoisted himself into his leather seat. A determined Earl Johnson held himself upright; he would maintain his dignity even though others did not.

A suicide. He knew the interrogations would come, and the media coverage.... His family would be harassed. It would be a miracle if he didn't lose his job. The repercussions of another man's decision to end his life would be like the ever-widening circles on the surface of the gator pond. Johnson had not thrown the pebble that caused the disturbance, but he suspected that, unfairly, he might bear the blame.

When the pressure in his chest overrode the dark thoughts swirling through his consciousness, Johnson felt only a mild curiosity. He flashed back to the only other death that had occurred on his watch, that of an elderly heart attack victim in 1973. When the first stabbing pain stole his breath, Johnson remembered kneeling and taking the old man's hand. The moment of realization, and acceptance, had been clear in the man's rheumy eyes. There it was again, that look, mirrored in the reflection of the windshield of the 49.

Jim Henderson and Willie Thomas were the first two cops on the scene. They had been two blocks away when they heard 49's steel wheels screeching to a stop. This was their regular beat so they knew the EL wouldn't make an unscheduled stop unless there was trouble.

"Holy Jesus, give me strength," Thomas muttered. There, no more than four feet from the last car, illuminated in the beam of his high-powered flashlight, was a mangled torso. The victim's legs were flattened against his chest and pointed toward his head as though he'd simply been tumbled and folded onto himself. His right arm was missing, and the left was bent at an impossible angle. The face was gone, sheered cleanly off, with a tuft of hair clinging to the only remaining flap of scalp.

"Jesus, Jesus," Thomas repeated, louder with each effort.

"Get a grip, Willie; we gotta get some order here. You call it in." Henderson had been on the force longer than his partner, and had seen more carnage. It wasn't as though the bloody scene didn't get to him; it did, but he was made of sterner stuff.

There were still a few passengers milling about. "We'll start asking questions, Willie. Do what needs doing. And make sure they don't touch that damn electrified rail. Shit...that's all we need now, someone getting fried."

Henderson knelt closer to the body and braced one hand against the rail. The victim's trench coat was wrapped around him, and the belt remained neatly tied. *Go figure*. Struggling to reach, he patted the pockets of khaki pants in search of a wallet or some other identification without contaminating the scene for the forensic guys who would be all over his ass if he moved so much as a stone. Henderson traced the outline of a wallet in the man's right rear pocket. He wormed his hand under the coat and into the pocket, carefully liberating the worn tri-fold with two latex-gloved fingers.

"Give me your flashlight, Willie," he shouted to his partner. "Over here." Henderson opened the wallet as Thomas flashed the light onto the contents of the billfold. There were enough credit cards to command some serious debt, and a faded Illinois driver's license. The face of the victim was solemn, unsmiling. The face that was no longer...

"What's his name, Jimmy?"

"Vinson. Edward Vinson."

"Poor sap. Wonder why he did it, why he offed himself?"

"Shit, why does anybody do something like that?" Henderson glanced up at the coach and saw several people standing at the window, looking lost. "C'mon," he said.

Both policemen boarded the train and told the passengers that a CTA bus had been called to take them on to the station. Henderson told his partner to convey the information to the occupants of others cars, and he headed to the front of the train. It had finally occurred to him that the EL conductor had been nowhere around, and that was mighty strange. Had he skipped when faced with the emergency? That didn't make sense. As a group, EL conductors were a dedicated and cohesive bunch, one of the more proactive groups of city servants.

More likely Henderson had just missed him...probably he was sticking close to the radio. That made more sense. He'd get some preliminary information.

As he approached the front compartment, Henderson could see immediately that the conductor was slumped over, his head resting on the side window. "Oh, no," he whispered, making the sign of the cross. Climbing the steps into the car, Henderson felt for the pulse he knew was not there. Gently he closed the conductor's eyes.

Moving back through the coaches, Henderson met his partner halfway. "Conductor's dead, too," he said, shaking his head wearily. "Probable heart attack."

"What a night," was all Willie could think to say. Then he had another thought, "Aww, Lord! Think of all the paperwork."

CHAPTER TWENTY-THREE

When the phone rang in the Cook kitchen, Sonya Vinson was just pouring the first cup of coffee of her day. Her father, Tim, already a half pot ahead of her, was wide-awake even though it was only 5:00 a.m. He snagged the telephone receiver on its first ring.

Sonya watched as he muttered a few "Uh, huhs," and his face darkened. He glanced at her, then turned his back, and although it was apparent that the caller was simply relaying information which did not require further response, Sonya felt icy fingers of fear grip her throat.

"OK, we'll be there at nine," Cook finally replied. His hand trembled as he returned the receiver to its cradle, but didn't turn around. His shoulders were bowed, and the caffeine-induced energy vibrating through him only moments before drained from him as though he had sprung a leak.

"What is it, Daddy?

"Daddy?"

"It's Eddie, honey."

"Eddie? That was Eddie? What did he want?"

"It wasn't Eddie, Honey. It was the Chicago police. There was…there's been an accident."

"An accident?" Sonya circled once around the kitchen. "He's working an accident? Did he get hurt? What is it, Daddy?"

"Eddie's been killed." As he folded Sonya into his arms, Cook looked up to see his wife, Dorothea, at the door from the dining room. He'd never known her to show her beloved face before 8:00 am, not once in all their years together, but then, he'd never known her radar to fail when her family needed her either. Belting her bathrobe tightly around her, she stepped forward and embraced them both.

"I'll go shower," Cook said, clearing his throat. "We have to be downtown at 9:00 to make the identification. I'll go with you, and Mom can keep Dottie busy, huh?

"There's room for two cooks in this kitchen if you just take her under your wing. She's been beggin' you; now's a good time." He kissed the back of Dorothea's neck, and inhaled. He'd need her strength, her essence, in the hours to come, just as their daughter would. *We'll get her through this.*

CHAPTER TWENTY-FOUR

Foster was preparing for his Friday. TGIF. Joyce brought morning coffee and a folded newspaper, and set them on the bedside table. His eyes tracked the drift of the steam rising from the mug. *First sip is always best*, he thought as it warmed its way down. Foster propped himself against the carved headboard, punching two pillows together to support his back. Another sip of coffee. "Ahh, that's good Joyce." No response, but he knew she heard him.

Foster often talked to himself, providing a running commentary as he perused the newspaper. "Another peace initiative in the Middle East...gimme a break. More Presidential promises, a tax break for the American people...OK, who? The top 1%? To be sure, even if it doesn't say so."

When he finally turned to the classifieds, Foster glanced at the columns for classic sports cars. There were ads for a Studebaker Golden Hawk and several Avantis. For a moment, his fantasies took him to a deserted road, wind in his face, the Golden Hawk soaring to his lightest touch....

"Hey, Joyce. Beautiful day, high seventy-five, low mid-fifties. Spring is in the air!"

Foster turned to scan the local news: Two teenagers were arrested for cruelty to animals. They set fire to cat and threw it off a roof. *They need a good shrink!*

A local man had been killed Wednesday night on the west side of Chicago, an apparent suicide. The victim, Edward Vinson, thirty-five, was pronounced dead at the scene. Apprehension curled along Foster's spine. His eyes fixed on the two-inch column at the top of the page, and a cold, sucking feeling caused his stomach to contract violently. *Edward Vinson? Eddie Vinson? My client, Eddie Vinson? Couldn't be. No way he was suicidal. What the hell?*

"What, John?" Joyce asked as she walked into the bedroom. "John? You look like you've seen a ghost."

"Vinson."

"Who?"

"Eddie Vinson. It says here an Edward Vinson got run over by an EL, probable suicide."

"Oh, John. Run over like that?"

"The EL conductor died, too, an apparent heart attack. Check this out. Vinson had just become a *person of interest* in an investigation into the death of a local pub owner who had his head bashed in. "'Vinson was allegedly distraught over a recent separation from his wife.' Aww, jeez, Joyce, it's *my* Eddie Vinson. Police think he committed suicide to avoid prosecution."

Foster was not accustomed to having his patients commit suicide. Since he'd begun to practice, it had happened only once before. On that occasion, too, he had been blindsided by the patient's action since there had been no prior indications of suicidal thinking.

That first suicide had been a psychiatric social worker, late-thirties, who had been committed to the psychiatric hospital where Foster worked while receiving his post-doctoral supervision. The man's admitting diagnosis had been a Major Depression without psychosis, and a secondary diagnosis of Alcohol Abuse. Rather straightforward, and treatment had been uneventful. The man responded well to an antidepressant, and gave every indication that he was recovering. His first home visit was staffed carefully the day before it was to take place, and he seemed ready and eager. Later, Foster learned that, on the first night of his visit, the man began to drink heavily and confronted his wife about signing his commitment. He held a pistol at his side while sobbing, and before his wife could react, he placed the pistol to his temple and fired.

Foster and his treatment team had performed an intensive psychological post mortem under the eagle eye of the hospital administration. No fault was discerned, and the man's wife blamed herself, but the suicide had rocked Foster's professional assurance. In the dark of many a night, he had reviewed that suicide from every angle. However, even hindsight wasn't always 20/20, and he was wise enough to know that guilt continued to distort his analysis. Only the patient had known what personal demon had caused him to surrender his life.

Now, Foster knew he would conduct an exhaustive analysis of his interactions with Vinson and his wife, and, of course, he would support Sonya Vinson, if that was what she wanted, or he would refer her to another therapist, if that was her choice. As Joyce topped off his coffee, he said, "I'll call Ms. Vinson today to find out how she is doing. Maybe she can shed some light on what happened."

When Foster arrived at the office, he was preoccupied, and only Louise's inquiry stopped him from drifting past her desk without saying good morning. "Dr. John, did you hear what happened? It was on the radio this morning."

"Yes, Louise. Vinson? Yes."

"They say he was a suspect in a murder."

"We never know who's gonna come through our door, Kiddo; it should keep us on our toes."

By 10:15, it was apparent that his ten o'clock patient was not coming. Foster fiddled with a pen, slipped it over, under, and through his fingers repeatedly; he tapped a rapid staccato on his legal pad while he prepared himself for the call to Sonya Vinson. As he pressed the intercom to ask Louise for her number, however, she announced that Ms. Vinson was calling on his private line.

Foster acknowledged the apprehensive flutter in his chest. He took a cleansing breath. *Anxiety, meet the doctor,* he thought, reaching for the telephone.

"Ms. Vinson, I'm so sorry."

"Thank you, Dr. Foster." She paused, then asked, "Do you know anything about why Eddie would take his life?" There was accusation in her tone, if not in the words themselves, not at all what he had expected considering their previous contacts.

"Ms. Vinson, your husband had some very serious issues to deal with, but he was not suicidal. Naturally, we can't always predict, but Eddie just didn't fit the profile of a suicide.... I have to qualify my statement, however, because I had not seen him since he came under investigation. You knew he was a suspect in the murder investigation, yes?"

"Yes, but Eddie couldn't have done that. He was too sensitive. He's devoted himself to saving lives, not taking them."

Foster could hear both anger and tears threatening in Ms. Vinson's voice. It was a normal reaction to the helplessness of sudden loss. *She needs to let loose on someone; might as well be me.*

"Ms. Vinson, it's not inconceivable that Eddie's daily exposure to violence and death in his work might desensitize him, lower his threshold, make it easier for him to take a life in anger."

"What do you mean by that, Doctor?" Ms. Vinson snapped. Nowhere was the fearful woman who had first contacted him because she believed her husband had defaced her niece's room while in a violent, drunken rage.

"I mean, Sonya, that the man you described to me during our first meeting seemed more likely to commit a violent act toward someone else, not himself. There was nothing in the background you or your husband provided to suggest a potential for self-injury. Therefore, an aggressive act, in this case, a murder, would have seemed more likely than suicide."

In the silence that followed, Foster heard several sobbing gulps. He did not rush to fill the void.

"I'm sorry, Dr. Foster...John. I'm just at such a loss. I didn't mean to imply that Eddie's death was.... I'm just trying to make sense out of this. You've reminded me why I first came to you, as well you should. If I stop to think about it, his behavior was out of character, even then. Something was happening, and I didn't understand, didn't see a pattern emerging..., if there was a pattern."

"I understand, and Sonya, you may never know.... Shoot, *I* may never know. I can assure you that I will review my involvement with Eddie intensively, knowing what I now know, but he didn't give many clues."

"You think so?" The plea in her voice was heart breaking, and signaled to Foster that Ms. Vinson's anger had dissolved once she was reminded of the significant changes in her husband's behavior that had precipitated her coming to him in the first place.

Foster settled into his chair and put his feet on his desk. As he encouraged Ms. Vinson to say whatever was on her mind, his deep FM voice emerged to calm and reassure. He could hear her breathing return to normal and tension fade from her voice. As she gained a measure of composure, Foster felt his own unease return, as though it took on a life of its own when he was otherwise occupied.

Foreboding, that's what I'm feeling. Although there was nothing he could put his finger on, he felt compelled to warn Sonya to be careful. He did not, of course; it wasn't appropriate, although he wanted to…really wanted to, but, be careful of what? The available pieces of the puzzle that was Eddie Vinson did not fit, and there were pieces missing, of that he had no doubt.

As their conversation drew to a close, Ms. Vinson assured Foster that she would get back to him after Eddie's funeral as she began to put their affairs in order. He reminded her that she could contact him at any time if she needed his assistance or support. That was as far as he could go.

Ten days passed, and Foster found himself involved in a high-profile custody case. Dismayed that details of the litigation and the nasty charges and counter charges by the estranged socialite spouses were being leaked and making the daily news, the Court ordered Foster to evaluate all parties and deliver his written reports to His Honor *only*. Because custody evaluations were often the most difficult of all cases, he knew from experience that the coming weeks would find him wrapped up in the public and private lives of a dysfunctional family.

The absorption that was required for Foster to ferret out the truths that each family member sought to keep hidden, while also putting forth his or her own agenda, was draining. For this reason, he would cram the evaluation into as few days as possible, thereby keeping family members off balance and more likely to let slip bits of useful information. Psych testing came next, then follow-up interviews to check for consistency.

For this particular family and the two children involved, Foster knew to expect that the adults would try to hide behind their social status; rules were different for them, after all. When he failed to be impressed, they would weep and wail to their attorneys that the process was invasive, unfair, and demeaning.

Although he would not bend to the manipulations of the parents or the machinations of their well-heeled attorneys, Foster would jump through hoops to establish rapport with the children. It was imperative that they trust him and know that they could discuss their feelings openly without fear that what they said would be reported to their parents. When all was said and done, the best interests of the children would be the sole focus of his assessment.

Foster was no longer saddened by the adversarial nature of divorce and custody litigation. Parents, who supposedly conceived their children in love, thought little of using these same children as pawns in the litigation game, a game in which there were never winners, only losers, and the losers were almost always the children. Fortunately, word had spread through the judicial community that Foster was a fair and fearless child advocate, and to his way of thinking, that was as it should be. Furthermore, the evaluation reports provided him with a forum to advocate mediation or collaborative divorce in lieu of litigation, as area judges also knew. Progress, however, was slow in coming.

The intensity of the custody evaluation consumed Foster, and another two weeks passed without any word from Sonya Vinson. He hoped that she was finding the support she needed within her family. The reasons for her contact with him had ceased to be when her husband took his life, but knowing that to be the case did not end Foster's unease about the circumstances that caused Eddie Vinson's suicide.

His assessment of the Vinson case changed three days later when Sonya Vinson called during the noon hour on his private line. Their conversation recalled for him the amorphous angst that had accompanied their previous conversation; however, there was no ambiguity now in the alarm that was triggered by her words.

Ms. Vinson stated that she was afraid she was being followed. Additionally, someone had broken into her house again while she and Dottie were staying with her parents in the days before, and immediately after, Eddie's funeral. She returned home alone the following week to find that a large amount of cash had been removed from a floor safe, and several of her husband's sentimental possessions were missing, among them a prized, autographed Nellie Fox bat that had been given to him by his only uncle.

Foster allowed genuine laughter to break the tension of the phone call when Ms. Vinson concluded wryly that she had a full plate these days. From a clinical perspective, however, the second break-in, which followed her husband's suicide so closely, seemed to have triggered symptoms of acute stress. Ms. Vinson requested an appointment to come in so Foster could, in her words, "debunk" her fears, but when she told him she thought she'd seen Eddie ride by their house on a bicycle, he instructed Louise to give her the first available appointment.

Following the conversation with Ms. Vinson, Foster requested her file and her husband's. From his notes, he began to construct a timeline of events since Sonya had first contacted him: her husband's strange behaviors, the drinking, his personal and sexual withdrawal from her; the amount of time he was spending on the computer; a break-in and vicious vandalism of their home; the murder investigation into the death of the barkeep; Eddie's suicide, which simply was not in character given his overall clinical presentation; and a second break-in and theft after his funeral.

Ms. Vinson had disclosed that all leads in Michael O'Hearn's beating death stopped at her front door. According to police, the reports implicating her husband came from bar patrons who had witnessed his shouting match with O'Hearn, although no one could say with certainty that Vinson had threatened the tavern owner with harm. Their argument had not appeared to be all that serious; more than one patron had alluded to an alcohol-induced confrontation, nothing more. If that was the case, then who killed O'Hearn, and why Vinson's suicide?

Late into the afternoon, Foster again perused his case notes and the timeline he had constructed for Eddie Vinson. His brain ordered and reordered known facts and suppositions. *What am I missing?*

CHAPTER TWENTY-FIVE

When he had been released from prison, Tim Cook promised himself that he would miss no more significant events in his daughter's life. Although he and Dorothea found it difficult to break through the barriers Sonya had erected after she was removed from their custody, once they had reconciled, there were no recriminations and no looking back at the lost years. They treasured their relationship with Sonya, and were blessed tenfold when she stepped forward to adopt her niece, Dottie, following the deaths of her brother and sister-in-law. Naturally, he and Dorothea would have provided for their granddaughter, but it was far better for Dottie to have a *young* parent. Like it or not, he and Dorothea were no longer spring chickens, and on days like today…well, he was feeling every one of his advancing years.

Cook moved a flavored toothpick from one corner of his mouth to the other and back again. His girls would say he was cogitating, but they would be wrong. He was worrying, plain and simple. Until this morning, his strong and independent daughter had kept him in the dark about the events of the past several months. He'd known Sonya was under a lot of stress, but she had shrugged off his inquiries and fed him only vague generalities. Now, he knew that she was just plain scared, and given what she told him this morning, he believed she might not be scared enough. He pondered how to impress upon his girls the need for caution and vigilance without making them more fearful.

After some give and take with Dorothea, and finally having to stand his ground, Cook decided that he would keep an eye on Sonya's house at night and sleep days while Dorothea kept her eye on Sonya and Dottie. It had already been agreed that one of them would pick Dottie up at school, and she would stay with them until Sonya got off work. Sonya had allowed that she and Dottie would stay and share their evening meals despite the hardship of eating her mother's cooking. Only Cook and Dorothea knew that he would follow the girls home and stand watch through the night.

Cook had gone to the attic and rummaged through his old Marine footlocker to find his camouflage fatigues. Much to his chagrin, Dorothea had caught him preening before the mirror, but he figured he was entitled since the uniform still fit after all these years. She'd patted his buns and made some smart remark about being the one responsible for his diet and exercise.

Cook sat quiet and still in a clump of bushes two houses down and across the street from his daughter's home. Further on, O'Hearn's Pub was closed, and someone had pulled the plug on the neon sign that had given Sonya's block its distinctive pulsing shamrock-green glow in the night. Sitting there, alert and watchful, Cook swiped a leathery palm over the hills and valleys of his face, wiping away the smile tugging at the corners of his mouth. He may have been retired for more years than he cared to count, but the old skills were still sharp, still his to command. He might be an *old* Marine, but by God, he was still a Marine! "Semper Fi," he whispered.

Cook hadn't shaved in several days, and his neck was beginning to itch. To make matters worse, he could hear mosquitoes who'd pegged him for a hot meal and were pissed by the high-powered repellant he'd used. In retaliation, they flew into his ears and up his nose, and he'd already swallowed one or two.

Forget the damn bugs. Pay attention, amigo! Cook set his jaw and peered into the night. The first floor of Sonya's house was dark and shades were drawn upstairs, but he could see occasional shadows as she and Dottie prepared for bed. He turned his attention to the street and black between buildings, scanning continually, all senses working in concert. It had been nights in Bogota that prepared him for such surveillance; he was an old hand. He looked under cars, watched for shadows or movements that might break the glare of streetlights, sniffed the night air. Smells were a dead giveaway. You might not see or hear a truly skilled adversary, but the human animal carried a smell that was clearly detectable to those in the know...and cigarette smoke? Cook snorted. Smokers hadn't a clue how far *their* scent carried.

Behind the junipers, Cook sat on an inflated canvas chair, his butt resting comfortably on a cushion of air, thanks to the manufacturer and his own lung capacity. Cars passed intermittently. Nothing suspicious. Crickets serenaded to a Latin beat, and he tapped a thumb silently on his knee to their rhythm. Crickets must have excellent audition. All you have to do is whisper when you're with them, and they shut up. "Whhhh," he went. Sure enough, no more chirping. He grinned and swallowed another mosquito. *Dang*!

How much time passed, Cook couldn't say. He'd forgotten his watch, the one lapse in his preparations for this first night of protecting his girls. In his peripheral vision, he caught the familiar blue pulses of a police vehicle before it turned the corner and started down the block. Behind it followed a second car, and both stopped directly in front of him. He sucked in a breath and held it.

One policeman emerged on the passenger side of each vehicle. While Cook's attention was on their approach, the driver of the closer car hit him full force with a high-powered beam, blinding him. Before he could get his hands up to shield his eyes, cuffs were snapped on his wrists, and he was being manhandled by an Amazon with a deep sexy voice and fragrant floral scent. *What's wrong with this picture?*

"What you doing here, man?" the policewoman rumbled in his ear as she dragged him to the patrol car. She dug him with her elbow. "Give me the position." She patted him down, and didn't miss much. She snickered, and Cook cringed. He could feel the heat painting his neck and ears red.

"We had a call 'bout a suspicious dude skulkin' around in the bushes. That would be you, it seems. What are you doin' here?"

"Ma'am, Officer, please. My ID's in my left rear pocket. You'll see that I'm Timothy Cook, and I'm an ex-Marine."

"Oh yeah? Well, so am I, Mr. Cook, but I'm not lurking about trying to sneak looks at unwary folks just goin' about their lives. Besides, I already know what's in your pocket."

"I wasn't trying to cop a look. Er...uh, no offense intended."

"What did you say?"

"I said no offense intended, Officer."

The woman backed Cook against the police cruiser. As close as she was, he could tell what she'd had for supper, probably lunch and breakfast, too. He could also tell she was solid muscle, and she was waiting for him to give her an excuse, any excuse, to take him down a notch or two.

Unable to focus his watering eyes long enough to read the officer's nametag, Cook tried to lift his cuffed hands to wipe away the tears. Because the damn woman was still crowding him, the backs of his hands grazed her breasts. He wasn't too old to know DD's when he felt them.

"Sorry," Cook muttered as he scrubbed at his weeping eyes with his sleeve. In the time that his eyes were shaded by his arm, he was able to make out the name, Headstrom, on the officer's nameplate. Carefully he lowered his hands, sliding them down his own chest to avoid further contact. Nevertheless, he brushed one rock-hard nipple on his descent. *Aw, hell!*

Knowing full well that his face was flaming, again, Cook dropped his eyes and cleared his throat.

"Uh, Officer Headstrom, I need to explain. Please?" he added miserably.

Headstrom took a step back and nodded.

"I'm Timothy Cook, and my daughter and her niece live over there at 4506. Sonya's been through a lot recently, had a couple of break-ins, and her husband recently passed. I was just watching out for her and my granddaughter."

"Really?" Headstrom's tone said she didn't believe a word. "Let's go over and meet this daughter." As the second police car pulled away, Headstrom's partner, a pixie to her Amazon, led the way to Sonya's front door and rang the bell.

When Sonya opened the door as far as the security chain would allow, the pulsing lights of the patrol car—and her father—were in her narrow field of vision. She closed the door and dropped the chain. When she opened the door wide, Sonya looked from one police officer to the other, and then at her father.

"Daddy? What's going on?"

"This is your father, Ma'am?" Headstrom's deep bark clearly startled Sonya.

"Yes, of course. Daddy?"

"Don't worry, Baby. I was just trying to look out for you."

"I'll see that ID now, Mr. Cook." Headstrom turned back to Sonya. "And your name is?"

"Sonya Vinson. What is this all about?"

"We got a report of a peeper in the neighborhood. Appears to be your father, Ms. Vinson.

"You've had some problems, a death, haven't you, Ma'am? Your name is familiar to us."

"Yes, I have." Sonya rubbed her eyes wearily.

"We're sorry for your loss, Ma'am." Headstrom and her partner spoke almost in unison.

"We're going to speak with your father for a few minutes, Ms. Vinson. Then he can stay with you, or we can see that he gets home, whatever."

"I'll stay, Sonya."

"No, Daddy, I'm fine. We're fine. Go home to Mom. We'll be OK. I'll talk to you tomorrow."

Cook watched his daughter swing the door shut. At the last moment, she sniggered, "And no more of this Marine to the rescue shit." He heard her shoot the deadbolt and replace the security chain.

Headstrom eyeballed him as they reached the sidewalk. His face flamed again, and she gave an unladylike snort.

"Under the circumstances, we can understand wanting to protect your daughter and granddaughter, Sir," the diminutive policewoman offered, placating, "but we can't have you lurking about in the bushes and upsetting the neighbors. We'll see you to your car now."

CHAPTER TWENTY-SIX

Sonya tossed restlessly in a twilight sleep. The visit by her father and the two policewomen had disturbed what little sleep she was usually able to catch between 10:00 p.m. and 2:00 a.m. After that, she was awake and alone with her demons. At 3:00 a.m., she glanced at the glowing clock face, and wondered what internal mechanism always caused her to look precisely on the hour.

Goading herself to take decisive action, even for something as stupid as unplugging the damn clock, Sonya swung her feet to the floor just as she heard what sounded like the tinkle of breaking glass. Soundlessly, she moved across the hall to Dottie's room. She shook her niece gently, and when Dottie's eyes opened, she put her finger to her lips to indicate silence. Dottie's eyes focused and she nodded to show she understood. Sonya grabbed the bathrobe at the foot of the bed, and tugged Dottie to get up. She gestured for Dottie to get into the back of her closet and remain silent. It was the best she could do at the moment. As she left Dottie's room, she turned and pushed the locking mechanism of the doorknob, and closed the door silently behind her. It wasn't much of a deterrent, but it would slow an intruder momentarily.

Sonya returned to her room. As she passed her dresser, she grabbed a heavy crystal candlestick. She climbed into bed, concealing her poor excuse for a weapon. There was no escape from the second story except for the safety ladder she kept in her closet in case of fire, and there was no time for that now. Surprise was about all she had going for her. She tried to slow her breathing…to find a relaxed cadence that would suggest she was asleep and defenseless.

Minutes passed, and Sonya heard nothing. *Did I over-react?* Raising her lids fractionally, she scanned the shadowed bedroom landscape. A weary resignation settled over her as her eyes came to rest on the figure filling her doorway, arm raised, gun extended. A flash of light was her only warning, and by then, it was already too late. The bullet pierced the left side of her chest. *It doesn't hurt.*

Dottie heard the single gunshot. She scrambled for her winter quilt in the far corner to cover herself, and dislodged some books she had thrown carelessly into the closet. The shooter heard the muffled thunk as the books toppled to the floor; he paused, oriented toward the sound, and jiggled the handle of the locked door. Then, abruptly, he moved down the stairs and out the front door, leaving it open to the humid night.

Bill Nafus was at the console when Dottie's 911 call came in.

"Nine one one, emergency, Officer Nafus speaking. What's your trouble?"

"I'm Dottie; my Mom's been shot."

Nafus went rigid. "OK, honey, how old are you?"

"I'm fifteen."

"Where are you?"

"In my Mom's bedroom."

"What's your address, Dottie?"

"4506 Stanton."

"Good, that's good. Are you hurt?"

"No."

"OK. I'm sending help. The police and ambulance will be there in just a minute. You just keep talkin' to me. That's what I'm here for, Sweetheart."

"I don't think she's breathing!" There was an audible gulp.

"OK, can you tell where she's hurt?"

"Her chest is bleeding. We heard someone come in and she made me hide in the closet. Then, I heard a shot."

"OK, Dottie. Do you hear anything now? Do you think the intruder is still in the house?"

"I don't think so. I don't know.

"She's really my aunt, but I call her my mom."

"That's wonderful, Dottie, that the two of you are so close, I mean.

"Now, listen carefully. I want you to check and see if your Mom is breathing. Put your ear right up to her face. Can you feel her breath?"

"I can't do it. There's blood everywhere."

"OK, Dottie. I understand. Try laying your hand on her stomach. Can you feel her breathing now?"

"I'll try...yes, I can feel it!"

"That's great! Take hold of your mother's hand, why don't you? It'll make you both feel better"

Dottie scooted as close as the phone cord would allow and tucked the receiver under her chin. She grasped her mom's hand in both of hers and closed her eyes tight. *I believe in miracles. I believe in miracles.*

Dottie could hear approaching sirens.

"They're coming, Mom. Please hold on a little longer."

"I think her hand is growing colder," she said into the telephone.

"You might be right, Dottie," Nafus said matter-of-factly. "She's had a serious injury, and she could be in shock. That's the body's normal response. Just hold tight; the ambulance will be there any minute."

Dottie felt a squeeze of her fingers.

"Dottie?" Sonya slurred, "What happened?"

"It's OK, Mom, the ambulance is here. Just be still. I love you."

"I love you too, Sweetheart...

"Dottie, where's...Eddie?" Sonya asked, her voice fading.

"Oh, Mom. Eddie's dead...remember?"

Dottie heard muffled noises from the foot of the stairs, and a husky voice calling her name.

"We're up here," she answered.

There was a blur of activity as two policemen and two paramedics appeared. Gentle but firm hands lifted her up and away. "Let's move you away, Darlin', so the medics can do their job."

Dottie was passed to a bear of a man who smelled like fresh-roasted peanuts. He scooped her up into his arms, and turned her face into his chest to hide her eyes. He carried her from the room.

"My friends call me 'Ski.'" His voice rumbled in Dottie's ear, and when she looked up at him, a warm smile emerged from within his beard. "This your room over here?" She burrowed into his shoulder as Ski bent to put her on the bed. He grinned, "All right, we'll do it this way." He turned and sat on the bed, his back against the headboard, and settled Dottie at his side. He ran his huge hand soothingly down her hair and began to hum.

How much time passed, she did not know. When the policeman stopped humming, Dottie could hear the paramedics. "Looks like a nine millimeter. Damn. This is going to be touch 'n go." Then there was only silence.

"The IV's goin'. Let's get the hell out of here."

Pilarski was the name on the officer's chest. He stood and supported Dottie while she gained her footing. "I'll wait down stairs, Dottie, while you get dressed. I'm appointing myself your guardian angel, and I'll drive you to the hospital. Can you tell me who I should call while I'm waiting?"

"My grandparents are Timothy and Dorothea Cook. Their number is by the phone in the kitchen. I can't seem to remember it right now." A tear slid down her cheek. Ski gently wiped it away with his thumb, and gave her a pretend sock to the jaw.

"Buck up, Dottie, you'll have to be strong, but there are lots of folks to help you. I'll send police officers to your grandparents so they don't have to learn about your Mom over the telephone. They'll drive your grandparents to the hospital, and you and I will meet them there. Now, scoot and get dressed."

Pilarski made the necessary arrangements to get Mr. and Mrs. Cook to the hospital. Dottie had not come down. From the foot of the stairs he could see that she was dressed, but she was sitting on the top step, a hightop dangling by its lace from her fingers. Tears were streaming down her cheeks.

"Looks like she's shutting down," one of the forensic guys muttered to Pilarski as he approached the stairway. "Poor kid."

Ski preceded the technician up the stairs. "Slide over, Kiddo."

Dottie made room for him, and he sat down beside her.

"My mom asked about Eddie," she whispered, "but Eddie's dead."

"Your mom spoke to you, Dottie?" Surprise was evident in Ski's voice.

"Eddie is...who, Dottie?"

"My stepdad."

As the crime lab technician skirted around them to reach the second floor, he leaned down to Pilarski. "Eddie Vinson. The EL suicide three-four weeks ago. Remember?" he said softly.

Officer Headstrom shook her head sadly as she approached the Cook home to see Tim Cook for the second time in three hours. This time, she and her partner were to take Mr. and Mrs. Cook to the hospital where their daughter was clinging to life. In her mind, Headstrom replayed Cooks' urgent plea when she had followed him to his car and sent him home. He had spoken politely enough, but she had to admit she had been aware of the frustration coloring his words. She had ignored his intuition, at what cost to Cook and his family?

"Officer, please, listen to me. My daughter and granddaughter are in jeopardy. I know it. You've got to let me stay, or at least send someone to protect them."

Now, what Cook said would happen had come to pass. Headstrom figured her broad shoulders would be toting a boatload of guilt for weeks to come, and rightly so. She knocked firmly on the Cooks' front door. *I need a long vacation.*

Officer Headstrom supported a wobbly Ms. Cook as they approached the Emergency Room double doors. With a speed that belied his advancing years, Cook himself was already through the swinging doors, and Headstrom would bet her next paycheck that he was already barking out demands.

Sure enough, even from the entrance, Headstrom could hear Cook though she couldn't see him. Momentarily, he came around the corner, his arms around a sobbing adolescent.

"Grandma!"

"Dottie! Tim...?"

Dottie broke from her grandfather's gentle hold and flung herself into her grandmother's bosom. As tears flowed, Dottie told them what they already knew. "Mama's been shot, Grandma."

The words pierced Cook's gut like a double-edged blade. Beyond his wife and granddaughter stood Officer Headstrom. He held her gaze until she broke eye contact, and an entire conversation passed between them. A feeling of heaviness radiated through Cook's chest and his field of vision narrowed to black. Though he didn't see her move, Headstrom was there to catch him when his knees buckled.

When he came to, Cook was lying on a Naugahyde sofa in a narrow cubicle across from the ER intake center. The pea-green plastic couch emanated the odors of fear, frustration, and sorrow accumulated in its lifetime of service to families, cops, and medical staff, of which Cook was now one. The smell made him sick to his stomach. "Where am I?" he asked, struggling to sit up.

"Don't worry, Mr. Cook. You're going to be alright. Let me give you a hand."

"I am alright; I'm OK," Cook spat, swinging his feet to the floor. At a glance, he took in Dorothea and Dottie, a uniformed police officer, and a civilian dressed in a brown business suit, but a cop, nonetheless. "Lieutenant Jack Swasas" his nametag read. Cook looked into Swasas' cool blue eyes. He saw strength of character, and, if the crows feet were any indication, a man who could laugh. *A good man to know.*

Swasas' assessment of Timothy Cook was equally favorable despite the background check that had turned up a long-ago felony drug conviction. The computer check had been routine after Cook's tangle with Headstrom earlier in this hellishly long night.

Without inflection, Cook asked, "Tell me the truth, Lieutenant, how's my daughter?"

"The last report was that she was in critical condition, but holding her own. She sustained a serious chest wound...." That was all Cook heard; although Swasas' mouth continued to form words, he did not hear them.

When Cook regained consciousness a second time, he and Dorothea were informed that Social Services had been called because of Cook's drug conviction. An investigation and home study would be required before Dottie could be released to their custody. The system had been set in motion. *The goddamned system.*

As Cook returned to the ER from a few moments of respite in the beauty of an approaching dawn, he glanced at Headstrom who sagged wearily against the rear fender of an empty ambulance. Her back was to him, and she was running her hands repeatedly through her spiky hair. As he watched, she crossed her arms at her waist and bent forward, as though she was holding herself together. Tremors in her back and shoulders indicated that she was sobbing although she made no sound. Not allowing himself to censor his actions, Cook detoured toward Headstrom. He put a hand on her shoulder as he addressed her. "Officer Headstrom?" The eloquent message in her eyes was all that Cook needed to know that Sonya was dead.

CHAPTER TWENTY-SEVEN

Foster hadn't seen Erik von Kovska for a number of weeks. Erik's office had notified Louise that he was on an emergency medical mission to Afghanistan. As an active participant in the Doctors Without Borders program and an immigrant himself, von Kovska served extensively overseas treating the severely injured who had few other resources. Foster anticipated that von Kovska would probably show symptoms of a PTSD relapse after his immersion in the carnage. It was 5:05 p.m. and Louise hadn't announced von Kovska's arrival. It was possible that his return from overseas had been delayed.

"Dr. F.? Dr. V. is here."

"OK, send him in, please," but as Foster looked up, von Kovska was already standing in the open doorway. Without saying a word, he collapsed in a heap into an overstuffed leather recliner.

"Erik?"

"John, my friend, I missed our sessions," von Kovska sighed, not lifting his head to meet Foster's eyes.

"Rough trip?"

"Rough. I think too rough. It surprises me that I am getting old. I am back one week, and still not sleeping." In his shorthand session notes, Foster briefly recorded the absence of von Kovska's usual erect, military bearing and the deterioration of his precise diction and grammar.

"I take Ambien now, so, I will be OK, but, John, something happens over there. It all comes back. It is terrible burden for me."

"Tell me," Foster encouraged.

Von Kovska paused at length and seemed to be gathering his thoughts. "She was twelve years old. When I first see her, she was in local hospital, in triage. Somebody says she had been playing with a grenade; children were throwing it to one another, running away and laughing. A witness reported she threw grenade into a group of children when it finally discharged. All of those children killed outright. The girl received multiple fragment wounds and her right arm was severed. Somebody had good sense to bring arm wrapped in dirty rag along with her unconscious body to hospital. When I first saw her...she...."

"Take your time, Erik."

"She opened her eyes, so deep, and our eyes met. I could see same look as in Budapest so long ago, and suddenly, I was there. Not Afghanistan, but Budapest. I could do nothing, froze up, you say, and had to be relieved until I regained my composure. Damn frightening. The flashback was unexpected."

"Right. Memories ambushing you and running amok."

"Yes, amok, all right. When do you think I get over these, John?"

"Honestly, I don't know, Erik. The bloody intensity of your experiences, and we both know I mean that literally.... The best we may hope for is that you learn to ride the wretched waves of your memories when they swamp you, knowing that they resolve eventually, and that you are fighting back the only way you know how, with your medical skills."

"That is what I did, John. As you instructed, but I sure miss you when I am over there."

"How are you doing at the hospital? Any problems since your return?"

"No. Am in good routine and, with medication, finally will be able to sleep. Oh, yes. First day back, I saw your client, I do not recall name...nice fellow, good paramedic, too. I don't think he saw me. You remember? I meet him the night of gang violence. Then I see him here last appointment."

"I don't have a paramedic client." Foster sorted mentally through his recent patients. "Ah...uh...I used to, but he died."

"Come on, John. You are growing old and forgetting. I meet him few weeks back as I was leaving my session. Remember? We all three talk about the gangs conflicts."

"No, you're mistaken, Erik. You're recalling the paramedic, but he committed suicide, probably right after you went overseas. Then, not long after, his wife was killed by an intruder."

"Is same guy! I am telling you." Erik was emphatic. "I do not forget faces."

Foster made it a policy never to argue with his patients. Thus, he let slide Erik's assertion that he had seen Eddie Vinson on his first day back in the hospital. The next forty-five minutes were spent processing Erik's flashback caused by both recent and remote traumatic experiences. However, as Foster documented the sights, sounds, smells, and even tastes that had triggered Erik's distress resulting from his treatment of the injured child, he couldn't dismiss von Kovska's report that he had seen Eddie Vinson.

After von Kovska's session, Foster retrieved Vinson's file and read his notations following their last meeting, "Probable sociopath; chameleon-like; use caution." Slowly he perused the entire file again, beginning with his interview of Vinson's wife. When he finally closed the folder, his conclusions remained the same. Vinson had not presented as a potential suicide; he was more likely to kill another and disappear than die himself. And what about his wife's death? Coincidences? *Don't believe in them. Something stinks here.*

Foster's FBI profiler personality was awake, restless, and prowling. He realized it had been running possible scenarios deep in his brain, and without his permission, for some time. *Damn. Son of a bitch! Vinson could be alive and well and still in the area. Not just could be; probably was.*

Foster tensed as a visceral rush of fear buffeted him; sweat rolled down his chest and back, dampening the linen shirt beneath his sport coat. A wave of nausea swept over him and bile surged to the back of his throat. He swallowed convulsively, trying to tame the physical manifestations of an adrenaline onslaught. *Am I the only one to have considered the possibility that Vinson might have orchestrated his own "suicide" to get his ass out of the proverbial fire? And why am I reacting so strongly to the prospect?*

Could it be? Look at the big picture, not just the puzzle pieces. Vinson's body was unidentifiable, mangled beyond recognition. Because the watch and clothing were his, and his ID was on him, no one thought to question the obvious. He was recently estranged from his wife, had been erratic at work, and was showing distinct personality changes; he was drinking and aggressive, and was the primary suspect in the unsolved murder of a man with whom he was known to have quarreled only steps from his home. To many, suicide would seem to be a logical response as Vinson's world spun out of control. But was it only a near-perfect ruse? DEAD, he was free to come back as the unknown intruder and kill his wife whose contact with me would be perceived as an unforgivable betrayal.

Foster stood and removed his jacket; holding it at arm's length, he sniffed and grimaced. He might as well drop it at the cleaner on his way home. He dropped the offending jacket in his chair and began to pace. He thought back to the visit from Police Detective Branan to his office only a few days following the Vinson suicide. The questions had been routine, innocuous: How long had Mr. Vinson been in counseling? Was he despondent? Was suicide an aspect of his clinical picture?

Foster reckoned that Sonya Vinson had given the police his name. He tried to give the police useful information about Vinson's clinical presentation without providing specifics that could be embarrassing to the family. Of course, Sonya Vinson had not yet been murdered, and he'd not yet been bushwhacked by the possibility that Vinson had staged his own death. At the time, no mention had been made by the detective about the bartender's death, but.... Get real! What were the odds of a suicide and two murders in one very small geographical area in a matter of weeks?

"Curiouser and curiouser," Foster said aloud. He was seized with the impulse to call Detective Branan, but decided he would wait for the moment. "I need to let this percolate awhile, and not go off half-cocked."

"Good idea, Dr. John, you have a sterling reputation to uphold." Louise stood in his doorway grinning like the imp she could sometimes be.

"How long have you been standing there, girl?"

"Just a few seconds. What must you think about some more? Anything wrong with Dr. V.?"

"No, something else. Another patient. I'm just thinking things through, for now." *That's a lie! There's not a shred of doubt in my mind that Vinson is alive and continuing his schemes.*

"Can I go home now, Dr. John?"

"Sure, Louise. What's on for tomorrow?"

"Another court-ordered sanity evaluation in the morning; the defendant was indicted on obscenity charges. After that, your day is clear...for paperwork and dictation, that is. You can catch up, maybe?" She snickered and waggled her fingers at him over her shoulder as she headed for the back door.

"The answering service is at the helm."

"And I think I'll run some errands." Foster addressed the air where Louise had been only a moment before. She gave him no chance to change his mind about going home early. "So-o-o, I'm outta here, too. Flowers for Joyce, dry cleaner, and yeah! I'll go by the District and see if the good detective thinks I've taken leave of my senses." *So much for waiting.* Foster retrieved a business card from the center drawer of his desk:

Michael J. Branan, Detective First Class
Twenty-sixth District, Chicago Police Department
North Avenue at Kedzie, Chicago, Illinois 31250
312-555-7654

Detective Branan had loosened his tie, and was peering at what appeared to be marinara sauce lurking among the subdued blue and gold diamonds on the fashionable noose. "Costs a fortune to clean the damn thing," he muttered, "and it'll never lay flat or hang right again." Halfway down the stairs from the second floor, he looked up, startled, to catch Foster's look of sympathy."

"Branan," Foster paused, "I'm John Foster, Clinical Psychologist. You came to my office after the Vinson suicide.... If I were you, I'd just throw the darn tie away!"

"Oh, yes. Dr. Foster, I remember." Branan slid the tie from under his collar; with a grin, he dropped it in the wastebasket. "How can I help you? Is this about Vinson?"

"Well…today I received some information that might have a bearing on the suicide and, maybe, Sonya Vinson's death. It's bothering me; I can be clear about that, but you may think I'm off my rocker when I've said what I came to say."

"OK, Doc…tor, but we've already arrested someone in the Sonya Vinson murder."

"You have?"

"Yeah, a guy who'd been burglarizing in the area for quite awhile. They think he was surprised by Ms. Vinson, panicked, and shot her."

"Oh, well…are you sure?"

"We haven't found a weapon yet, and the poor fool insists he's innocent of the murder, despite his admission of three break-ins. Doesn't mean squat, and we've got a strong circumstantial case. The DA thinks he can convict. If you want to talk, I'll be glad to hear what you have to offer, but it'll have to be tomorrow because I have a hot date with my wife."

"Alright, maybe it's nothing, but, then again…stranger things have happened. I could be here around four tomorrow if that would be OK with you."

"All right, Doc, see you then."

CHAPTER TWENTY-EIGHT

7:30 a.m. arrived way too early. Most of the night had passed in the play and rewind of repeating dreams. Foster slept lightly as he wandered a dreamscape of unfamiliar people and places. His first waking thoughts were tainted by dread. When he didn't heed the alarm, Joyce nudged him gently.

"I'm awake," he rumbled from beneath his pillow. "Just need a few more minutes."

Sheets rustled, and a silky, sleep-warmed derriere descended on his buttocks. Strong fingers kneaded the tense muscles of his lower back. "Rough night, hmmm?"

Joyce's soothing massage ended with a love bite to his shoulder and a bawdy solicitation for the evening to come. It was enough to get him moving, as she knew it would be. The sooner his day began, the sooner Foster could get home to accept her invitation, and he knew he would not be disappointed.

After a quick shower and shave, Foster nabbed the oversized insulated coffee mug that Joyce had filled for him, but stopped at the back door. "You're too good to me. I'll return the favor, and please, please don't forget about tonight, OK?" He winked and grinned. A giggle floated down the hall as the door closed behind him.

Foster reviewed the court order, arrest record, and police interviews that had been sent with the referral for his morning sanity evaluation. By 9:30 he began to anticipate a cancellation, which would give him three hours to dictate reports and tackle the never-ending paperwork, but it was just as likely that the inmate and sheriff's deputies would arrive one to two hours late and put him behind schedule for the remainder of the day. Half-heartedly he asked Louise to check with the jail and verify that they were transporting the inmate to the evaluation. Louise fielded the "I don't know...not my job...she's on maternity leave" excuses in the Sheriff's Department until one courageous soul finally admitted that the deputies hadn't received the transportation request until that morning, and they couldn't find the inmate who wasn't where he should be.

Ordinarily, Foster would have been disgruntled by the waste of his time. Instead, he grabbed his suit coat and the Vinson file from his credenza, and headed for the back door. "Bill those inefficient civil servants for the three hours they didn't use! I've got more pressing matters. I have my cell if you need me."

The door closed on Louise's sputtering about phone calls and paperwork.

The drive to Evanston was pleasant; with the top down on his Porsche, the wind in his face scoured away the last vestiges of his troubled night. Any break in his routine was a gift. Foster felt like a kid skipping school; a "stolen" day seemed better than all others. Stealing a day...a candy bar...a life. Could they all be served by the same brain center; were they only matters of degree? *Now there's a scary thought.*

The speedometer cruised past seventy on Lakeshore Drive. *Just keeping up with the flow of traffic, Officer. Honest.* Lake Michigan was the color of ripe blueberries with whipped-cream whitecaps that rose and fell. For a workday, there were lots of sun worshippers on the beach and psychedelic sails glinting on the horizon.

Foster's thoughts returned to last night's dream encounter with Eddie Vinson. There he was, sitting quietly in his office, his feet propped on his desk, only it wasn't a desk; it was a coffin. On the side of the plain pine box was a brass plate inscribed: Edward Vinson 1965-2000.

From over his shoulder, Foster heard, "Hey, Doc. How ya doin'?" As is the way only in dreams, he was unable to turn around to look at the person who addressed him, but he did not want to turn; nor did he need to. The voice was Eddie Vinson's. Foster waited.

"John, John?" The voice grew louder, strident, and demanding. Foster remained still, while all around him drummed a cacophony of violence and destruction. He was inundated by a rage so intense that, surely, all that was good within him would wither and die if he did not respond.

"Your rage enables me," Foster said in a voice that whispered from his parched throat and was barely audible to his own ears. Then, louder, "Do you hear me? You cannot, you will not prevail." Into the thunderous silence that followed, there was only the sound of his feet when they hit the floor. The coffin was gone.

As Foster approached the Emergency entrance of Evanston Hospital Center, it began to rain. Apparently, the sun was shining only on the lakeshore today. He struggled with the Porsche's cantankerous canvas top, getting soaked and earning piteous glances as the shower became a deluge. His summer-weight slacks pasted themselves to his thighs and calves, and his Oxford cloth shirt, light on the starch.... "The starch is now in my socks," he said to no one in particular.

A glance at his reflection in the sliding glass door confirmed that he looked like a drowned rat. Foster slicked the rain from his hair and began to whistle "Singing in the Rain" as the door swished open to admit him to the intense atmosphere of a big city ER and the shock of air conditioning.

At the admitting desk, Foster addressed a harried Bertha Schultz, RN. "Ms. Shultz, I'm Dr. John Foster, Clinical Psychologist. Can you tell me where I will find Dr. von Kovska? I need to speak with him."

"Do you have insurance?" Shultz asked, never looking up from her paperwork.

Foster gaped.

"I **said**, 'Do you have insurance?'" This time there was more snap to her words.

Foster censored several pithy retorts as unprofessional and remained silent.

Shultz pitched a "Jesus, what is wrong with you? Are you deaf?" at him, but still did not raise her eyes. The ballpoint with which she was scrawling unreadable chart notes leaked a glob of ink on the page. She uttered one of the epithets that Foster had already rejected. She threw the pen across the desk.

Good for ya, you old bat!

Schultz finally looked at him. "Nothing is wrong with me that one moment of your time and a little courtesy wouldn't fix," Foster smiled insincerely. "I'm looking for Dr. von Kovska.... You know? Head of Emergency Services? Your boss, I do believe."

Shultz swallowed audibly and her double chin jiggled. "If you'll have a seat, Sir, I'll call his office. Who shall I say is asking?"

"Foster. Dr. John Foster is asking."

"Well, you don't have to get huffy."

Foster glared and turned away. He chose an orange plastic seat because he hated turquoise. The rigid, molded chairs must have been designed by a torture expert; the seats were too low and the backs, too short. To make matters worse, Foster was sure he could see frost on the bathroom-beige walls. He was shivering and his nose began to run. "Freezing," he muttered.

"It's only gonna get worse," commiserated the young man sitting next to him. "They could hang meat in here!"

Foster turned to smile his agreement, and his teeth chattered. "What brings you here?"

"I lost a finger last night."

"Last night?"

"Yeah. Working. I'm a carpenter's helper."

Foster glanced down to a pancake-size puddle that rippled each time a drop of blood fell. The young man was resting his battered hand on a blood-soaked towel that was funneling droplets neatly to the pool on the floor. "It doesn't hurt much, not anymore," he volunteered.

"How long have you been here?"

"About six hours."

"Six hours?" Foster's eyebrows flew up a good inch.

"Don't sweat it, man. There are people here lots worse off than me. Been coming in all night, steady-like. Heart attacks, OD's, auto accidents, fights. Don't know how the doctors and nurses handle it all. Me, I sawed off my own damn thumb. Pretty stupid, huh?"

"Where is your thumb?"

"A nurse took it. She gave me a shot and told me to wait; said I'd be alright for a while."

"So you are. What's your name?"

"Tyro."

"Well, Tyro. You're a patient man. You have my admiration. I was only grumbling about being cold and wet."

"John! What are you doing here?"

Foster rose to his feet and extended his hand. "Erik, I've got to speak with you for one minute; this young man was telling me how busy you've been. Sorry I don't look very professional; it's the price I pay for owning a vintage sports car. I know I look like a survivor of the great flood who refused Noah's hospitality!"

Von Kovska chuckled and thought better of clapping Foster on the back. "Come with me. I will find you dry clothes."

Within a few minutes, Foster had toweled himself down and dried his hair. He was dressed in borrowed boxers and surgical blues. "At last, a *real* doctor," he quipped,

Von Kovska gestured, "I could use a break; let's go to my spacious private office, John. You brought the bad weather with you?"

"I could have brought worse." Foster's sarcasm wasn't wasted on von Kovska who saw worse every hour of every day.

Foster had been to Evanston Hospital several times before, but never to von Kovska's office. It was spacious only in one's imagination, but the muted blue of the cinder block walls was pleasing to the eye, and von Kovska's diplomas and board certifications were framed in handsome antique gold frames. A scarred oak desk faced the wall, and there appeared to be an order to the hundred or so files that covered the entire surface except for the very center where a calendar desk pad delineated the workspace. Two small sofas were the only other furniture. The glass wall, which overlooked Erik's domain, was flanked by mauve drapes that could be drawn for privacy.

"Mauve drapes, Erik? I would never have guessed."

Von Kovska shrugged. "My predecessor was a *she*. And they do not distress me enough to replace them."

"I guess you're wondering why I'm here, Erik."

"You can say so," von Kovska replied.

"Erik, you remember, yesterday, telling me you had seen my paramedic client your first day back at the hospital?"

"Sure, I am not senile like you," he said, winking.

"Look, Erik, this is serious. I think that the man you saw, the paramedic, may have faked a suicide and then killed his wife."

"John, all I know is I saw this man or someone very like him."

"Erik, do you recall which ambulance service the man worked for?"

"No, have no clue. They all wear insignia of their service, of course, but I did not pay attention at the time. Emergency support personnel from all over the city come and go from here all day and all night."

"Do you know, by chance, who he brought in when you saw him?"

"No."

"What day it was?"

"Uh…a Tuesday, I think, but whole week was very busy, and I was out of my routine. Not so focused after being away."

"Darn. I was hoping…."

"I am sorry, John. Maybe I was wrong about him."

"It was Vinson."

"Right, Vinson. You know, it could be a doppelganger, John?"

"Right. Doubles. I know. I once met myself in New Orleans. There I was, twenty years younger, seated on a racing bike in Jackson Square. Freaked me out! Especially because, as the cab drove past him, he never moved a muscle, like he was posing. Very weird, but it convinced me that doppels exist."

"Yeah, I remember going through the Metropolitan Museum in New York and saw my cousin, Laura, in one of the Greek busts. Faces have only so much variation it seems; over the ages there must have been hundreds of Vinson lookalikes."

"You're probably right," Foster replied, "but still, there is something awry."

"John, I've must oversee a reattachment surgery. I really must go."

"I understand. Thank you for your time, Erik. I know you don't have a minute to spare. I've got a bug up my ass, and it doesn't feel good. Something's very wrong here, and I'm going to find out why."

"Be careful, my friend. If you are right about Vinson.... Well, no one knows better than you of the possible danger. Some missing people do not wish to be found. Ciao, John."

"Can I keep the scrubs?"

"Sure. No sweat, as you say."

When von Kovska had gone, Foster sat for about fifteen minutes arranging and rearranging what little he knew to be factual. He still had four and one-half hours before his appointment with Detective Branan, and was uncertain how to use that time productively. As he sorted through possibilities, he noted that the young man with the missing thumb was finally taken into a treatment room.

On the drive back into the city, Foster admitted that he had lost his professional focus when it came to the enigma that was Eddie Vinson. Had he not been the one to request the 4:00 meeting with Branan, he would probably have cancelled. There weren't many facts to substantiate the claim he was about to make to Branan, but he did have von Kovska's identification of Vinson, and he trusted Erik implicitly.

Joyce met him in the driveway, which meant that she had been watching for him. There were leaves and broken branches, and one large limb on the lawn attesting to the intensity of the morning thunderstorm. The look on her face told him that Joyce's mood was stormy too, and that was not like her. When she eyeballed his surgical garb, however, he could see she was fighting a smile.

"You've been shopping," she deadpanned. "Couldn't you have turned your cell phone on while you were selecting a wardrobe? Or did you hope to surprise me with the new you?"

"Got caught with the top down in Evanston. Erik took pity on me—right down to the underwear. How's that for friendship?"

"Von Kovska? I thought he was your patient."

"Yes, he is, but there is some collegial cross-over, and he provided information that could be crucial to the Vinson case."

"Vinson?"

"Yes."

Joyce sat down abruptly on the front step. "OK, you've got my attention."

"All right. I wasn't going to tell you until I had something more concrete. Actually, I don't have anything concrete. I thought von Kovska could give me something I needed, but he didn't. It's about Vinson."

"Go on."

"I don't think he's dead."

"OK. That cuts to the chase. Why not?"

"Intuition, mine, and the fact that Erik said he saw 'my paramedic' last week in his ER. He was sure, and I couldn't shake him. Vinson's suicide was after Erik left for Afghanistan. He didn't know."

"I know you keep telling me you have a bad feeling about Vinson?"

"It won't go away, and now Erik's assertion has really stirred things up!"

A protracted silence was punctuated by her deep sigh.

"I smell brain cells burning, Joyce. You've stuck by me all these years. Are you gonna bail out on me now, just because I'm out on a limb with saw in hand?"

"I s'pose you're going to tell me that the old intuitive edge is as sharp as ever, but come on, John. Gee whiz! Faking your own suicide so you can snuff your wife and beat two murder raps? That's what you're saying, isn't it? That's a big leap, even for you! You're no longer the darling of the FBI who solved cases with deductive reasoning alone—oh, and an occasional dash of omniscience when there were no clues to be had."

"Yup, I guess that's what I'm asking you to believe. With you, at least, I have a history of doing the impossible! Detective Branan doesn't know me from Adam, and he's gonna laugh me right out of his office. The one benefit is that our meeting will be short, and we can both get a jump on the weekend…if he gets a weekend, that is. On the other hand, maybe he'll suspend reason, and give me enough rope for what he assumes will be the inevitable outcome! Think so?"

"I don't know, John. You've been right before in the face of insurmountable odds. We both know I have no problem suspending reason where you're concerned. You're just too damned cute! I would never bet against you, so, hey, go for it! If nothing else, Branan will tarnish your image in the Police Department, and, just maybe, he'll eventually have to eat crow!"

"Your faith in me is overwhelming!"

"Well, what is a good wife for, if not to stand behind her man? I love you, John."

"Back to you, Sweetheart.

"What's for lunch?" he asked out of the blue.

"Lunch? It's two-thirty. Didn't you eat? Stupid question. You wouldn't ask if you had. I've got some ham and Swiss. I can make you a sandwich before you leave to see Branan."

"I don't have much time. Don't want to get caught in traffic. A sandwich would be great."

"It's portable. You can take it with you."

"What? Get crumbs in my car? Be serious!"

CHAPTER TWENTY-NINE

The Twenty-sixth District of the Chicago Police Department was located in a blue-collar business and residential neighborhood. Its presence afforded the close-knit area a sense of security that was at odds with crime figures compiled by the political bean counters. The station's brownstone facade was in keeping with homes in the area. The double doors of the entrance were oak and leaded glass, beautiful, but impractical as hell.

Foster entered the brightly lit reception area for the second time in twenty-four hours. A maze of corridors radiated from the information desk. Terrazzo floors both amplified and echoed conversations, and the ringing of telephones, the clattering of printers and typewriters. A grizzled old sergeant commanded Foster's attention with only the quirk of a brow. He might have retired from walking a beat, but Sgt. Pellegrino's reputation, Foster knew, was legend throughout the city. Now the formidable lawman was the heart of the Twenty Sixth District, and he didn't miss much.

"Can I help you, sir?" asked Pellegrino.

"I have an appointment with Detective Branan at four o'clock. John Foster"

"Sure, have a seat, Dr. Foster. I'll find him."

Foster was startled by the sergeant's use of his professional title. A quizzical glance at Pellegrino was met with a smile and a shrug. Foster crossed the terrazzo floor to a massive oak bench that quickly proved to be as hard on his ass as any pew in his boyhood Lutheran church. Obviously, comfortable accommodations were not provided for those who had business in the District.

To take his mind off his complaining backside, Foster had only to observe the goings on around him, live and in color! One very junior patrol officer was trying futilely to placate a heavy-set woman who was railing against her "...no-good husband. The son of a bitch has to pay," she sobbed repeatedly.

"I know, ma'am, but we have to fill out the necessary paperwork."

"Paperwork? Paperwork? Do you see my eye? The bastard didn't need any paperwork to bruise my eye."

"Ma'am, you'll have to calm down," pleaded the rookie."

"Calm down? How would you feel if your eye was throbbin' like a sonofabitch? The bastard."

Foster glanced to the opposite side of the room where a blond with squared-off, mannish features studied her magenta nails—talons, actually. A yellow spandex bandeau barely contained her generous breasts, and pebbled nipples suggested the lady could use a sweater. Although a half wall obstructed Foster's view of her lower body, he imagined satiny black short-shorts and three-inch heels. Despite her daring couture, the lady looked like she'd had a hard day in a string of hard days. She was heavily made up, but there was a coarseness to her complexion; the bone structure beneath was angular, harsh, not soft and rounded, and the prominent Adam's apple....

Well, damn! A little slow on the uptake, aren't you? Awareness dawned, and Foster grimaced. She was a *he*, definitely a transsexual. *How did I miss that?* Her movements were effeminate, not feminine, and the tears were a dead giveaway, as false as the eyelashes that were beginning to drip cobalt blue mascara.

Foster's surveillance moved on to a beefy police officer who was manhandling a cuffed and whining scarecrow down a stairway in the far corner. When the man lost his struggle for balance, the cop grasped him about the waist and effortlessly hiked him down the remaining stairs. A vagrant or addict, probably both, the fellow was getting the heave ho. As they passed in front of Foster, a miasma of vomit and urine polluted the air. By now red-faced, the policeman released the handcuffs and propelled the man out the front door, closing it firmly behind him. Only then did he gasp for breath.

"Dr. Foster?"

"Yes?"

"Detective Branan will see you now. Up the stairs, turn left, third office on the right."

"Thanks," said Foster. As he climbed, he imagined smoke-filled cubicles; the nervous sweat of cops who flicked ashes into paper cups, donut and pizza boxes thrown into corners, and coke cans littering desktops. Reality was mossy green walls with varnished pine doors and woodwork, natural daylight from numerous windows and skylights, and a sophisticated commercial carpeting that muffled the day-to-day business of law and order. There wasn't a discarded box or aluminum can in sight. A PBX-type phone system and computer sat on every beige desk in every soundproofed cubicle. A central hub provided a high-speed laser printer and a copy/fax machine that looked as though it could function without human direction. The entire setup was efficient to the nth degree. A discreet sign above the copier announced that Foster was entering "a smoke-free environment."

"Come in, Dr. Foster," Branan offered his hand in greeting. He scrutinized Foster's casual attire, and dropped the formalities. "How ya doin', Doc?"

"Just fine."

"Have a seat." Branan himself was a sharp dresser, stylish, but not blatant about it. His thick, black hair was graying at the temples. Foster estimated that Branan had to weigh 300 pounds, at least, but he looked fit, as in solid muscle.

Foster hooked the lone straight-back chair with his toe and pulled it up to Branan's desk. As he sat, he observed a pearl-handled .357 magnum in a leather holster at the detective's waist under his camel blazer. Foster nodded toward the weapon. "You're a lefty, huh?"

"Don't let it fool you," Branan grinned.

The screen saver on Branan's computer showed the Twenty Sixth District's logo floating randomly across the monitor; it was an American eagle perched atop a cactus, holding a snake in its beak.

"An unusual logo for a Chicago police district.... What's its meaning?" Foster asked.

Branan glanced at the monitor, then back at Foster with a shrug. "Damned if I know. Never thought to ask."

Foster knew he looked disappointed at Branan's answer.

"Just kidding, Doc.

"After all, what kind of detective would I be if I didn't know what my District's logo means? It seems that, hundreds of years ago, there was this Aztec tribe in Central America. Legend says that they were a wandering tribe in search of a promised land. Their own Charlton Heston saga, so to speak. When their elderly chief saw an eagle atop a cactus, feeding on a snake, he took it as a sign that they should build a city on that spot. Despite the fact that the cactus would suggest a desert environment, the predominant feature of the chosen area was, in reality, a vast marshland. Undeterred, the chief and his people hauled sand and stone, and built a great city for their tribe. So, you see, our logo means that no matter how difficult a crime we face, we will build a case on facts, and it will stand."

"Interesting, Detective," said Foster, leaning back into his chair, "Why do I suspect you have just served me a plateful of steaming bull?"

"Suspicious are we, Doc? It's Mexico City. You'll just have to get to know me better! Now, bring me up to speed."

Foster outlined the bare bones of his theory about the Eddie Vinson suicide. Without revealing the details of his therapeutic relationship with Vinson, he built his hypothesis on the generally accepted psychological characteristics of a personality like Eddie Vinson's, and he capped his argument with Erik von Kovska's identification of Vinson, the paramedic, in his ER the previous week.

"Of course," Foster concluded, "Dr. von Kovska was on an overseas medical mission when the Vinson suicide took place, so he knew nothing of Eddie Vinson's death."

Branan listened and did not interrupt. When Foster finished speaking, Branan did not rush to fill the ensuing silence. He chewed his lip and buffed his nails against his pant leg. His eyebrows rose and fell, but his eyes showed nothing of his thoughts.

When he could stand it no more, Foster asked, "Well? What do you think?"

Detective Branan rose and went to the coffeepot just outside his cubicle. "Want some sludge?" he inquired as he filled his mug with the black syrup of day's end. When Foster shook his head, Branan shrugged. "Me neither," and he shuddered as he took a swallow.

Returning to his chair, Branan set the mug on his desk with a thunk. He spread his hands in front of him, and studied his nails. Finally, he responded. "That's an interesting story you tell, Dr. Foster. Did you say you're an ex-FBI profiler?"

"I didn't say."

"But you are, correct?"

"I was."

"C'mon, Doc, quit splittin' frog hairs. You haven't retired your profiling skills. They're evident throughout your portrayal of Vinson and what might be expected of him. Despite your dad gum humility, I know for a fact that you were reputed to be one of the Bureau's best. I looked you up and made a few calls. Were you clairvoyant or something?"

"Naw. Profiling is nine-tenths grunt work and a single-minded attention to details. The predictability about a suspect's likely characteristics and possible actions or reactions, the *magic*, if you will, comes from a thorough grounding in human behavior."

"Doc, I'm going to tell you something confidential. You'll keep this to yourself?"

"Detective Branan, I'm in the business of keeping secrets."

Branan nodded and continued, "I've had a bad feeling about this case from the beginning. The shooting of Ms. Vinson looked like cold, calculated anger, revenge, perhaps, more than anything else. Nothing was taken from the home, and no attempt was made to cover or distort what went on. According to her parents, Ms. Vinson had no enemies.

"Then, as you know, before the shooting of Vinson's wife, was the brutal beating death of the bartender in the very same block. What kind of coincidence is that? The regular patrons of O'Hearn's pub were of one accord about Vinson's animosity toward O'Hearn, and those who were there the night of the altercation between Vinson and O'Hearn provided almost verbatim accounts of their heated exchange. The investigation of O'Hearn's death was pointing clearly at Vinson although he had no known history of violence; it all came to a screeching halt when Vinson offed himself. I gotta say, however, your portrayal of the man as an unlikely suicide, more likely a murderer, raises all kinds of interesting avenues for investigation, and it would surely explain many of the details from both crimes that have, until now, remained seemingly unexplainable."

Foster felt the raising of gooseflesh across his neck, shoulders, and arms; he barely suppressed a shudder and hoped Branan hadn't seen his emotional response.

"Cold, Doc?"

"Not much gets by you, does it Branan?"

"No, Doc. Those details you said you rely on as a profiler and psychologist.... Well, the devil is in those details for me too. Details make or break a case.

"Tell you what. I'm gonna ask my favorite red-headed ADA to wave an order to exhume Eddie Vinson's body in front of a judge." He smirked when Foster looked stunned. "I won't need to get any other permission since the guy had no family of record other than his deceased wife and his minor niece. I'll call my captain in the morning and get the ball rolling.

"Uh, listen, Doc, would you consider consulting with me on this case? I know you considered that I might think you a crackpot, or resent your unsolicited theory about Vinson, but to be honest, you've just energized what I thought was a moribund investigation of two murders. An autopsy will tell us yea or nay in a Jackson second. I doubt the department could pay you much, but I'll look into it, and bringing a double murderer to justice should be a powerful reward for both of us. Will you consider it?"

"I've got my caseload to consider, but, yes, I'd like to work with you. If Vinson's done what I suspect he's done, then he's got my professional curiosity up; I'd like to follow through and learn what I can about him."

"We can do much of our analyzing/brainstorming by telephone. That might be a wise use of your time. Maybe you'll tell me how your days run, and we could find a time to confer—a time we can touch bases each day that fits into both our schedules."

"I'll have my secretary call you. Her name is Louise. Just tell her what you need."

"Great. I'll expect to hear from her."

Foster stood and stretched his lower back that was protesting Branan's rock-hard *suspect* chair. "Maybe you could find a more comfortable chair for us non-criminal types?" he tossed over his shoulder as he exited Branan's cubicle.

Just as he turned the corner to the stairway, Foster heard "Wuss!" come floating down the hall after him. Damn! He really liked Branan. He should have told Branan right up front he wouldn't take payment for consulting with him. Or, maybe, if they came up with some funds, he'd pass them on to the District's highly innovative academic and sports program for neighborhood children. There had been city-wide acclaim for the program; other Districts had soon followed suit, but the Twenty-sixth had been *numero uno*. Foster had seen a commendation on Branan's wall recognizing him for ten years as a volunteer with the program.

Foster failed to register any details of his one-block return to his car, and he almost walked right by. His thoughts were flying and he was unable to order them into anything resembling coherence. He hadn't expected Detective Branan to endorse his theoretical assessment of the two homicides as being the actions of Eddie Vinson, and he certainly hadn't expected to be offered a collaborative role. *Hot damn! I'll enjoy being back in the action for a bit, but Joyce won't like it at all, at all!*

Back at the Twenty-sixth, Detective Branan was pulling together his notes on the Vinson case and jotting down what Foster told him while also dialing the phone.

"I hope the DA is in," Branan said out loud while the phone rang.

James Fender was one of many Assistant District Attorneys serving Cook County. He had been an ADA for about five years and racked up a string of prosecutions that earned him a reputation as a winner. The wins came from hard work and exhaustive preparation, however, and Branan needed his help. Besides, Fender owed him a favor or two.

Fender was thinking about leaving his office early when Branan's call came through. He almost let it ring, but his compulsive nature wouldn't allow it. "Fender, here."

"Yeah, Jim. This is Mike Branan at the Twenty-sixth. How are you doin', buddy?"

"Mike! Hey, what's up, man? You calling to ruin my weekend?"

"Look, I got a lead on a double homicide over here, a case that seemed to have gone stone cold. I need your help."

Fender's first reaction was to sit down. In the past, Branan had asked for some damn big favors. "Don't tell me. Another exhumation? Right?"

"How'd you guess? Shouldn't be a problem, though. The deceased doesn't have any living family. It's vital that I get the guy's fingerprints, DNA testing, whatever, to confirm his identity."

"Why do you always saddle me with these requests? Can't you spread yourself around a little? There's certainly more than enough, Big Guy."

"Sorry!" but laughter was evident in his voice, despite Fender's grumbling.

"Aw, hell, Mike. Tell me what I can use to justify this one. And remind me what poor judge we collared last time. I can't afford to wear out my welcome with them, you know."

"OK. I've got this witness...well, he's not really the witness. He's a psychologist, and the dead guy was his patient briefly. The shrink knows a physician who saw the deceased in his ER weeks after he supposedly committed suicide. The guy was a paramedic, and the doc had seen him before and recognized him."

"Look, Mike, have you been hitting the sauce?"

"No, Jimmy, nothing like that. Let me start over...."

"OK, OK, go on," Fender sighed.

"This is the case of a dead pub owner and a woman who was killed in her home, both in the same block. No obvious motive, no robbery, nothin', for the woman. I figured it for a hit or a revenge thing, although family says she had no enemies. She had recently split from her husband; that's Vinson, who turned up shortly thereafter as the mangled suicide on the EL, remember? Interestingly, her hubby was the odds on favorite suspect in the bartender's death because a number of patrons witnessed a pissing contest between the bar owner and the man who turns up diced and sliced on the EL tracks. His wife ID'd him from clothes and personal effects, and no autopsy was done.

"Now, and this is what...eight weeks later? My, uh, informant tells me his ER doc saw the suicide guy, Vinson, the EMT, delivering an accident victim to his ER only last week. Vinson *was* a paramedic, and the doc had met him at least twice before. He was positive about his identification. So...maybe Vinson whacks the bartender for dissin' him, and whacks his wife for leaving him. To get away with the murders, he must not be a suspect, and he can't be a suspect if he is dead.

"The way I see it, all he needed was a cooperative stiff of similar height, build, and coloring, etc. to shred on the tracks as his stand-in, and let's face it, as a medic, I'm sure he was familiar with any one of several morgues in the area, and we both know unclaimed bodies are a dime a dozen."

"It's a bit of a stretch, isn't it, Mike?"

"Yeah, but according to the psychologist, all the pieces seem to fit when you factor in the guy's personality characteristics, in combination with his wife's fears about sudden changes in his behavior and emotional state."

"Look, I'll draft an order; get it to a judge for his signature tomorrow. I'll need the particulars on the suicide ASAP."

"OK, Jimmy. Thanks a lot. I've got the info right here. A fax is on its way in the next sixty seconds. How's that for being on top of things?"

"You owe me one, Mike. A big one!" Fender said in closing.

"I know. I won't forget."

"I'll get back to you, Mike, when I have the signed order," Fender said and disconnected.

Branan fed a synopsis of reports from police, crime scene investigators, and the coroner into the fax machine, and at the last minute, he added the notes from his conversation with Foster. He knew Foster had clout with the judges, and it just might tip the decision in his favor

Foster spent the late afternoon drive home mulling over the best way to explain to Joyce his willingness to work with the police on the Vinson suicide and murders. "She puts up with a lot of crap from me," he muttered. Nevertheless, only in the face of her most strenuous objections would he withdraw from his agreement to collaborate with Branan.

It was five-thirty when Foster strode through an empty kitchen. He knew he would find Joyce reading in the sunroom that spanned the back of their home. "Joyce?"

He heard a distracted, "Hmm?" as he stepped down onto the old brick floor that he and Joyce had laid themselves. When she did not look up, he stepped behind her and nibbled on the silky column of her neck. He inhaled deeply.

"I charge extra for smelling," Joyce murmured, but tilted her head to give him greater access, at the same time, putting her finger between the pages to mark her place. She was curled into a battered and tattered Papa-san chair that she would not surrender. It had been her reading chair since college, and although she had recovered the cushion numerous times, it always looked like the ugly stepchild among their tasteful, but comfortable, furnishings.

Leaning over Joyce's shoulder to nuzzle, Foster's eyes fell to the book on her lap. "How is the good Captain Ahab today?" he asked, seeing that she was reading *Moby Dick*. "Did you finish the new Grisham, and can I have it now?"

"It's on your bedside table. How was your meeting with the detective?" Joyce asked.

"Oh, it was good. You know how detectives are."

"I do?" Joyce answered.

"Not literally, Joyce. I mean they can be overbearing and such."

"And such?"

"Right. Overbearing and such." Foster moved to the pine rocker and stretched out his legs.

Joyce put her book on the wicker table beside her, and deliberately lined it up with those beneath it. "OK, John, what is it?"

"What do you mean?"

"John Foster, my always love. You're being evasive... non-disclosing, and vaguely argumentative. Just tell me what you don't want to tell me and get it over with."

Damn! "Well, I s'pose there's no help for it. You're gonna be disappointed in me for goin' back on the streets again, but, Joyce, I've agreed to help the police in the Vinson murder-suicide. They're wanting to draw on my profiler skills."

Joyce leveled an unblinking stare at him, and he could swear his collar shrunk an entire neck size. "Well?" Foster asked.

"How are you going to manage such a collaboration with an already full practice?"

"I'll have to scale back some for awhile...so I can be available for Branan, although he seems to think much of it can be accomplished by telephone pow-wows."

"Is it dangerous?"

"Nah," Foster scoffed. "Nah. Why would you think that right off the bat?"

"John?" Joyce said, drawing out his name as though he were the naughty boy he was feeling like at the moment.

"A little, maybe. Depends on Vinson."

"OK, I can deal with that." Joyce continued to study him, but he did not feel any anger from her.

"You're letting me off easy. Why? Not that I don't appreciate it, mind you."

"You've been restless. I think you need a diversion, and Vinson has gotten under your professional armor. Am I right?"

CHAPTER THIRTY

Foster hadn't heard from Detective Branan for a week and he was getting antsy, or as Joyce had put it that morning, he was "all dressed up with no place to go." A telephone call to Branan seemed in order, although Foster played mind games with himself all day, putting off the call as long as possible, hoping that Branan would call him so he wouldn't show his eagerness. No such luck.

"Detective Branan, here. How can I help you?"

"Detective, this is..."

"Oh, hiya, Doc. How are you? I was just reaching for the phone to call you. Got permission to exhume Vinson's body. He's with the lab guys now. I was there when they dug him up. The body's totally unrecognizable, already starting to decompose. It wasn't too pretty, and to say it smelled bad would be the mother of all understatements. Looked like they just plopped him in the casket without any preparation or preservation. Closed coffin. Why bother? With all the damage, they couldn't exactly make him look like himself! Anyway, the preliminaries suggest it is Vinson, but we'll know for sure when all the results are in."

Foster could think of nothing else to ask. Branan had answered all his questions without his having to open his mouth.

"Don't worry, Doc. I'm gonna see this through to the end. And when we get there, I think your hypothesis will prove to be right."

"Do you need me for anything right now?" Foster asked, squashing any hint of eagerness that might leak through. *I am not gonna beg.*

"No, not at the moment. We're waiting on his holiness, the Coroner."

"Well, I've trimmed my schedule, so if you need me, just call."

"Will do, Doc. Bye." Click.

Looking idly at his daily schedule, Foster noted that his therapy appointments for tomorrow didn't begin until after lunch. He could find it easy to enjoy this less intense schedule! He supposed he could use the time to catch up on dictation so Louise wouldn't nag, or he could do some legwork on his own. He was particularly curious about Vinson's last place of employment. If Eddie had been decompensating, surely his fellow paramedics would have noticed.

"Louise, I'll be in at 12:45 tomorrow. I have my cell. Let me know if that obstinate what's her name at one o'clock cancels again, OK? Oh, and please tell her that our office policy is not to reschedule a new patient who cancels or misses two consecutive appointments."

CHAPTER THIRTY-ONE

Paramedic Jenny Fox was not the same after Tony Rizzo's death. She held herself together, and she did not believe that her work suffered, but after the night Tony was killed, she was always afraid. While on the streets tending to victims, she imagined a bullet from nowhere moving toward her forehead. Jenny's fear and social withdrawal had ended an already shaky relationship, and she seldom left her apartment when she wasn't on the job. Then, Eddie Vinson's suicide had been another blow. Even though they had not been as close as she was with Rizzo, professionally they had been a good team, and he made her feel safe. She missed him, and she couldn't understand the suicide.

Foster drove to the side of the First Alert headquarters where a sign in bold, red lettering designated the entrance. He walked into a sterile-looking office area that was bathed in noxious florescent light. Instinctively Foster raised his hand to shield his eyes from the glare. "Do you hand out sunglasses?" he asked of the young woman sitting at a computer console.

"We certainly should, shouldn't we!" she smiled and stood up. She gave her wheeled task chair a forceful bump with the backs of her legs, and it careened into the files behind her. "Oops! Been sitting too long; lost all sensation in my backside!

"Well now, if that isn't a thoughtless thing to say to a complete stranger. I apologize. I'm Jenny Fox, paramedic and working stiff, who obviously needs to polish her social graces!"

"Maybe all of this florescent light is getting to you!

"I'm John Foster, a clinical psychologist."

"Foster, you said? I remember you."

"I don't think we've met."

"No, you're right. Eddie told me about you."

"Eddie...?"

"Eddie Vinson. He spoke about you."

At Foster's clear surprise, Jenny continued, "He said his wife was seeing some shrink because she was having a breakdown, or something. He mentioned your name. I met her a couple of times. She didn't seem like the breakdown type."

"Really?"

"Really. Eddie didn't think much of the shrink idea. Oh, don't get me wrong, I think you guys are great…necessary. I even went to one a few years ago after our ambulance wrecked. I was afraid to get back on my horse for a while, if you know what I mean. The therapist helped me a lot. Terrible about Eddie, though. I never would have thought he'd do that to himself."

"Me either, Jenny." The two stood silently for a few moments. "Is there anything about Eddie that you can think of that might explain his actions? Did you see any changes in him, personality or behavioral changes? Was he letting his work slide? Acting differently?"

"Eddie? He never talked much about himself; he was private. He didn't solicit personal information from me either. The one thing he did say was that he was raised right here in Chicago. Oh, and that he'd never traveled outside the state...never had a vacation to Wisconsin, for example. He said he'd live and die right here."

"Please, go on."

"Eddie knew more about this city than anyone I've ever met. Granted, we have to know the city; getting lost on a call would waste critical time, but Eddie knew more. He could take you on back streets that connected to alleys that connected to more back streets, the back sides of warehouses, parking garages. He used to say he could disappear from anywhere in two minutes or less. I believed him. When he was driving, we were always first on the scene.

"Not too long ago, Eddie took me on "a tour of his city" is what he called it, places I'd never been before, and I've worked in Chicago since my very first job. It was kinda scary, but it was interesting, too. Eddie was trying to distract me. It was right after the gang shootings. I was scared, gun shy, I guess you could say. He was supportive, considerate, and funny, less reserved than at any other time since I'd worked with him. So, when you ask if he had changed, I'd have to say not really, but he did seem more approachable, maybe."

Foster had been listening carefully to Jenny's description of Eddie and her interactions with him. There was nothing glaringly evident or alarming from a psychological viewpoint. When he asked if Vinson had ever shown any tendencies toward strong anger or violence, Jenny's response was an immediate, "No! Not Eddie."

However, as Foster watched, she frowned and there were lines between her eyebrows. She thought for a moment, and said, "There was one thing…an incident the night of the gang violence. After our partner was wounded, just as we were leaving to take him to the hospital, we came across two medics who had been stranded when their tires were shot out. We picked them up because they were sitting ducks. I was driving, and when we pulled away, Eddie stepped out of the back of the van. He told the other EMT he was going to look for Rizzo's shooter, and the EMT said he had a gun.

"Later, we heard that a young woman's body had been found in the alley at the side of that building where we were. Given her injuries, it was evident she had fallen from the rooftop. By that time, however, there were no witnesses, and no forensic evidence to suggest what might have gone on before her death although it appeared that she had fired a gun that was found on the roof.

"You know, police and medics talk; there were lots of rumors for a while, but I don't know if anyone other than me, and probably the one paramedic from the disabled ambulance, knew that Eddie could have been in that building. For sure, nobody did anything about the girl's death. Things were so out of control in the days right after the violence, and besides, the victim was a gang-banger; nobody seemed to care. Everyone seemed to be holding their breath, waiting to see if it was an isolated incident or the start of something more serious. I figured the girl's death got lost in the shuffle; she was just another statistic."

After a protracted silence, Foster asked, "Why do you think Eddie killed himself, Jenny?"

"That's a good question. It seemed out of character at first, but the more I thought about it…Eddie was always saying how nothing really matters or makes sense; everything is random. It was like, for him, the only thing that mattered was the moment. The thrill, the 'rush' he used to call it. 'Boring' was the other word he used a lot; it was everything else that didn't cause a rush for him.

"Don't get me wrong, Eddie was a great paramedic. His instincts were always right on, even when logic said otherwise. He saved more lives than Rizzo and me together. But he made no bones about the fact that broken bodies, blood and gore, fire and twisted metal, the intensity of the job were things that gave him a rush. What that might mean with regard to his suicide, I haven't a clue, and I don't know if anything I've said helps you to have a better understanding of him. Without a doubt he was the best medic—technically—I've ever seen; if he was lacking…. Well, I guess I'd have to say it was compassion that he was missing. I can think of only once when he offered comfort, and that was to a child."

Foster noticed that Jenny's cheeks were red; tears filled her eyes and spilled over. She turned away from him while she brushed them away and fished for a tissue in her pockets. When she came up empty, he handed her his handkerchief. He always kept a clean one for situations like this. It was something his father taught him. Jenny's chin wobbled, but the smile was genuine and she thanked him.

As a means of distracting her, Foster put an off-the-top-of-his-head question to her. "Just suppose, Jenny, if Eddie Vinson wanted to disappear in this city, could he do that?"

"Could he ever! Dr. Foster, Eddie had stuff he'd collected from all over. Said he could never tell when he might need whatever. And he networked, too. He used to say he knew people who knew people who knew people! If he wanted to disappear…no sweat."

"Like what stuff? What did he collect?" Foster queried.

"Oh, man. He had security and name badges, licenses, keys, pieces of uniforms, a policeman's hat from somewhere. He even had a key from Cook County Morgue."

"How do you know that?"

"I saw him use it. He let us in one time when we were delivering a body for autopsy.

"Eddie also carried a 9 millimeter, but don't tell anybody I'm the one who said so."

"A 9mm? A gun?" Foster stammered stupidly. "You're serious?"

"Yeah."

"Why a gun?"

"Heck, you never know where you may need one on this job. These riots were my first, but I'm sure they won't be the last. And the gangs...their violence is what really scares me. It's so mindless, so much anger that spills over onto anyone and everyone who gets in their way, even those of us trying to help. I could never carry a gun myself, but I can understand why Eddie would."

"Jesus, I hope they pay you enough."

"Not hardly," Jenny said, as she sat down on the chair behind the counter.

"Did Eddie ever talk to you about working for another paramedic agency?" Foster asked.

"Hey, why are you asking all these questions about Eddie?"

"Well, you know I was counseling Vinson and I'd seen his wife; Eddie told you that himself. Now he's dead, a very unlikely suicide victim, and Ms. Vinson has been killed, as I'm sure you also know. I have so many unanswered questions. It's like a puzzle with pieces that don't seem to fit, that don't even belong to this particular puzzle. I won't go so far as to say that my professional confidence has been shaken.... Oh, hell! Yes, I will! The Vinson case has me questioning myself. Did I really miss something crucial that could have prevented one or more deaths?"

"Dr. Foster? I didn't say anything earlier, but I'd heard about you before Eddie told me you were treating his wife. We hear things in our jobs, everyday...on the streets, from doctors and hospitals, in the courts and legal community.

I've always heard good things, that you can always be counted on, that you do more than is required, often for free, and that you try to share your training and knowledge with other professionals...and, I suspect, with your patients. It seems to me that these doubts you're having are part of what makes you good at what you do.

"Whew! That's quite a speech for me! Would you believe I tend to be a very quiet individual? No? I guess you wouldn't. I'm being downright loquacious; isn't that the right word?"

"Yes, it's the right word, and it's been helpful that you are willing to talk to me, give me your insights. Can we go back to a question I asked earlier? Do you recall Eddie saying anything about working with another agency?"

Jenny's eyes roamed the room for a moment and she chewed on her lip. "Eddie once said something about a temporary gig he had up on the northeast side...uh, the Lakeshore Agency, I think it was. He said he was moonlighting sometimes for extra bread. He hadn't been married all that long, and they had his wife's niece living with them; he said he had extra expenses."

Jenny swiped a hand across her eyes, then rubbed them vigorously. "I really need these glasses," she admitted sheepishly as she pulled them from her pocket, "but everyone says my eyes are my best feature, and I can't afford to hide them behind coke-bottle lenses. It's my one bit of vanity!"

Foster could see the fatigue in her drooping shoulders. "It must be nearing the end of your shift, time for me to let you go so you can finish up here and get home. Thanks a lot for your time, Jenny. You've been a tremendous help."

"You're all right, Doc. That's what they call you behind your back, ya know! Someone once heard you joke you're not a *real doctor,* but I know better. Now I understand for myself why you're so well respected. I'm glad to have met you."

As he pushed the door open, Jenny tossed after him, "And you asked better questions than the cops."

Jenny's statement stopped Foster cold. "What's that?"

"The cops. They were here about the Vinsons, too. They never asked me any of the questions you did. It was like they didn't have a clue."

"Do you remember who questioned you?"

"Nah! It was some gum-poppin' greenhorn who was trying to wrangle a date. My little brother is more mature than he was! And he sure wasn't doing much to advance the Vinson investigation. What a jerk!"

"Thanks again, Jenny, I'm sure the lead detective will be happy to hear what you have to say! I'm going to tell him about you, and he may be in touch with more questions based on the data he's acquired. His name is Branan.

"Take care, Ms. Fox."

"The northeast side," Foster grumbled. *Shit, I was just there!* The spring-loaded steel door closed behind him. Foster leaned against the side of the building for several minutes ordering his thoughts, cataloguing what he'd learned about Vinson, and slotting new data in his mental files. He saw none of the vehicles that passed until his concentration was broken by the wheeze of an accelerating bus and the diesel fumes that enveloped him.

Talking with Jenny Fox had provided him with fresh glimpses of Vinson. Had what she told him eased his feelings that he wasn't getting the whole picture, however? Some, he guessed, or maybe the jury was still out. He closed his eyes and permitted himself a gusty sigh. He hated when professional insecurity shook him; it was so damn counter-productive. He had lectured on the subject of insecurity many times, and his listeners always told him how illuminating his presentations were, but it seemed that no matter how thoroughly he understood the dynamics, he couldn't always harness his own insecurities, whether personal or professional.

Quit feelin' sorry for yourself. All you can do is roll with it…. Don't focus on the problem…only on the solution. It was the same litany that he suggested to his patients when they seemed content to wallow in their insecurities. Any step toward a remedy is better than dwelling on the problem.

So, here I am, talking to myself on the sidewalk. OK. Let's make it good; let's try some cognitive mitigation with a stupid metaphor:

"Look, Your Honor, this defendant, supposedly a licensed professional, has made mistakes so many times, we can't trust him anymore. Your Honor, remember the evidence...Dr. Foster recommended probation for a convicted rapist because he showed insight into his paraphilia. Your Honor, within two short weeks of his release, the animal raped a delicate and vulnerable old woman who has never recovered from the trauma. In effect, her life ended with that rape! Therefore, I respectfully request that the Court find this psychologist incompetent, and further, that he never be allowed to work in the field of mental health. Never again! It would be a travesty, Your Honor. The prosecution rests."

"Your Honor, I represent Doctor John Foster, a clinical psychologist well respected in his profession. I wish for the Court to know that this man has devoted his life to helping those who are troubled. Dr. Foster has endeavored to encourage emotional awareness and understanding that illuminates the barren corners of his patients' desperate lives. His decision to recommend release of a known rapist was based on his educated prediction that the man had gained self-control through insights acquired in treatment. Your Honor, that decision was proper. Who is the Prosecution to say that it wasn't? They have provided no expert testimony to refute Dr. Foster's decision as erroneous. John Foster relied on his professional knowledge and experience derived from an illustrious career, in conjunction with his many hours of contact with the individual, and, *now,* with the benefit of hindsight, the esteemed Prosecutor wants you to condemn him because the results were not what we would have hoped.... Your Honor, how many mistakes have all of us made here, right here, in this very Courtroom. We are, none of us, all knowing or all-powerful, and we should not be judged when we have made honest mistakes where results prove to be beyond our control. Thank you, Your Honor."

"That old man, Anxiety! He just keeps rollin' along," Foster sang to himself. *Screw it. Go! Johnny, go!* His mother had always called him her "Johnny Be Good" when she was intent on motivating him to try something new, to face fear, and push himself to his potential.

Foster did an about-face and returned to the ambulance service front office. Jenny was where he had left her.

"Hey, Doc. I thought you were leaving?"

"Yeah, me too. Look, Jenny, you don't really know me, but...."

"Are you coming on to me, Doc, because if you are... well...that's OK, cool!"

"No, no, no," Foster said, embarrassed. "Look, I'm not coming on to you. Nothing like that, but I would like to spend more time talking about Eddie. Would you help me out?"

"What?" Jenny said, moving away from the counter and approaching Foster. "What do you need?"

"Well, I thought maybe you could take me around to places where Eddie took you. Point out the places, relate things that he told you. You said he spoke of some of his old haunts. You saw a side of him even his wife apparently didn't know. It could be really helpful."

"Yeah, I guess I could do that," Jenny nodded, "but you'll have to buy me dinner first. I'm starving!" Having plunked down her ultimatum, Jenny pushed through the swinging door that led to the ambulance garage.

"I'll come back for you at five!" Foster bellowed, not knowing if she heard him.

Foster called Joyce on his cell phone. "Joyce, it's me."

"John? Where are you?"

"I'm at Eddie Vinson's last place of employment. I think I've got a lead, here. I spoke to one of his co-workers, a woman paramedic, and she has some good insights, some useful information. Eddie talked to her when they teamed up. She knows some of the places he used to hang out. After I see a couple patients, I'm going back to pick her up, and she's gonna show me places where he took her or talked to her about. I just wanted you to know that buying her dinner was her only request in exchange for the tour, so I'll be home late. You have some time for pampering yourself. Maybe you'll smell really sexy when I get home. Huh? My little chickadee?"

"John?" His silliness hadn't deflected Joyce's worry. He could still hear her uneven breathing.

"Don't worry, Joyce. I know what you're thinking. It'll be alright. I'm just snooping around a little. I'm too cowardly to get into any real trouble. Remember?" he lied.

"Be careful, OK?"

"OK, I'll call you if I'm going to be later than ten. Don't wait up."

"Right. Don't wait up. Sure thing." Joyce said sarcastically.

"'Bye." He slid in a Traveling Wilburies CD and hummed along as he drove to the office. Two patients, then he'd be free to snoop to his heart's content.

At 4:50, Foster was back in the ambulance parking lot. He leaned back against the leather headrest and closed his eyes. He could catnap at will; it was a trick he learned while in graduate school. Long hours of research interspersed with brief periods of dead time...you quickly learned how to sleep on command. Within minutes, Foster was in a light sleep. He could still hear the gravel voices of the Wilburies and indistinct road noises, but he did not sense Jenny's approach. She tapped gently on his window, and he opened his eyes. Because she was bending at the waist to look in his car window, in his immediate line of sight were her breasts in a hot pink blouse. *Awesome; how did I miss those?*

Foster struggled to sit erect and lowered his window. "Give me a moment. I was catnapping."

"You don't need to play the gentleman; you'll make me nervous. Unlock the passenger door."

"Jenny settled into the embrace of the leather seat and sighed. "You can smell the leather! What's for dinner, Doc?"

"Call me John."

"All right, John. My friends call me Jen. What's for dinner? Your biological clock may be saying sleep time, but mine is saying dinner time! Big time!"

"OK. Where to? Do you have a taste for something? There's this little Chinese place a couple blocks down and over...."

"Ah-So! General Tso...Colonel Sanders...chicken's chicken to me! Let's do it!

"Darn! Wait, I forgot! I musta been dazzled by your wheels! Before we eat, John, I'd like to take my car home. I can't leave it in the agency parking lot when I'm not here. Company policy."

"OK, how far away do you live?"

"It's not far...ten minutes, maybe fifteen, since traffic is heavy."

"OK. I'll follow you home. Just don't lose me." Jenny cocked her head as she surveyed the flashy hi-tech dash of his Porsche and said, "Not much chance of that!"

Jenny walked to the far side of the parking lot and put her key into the door of a bright white '96 Chrysler LHS. As she pulled up to him, she rolled down her window. "Just follow my boat," she grinned, and gunned the engine, which snarled in response.

The ride to Jenny's home was uneventful. She lived in a small quiet neighborhood, only a couple blocks long and wide. Her townhouse on the north edge of the neighborhood was new and fashionable, of coral-colored brick construction. Foster noted a foot-wide firewall separating each townhouse from its neighbor that would serve the added purpose of muffling noises from one unit to the next. He followed Jenny to a carport in the rear of the complex and noted a well-lit entry only steps from her car. She parked and locked the LHS. As she walked toward him, Foster observed that her gait was confident, with long, deliberate strides. Nevertheless, she was feminine in every way, and a bit of a coquette, he suspected, when she was out socially.

"Really nice car, John."

"Thanks. I like it. I've always had sports cars.

"I like your car, too. It's a '96 right? It's got such classic lines, or should I say curves, and it shines like a pearl! You obviously baby it!"

"Hey, it's my wheels we're talking about!"

The Peking Palace wasn't difficult to find; on the other hand, a parking space *was*, even a Porsche-size space. On their second time around the block, a car pulled out, and Foster executed a deft little maneuver that caused Jenny no small amount of jealousy. "There are definite disadvantages to driving a big car in the city," she grumbled.

The fragrance of won tons and fried rice seemed to pulse with the blue and red neon sign in front. The restaurant itself was small, cozy, and hushed since all conversations seemed to be in whispers. Foster could see one empty table toward the rear, and when no hostess appeared to seat them, he guided Jen by the elbow to claim it. He held her chair. "This is nice, Jen. It's been a long time since I was here."

"It's my favorite," she replied. "I like the peacefulness. Some of my days can be pretty hectic, and it takes quiet time to unwind."

A delicate young woman of about seventeen greeted them. She poured water and directed Foster's attention to the menus under the glass on the tabletop. Jenny ordered a #3, almond chicken with an egg roll and egg drop soup. Foster ordered an egg roll, Lobster Cantonese, and shrimp fried rice, and they agreed to share. Their meal was served steaming hot within five minutes.

"A delicious meal," Foster said, struggling to contain a burp.

"Don't hold back on my account," Jen laughed. "I sure won't if the need arises!"

Foster ordered a second cup of tea for each of them, and they drank without speaking. It was a comfortable silence. Finally Foster said, "My wife would love you. She enjoys people who can share quiet without needing to fill it with words!"

When Jenny had placed her empty cup on the table and folded her napkin, he asked, "Are you ready? I don't want to rush you, but I'm anxious to get started."

"I'm ready."

At 6:30 on a week night, the traffic into downtown was unexpectedly light and moving quickly. It wasn't until they reached Lakeshore Drive that Jenny looked at him. "You spoke of your wife, John."

"Yes. Thirty-three years of marriage to the same woman."

"What's she like?"

"Joyce? She's my best friend...always has been, always will be. She's been there for me every step since grad school. I think I've been the same for her."

"Is she pretty?"

"I'd say by most standards, Joyce is beautiful, inside and out."

Jenny sat silently for the next few minutes. "Ever mess around, Dr. John?" Her question surprised him, but he had no difficulty responding.

"No. Of course, I see people who do every day in my practice. Under normal circumstances, I can't think of a single thing to justify infidelity. I find that supposedly committed individuals who are unfaithful do so because something is very wrong at the heart of their relationships. Usually it's a lack of emotional connectedness; you know, you feel alone and your partner doesn't understand you. The sexual straying is incidental, a symptom, not usually the cause, of a broken relationship."

Jenny just looked at him, "Incidental?" she asked incredulously.

"Right, sex is not usually the primary unfulfilled need when someone starts an affair. It comes into play naturally, but the real attraction is the sense of belonging and acceptance that was missing within the marriage."

"I never thought of it that way. It's a new perspective." Jenny looked toward the lake and back at the tall, gray buildings of downtown. The sun was setting and bathed the city in a soft orange luminescence. "Beautiful town, hey, John?"

"Absolutely."

Within ten minutes, Foster and Jenny reached Evanston. "Where do we go from here?"

"Uh...stop over at that gas station. I want to get my bearings."

Foster pulled into the brightly lit Mobil station and parked beside a high tech, white and glass building. Jen chewed on her lip for a moment as she looked around them. "See, John... the problem is, Eddie took me through unfamiliar Chicago neighborhoods, not up Lakeshore. It was dark, too, and I wasn't thinking about having to find places again at a later time. I know we're in the right ballpark, but I'm not sure which direction to take from here.

"I remember that it was a rundown warehouse district, mostly abandoned buildings and empty lots; old wooden garage doors leading from loading docks, discarded machinery and equipment. We saw only one sleeping vagrant in his refrigerator box, which seemed so sad to me. Tell you what, take a left up there; I can see the top of a rusted smoke stack that looks vaguely familiar."

Foster began driving a ten-block grid pattern through the area. They passed through neighborhoods that were only a few blocks in each direction. Some boasted well-cared-for residences and manicured lawns and sophisticated landscaping. Then, only a block or two away, were crumbling foundations and sagging porches, broken windows and shutters; the accepted ornamentation for every patch of dirt or weed-choked yard appeared to be a stripped junk car.

As they passed through a neighborhood of two-story brownstones where pride of ownership was evident, Jenny suddenly shook his arm and pointed, "Take a right up there, John. I definitely remember that glorious tree." She referred to a magnificent weeping willow that stood on the corner of a grassy double lot, its branches sweeping the ground. "Beautiful, isn't it? I remember Eddie saying something about there being a sadness to the tree, but he was smiling when he said it. It struck me as odd, like a mixed message."

"Weeping," Foster said, "and he smiled?"

"Yeah, weird, huh? Pull in there."

Following Jenny's directions, Foster maneuvered the Porsche into an alley where an uneasy darkness had already settled in for the night. As he looked beyond the beams of his headlights, Foster shuddered involuntarily. It seemed that, having simply turned a corner, they had pierced a shroud of decay, despair, perhaps even death, all that remained of the once vibrant industries that had spurred Chicago's growth. When had a man last whistled as he shouldered a bag of cement or unloaded lengths of copper pipe? Where, for that matter, was the reasoning that allowed these abandoned businesses and factories to crumble and fall? The land that these decaying structures occupied would be worth millions of dollars. The magnitude of such waste made no sense!

Foster and Jenny drove slowly through an industrial maze of intersecting alleys and narrow streets. Foster felt vulnerable with the top down, but kept it down to afford them a better view. Just ahead, Jenny noticed a building that she said looked familiar, "Pull up there." Ahead, was a narrow, two-story wooden building that looked to have been built in the thirties. The vertical plywood sheets, which sealed first floor windows, were unpainted and warped by weather.

"Stop here."

"Eddie told me this was one of his favorite spots."

Knowing what little he did about Vinson, Foster could see why. The building was situated at the corner on a four-way intersection. "Look at that. The alleys go in four different directions."

"This *is* the place he showed me."

"Let's get out, Jenny. I want to look around. If you want to stay here, it's OK. I'll be just a minute or two."

"Not a chance," she said, "I'm coming with you."

Foster reached for the door latch and felt Jenny grab his arm and squeeze hard then let go slowly. Both of them emerged from the car, and while Foster examined the structure in front of him, Jenny walked behind the car and came to his side.

"I don't know why, but I'm scared," Jenny said sheepishly. "There's no one here. The place is too quiet, creepy. No one has been here in a jillion years."

"Look. There is a window that's not boarded up; I want to see inside." Foster walked cautiously across the littered alley. An acrid smell rode the occasional gust of wind.

"Jenny, would you get my flashlight from the glove compartment?"

"Do I have to?"

"Yes. Please?"

Jenny moved quickly to and from the car. She thrust the flashlight at Foster who was standing on tiptoes, trying to look through a haze of dust and mildew or mold that coated the glass. The flashlight's beam bounced off the grimy window; only a few feet of the interior was illuminated and nothing but scrap metal and 2x4's were visible. There were hulking shadows beyond the immediate path of the flashlight that suggested equipment of some sort around the perimeter, but the center of the room seemed to be empty of all but litter and industrial debris.

Because his calf muscles were beginning to knot painfully, Foster stepped back from the window. *Too much sittin' on your arse, old boy!* He looked down the alley and saw a section of broken wooden ladder that contained only three or four rungs, but it would be enough to give him the boost he needed. Foster leaned the ladder against the brick wall and tested the first step. It cracked ominously, but held. The second rung snapped even before he could place his full weight on it, so he stepped over it to the third, which also held. Not wanting to press his luck, and grateful for the three feet of added height, Foster pulled the flashlight from his back pocket and scanned the interior as far as the light would allow. Glimpsing nothing that he hadn't already seen, he turned his head to look down, and as he did so, he caught a glint of orange in the far rear corner. He tried to angle the flashlight to catch the color again, but the beam was fading. With a frustrated huff, he jumped to the ground.

"There's something in there besides abandoned machinery and equipment. I'm gonna find out what."

Like two thieves in the night, Foster and Jenny circled the building, but ended up back at a pair of large wooden doors that spanned about fifteen feet. Judging from the gleam of the lock that hung on a rusty, but stout, chain, it was a recent addition.

"Locked," Foster fumed. "I can't count lock picking among my many accomplishments."

"Nor can I," Jenny grinned, "but it wouldn't be the first time I had to break a window and climb in where I wanted to go."

"Jen, that's illegal." She shrugged and began unbuttoning her sweater vest.

"What are you doing?"

"Don't worry." She removed the vest to reveal a silk blouse and filmy camisole that accentuated more than it covered. Foster swallowed and stepped back.

Jenny wrapped her arm and elbow with the sweater. "Should have brought my brass knuckles, huh?" She climbed the poor excuse for a ladder and balanced herself by leaning her left hip against the wall. With short, sharp taps of her elbow, she cracked the glass. When it didn't fall away, she wrapped her hand, and pushed on a piece of glass that appeared to be fractured on all sides. The piece popped out and smashed on the concrete floor inside, but the window maintained its integrity.

"It's all that dirt and grime holding it together!" Jenny joked. Patiently, she pushed the broken pieces of glass to the inside until she had cleared the lower frame and had an opening of about two by three feet. She folded her vest in thirds and placed it on the narrow ledge to protect her hands, then look down at Foster.

"I know it's an imposition, John, but I need a boost. Put your hands on my butt, and push! On three."

"Wait, Jen. WAIT! Let me go."

"John, be reasonable. I can't give you a lift, svelte though you may be! And, believe it or not, I am trained to do this. You know, fearless EMT and all! Don't get all macho on me. Just push!"

"OK, I'll push. Just don't go breaking your neck once you're up there. I'd have a heck of a time explaining what we're doing!

"I'll hand you the flashlight once you're in; see if you can't find a way to let me in."

Jenny was up and over the window ledge in an instant. She disappeared into the dark interior. When Foster tried to climb the ladder to follow her progress, the top rung snapped resoundingly. He could hear her talking to herself, but the words were garbled. Suddenly he heard a chortle, and then a whoop of triumph. A moment later, Jen appeared beneath the open window. "Your wish is my command! Stand back, John. Here comes the one tool that will let you break the lock and walk in the door."

Foster retreated about four feet and waited. "OK, I'm standing back"

With a grunt of exertion, Jen tossed a heavy-duty bolt cutter through the window opening. It landed at Foster's feet. *Well, I'll be!*

It required some exertion of his own, but Foster was able to cut one link of the chain that was strung between the two door handles and padlocked. The doors opened in to a rusty tune, and he found himself staring at Jen who was grinning like a loon. "Welcome, good Sir," she bowed gracefully. "You'll never guess what's here!"

Foster accepted the flashlight from Jenny and surveyed a two-story room that was, as the shadows had suggested, lined around all four walls with metal drums, bales of wire and cable, pipes in all diameters, and tables laden with tools. There was nothing familiar, however, to tell him what kind of enterprise had gone on here or how long it had been abandoned. Only a stale, metallic odor and the accumulation of dust and dirt hinted at the length of the vacancy.

When he had completed a full turn around the building, Foster walked toward a windowless corner where he had seen the glimpse of color from the window.

"Red, not orange...," he groaned. A black tarpaulin covered what was obviously a vehicle; long and low, it could only be a sports car. Although it had been hidden, the tarp did not cover the spoiler on the right front side, and it was there that Foster had seen the unexpected strip of color in the otherwise black and gray interior.

A glance at Jenny told him that she knew what was beneath the tarp; Foster suspected that he did too. With a sharp snap, he pulled the cover to reveal the showroom sheen of a cherry red Corvette. "Vinson!" was all he said.

"Hello, baby. What's a nice car like you doing in a place like this?" Jenny murmured.

"You knew immediately that it was Eddie's car, didn't you?"

"Yes, there's no color like that.... I just thought the police would have it...after his suicide and all."

"I never even thought about his car. I had seen it twice near my office; it's not the kind of detail I should miss. I wonder if the cops realize. Perhaps not, if Ms. Vinson didn't tell them it was missing."

Foster glanced at his watch; it was 8:33 p.m. "Let's get a move on. Maybe I can still reach Detective Branan."

CHAPTER THIRTY-TWO

John woke early. He had not reached Branan the previous evening so his brain was already humming with the ramifications of finding Vinson's car and needing to share with Branan the insights Jenny Fox had provided.

Despite his preoccupation with the enigma that was Eddie Vinson, Foster smiled to realize that Joyce had kicked off the blanket, and the curve of her hip was sufficient to send all other thoughts scattering for the moment.

Morning was their favorite time for loving. The reasons were pragmatic because, after long days of listening to the problems and stresses of his patients, sex was usually the furthest thing from his mind. Thankfully, vacations always provided an instant cure!

For several moments, John scanned Joyce's face, remembering. The years had not dimmed the intensity of their passion. If anything, the familiarity with each other's physical and emotional needs heightened the desire. John stroked gently down his wife's back and over her elegant hip. She rolled toward him with a sleepy smile.

Several years ago, Foster had served on staff at the University of Illinois Medical Center. His teaching duties included instructing family physicians-to-be about psychosexual dynamics. Following one of his lectures, he was asked by a young woman resident to describe in words the feeling of sexual tension, the build-up of sexual tension in both men and women, and to address whether or not the feelings were similar for both sexes.

Foster remembered pausing for a moment while he considered possible descriptors. When he continued, he asked the young woman if she'd ever had heartburn, to which she answered that she had. Foster then turned away from the lectern and said, "Now, imagine that heartburn and move it to your genitals." The resident blushed and the audience howled with laughter. "And yes, Ma'am, the feelings are the same for both sexes!"

There was no lingering about after lovemaking. Foster had to get to Branan PDQ. As soon as he had showered, he hunted down his cell phone and dialed Branan's number.

"I'm sorry, sir, Detective Branan isn't at the District right now. Is this an emergency?" The voice on the line sounded familiar to Foster. "I'm Doctor Foster. Do you remember me?"

"Oh, yes, sir, I remember."

"Look, Officer, it's Pellegrino, right? I have something critical to tell Detective Branan. It's imperative that I speak to him as soon as possible."

"OK. I can track him down and have him call you."

"Thank you, and please tell him it's urgent."

"Will do, Doc."

"Bye. Thanks again."

Foster was feeling antsy. It was akin to driving his Porsche with one foot on the accelerator and one on the brake. He wandered to the kitchen where a still glowing Joyce was making tea. She correctly interpreted his body language in a glance.

"What's wrong, John?"

He shrugged and stood before a window that overlooked the back courtyard. Joyce put her arms around him from behind, and ran her fingers up and down his chest.

"Joyce, please? I know I've done an about-face on you, but...."

Slowly, Joyce's hands dropped to his hips, and then she stepped back. Although her facial expression remained carefully neutral, her reflection in the window clearly showed the hurt in her eyes. She fiddled with the neckline of one of his long white t-shirts, which was all she wore. He thought, in passing, that it was nothing short of a miracle that a woman could wear a T-shirt that stopped just shy of her buttocks and still remain discreetly covered.

"Is everything all right, John?" She handed him her cup of Earl Grey.

"No, I'm sorry, Joyce, for snapping. Our paths have diverged rather suddenly, huh? I feel like I'm flying in forty directions at once."

"What happened yesterday?"

Because Joyce had been dozing when he arrived home last evening, he had told her nothing of his dinner and explorations with Jenny. "I think I may have found some crucial evidence in the Vinson case. I'll have to check it out with Branan, but he's not in. Where's a cop when you need one?"

"Did you check the Donut Xpress?" Joyce said coyly.

Foster turned and smiled, "You're a real comedian this morning."

"You betcha!"

The phone began to ring, "I better get that. I called the District and begged special favors!"

"Foster, here."

"Doc, this is Branan. What's the emergency?"

"I've got what could be vital information relating to the Vinson case."

"Have you been snooping around on your own, Doc? You could get yourself into trouble...."

"I'm all right. Can you meet me?"

"Yeah, OK. I'll meet you at McDonalds on Home Avenue, thirty minutes plus or minus."

It didn't talk long for Foster to finish dressing and drive to the restaurant. He found Branan sitting peacefully, sipping a cup of coffee and smoking a cigarette. "I thought you didn't smoke?" Foster sat down on the plastic swivel chair and squirmed to find a comfortable position.

"Oh, this? I don't smoke really, at least not at home or in the office. My wife hates it; the kids give me all kinds of grief, and word has come down from the Commissioner that all Districts will be 'smoke-*free*' environments," he said sarcastically. "At least a guy can still enjoy a smoke and a coffee at McD's, hey, Doc?"

"Look, I don't care if you smoke a truckload of these cancer sticks."

Branan looked up, surprised, at Foster's remark, but he let it pass. "Tell me what's so important, Doc."

"I found Vinson's car."

"Oh, that."

"Oh, that?"

"Cool it, Doc. I know you found the garage."

"What do you mean?"

"We've had an eye on that place for the past few days. I'll tell ya, the stakeout team flipped out when you and that paramedic chick showed up. They fixed the window this morning and put everything back in place." Branan grinned.

"I don't believe it! You had surveillance on the car all along?"

"Yeah, we found it three days ago. We'd been looking for it since Vinson's death. From the beginning…thought it was fishy that the guy would take himself into one of the worst neighborhoods in the city, kill himself on a railroad track, and leave his fancy sports car behind. The Captain said to drop it; he thought sure the car had been stolen, but I've got connections up, down, and sideways when it comes to stolen vehicles, and there wasn't one peep about a red Vette. If there had been, I would have known within two hours. A car like that, there's always a trail. So I came to the conclusion that Vinson had done something on his own…used the car to settle a debt, bookie or drug connection, something. Maybe had hidden it…or, of course, there was always the possibility that he wasn't dead.

"Now, the DNA results make it a done deal. The body wasn't Vinson's, just as you suspected."

"Ya, but…?" Foster felt disoriented momentarily. *Erik was right; I was right.*

Branan was watching him closely, "Are you OK, Doc?"

"Just shook up. Didn't expect…well, this puts a whole new twist on things, particularly Sonya Vinson's death."

"Here, take a sip of my coffee."

Foster took more than a sip and felt better for the jolt. "So, you've suspected all along that Vinson is alive."

"Uh, huh," Branan said, wiping a broad grin from his face. "Great minds and all that!

"When I asked you to consult on the Sonya Vinson case, I already suspected her husband. I know he killed the barkeep, even if I never prove it. That trail has gone stone cold. Vinson being an EMT in Chicago…he knows this city like it's part of him. He can move around so fast, go places no one could anticipate, and close doors so completely.... Elusive doesn't begin to describe him. You've got a handle on his personality. I need you to see what I can't. You know, the nuances. Sophisticated word for a cop, don't you think, Doc?"

"Please, call me John."

"I prefer Doc. Besides, I'm used to it now."

"Whatever," Foster slumped into his seat, the picture of dejection.

"Don't despair, Doc. With our two heads together, Vinson doesn't stand a chance. Not that I think it's going to be easy; in fact, I'm sure it won't, but tenacity will win the day! Can I buy you a coffee?"

"No, thanks."

"Burger?"

"No."

"Fries?"

"NO!" Foster said more emphatically, looking away.

"Well...can I offer you a hot apple pie?"

Foster turned back abruptly to see Branan chuckling, "Get a grip, Doc."

Foster got the joke. "What do we do first, Detective?"

"Besides wait, you mean?"

"Right."

"Well, I think.... Were you tempted...to put the moves on the paramedic? My boys said she was built like a brick tollbooth."

"A brick what?"

"Tollbooth. More twenty-first century than 'shithouse.'"

"I can't believe you're asking me this. Jeez!"

"Hey, don't get all in a dither; I was just wondering. Great tits, I'm told."

Foster sat, mouth open, wondering where his day had gone wrong. His mentor would roll over in his grave, and his colleagues would probably refer him to the program for impaired psychologists sponsored by the Illinois psychology board.

Clearing his throat and looking the jovial detective in the eyes, Foster asserted himself. "Branan, I can't work with you if I suspect that you're keeping information from me. If I'm gonna be of any help to you, you've got to give me everything you have, including your hunches. I am willing to do the same."

"OK, you've got it," Branan said matter-of-factly.

"No, really, I mean it," Foster said, louder.

"OK, Doc, I got your point. We'll drive over to my office and go over chronology, what we know, what we suspect, the works."

"OK, sounds good. Just give me just a minute to call my wife."

"Me too. Got a quarter? I don't have a fancy silver phone like yours."

"Here, use mine. I'll call after you."

Branan punched in the numbers then asked, "How do you send it?"

"Just hit the yellow button that says 'Send.'"

"Oh, yeah. Right here. Hello? Frances? It's Leslie. I'm finally using a cell phone!"

"Leslie? I thought your name was Mike," Foster frowned.

"Middle name," Branan mouthed. "No, won't be home this afternoon. Right. Something came up. I'll check with you later. Love you too. How do you turn it off, Doc?"

"Press 'Send' again."

"Really? 'Send' to call and 'Send' to end? Wild. Here, thanks. Maybe I'll get me one of these little gizmos someday soon."

Foster pressed Memory 1 and Joyce answered on the first ring, "I know it's been one thing after another, J, but this is important." Foster could hear the irritation in her voice as she responded to his statement. "You're right, but I'm into this in a big way now, and I've got to go with it. I've made a commitment"

Into the silence that followed, he said, "I love you."

Branan's eyes reflected understanding, but rather than offering manly commiseration, he swept Foster's discomfort under the table. "Are you sure you don't want a burger?"

"I'm positive," Foster said, smiling his thanks. He was getting used to Branan's brand of humor. "You're worse than my grandmother. She was always pushing food!"

At the District, Branan provided Foster with a cardboard box filled with reports, interview notes, and photos, all dealing with the Vinson case which, ostensibly, included two homicides and a suicide; the relevant names were O'Hearn, Vinson, and Vinson. For the remainder of the morning and much of the afternoon, Foster plowed through the files. He did not take notes; he wanted simply to immerse himself in the details that had been assembled to date. He paid particular attention to photos of the crime scenes, trying to get a read on both the obvious information provided by the photos and the more subliminal details. One photo caught Foster's eye; it documented the scene at the EL tracks where the mangled body had been recovered, the body they now knew was not Eddie Vinson. Because of the wide angle of the photo, in the background were passengers and curious onlookers who seemed always to congregate when tragedy struck. Beyond the sharp focus of the mangled corpse, Foster noted something that appeared to be out of place.

"What do you think this is, Mike?" he asked, pointing.

"Darned if I know; looks like...uh...haven't got a clue."

"Can you get it blown up?"

"Sure, why?"

"I don't know, but I've got a funny feeling."

Branan took the photo and left the room. Foster continued to study the file materials.

Ten minutes later, Branan strode through the door. He pushed the photo at Foster. "Well, what do you think you see?"

"Do you have a magnifying glass?

"Whaddya think, I'm Sherlock Holmes?" Then, with a flourish, Branan pulled a large magnifying glass from the top of a filing cabinet. He blew on it and dust flew up his nose, precipitating a trio of gusty sneezes.

While Branan blew his nose and wiped his eyes, Foster studied the photo through the glass. "Come over here a moment. Tell me what you see. Look to the left, behind the row of trees and brush that run along the tracks."

Branan held both the photo and the magnifying glass at arm's length. He cocked his head, squinted, and mumbled something about not needing glasses.

Foster prodded, "White guy...sitting in...assuming that blurred outline is a vehicle, a red one?"

"Damn straight," said Branan grabbing the photo, "I'll be back in a few minutes. I'm taking this upstairs...got a guy who's a whiz at computer enhancement."

"You think it's Vinson?" Foster addressed Branan's retreating back.

"Absofuckinglutely!"

Mike Branan returned to his office about a half-hour later. Foster looked up from the file he was reading, expecting to see the detective dancing a jig and affirming that the blurred image in the photo was Vinson's vehicle near the accident scene. What he saw frightened the bejesus out of him. He scraped back his chair and stood to help a gray and perspiring Branan into it.

"Are you all right, Mike?"

"I think so, but...." Branan missed the chair seat and fell on his butt. Foster didn't need to see him clutch his chest to make a diagnosis. He slid Branan to the floor, and with his left hand, he snagged a small pillow from the love seat that was crammed into a corner. With his right, he punched the phone on Branan's desk, hoping that zero would get him the PBX operator. It did. Clearly, concisely, Foster requested an ambulance, oxygen if it was available, and some aspirin and water. Before he hung up, he could already hear rapid footsteps on the stairs.

"Mike?" Foster used his handkerchief to wipe Branan's forehead. When Mike focused his eyes on him momentarily, Foster squeezed his hand. "An ambulance is on its way, Mike, and here comes the cavalry."

Pellegrino wedged himself between Branan and the desk. He held a portable oxygen cylinder and mask. Another detective handed Foster the aspirin and small cup of water. Pellegrino lifted Branan's shoulders just enough for him to be able to take a few swallows, and Foster popped the aspirin and held the water to his lips. Just as the oxygen mask was lowered into place, Branan's sighed and said, "Thanks, Guys; I'll be OK."

The EMTs were in and out rapidly. Pellegrino advised them of the aspirin that Branan had been given. Foster went down the stairs while the medics took Branan in the elevator. He felt as though he was wearing lead shoes, and he broke out in a sweat now that Branan was in capable hands. Sgt. Pellegrino came up behind him and squeezed his shoulder as they watched the ambulance pull away. Foster heard the word being passed about Branan's heart attack. There was no doubt it had been serious; sudden and hard, it had knocked the big detective off his feet. He heard one loud outburst, "Not another one?"

The response, from someone Foster couldn't see, was, "Yes, another one. This makes number three."

"Sir, are you Dr. Foster?" A young woman approached, shaking her head sadly. "Detective Branan requested this computer enhancement, and said to give it to you. He indicated you are consulting with him on the Vinson case. Is that correct?"

Foster turned slowly to make eye contact with a delicate and slender Eurasian woman wearing a no-nonsense, brown business suit that served only to call attention to her femininity, quite the opposite, Foster suspected, of her intentions.

"Detective Branan wanted you to see this enhancement, but before he could bring it to you, he began experiencing chest pains. I printed it out and wanted you to have it before you left. I hope it helps." She extended a glossy 8' x 10' color photo to Foster.

Foster thanked her before looking down at the photo. Although images were still blurred, the resolution was sufficient for him to recognize immediately the front fender of a red Corvette that was only partially obscured by weeds and scrub brush that paralleled the tracks of the EL.

"Vinson, you bastard!"

CHAPTER THIRTY-THREE

"Bobby, are you awake? Time to get up."

Marnie Dubroc slumped against the doorjamb; her forehead was pounding to a brutal staccato. New Boyfriend, she doubted Bobby was his name, was dead to the world, face down and drooling on the stripped and stained mattress. *Oh gawd, what a night!* "Where the hell is the Excedrin?"

Moving into the grungy bathroom, Marnie relieved herself. She hovered over the scarred and urine spattered toilet-seat.

Marnie was a prostitute who'd seen better days... certainly better paydays. Long gone were the engagements for which she could command five hundred dollars a night from real gentlemen. Her success had ended on a rainy night in the company of a drunken corporate executive from Nowhere, USA. "Butt sex is not part of my gig," she remembered saying to him.

Marnie awoke in a hospital ER where she had been sutured from stem to stern and shot full of painkillers. It didn't take a rocket scientist to know that her beating had resulted from her smart remark to a dissatisfied customer.

During her recovery, while she was out of commission, Marnie decided there would be some significant changes in her life. She figured she was organized and methodical enough that she would make a fine administrator, and because she knew the business inside and out, she would make a far more caring madam for the girls who would choose to work for her. That was the plan; as it turned out, it proved to be an unworkable plan, and she was a working girl again. If anything had changed, it was that she listened to her "radar" more closely, and didn't accept every John who requested her services. She had also acquired a boyfriend for protection.

Marnie surveyed her face in the cracked mirror over the sink. The brown, purple, and gold bruises had finally faded, but she could still see them as they had been. There was a jagged scar that was all but hidden in her right eyebrow, a souvenir from that miserable night. Her unusual azure eyes, once her most striking feature, were now a watery dull blue; the color of disillusionment was how she thought of them. *And you know what? I don't give a damn!*

"Are you awake? Bobby, you got to look for work; we don't have any money. Hey!" She prodded his inert figure. The primary qualifications for a position as boyfriend had been a car and quick fists, and a willingness to use them. GQ material Bobby wasn't. It was also becoming obvious that he was allergic to work. Marnie suspected her allure for ole Bobby was as a meal ticket; it sure wasn't the sex, and who could blame him?

"Where did you park the car, at the Late Night Garage?"

Bobby rolled over and levered himself up against the cracked headboard. "Yeah, Baby. Where's the Charter?"

"You drank every drop."

"Shit. I've gotta have some. I'll go for it." Bobby pulled on yesterday's clothes which were on the floor beside the bed.

Hell, those are last week's clothes, Marnie thought, suppressing a grin, *and I bet they've got a whole colony of little flea beasties after being on the floor of this dump all night.*

The door slammed behind Bobby.

I'll have to remember that Charter is a potent motivator! The wee dear didn't even bother to wash the important parts before he left. Marnie examined a broken thumbnail while idly debating whether Bobby had already outlived his usefulness. She parted the curtains to look out on the sidewalk below. A fruit and vegetable stand was doing a booming business. She watched as two kids set up a clamor to distract the aging vendor while their cohort pinched several pieces of fruit and stowed them beneath an over-size shirt. The three were gone in the wink of an eye. *That's free enterprise for you!*

On the street, Bobby's energy had already peaked for the day. Under the unforgiving glare of reflected sunlight, he struggled simply to walk a straight line. His head was on his shoulders crooked, and his eyes were gritty and swollen. His mouth…naw, he wasn't goin' there! He fished in one pocket after another, but couldn't find the ticket for his car, and he sure as shit couldn't remember what floor he'd parked it on. Maybe he should get the Charter first; it would give him a jumpstart.

When the next cylinder fired in his brain, however, Bobby remembered that his pockets also held no money, and he had only a fiver to his name. It was in the console of the car, and he would have to hope it would cover what he owed to spring his wheels. *You should have hit Marnie up for some cash, you dumb cluck!*

In his Old Charter fog, Bobby passed the parking garage and had reached the next block before he realized nothing looked familiar. The garage itself should have been unmistakable as its entrance looked like the roaring mouth of a cement dragon; at least it had when he was stoned. He backtracked, angry at his loss of focus. *Better keep your shit together, old chum.*

"I'm here for my car."

The cashier behind the plexiglass didn't even look up. "Ticket," was all he said.

"I lost it."

"No problem." The man was a behemoth, a tattooed giant! There were dragons everywhere! Detailed and stylistic, Chinese probably, from the looks…and all done in red.

"Nice artwork," Bobby offered while he waited uncomfortably under the man's scrutiny.

"It's a wonder you remember where you parked your car; you were feeling no pain when you dropped it off. When you didn't come back yesterday, we were laying bets how long it would take you to find it."

"I parked it here last night. You're thinking of someone else."

"I don't think so. Never forget a face."

The cashier held a ticket up to the glass, and Bobby's license plate number was written at the top in bold print. The ticket was dated two days ago, and the date and time had been stamped by machine. "Are you trying to fuck with me?" he asked without much conviction.

"Hey, man. I just work here." The cashier's response was mild, non-threatening, but his right hand dropped below the counter. Common sense said he'd reached for a gun.

"OK," Bobby shrugged obsequiously. "Didn't seem like I was *that* wasted. Give me the keys and I'll get out of here." He slouched and leaned an elbow on the narrow counter to wait for the guy to come up with his keys. It was then that he saw the two men who had been holding up the wall not five feet from him. Together, they might have tipped the scales at two hundred fifty pounds.

"Sorry about the holdup," Bobby mumbled, but he straightened to his full height and balanced his weight. His body language clearly spoke, "Don't fuck with me," but both men stepped forward and halved the distance between them.

"Something I can do for you gentlemen?" Bobby challenged.

"Maybe," the shorter man said defiantly, and took another half step. It wasn't the pugnacious jut of his chin that signaled intent, however; it was his eyes, and the two almost simultaneous snicks as each man raised an open and ready-for-business stiletto.

Two shots reverberated through the upper levels of the parking garage. *Leave it to street punks to bring knives to a gunfight.*

Before either man hit the cement, Bobby was facing the cashier, the gun now clear of his windbreaker pocket. The fact that the fat man was holding a gun on him as well told Bobby that the window separating them was glass and not bulletproof. When the cashier's eyes dropped to the two smoldering holes in his chest, Bobby fired one more shot between his beady pig eyes.

Taking a battered metal folding chair that leaned beside the cashier's booth, he slammed the window, which fissured before exploding inward. Bobby pulled his keys from the cashier's hand. He threw a quick glance over his shoulder. Maybe it was the five gunshots; maybe it was just good fortune, but there was not a witness in sight. Leaning over the counter, Bobby pulled open the cheap cash drawer and palmed as many bills as he could on a single pass from slot to slot.

Knowing he wouldn't get far on foot, and not being able to remember where he'd parked, Bobby did an about face and returned to the street. As two cop cars screeched to a halt midway down the next block, he strolled toward the hot dog vendor at the corner. The man's setup was a hotdog in a bun—on wheels, and it was angled such that the vendor had his back to the parking garage and other businesses on the block. Bobby was gambling that he had not been seen exiting the garage.

"What'll you have?"

"I don't know yet," he answered, and stepped back to read the menu on the side of the cart. A women stepped from behind him to order a dog with mustard and sauerkraut.

"You got it, lady."

When she had been served, the vendor looked at Bobby for his order. Because having the hotdog was only a ruse so that he could observe what was going on at the garage, he hedged and said, "Smells good; I'll take mine plain."

"Plain, huh? That's original."

"I want to get a taste of the hotdogs you use. Next time I'll load up on the toppings." He watched as the man pulled a steaming bun from a stainless steel chamber and laid a plump, oversize dog in it.

"Hope you like it. Regular customers are the best part of my business. Bought this rig and paid for it in the first ninety days. Now my profit is really profit!"

Bobby nodded agreeably while he munched, but he wasn't paying attention to the vendor's spiel. He was watching the police converge on the entrance to the garage. In a matter of moments, one yahoo appeared with the crime scene tape and began blocking off the area. He turned to the vendor and asked, "Do you know what happened there?"

"Heard four or five shots, but that's all I can tell you."

Bobby was wondering about the best way to get to his car. The more he thought about it, the more certain he was that he'd parked under a big, broken halogen bulb on the third tier just before the ramp to the fourth level. He knew he could talk his way past the police; he needed his wheels and he needed a drink. He pulled out a bunch of crumpled tens and twenties and peeled off a ten for the vendor. "Keep the change," he said. "Got to sweet talk the cops into letting me get my car out. Wish me luck!"

Bobby walked up to the uniformed officer who appeared to have done all the damage he could with the roll of fluorescent tape. "What happened?"

"Triple murder."

"Man, I was just on my way there…stopped for a dog. Did they shoot the big guy with the dragon tattoos?"

"Sure did. Did you see anything?"

"Naw. The hotdog guy and I heard the shots, but didn't see anyone go in or out. Was it robbery?"

"Appears to be." The cop turned to admonish two teens who ducked under the 'Do Not Cross' tape, and his attention strayed for the moment.

When he had the officer's attention again, Bobby began to whine. "Jeez, Officer, I gotta get my car. It's paid for; it's on the third level. I need my car to get to work. Plus, my wife is gonna kill me if I don't pick up my kid's birthday cake for the party this afternoon."

"All right, already! Go on. Get your car and get out of my hair…. Benson, let him through. He's going to the third floor."

Bobby moved purposefully into the garage. Like Mr. Average American, he slowed to gawk, and to admire his handiwork. The two stiffs were covered with the same white sheet, and blood was seeping through. The whale in the booth was sitting up, but his head was thrown back at an odd angle. The final bullet had entered just above the bridge of his nose. As he passed, Vinson overheard three cops talking about how they were going to get the guy out because of his mammoth size and dead weight. *Dead weight, that's for sure!*

Within a few minutes, Bobby reached his car. He opted to use the rear garage exit because of all the crime scene goings-on up front, but he was stopped as he approached the exit.

"What are you doing, pal?" asked a very young cop.

"I was told I could get my car out of here by the officer up front."

"Hey, Joey, did you let a guy come through here to get his car?" he asked over his radio.

"That's a roger," came the response.

"OK, move out."

"Thanks officer, I'll remember next time I get hit up for a police fundraiser." The cop didn't look amused.

That was too easy! "Stupid friggin' cops," Bobby muttered as he headed for the nearest liquor store.

Marnie chewed a ragged cuticle. Bobby had been gone for almost an hour, and she had to consider that he'd split. It wouldn't be the first time, and their night of alcohol and drugs probably made it more likely. She had been pacing for the past twenty minutes, but it was only now that she realized Bobby's duffel bag remained in the corner. Surely, he wouldn't go off and leave it behind...or maybe he would, as hung over as he was.

Marnie had known Bobby for two days, and he seemed like a nice enough guy. He'd bought her drinks and sweet-talked her. She'd been up front with him, and he didn't seem to be put off by her choice of career. He was a little rough in bed, but hell, she'd been with worse, and she suspected that his acceptance of her as a working girl probably meant he used prostitutes regularly.

Marnie sat down on the rumpled bed and stared at the duffel bag. She was curious about Bobby, and he had provided her with few answers to the questions she had asked under the guise of "getting to know you." When she realized that her mind was already made up, she pulled the bag onto the bed and worked methodically from one end to the other, opening the Velcro fasteners and zippers. She put her hand into the pocket closest to her, but yanked it back when she felt the cold, sleek butt of a gun. She pulled the pocket open to peer at an ugly, snub-nosed pistol. She moved on to the other storage pockets around the exterior of the bag. In each, she found a different set of ID's with what appeared to be simple elements of disguise, colored contacts, several mustaches and a goatee, glasses, and a man's wig. As she examined the documents, it became immediately clear that they were various driver's licenses, all bearing Bobby's picture, Social Security cards and credit cards. In some photos he wore the disguises.

From the last outside pocket, Marnie pulled out a small, blue cloth bag filled with keys, all neatly labeled, and several heavy metal padlocks. She arranged the keys neatly across the bed with each ID tag face up so it was readable. Then she returned to the licenses, and arranged each of the four neatly in a row with Social Security cards and related credit cards. The first Illinois license was for a Bobby Burton, and the photo was without disguise. In fact, Bobby was wearing the same shirt he'd had on when she met him. The second set of documents was for a Vincent Burton who had both a mustache and goatee, and graying brown hair. The third was for a blue-eyed and blond Vincent Edwards, and the fourth, for an Edward Vinson, again, no disguise. This fourth group of documents also contained an Illinois paramedic's certification."

"Well, what do you know?" Marnie mused aloud as she considered the implications of her find.

"I don't know, Marnie, what *do* you think?" Bobby spoke softly behind her. She had not heard him enter, and she jolted, dropping the license she held in her hand.

"What are you doing in my things, Baby?" Bobby stepped up behind her and rested his hands on Marnie's shoulders. His touch was light, non-threatening, but his voice was low, almost a hiss.

Despite the cold sweat that suddenly bathed her from head to toe, Marnie resorted to bluster. "Hey, look, I don't give a shit who you are; it's none of my business. I'm sorry I snooped, but I was curious. You kept dodging my questions. Where have you been, anyway? I was worried."

"Oh, I had a little trouble at the garage. Took longer than I expected." Almost as an aside, he added, "I had to kill three guys."

Marnie's jaw dropped. Every bit of spit dried up instantly, and she felt like she had a mouthful of gritty, just-picked cotton. She scanned the pockets of the duffel bag trying to recall which one held the pistol, but her brain had emptied of all coherent thoughts. She turned her shoulders and raised her eyes to Bobby who was now standing at her side. A sleek, gunmetal semi-automatic had appeared in his hand. He smiled as he stroked her cheek with its cold barrel. Marnie was terrified by that smile.

"What are you thinking, girl? You know I'm not gonna hurt you. Besides, I was only joking about killing anyone."

Bobby reached into the left pocket of the duffel and removed the second pistol. "No sense in tempting fate, now, is there? Are you planning to get dressed today?"

Bobby moved toward the bathroom where a small, beat-up safe had been provided to safeguard the hotel guests' valuables. They had joked about it when they first arrived; the safe was not secured in any way, and was so lightweight that even a woman could carry it. Now, however, Bobby put the small pistol in the safe and pocketed the key. "Want some Charter? I've had a sudden influx of cash."

"Sure, I'll take some. Shall I get some ice?"

"No." Short and curt, the word stopped her in her tracks. Bobby handed her the drink in a flimsy plastic cup. As she sipped, he ruffled through a wad of bills and then fanned them on the bed in front of her. When she put out her hand to touch, the gesture was halted by a simple, "Uh uh uh."

Despite the morning hour, Bobby kept the drinks coming. The warm Charter lost its appeal after the first few swallows, but the unwinding of tension was a relief. Marnie settled back against a foam rubber pillow. Trying to make her actions look natural, she closed her eyes and slowed her breathing. She had to think about what was going on here, but pretending was easier than thinking, and she surrendered to the alcohol haze.

Bobby sat against the headboard watching Marnie sleep. He was fuming and delaying the inevitable, which was simply to make her sleep permanent. "Stupid, fucking bitch. Why couldn't you mind your own business? You ruined it, just like Sonya," he grumbled softly. "I liked you well enough...for a whore." He reached for the gun on the bedside table. "Be thankful you never knew what hit you." On that thought, he buried the gun in a pillow, shoved the barrel against her temple, and fired.

He listened as Marnie's breathing slowed, then stopped. There was no thrill. Idly, he wondered if she would remain forever drunk in hell. He tried to order his thoughts; he needed to plan how to get rid of the body, but sleep beckoned. He closed his eyes.

Bobby woke to rain and darkness. He realized he ought to feel disgusted that he was huddled against a dead whore, but he didn't, couldn't. He flicked on the table lamp and looked to see that the curtains were completely closed. When he turned back to Marnie, she looked like she was asleep, and that, he decided, was the way he would remember her.

Bobby tried to replay in his head the events of the night when he and Marnie had checked into this dump. Who saw them together? She had remained in the car while he paid for the room—with her money, so the desk manager hadn't seen her, but he knew well that the night always has eyes, so they could have been seen by anyone or no one.

As he thought, Bobby ran his hand rhythmically over Marnie's hair. He finally decided that he would pay for another night, and he and Marnie would "check out" between three and four a.m. Although it left him feeling unsettled, he would have to avail himself of a certain abandoned construction dumpster near old man Ryerson's auto graveyard. The body wouldn't be found for days, and by then, Eddie Vinson, a.k.a. Bobby Burton, would have become someone else.

CHAPTER THIRTY-FOUR

Following Branan's heart attack, the detective who took over the Vinson investigation never contacted Foster about continuing to work with the department. As things stood, the police were certain that Eddie Vinson was alive, and that he had killed his wife and the pub owner. His picture had been on the tube and in print for several days, so if Vinson was still around, he had known to lay low. By now, however, Foster suspected he could probably hold a one-man show in the middle of a city street and not be recognized by citizens or police.

A few judiciously spaced phone calls by Foster to the Twenty-sixth District had hit a proverbial stone wall. Branan's replacement was a lackadaisical, waiting-for-retirement fellow who, according to Sergeant Pellegrino, seldom left his back corner cubbyhole, and then only for coffee and donuts. Foster concluded that there wasn't much he could, or even should, do with regard to the Vinson case, but neither could he resolve things in his mind.

Just when he was finally conquering the frustration caused by the demise of the police investigation, Foster received a call from an equally frustrated and very angry Tim Cook, Vinson's father-in-law. Cook explained that his daughter had told him about her meeting with Foster before she left Eddie, and he was seeking any information, any lead that might enable him jump-start the police investigation. "I intend to shame those lazy ass pig-bastards into doing their damned jobs," was what he railed to Foster, who didn't argue with his reasoning. That Cook's statement had been followed by a sob and a lengthy gulping silence told Foster much about the measure of the man.

Cook had been unaware of the myriad details that Branan had pulled together before his heart attack. Consequently, Foster agreed to meet him for coffee, and they went over what Foster knew of Branan's investigation. He acknowledged that he had been working with Branan, and together he and Cook groused about the police department's failure to pursue the investigation despite the body of evidence that was already available.

Foster sized Tim Cook up as they talked. He was certain that the man was a cream puff when it came to "his girls." Cook's facial expressions softened when he spoke of his grieving wife and granddaughter. That same face seemed hewed from granite, however, when he spoke of the horror and injustice of his daughter's needless death.

Foster soon noted that much of Cook's anger was turned inward because he perceived that he had failed Sonya by not recognizing her husband for the monster he had shown himself to be. It was this self-directed anger that was the foundation for Cook's dogged pursuit of Eddie Vinson, and Foster suspected that Cook would hunt Vinson until justice was served or he died trying. In fact, when they had argued good-naturedly about who was going to pay their tab, Cook summed up Foster's assessment of his commitment to finding his daughter's murderer. He put his hand on Foster's shoulder, and said wearily, "Doc, men like me, we never give up. As long as that bastard, Vinson, is free, I'll find the energy to hunt him. I'll run him 'til he drops...or I do. I'd be obliged if I could call on you every now and then. Between you and my wife, I might be able to stay within the letter of law—just!"

As things turned out, Foster volunteered to assist Cook with much more than a few phone calls. He slipped back into the investigation, picking up where he and Branan had been when the detective was forced to take convalescent leave. He was able to balance the demands of his practice and his sleuthing with Cook; he could still pay the bills, and Joyce had accepted that he had to follow the evidence until he felt he had done everything he could.

Foster had gone with Cook to Lakeshore Ambulance Service downtown where Jenny believed Eddie had moonlighted. The owner didn't recognize Eddie Vinson by name, but when Cook produced a photo of him with Sonya on their wedding day, he identified Vinson as Bobby

Burton, and confirmed that Burton had worked for him intermittently. "He was a good medic, I'll say that," offered the old-timer who had run the ambulance service since its inception. "I've owned this company, oh, probably...a lot of years. I've seen them come and go, but Burton, he was a good one. I wish he'd stayed longer. Just came in one day, looked like he'd been on a helluva bender, and got his gear. No explanation. Haven't seen hide nor hair of him since. That was about, I don't know, eight-ten days ago, at least. I remember because both my crews had been called out on that triple slaying at the parking garage...one-way trips to the morgue, those were. Made all the headlines. Then, there was a woman's body found in a dumpster not far from there. It didn't make the papers, and I never heard any more about her shooting, but it seemed strange, the two incidents in the same neighborhood and all."

"Anything else you remember about Vinson? Sorry, I mean Burton," Cook asked.

"Where was I? Oh, yeah. Anyway, Bobby had come to fill in on a mid-shift when we got the call to pick up the woman's body and get it to the morgue—fast. Don't know why the rush, but he jumped right on it. He was back from the morgue in record time, and I joked that he must have had her in the van already when the call came in. He was a solid employee, had great instincts when it came to the really serious injuries. I would have hired him fulltime in a heartbeat."

Cook and Foster looked at each other in dismay. "Remind me, where was that triple murder?" Foster asked.

"Thirty-sixth and Fullerton. Around that area...a parking garage."

From the ambulance service to the parking garage took about thirty minutes in early evening traffic. Cook was chauffeuring in his 1999 Honda EX, standard transmission and a few *extras* to make it fly. By the time they arrived, it was already dusk. He and Foster approached the garage entrance where an attractive young woman in her early thirties greeted them. In a lilting Jamaican accent, she addressed Cook with a smile, "Hey, Mon. How can I help you?"

"How long have you worked here?" Cook asked.

"Why you need to be knowin' that, Mon?" She was no longer friendly.

"Well, a friend of mine was killed here. The guy whose job you have."

"You knew Big Bruno?"

"Oh, yeah. He and I did some time together. What happened? Not like him to be taken sittin' down."

"All I know is some white guy come in here and start shooting."

"What's the word...on the street?"

"That some girl got killed by the same white man. Same day, just a few blocks from here.

"What did Big Bruno do to go to jail?"

"He ripped off a donut truck," Cook said sardonically.

"No foolin'? They put you away for that?"

"Sure, they found him holed up in a motel, still eatin' the loot." The woman was gullible or playing dumb! "Did that woman live around here? The one who was killed?"

"She was staying in some hotel, next block down and over. Can't miss it. Kent Arms or somethin' like that."

"Thanks a lot, Miss."

To reach the Kent Arms, Cook and Foster entered a dreary neighborhood where many of the small homes and businesses had been abandoned. The Kent had seen better days, and its current incarnation seemed to be as a residential hotel where many occupants were transients, one step above homeless. Many were milling about on stairways and landings as though loathe to shut themselves in for the night. There was a collective suspicion that focused on the two men as they approached the entrance to a dingy lobby where only a single bare bulb swayed as the door opened and closed behind them. The smell of whiskey wafted from the manager with each sonorous snore. Foster was a little spooked by it all. Cook, sensing that he was unnerved, punched his shoulder and said, "Don't worry, John. I know all the moves if we get jumped. Just get out of the way...so you don't get in my way, if you know what I mean"

To the right of the reception desk where the manager was resting his head, there was a marquee of sorts that displayed the names of residents, although most slots were empty or sported a red *Vacancy* tag. Of the names listed, all were men. No help there. Cook shrugged. "OK, John-Boy, what do we have to lose? Do you want the honors?"

"Be my guest," said Foster. Of the same mind, they both took a step back, looked at each other and grinned.

"SIR!" Cook boomed.

The manager's head whipped off the desk, and Foster winced, suspecting that the sudden movement was playing havoc with his drunken state. Sure enough, the man groaned and put both hands to his head, probably to keep it from flying off. He gulped convulsively, and Foster wondered if they were to be treated to the remains of his last meal. The whiskey fumes alone were testing his gorge.

When the manager's eyes stopped rolling around, Cook stepped a little closer. "I wonder if you could tell us which room was occupied by the woman who was killed around here ten days or so ago...same day as the shootings at the parking garage. We were told she was staying at your hotel."

"What's yer business? Are ye cops?"

"No, not cops...family members of another woman who was killed a couple months ago. Similar MO. The police have let the investigation die; we're looking for a way to persuade them to revive it." Cook's tone was firm, no-nonsense, but respectful.

The man took considerable time to process what Cook told him, but, apparently, he found the statement a reasonable justification for his cooperation. "Room 201. It's vacant; it ain't locked. The police never came to investigate. She must have been with the man who registered 'cause I never saw her."

"Then you don't know her name, don't know what she looked like? What about the man she was with? How did he pay? A credit card maybe?"

"Nah, cash; folks coming here don't have American Express Gold." the manager snickered.

Foster stepped forward and put a cautionary hand on Cook's arm. "Whoa, Tim, slow down; can't you see this man's head is killing him? Let's go look at the room, and then if we have more questions, we can stop on our way out."

They climbed the warped wooden stairway to the second floor. Cook reached for the door handle of 201, which looked to be held in place by a single screw. When he turned, nothing happened. Using his foot, Cook pushed at the bottom of the door panel and it swung open. The manager was obviously mistaken about cops having been on the premises. A Police Department notice was shut in the door which warned against trespassing, and every surface of the room had been dusted for fingerprints.

"Guess the manager doesn't keep himself informed about goings-on in his hotel. Must be all that whiskey! How do you feel about ignoring police directives, Tim?"

"I got no problem with it. You go first," Cook grinned.

"What are we looking for?"

"Shit, I don't know...anything out of the ordinary."

Cook and Foster worked their way methodically around the room, looking but not touching. While Cook stood in the door of the grimy bathroom, Foster circled the double bed that had been stripped of sheets and blankets. Before he could think better of it, he lifted the mattress and looked at the underside.

"Look at this." Foster lifted the mattress a little higher so that Cook could see the large circle of dried blood on its upper half. "Do you think the police even saw this?"

"No tellin', but if I were a betting man, I'd lay money on odds that the victim was killed right here in this room. A riskier bet would be that her companion was the shooter. Do you think the manager could come up with a name?"

"We'll ask. We also need to talk to the residents; surely someone saw the man coming or going—maybe the woman, too.

"You're right, Tim. Let's start knocking on doors. Maybe we can find witnesses more reliable than the pickled guy at the front desk."

Foster knocked first on the door to Room 203. When no one answered, he turned to 202 across the hall, only to be stopped by the rattle of a safety chain from inside 203. A frail, elderly woman opened the door only as far as the chain would allow. Through the opening wafted the fragrance of fresh-baked bread.

"Good evening, Ma'am. My name is…uh, Foster. This is Mr. Cook. We'd like to ask you a few questions about the woman next door who was killed"

The woman looked him up and down, and Foster suspected she didn't miss much. Cook got the same thorough once-over.

"Ma'am?" he said a little louder, in deference to her age.

"What? I'm not deaf, you know. You goddamn people never let me alone."

Another silence was accompanied by the woman's disconcerting glare. Then, the door snapped shut while the chain was removed. When it opened, they were allowed to enter.

"Hell! I'll talk to you now. I'm tired of turning you away."

The woman appeared to be in her mid eighties, and she wore a tattered gray shawl that did not hide a pronounced dowager's hump. Her facial features and manner of dress suggested she was of eastern European descent. "Sit. I'll be right there. I don't want to burn the bread," she said, moving to a small toaster oven in one corner that she clearly used as a kitchen.

The single room, larger than 201, was overheated and crowded. The window shade was drawn, and a small lamp provided the only light. Several dark wood tables and chairs and a daybed filled the room; the furniture was scarred and the fabrics worn, but everything was neat and clean. On one small library table were several pieces of exquisite crystal. When she noted Foster's interest in the beautiful old pieces, a faint smile softened her face. "Polish," was all she said.

"I am Berta. I have been ornery with the others who came asking questions. I was upset by what happened, and frightened. I did not wish to reveal what I know, but now...." She shrugged and turned her arthritic hands, palms up, in a gesture of resignation. "What do you want to know?"

By tacit agreement, neither Cook, nor Foster, corrected Berta's supposition that they were police detectives. Foster's conscience pricked, but he decided he would play the interview by ear. They could always disclose the reasons for their interest in the dead woman if it was the right thing to do.

"What do you know about the couple who stayed next door...for how long, a day or two?"

"He was Bobby, and her name was Mardy or Marnie, it sounded like. Unfortunately, I do know about them. They were here three nights; he was gone part of the second day, in the late morning. I could hear them talking through the vent over there." She pointed to the far wall which adjoined Room 201. "If you are very quiet and sit just there, you can hear everything." She grinned mischievously.

"Go on," said Foster, encouraging.

"After Bobby killed her, I heard him talking to himself."

"Wait a minute? You heard him kill the woman?"

"Oh, sure, I heard; it was only a *pop*...not very loud. He was angry. Drunk, too. Cursing, all the time cursing some man for an imposter, and a woman, too. I forget name."

"Sonya, maybe?" Cook spoke for the first time.

Berta's eyes flew to his face. "Yes! You know...?"

"Please tell us what Bobby was saying."

"It was rambling, did not always make sense. I remember he blamed them both for ruining his...what did he call it? This *Chapter*, you know, like in book. He was very mad, making threats; said he would make the imposter suffer.

"Later, maybe one hour, he became very quiet and I didn't hear any more. Figured he passed out. Then, by chance I saw him below the window, 3:00 a.m. maybe, carrying the woman as if she were injured, as I said, shot. I did not see where they go. She was nice girl; she had time to talk with an old woman, but she was a prostitute. She told me this. She made a bad choice, and she died for doing so. It is sad."

Foster looked to Cook when Berta concluded the account of her interactions with the couple who had stayed briefly next door. Cook looked stunned; he had provided Berta with his daughter's name, and had received confirmation that Sonya allegedly bore much of the blame for the perceived suffering of the man who was once her husband, now her murderer.

Foster, too, was reeling. He had no doubt that *he* was the "imposter" that Berta heard repeatedly in Vinson's angry diatribe. Until now, he had not considered that he, and by association, possibly Joyce, could be at risk as Eddie Vinson, a.k.a. Bobby Burton, continued to decompensate, which was clearly what was happening. So far, everyone known to have tangled with Vinson was dead.... If Foster, too, was to become one of the hunted, then his search for the hunter was suddenly all the more urgent.

Somehow, Foster and Cook marshaled enough manners between them to thank Berta for the information she had provided. They did not disclose the reasons for their interest in Bobby Burton, and Foster concluded that if Bobby should return to the Kent for some unknown reason, she was probably safer if she believed that police had questioned her again.

They walked silently past the hotel manager, who lay snoring just as they had found him. When they reached Cook's car, Foster's spoke suddenly, "Look, Tim, we've got to go back to Lakeshore."

"The ambulance agency? What for?"

"I'll tell you on the way."

Cook headed back along Lakeshore, the way they had come, and waited while Foster pulled his thoughts together. As he summarized his own response to what they had learned from Berta, Foster learned that Cook shared his concern for those individuals who had moved within Vinson's orbit. The agency owner was one; Jenny Fox was another. Though they didn't say so, both realized that they and their families were also on that short list. Foster wondered, in passing, whether Erik von Kovska should also be considered. Where would Vinson draw the line that encircled those he perceived to be threats to him?

Cook indicated that he would see if the owner was still there while Foster tried to reach Joyce to tell her what time to expect him home. No more than two or three minutes passed before Cook exited the building, and it was clear from his expression that there was trouble.

"The old guy?" Foster asked.

"Yeah."

"Dead?"

"Uh huh."

"How?"

"He was shot. Like all the others. His staff is handling it. Two of them were right in the building, and they couldn't save him. The police have been called."

Cook looked like he'd aged ten years since he walked into the agency. "It's him, John; he's on us like fleas on a hound. He's probably been on us from the beginning."

Foster felt every bit as weary and defeated as Cook looked. "He has unfinished business, Tim. He has the instincts of a hunter, and the skills, but when you factor in his deteriorating psychological status, he's as unpredictable as a wounded animal."

"It's a nightmare, a waking nightmare. John, do you suppose we led him to the Kent, to Berta?"

"Tim, I honestly don't know. I don't see any alternative to taking what we now know to the police. We can tie Vinson, or whoever the hell he is, to the parking garage murders and the prostitute, and now the old man. There are people who need police protection including Berta and Eddie's partner at First Alert, possibly other employees there or at Lakeshore. We don't know what they might know, or suspect, or what Eddie thinks they know...."

"If this doesn't light a fire under that lazy-ass detective at the Twenty-sixth, then we climb right over him and pressure whoever we have to—to get results. Surely the trail of dead bodies alone is enough." Cook's eyes filled with tears. "I want to go home, John. I can protect my family."

"Tim, don't you think we should send them away, out of harm's way?"

"I hate the thought of being away from them, but you're probably right. It *would* be prudent. If we're going to pursue Eddie, and we certainly have a good chance of flushing him out, then we can't provide the protection they need. Aw, geez, John. When will it end? And how?"

"Tim, it seems to me that the best defense is to find him before he finds us." Foster's fear was fading, and rational thoughts were returning. "I think I'm beginning to understand Vinson. Do you suppose that is his real name? Regardless, Vinson needs always to be in control. If killing is what it takes to maintain that control, then he kills. If drawing attention to himself is needed, then he puts himself out there. If disclosing his psychopathology is required, then he'll talk about it or make it up as he goes along. He's a true chameleon, becoming whatever, whoever, so long as he remains in control.

"There's another level to Vinson, too. When he is at his best, there's an artistic or aesthetic quality to his actions. Random or disorganized acts of violence would probably be repugnant to him…the antithesis of control. He plans, manipulates so that those who move within his sphere follow his lead, dance to his tune, whatever you want to call it, without ever knowing that he pulls the strings. If you take it to a metaphysical dimension, he may see himself as a god, all-seeing, but unseen, the master of his universe.

"You know, I once looked up the derivation of *chameleon*. I forget exactly, but it comes from the Greek, and means, literally, lion on the ground. That's a good metaphor for Vinson. He's like the lion on the African plain, the consummate hunter moving unseen through the waving yellow grasses until the moment of attack.

"So, if we're to hunt the hunter, we've got to stop chasing him, Tim. Get it?"

"Well, actually no. You lost me back there somewhere on the plains of Africa."

Foster took a deep breath and let it out slowly. "The way to catch a hunter, like Vinson, is to create an opportunity for attack that he can't resist. He cannot conceive of himself as the hunted, so we have to give up the hunt. Instead, we set a trap and use the one bait that he would never anticipate. We go about our normal lives. That means, of course, that removing our families from danger has to appear to be for some very logical, "normal" reason.

"If he responds as I think he will, he will become confused, then distracted. Since he has already shown that he is losing control more often, it should happen quickly. To reassert control, he will attack—without having anticipated our trap—and when he does, we'll have him."

"What trap, Doc? I don't follow." Cook was becoming agitated, and Foster knew he needed to let the matter drop for now. Cook was a hands-on guy and metaphors made little sense to him, especially as tired as he was. Hell, as tired as they both were!

"I don't know just yet what it will be, Tim. It'll take some doing, but let's just give it a rest for tonight. For now, I'll say only that I'm going to call an ex-FBI buddy who has the thought processes of an ex-con; I think I can get him to help us set a snare that will be undetectable by Vinson. By the time Eddie feels the pull, he'll have been caught."

"Why won't he just get on with his life, too, John? He's already assumed another identity, even if it is unraveling pretty quickly."

"There's only one reason, Tim. We each know a facet of Vinson that he realizes we can't ignore. We represent a very real threat to him, and unless we're removed, he'll always be looking over his shoulder. As a hunter, he simply can't live that way."

CHAPTER THIRTY-FIVE

As Jerry Doonan groped for the phone, he was trying to figure out how he'd knocked over the bottle of vodka by his bed. His mouth tasted like the sweat-soaked wool socks he'd worn as a kid. "What the fu...ck?" were his first slurred words as he dropped the receiver. Like a bungee jumper, it dangled insolently just out of his reach.

Doonan swallowed a groan as he struggled to sit up on the narrow, steel-framed cot. The bed and phone, and the recumbent vodka bottle were the only furnishings in what passed for his bedroom. The center wall that held his small apartment together also prevented the bed from rocking since the right rear leg, for reasons unknown, had been hacked to an inch shorter than its mates. The metal caps of several vodka bottles—always handy—were stacked and placed under the leg to minimize the remaining wobble. But it wasn't the gimpy leg of the bed that had caused Doonan to place the cot against the wall; it was his life-long habit of always sleeping with his back protected and his eyes focused on the direction from which an adversary would come.

Doonan swung his legs to the side of the bed. A gong reverberated in his head and his stomach pitched like a rubber raft in a gale. He tried to focus on the swaying receiver; he made an ill-advised grab for it, and felt gravity take him down. He landed on his chin, and the concussion sent anatomical bits and pieces in his head sliding around like so many pinballs. The resulting howl was inhuman.

"Jerry?" Foster yelled into the phone, "What the hell are you doing?"

"John?"

"Yeah, me. What the hell is going on there?"

"Nothing...I'm just, well, you know...."

"Drunk?"

"Yep, plastered, still."

"Goddamn it, Jerry. Get a grip and listen to me."

"Ya. Can do...I think."

"Jerry, I need you for a few days. Are you up to it?"

"Up to what?" Doonan grumbled.

"I'm in trouble; I need someone at my back."

"Oh boy. Doesn't sound like you, John. Not good ole Doctor Straight and Narrow.

"John?"

"Yeah?"

"Why me?"

"Because, Jerry, when you're off the sauce, there's no one better than you. You're killing yourself, and I don't want to see that happen; you're my friend. I've been stewing about this for a while, trying to decide what would motivate you to sober up and stay that way, because no one can do it for you. Well, here it is, and it's damn basic. It's my life, and Joyce's; will you do it for me?"

"John, it's not just the booze. I've been out of the game for a long time. I'm rusty, slow. I don't trust my instincts any more. I could *get* you killed, for Christ sake!"

"Jerry!" Foster shouted, "I need you now. Will you help me?"

Doonan shook his head and the rest of his body seemed to follow.

"Whine! Whine! Whine! You got five days, old friend. If I don't hear from you in the next few days, I'll start on your obit 'cause that's the next time I'll see you." Foster hung up quietly.

"Fuck you and die!" Doonan muttered to dead silence. There were tears in his eyes.

Doonan and Foster first met in D.C. during the summer of '82. Doonan was at the top of the FBI game at the time, and his name was recognized by every newbie agent. Had Foster's first encounter with Doonan not been spur-of-the-moment, he would have been intimidated as hell. As it happened, Doonan walked into his hole-in-the wall office one day, eyeballed him, and fired away. "You John Foster?"

"Most of the time," Foster muttered.

"Is now one of those times? Cause if you're Foster, I'm here to welcome you and show you around.

"Jerry Doonan. Glad to make your acquaintance," he said, shoving a gnarled paw at Foster who remained stupidly seated and speechless. "Word is you're a hell of a profiler."

"Don't believe everything you hear," Foster said, standing and accepting Doonan's hand.

"Oh, I don't! I surely don't, like my own press, for example. Bunch of bull! What say we each start with a clean slate, agree not to rest on our laurels, and give this dang case our best efforts? I figure, between us, we know a thing or two!"

Foster had been called to Washington to join a task force to deal with an apparent kidnapping and serial murder case that had law enforcement agencies from coast to coast jumping at shadows. He was surprised to learn that it was Jerry Doonan's case, and Doonan was heading the task force. Later he would learn that Doonan had asked for him specifically, and that he would be the only profiler, which surprised him even more.

Foster remained star-struck for all of thirty minutes. That was when Doonan told him to snap out of it and get focused. Foster did. He could see that someone had done a tremendous amount of groundwork to pull together the volume of information that Doonan plopped on his desk. Turned out it was Doonan who had done the job. When Foster asked, Doonan just shrugged, said it helped him order his thinking and weed out what wasn't germane to the investigation.

"Shit, son, I just plugged in all the information that was gathered by some highly skilled police officers across this fair land of ours. Anybody could have summarized it. I just did it first."

Doonan's gritty humility made him less scary. Foster began to study him with less trepidation and more curiosity. Jerry had probably been in his mid-thirties, but looked older. He was already going gray. His nose had been broken and set badly. Thus, there was no doubt he'd lost a battle or two in his career. His skin was pox-marked and looked like the surface of the moon. His cheeks and jowls were puffy, and small scars here and there suggested plastic surgery that hadn't been done just to make him beautiful.

"Ever get into it, Jerry? Can I call you Jerry?"

"Into it?"

"You know, get physical...with a perp?"

"Shit yeah, every time. I like to get real close and personal. The closer the better, but it's a dangerous way to go, and it doesn't always *go* as planned, as I'm sure you know. From what I hear, you're not just a desk jockey with a brain and a pretty face."

When Foster flushed, Doonan guffawed and cuffed him behind the neck. They had become friends that day, and had remained so for almost twenty years.

In the weeks that followed their introduction, Foster learned things about Doonan that were not part of his vaunted FBI persona. At one point, over an evening of beer and pizza, Doonan told him about the one terrifying episode that had been his trial by fire.

"Me and a fellow agent were following up on leads for a suspected gang of Nazi wannabes in 1976. Word was that they wanted to disrupt the Fourth of July celebration in Washington. You remember?"

Foster nodded, "The Bicentennial; a hell of a good time, right?"

"Wrong. I spent it in the hospital. My partner was permanently disabled, but I made it back. We were on the street for oh...six weeks, maybe, undercover. We wormed our way into the group and even planned some minor sabotage that was really just a diversion for the 'Auschwitz Plan,' their term for the mayhem that was being planned. Still, we eventually learned enough so that the plan was foiled.

"Before we could get away clean, however," Doonan stopped to make sure Foster was listening, "we were discovered. To this day, I haven't figured out how they found out—maybe we didn't shave our heads close enough—but they did. They invited us to a dinner at one of the main guys' homes, ostensibly to wrap up final details. When we arrived, there were eight, large, sausage-stuffed, Nazi-looking goons milling about this guy's living room.

I can still see Adolph's picture over the mantle. I sensed something was wrong immediately, but once inside, with this huge, storm-trooper-looking skinhead blocking our exit, I figured the only thing we could do was hit first. My partner and I had worked out a code for a preemptive attack so I figured it was time. I was carrying a World War II .45 caliber and my buddy had a Beretta. When I said the code words, we caught them completely off guard."

"What were the words?" Foster asked.

"'When shit happens, make sure you don't step in it.' When the words were out, I felt my partner jolt. You should have seen those dudes when we pulled our weapons. Shawn instinctively put his back against mine as we took aim and ordered them to put their hands up. Unfortunately, they just stood there…looked at us like we were nuts, which I s'pose we were. One of them reached for his gun, and Shawn took him out with a clean shot to the neck. Before I could get off a round, I felt something hit me in the right temple. I later found out it was a cane baton one of the bastards had thrown with uncanny accuracy. Then the melee began. Shawn squeezed off a spray of frantic shots around the room, and bodies were hunkerin' behind couches, chairs…shit, anything they could find.

"I was on the floor, dazed, but not quite out. Blood was pouring into my right eye and I couldn't hear from all the blood in my ear. Then, four of them ran at us and took Shawn to the floor. I could see him twisting, turning, kicking, and punching. He had the tip of one guy's nose in his mouth, but for only a second 'til he spit it out with a 'foop' sound I'll never forget. Funny what you remember….

"I managed to pound on one guy's throat while his cohort was choking me from behind. A quick reverse head butt got him off me and I managed to crush the other clown's larynx. It was bloody, man. I spotted my gun near the fireplace and made a grab for it when the main goon hit me with an andiron across the face.

"Whack, whack! That's what it sounded like, 'whack, whack,' just like in the comics. See here? These scars that look like sevens? That's what an andiron will do. My jaw was broken; I couldn't close my mouth, but I reached my

.45 and just unloaded. I don't remember much after that; it's funny how it doesn't stay with you. I guess you'd know the reasons for that, huh, Doc?

"Anyway, when the smoke cleared, all of the goons were dead or dying. They may have been big, but they weren't too bright. I was a bloody mess, but Shawn's back was broken; he lay there, completely still, and his pants were wet, a sure sign something was really wrong.

"Did you ever walk into a slaughterhouse, John?"

"No, can't say I have."

"That's what it looked *and smelled* like. Blood everywhere...everywhere. Bodies were laid open; body parts had fallen out. One guy's heart was still beating. I mean, I could see it. Me? I had a ruptured spleen, six broken ribs, multiple facial fractures, and damage to my windpipe. I was out for six months, but I made it back. Told them what they could do with the desk job they had arranged for me, and I've been here ever since. So, when you ask me if I've ever gotten into it? I'd have to say, 'Ya, I've been in it.' Shit, I've been covered in it.

"How about you, John?"

"Nah, nothing like that...never had to get that close. Had a couple near-misses, a graze to my thigh once, but thankfully, that's all."

"If you ever do, John, you gotta stay one step ahead. Don't let them intimidate you. They want you to think they won't act, but they will. When the hairs on your neck stand at attention, strike first, and strike without mercy."

"I'll remember, Jerry," Foster had assured him. He thought how Doonan's long-ago advice took on new meaning for him now—with Vinson out there, waiting. If nothing else, he needed to heed his old friend's words, but what he truly needed was Doonan. *Don't let me down, Jerry.*

Foster shoved his fingers through his hair in frustration. He hoped Doonan would pull himself together, but it was out of his hands. When he was fresh, he would give some thought to contingencies, but in the meantime, he needed to contact Jenny Fox. His gut told him she, too, was in danger because Vinson would see her as a lingering threat. Foster hadn't spoken to her since the night she'd helped him retrace her route with Vinson and they found where he'd stashed his car. Wait 'til he told her they'd been under the watchful eye of the fine fellows at the Twenty Sixth Precinct the whole time! He would begin the call with that tidbit, and hope he could warn her to be cautious without scaring her.

Jenny readily admitted she was scared when Foster confirmed the likelihood that Vinson was at large, and methodically covering his tracks, but she said *knowing* was better than laboring under some nebulous suspicion. She put on a brave face and quipped that the acquaintances of Gacy and Bundy must have had similar reactions when they learned of the monsters residing within those seemingly harmless individuals. Jenny agreed to talk with the supervisory staff at First Alert, and discuss Vinson with her co-workers. She also promised she would be vigilant, and readily admitted she was glad to have John's emergency cell number…just in case.

"What do you think I should do, John?" Jenny asked.

"Got any vacation time?"

"Yeah, sure. I work all the time. I haven't got a life outside this place," Jenny sighed.

"Well, then, take some time off. Get in your car and don't tell anyone where you're going. Rather, tell only someone you trust. Be anonymous and unavailable until we get this worked out. I don't believe it, but hell, Eddie may just disappear and we can all get back to our lives."

"What are you going to do?"

Foster could hear genuine concern for him in Jenny's voice. "I feel good about working with Cook, and I'm arranging for some highly skilled backup. I'm going to stick it out."

"What are you planning?"

"Planning? Nothing firm, at the moment, and you'll be better off not knowing—safer that way. Just take some time off and disappear. Have fun while you're at it. Look for that life outside the agency!"

"OK, I'll do it."

"Tomorrow, Jenny. Do it tomorrow."

"I will. You be careful."

"I will; you, too. Call me if you need to."

"I'll let you know how to reach me. You're the one I trust, John. Good-bye."

"'Bye."

CHAPTER THIRTY-SIX

Foster's plan was simple really. He and Cook were going to pick up their usual routines and act as though Vinson no longer mattered, that they were unaware of the threat he posed to them and their families. Nevertheless, Joyce would be making a spur-of-the-moment trip to see her favorite aunt in Vermont, and Cook's wife and granddaughter were taking an extended jaunt to scout out colleges before Dottie began her junior year of high school. She would be seeking early admission in the coming year, and wanted to visit several of her top-choice campuses. They would be safe until Vinson could be stopped.

Foster was hoping fervently that he'd made Doonan feel guilty as hell about his down-and-out lifestyle. He and Tim could count on being in Vinson's sights, but Doonan would be their ace in the hole since Vinson wouldn't know about Doonan. It wouldn't matter if he stalked them, or laid in wait. Either way Doonan would give them the advantage. That, and the fact that Vinson would be forced to play by their rules, even though he wouldn't know it.

He and Tim were in agreement that Foster would probably be highest on Vinson's threat list, and thus, the first to come under the gun, both literally and figuratively. As doctor and client, they had already gone head to head in therapy so there was precedent for their conflict. Foster knew that, whatever the plan to take him out, Vinson would come prepared. He had shown meticulous planning and preparation for both therapy sessions, and had always believed that he was in control. However, Foster had learned from their interactions that Vinson could be rattled, and when that happened, his instinct was to withdraw and regroup. With Cook, Foster, and, hopefully, Doonan, Vinson wouldn't be allowed to retreat. Of necessity, he would choose the time and place for the confrontation with Foster, but the outcome...that would be out of his hands. Game, Set, and Match!

Using a copy of his appointment calendar supplied by Louise, Foster prepared a meticulous itinerary for the coming two weeks. When he had dotted every "i" and crossed every "t", the only unknown remained Doonan. He was rubbing the midnight grit from his eyes when his private line rang. He snatched it quickly so Joyce wouldn't be disturbed. His caller was a chastened and sober Doonan, who informed him that he would fly into O'Hare tomorrow morning. *Hallelujah*! He would rent a car and settle into the Best Western only two blocks from Foster's office. They talked logistics briefly because it was of paramount importance that Doonan remain invisible to Vinson.

When their conversation wound down, Foster was caught off guard by a surge of emotion that accompanied the reality of Doonan's willingness to protect his back. Doonan, too, seemed to be struggling to keep a rein on the feelings elicited by his commitment to his old friend. In the way of men everywhere, they ended their call by trading insults—and all was right with their world!

Joyce wasn't exactly gracious when John explained that she would be taking "a vacation" to her Aunt Vi's in Vermont. Not that she wouldn't enjoy being out of the city and in the cool green valley near Killington, but she was never one to worry from afar, and she didn't want to leave John alone to face Vinson without her, Doonan and Cook, notwithstanding.

This wouldn't be her first enforced "furlough" in the face of danger. There had been a couple others while John was with the Bureau. She didn't like it any better now than she had then, but she realized that arguing or outright refusal would only add to John's stress.

Despite her reluctance, Joyce was packed within a few hours of learning about John's plans for her. Aunt Vi was excited about her unexpected arrival, and Joyce knew her welcome would be warm—and probably fattening. Her aunt's home was snuggled into a verdant hillside off the beaten path. City folks flocked to summertime Vermont, fleeing the cloying heat of steel and cement and asphalt. By July and August, however, the air could be heavy and still, and without air conditioning, truly oppressive. It was also the time when black flies, "no-see-ems," began their torment. Sales of "Off!" would go through the roof, and shelves were often empty. Still, Vermont at its muggy worst was 100% better than the oppressive heat of the cities. You could take a chair lift to the top of Killington and experience a ten to twenty degree drop in temperature as you looked out over some of the most beautiful rolling hills in New England. Joyce would enjoy Vermont, even though she would worry.

Joyce's flight out of O'Hare was uneventful. The sky was clear, and the forecast to Albany was favorable for an excellent view from 33,000 feet. Vi had promised to meet her at the airport, and they would have a two-hour drive to her home.

As Joyce passed through the metal detector, she turned and gave John a last look. A single tear rolled down her cheek and plopped onto her lapel. When she finally waved and disappeared around the bend of the corridor, John remained for several minutes. He felt relieved that he would not have to worry about Joyce's safety in the days to come, but the loneliness would be no great shakes either. As he walked toward the O'Hare exit, he tried to reorient himself and set his mind to the task at hand, drawing Vinson out into the open and baiting the trap.

Foster had asked Louise to block most of his appointments for regular patients to free him to work with Cook and Doonan. He would take an occasional new client, if necessary, but in some cases, he might go to half-hour appointments so that he could focus on current problems and provide necessary therapeutic support. He struggled to divide his concentration between the office and his adversary. On the third day following Joyce's departure, he was due in court to testify for a sanity commission, and then to give a noon lecture, 'The Mindset of the Pedophile' to the Illinois Social Workers' Association meeting. Either Doonan or Cook, his "bodyguards," would follow him unobtrusively whenever he left his home or office.

To himself, Foster admitted his concerns for Doonan—who had now been sober almost a week, and in all likelihood, was getting itchy for a drink. Foster had made what he hoped was a low-key inquiry about how Doonan was getting along with sobriety.

"Don't worry about me, Johnny boy. I'll be doin' all right," was the response he received from an animated Doonan.

Foster didn't know whether to be encouraged or dismayed, but decided to take his friend at his word. He had debated whether or not to give Cook a heads-up about Doonan's drinking, but decided, for the moment, to protect Jerry's privacy. He and his compadres were all experienced in maintaining discipline during high-risk situations, but it would be hard to wait.

Doonan was already at the courthouse when Foster arrived. Cook was behind him following the same route. Both men were licensed to carry weapons, and they were armed. Foster, too, carried his pistol except at the office, and, of course, in court. All three were carrying cell phones, and they were in constant contact so that their movements were coordinated and there would be no surprises.

Foster felt insulated, but not necessarily safe, as he emerged from his vehicle and started across the cavernous parking garage that served the courthouse. Vinson's disorganization made him increasingly unpredictable, and, therefore, dangerous. He could be anywhere. Despite a cloudless morning, it was unexpectedly dark on the second level. Foster shied and reached for his absent weapon; he slammed his back against a concrete support column and scanned the immediate area for the threat he could feel but not see. His heart rate double-timed while his physical reactions seemed mired in mud. Into the light of the catwalk connecting the garage to the second floor of the courthouse stepped Doonan.

Foster flushed as Doonan gave him a smirking once-over. "Kinda jumpy, ain't ya, Doctor Foster?"

"Conditioned emotional response, my friend, but yes..., I'm jumping at shadows."

Foster would be testifying in the Davis case on the sanity of the young man who was accused of a double murder. Sullivan, the attorney for the young man, had not been pleased when he received Foster's report, although the DA had been happy as all get out. Foster anticipated a rigorous cross-examination from Sullivan about his findings that Davis was capable of proceeding to trial. The sanity evaluation had shown Davis to be of average intelligence, and to be able to read and write well enough to meet judicial standards. His emotional status was fragile because he was suffering from an acute stress reaction, but he didn't meet the criteria for the McNaughton Rule. Davis's statements that he didn't remember killing the two women were suspect because he had gone on to provide a detailed description of the layout of the house where the crime occurred, although he asserted he had never been there before that night. He also provided descriptions of the women's fatal injuries that had been known only to police. Davis might have dissociated at the time of the murders, but that was not sufficient for him to meet the criteria for an insanity defense.

"How's it going, John?" Sullivan materialized at his elbow. Thankfully, John's startle response was still recovering from the garage incident so he didn't make a fool of himself.

"Fine, how are you doing?"

"Oh, all right, for an old lawyer."

"How is Davis holding up?"

"You know, John, he's better. Your recommendation that he be placed on an anti-depressant seems to have done him a world of good. Brought him right back to the world of the sane. It's a good thing I referred him for your psychological work-up."

"Yes, it is." Foster didn't have the energy to argue, and it would be fruitless, anyway. Sullivan always had to be right.

"Haven't seen you around lately. Been at your place on the beach? Boy, some people got it made. I wish I could afford to take off whenever the spirit hits me."

John just shook his head; no response was required of him, and it wouldn't be heard if he made one. Just when he thought the attorney was winding down, Sullivan said, "By the way, I'm going to withdraw the insanity plea and go for manslaughter and a reduced sentence. The ADA doesn't want it to go to trial, so it should be a slam-dunk. The kid's obviously remorseful; hell, he hasn't got much of a record."

So, it's going to be a cakewalk after all, Foster thought. He wondered whether his insights changed the course of this case, and, if so, how. He'd never know for sure. Being a psychologist wasn't like being a fireman. When a fireman does his job, he sees proof positive that he's saved a life or prevented the total destruction of property. Not so in the field of mental health; if intervention prevents an individual from harming himself or another, well, there's no proof he would have done it in any case. Just goes to show...you can't prove a negative. As in the Davis case, there would never be proof that his evaluation had contributed to justice for the two women who had been murdered.

Sullivan finally put a sock in it and strolled off down the corridor without a word of parting. Foster huffed a sigh of relief, too soon, apparently, as Bill Lane, the dapper District Attorney, rounded the corner and held out his hand while he was still a full six steps away.

"John. How are you? Fine I hope. This is going to be an easy gig for you. We'll only need you to testify that your report is the one you submitted to the Court. Sullivan's not going to fight your findings. The other doctor, Wise, I believe, found Davis to be more impaired than you did, but still not insane."

"Right, I'll stick around until you call me."

"It won't be but another half hour or so, OK? Gotta go."

A half-hour of court time typically lasted about three hours. Foster considered whether to spend his waiting time doing dictation or listening to the trial; he opted for the latter. He slipped into a seat at the rear of the courtroom and settled in to listen and learn. There was always useful information to be gained from every court proceeding, and he was fascinated by the personalities of the players.

The prosecutor, for example, was known to be a lean and mean former defense attorney who had crossed the aisle to become an Assistant DA; he had served in that capacity for more years than Foster had been in the Chicago area. He had made all the money he needed with his own law firm, and Foster wondered if he had crossed over to prosecute criminals as a penance for getting so many guilty clients off. He had a reputation for ruthlessness, and there had been rumors that he was known to bury exculpatory evidence, although no one had ever made such allegations stick.

The District Judge for the Davis trial was an unknown commodity. He had been on the bench for only two months since the special election to fill a vacancy caused by the death of his predecessor. He had run a law-and-order campaign, but the press had unearthed his liberal past and paraded it in the headlines. Still, he had been elected, and it was only after he arrived on the bench that his true colors began to fly. As Foster listened, he thought, not for the first time, that a tribunal judiciary might take individual biases and politics out of legal proceedings.

Forty-five minutes passed before Foster was called to identify his psychological report for the Court. Each side stipulated to his report in lieu of testimony, and he was released by the judge although he chose to remain in the courtroom. Dr. Wise didn't show in response to his subpoena, and after a few moments of sidebar, each side stipulated that Wise's report could also be entered into the record. Foster only shook his head. There was no point to wondering why he had had to be present when the other doctor was given a pass for his failure to appear. It couldn't be because Wise was an M.D., could it?

Lawyers wouldn't mess with physicians, even ill-prepared ones, but they never missed an opportunity to rough up a Ph.D. Maybe that's because J.D.s and M.D.s have a longer history of court involvement, while Ph.D.s are relatively new on the judicial scene. Foster recalled his earliest court appearances when it seemed that he was asked every time, "You're not a *real* doctor, are you?" The first time he was asked this question, he was stunned, and, yes, intimidated. He fell for it once, but never again. It was simply a lawyer's trick to rattle him, and he quickly learned to turn the tables. Quite honestly, he found that overworked attorneys were far more likely to be unprepared to use the information his evaluations provided, and according to his friends, he had been known to eat complacent attorneys for breakfast.

The final outcome of the Davis trial was never in question. He was found guilty of manslaughter as Sullivan had predicted and sentencing would follow in three weeks. When Davis was finally led away by the bailiff, he glanced over at Foster, and gave a nod of recognition and, perhaps, gratitude. Foster hoped that Davis could move ahead with his life, own up to his guilt, and take his punishment. He had sensed a kernel of goodness in the young man, and wondered what his life might have been like had he had the nurturing of his mother and not run afoul of a selfish and manipulative young woman. Davis had also been done a disservice by his legal counsel; the insanity plea had been inappropriate, and had only delayed the inevitable while he sat in jail, waiting and worrying.

Sullivan and Lane spoke animatedly to one another. Foster couldn't hear what was being said, but he noted that the two ducked out of the courtroom through a back entrance, Sullivan's arm around the DA's shoulders as though they were the best of buddies.

Foster sat alone in the silent courtroom. He should have gone back to the office; he'd known he should go, and because he didn't, he would cope with the frustration and sadness that reared its head periodically when he observed first-hand the flaws in the legal system and their impacts on the lives of individuals.

While he brooded, Foster felt the vibrations of his cell phone against his hip. He pulled the phone from his pocket, unlocked keys, and pushed 'Send.' "Yeah? Foster, here."

"Where the hell are you, John? We're five minutes off schedule."

"Doonan?"

"Yeah, of course, Doonan. Who else would be calling you? Vinson?"

"Sorry, Jer. Lost my concentration there for a minute. I'm moving on."

"Well, thanks, Doc. It's your damn schedule we're trying to stick to. We've been watching, and it looks like all's clear. How's the trial going?"

"Simple for me; I've been released by His Honor."

"Great. Now get your rear in gear!"

"First gear, I'm in first, Big Guy. Let Cook know I'm off, OK?"

CHAPTER THIRTY-SEVEN

It was just after 1:00 p.m. by the time Foster made his way from the Social Workers' Association meeting where he had just completed his presentation. He had given his lecture on pedophilia numerous times to many different academic and civic groups. Because it was a prurient topic, however pertinent in current times, it was usually well attended. The unknown, however, was always whether or not there would be adult abuse victims-turned-survivors among his listeners. In those instances, questions from the audience following his discourse ranged from poignant to angry. When that occurred, Foster always tried to answer questions in ways that were factual, but also personal and therapeutic.

Driving across Chi-town could be easy as hell, or sometimes, just hell. So it was this muggy afternoon. Foster found himself gridlocked as he headed west on the Eisenhower Expressway, a highway that had probably been doomed since the first shovel full of dirt was moved. Built in the late fifties to transport suburbanites to and from work and educational, cultural, and recreational opportunities with ease, the Eisenhower was not designed to accommodate the expansion of a consumer-driven nation, the growth of suburbs, and the 2.4 automobiles for every family. A single fender-bender was sufficient to bring traffic to a halt, as was probably the case while Foster cooled his heels.

The longer he sat in stalled traffic, Foster found himself feeling exposed despite his struggle to maintain his composure. He didn't know where Cook and Doonan were, and he hadn't heard from either man. If Vinson had drawn a bead on him, now would be an opportune moment to challenge Foster in a situation where he had little room to maneuver or defend himself. With that thought, Foster shuddered. His plans for luring Vinson from his cover hadn't included a daily fact of life, gridlock, and he had to admit that there were lots of other ways that Vinson might gain the upper hand because he could take advantage of the unexpected where Foster couldn't plan for it.

By way of distraction, Foster entertained himself with a humorous fantasy in which Chicagoland became Disasterland. There, in the privacy of his vehicle, Foster began a silly monologue as Disasterland's favorite radio announcer delivering the evening news to citizens who were oblivious to their dire straits, having been desensitized over the years.

"Good evening, John Foster here to give you the news of the day: There was an explosion on Navy Pier today. First reports are that people were killed, yes, but no more than the suicide bombing of a few weeks ago, lucky for that. Oh, yes, it's still raining...Day 117. That's right, 117 straight days of liquid sunshine. Fishing is good on State Street, but the water is polluted. For their safety, the public is advised to avoid displaced manhole covers in flooded areas; people are missing in several neighborhoods, reportedly sucked into voracious sewers. There have been only forty-three murders in the city so far today, a percentage increase of five percent over last week. That's good news, though, since the city's police public relations officer had projected an increase of seven percent. So, overall, it's been a good day, it seems. This is John Foster reporting."

His monologue at an end, Foster looked around to see who might have observed him talking to himself. "Highway delirium, for sure," he muttered. Traffic in his lane had moved all of fifty feet in the past five minutes; fossil fuel was burning at a rapid and wasteful rate, and feeding global warming like oxygen feeds a fire. Foster turned on the radio, only to hear that the heat index was 110 degrees. That made him feel so much better!

Rather than focusing on his discomfort, Foster began to observe his surroundings. To his right, a pony-tailed blond in her mid-thirties appeared to be listening to rap music at a volume that caused her car to shimmy and shake to the pulsing bass. She was snapping her fingers and waving her arms to the music that only she could hear. To Foster's left sat an uptight administrative type, surely an ass-kisser extraordinaire who hated the very corporate asses he kissed day in and day out. A repeated jerking of his neck suggested a high level of stress or a too-tight necktie. He was fuming and muttering to himself.

Again, Foster glanced over his right shoulder. Maybe he found her, although he felt that she found him. Their eyes did not meet, yet the connection was instantaneous and profound. Sitting alone in her auto, the woman's desperation was palpable. Her wretchedness rolled over Foster in waves, triggering his every therapeutic instinct. He judged the woman to be forty-five, but a sagging jaw line, missing teeth, and a puckered mouth made her look to be in her sixties. Her short black hair was stiff and streaked with gray. She couldn't have been more than five feet tall as her view of the expressway barely cleared the dashboard.

As Foster watched, the woman wasn't simply crying, her entire body was wracked by spasms. For a few moments, she seemed to recover, and then, without warning, she was drawn back into her nightmare. Perhaps it was physical pain, Foster reasoned, because acute pain could cause such severe emotional and physical agony. He routinely treated chronic pain patients, and experience had shown him that unrelenting pain can and will strip the individual to his or her very core, to the true self. Perhaps, in this moment, the woman traveler beside him was facing essential truths about herself that would change her life.

Foster looked ahead and then back to the suffering woman. She was quiet for the moment. No more tears, most likely she had no tears left. Suddenly, traffic began to move, and she looked wearily about her. Her eyes slid over Foster without seeing him, unaware that, for a moment of suspended time, he had shared her pain.

When Foster reached his exit, he could see the woman's vehicle three cars ahead and to his left. As he sat at a stoplight, his stomach rumbled, reminding him that he hadn't eaten since breakfast. He had a powerful rush for fast food, and realized he was responding to the siren song of the burger joint across the way. Because his itinerary didn't allow for detours, he called Doonan, "Look,

Jer. I've got a yen for a burger and fries. I'm pulling into the restaurant here at my exit; can I get you anything?

"Have you talked to Tim? How 'bout if I just load up and we have a feast?

"Yeah. OK, I'll tell Cook."

As Foster took his place in the drive-up line, it began to drizzle. "A minor rain event," the Disasterland weather anchor would report. When the line for the drive-in failed to move an inch in more than five minutes, Foster pulled over and around the vehicles in front of him and found a place to park so he could go inside to place his order. He requested a ham and cheese bagel and a cup of coffee to stave off his hunger while he waited for burgers and fries, cokes, and hot apple pies. He was served quickly and retreated to a booth near the condiments. As he munched contentedly, to his surprise, the distraught woman he had encountered while stuck in traffic on the Ike Pike, walked up to the counter and ordered a chocolate milkshake in a voice still tremulous from weeping. While she waited for her drink, the woman turned to observe the seating area, and acknowledged Foster with a nod as her eyes rested on him. Foster stared for several moments before breaking eye contact, realizing she might find his intense scrutiny rude. He continued to observe from his peripheral vision as he mulled over the likelihood that this second encounter with the woman wasn't happenstance. Foster experienced a tingling at the back of his neck. *Surely, she's not following me….*

"Order Up! Number 499, here's your to-go order, sir. Hope you enjoy your meal." The come-hither smile of a blond cashier was wasted on Foster as he accepted the bags of food and drinks. Without acknowledging her courtesy, he turned and scanned the table area, exits, and the parking lot. The woman appeared to have left. Paranoia or caution, take your pick, he didn't believe in coincidences, and he was unnerved.

As was his custom when faced with unlikely situations, Foster reverted to his scientific training. By suspending judgment while cycling though a series of questions and probable responses, he was able to consider an issue from multiple angles. In the past, such methods had enabled him to break the seemingly unbreakable FBI case or unravel the thought processes of a troubled patient. In this instance, however, the circumstances were personal. He was the one involved, and thus, it was harder to be objective, to suspend judgment and think logically because emotions and fear, yes, fear, clouded his perspective.... Ergo, it was easier to get off on a wrong path. In the absence of any obvious theme or connecting events, he asked himself, "How many random occurrences does it take to establish a pattern?" His response: For the paranoid personality, the answer is "only one." For the emotionally healthy individual, the answer depends on how personal it gets.

When he returned to his car, Foster decided it would be prudent to check in with Cook.

"Cook, here. Is that you, John?"

"Is everything still good?"

"Perfect. How about you."

"OK, I guess. I just had a scare. I ran into an apparently distraught woman...twice. I hate random encounters, and I don't believe in coincidence."

"It's OK from my perspective. I just spoke with Doonan. He knows your location, and there's no evidence of Vinson."

"That helps. Thanks. All right, I'm moving. You've got my next location?"

"Like, duh, as Dottie would say," Cook wisecracked. "You've got the food. Should take you less than five to deliver it. I'll meet you at the office. How much can we eat before Doonan joins us?"

Foster was reassured by Cooks gruff and irreverent humor. He made it to his office through light traffic and reached the back door with the sacks of starch and fat just as Louise was leaving to drop mail in the box in time for the 3:15 pickup. She usually combined this task with a brisk walk around the block. Today, however, there would be no walk because the drizzle had, in fact, become a rain event.

"I'll be right back, Dr. John."

"Right. I like your umbrella! Snazzy!"

Louise held a huge psychedelic umbrella that reminded Foster of the tie-dyed fad of the sixties. "Thanks. Picked it up last weekend at a festival in Brookfield."

"Did you go to the zoo?"

"No, we didn't have time."

"We?"

"Yeah, my new boyfriend, Kenny."

"When did this happen?"

"Last weekend," Louise replied, smiling.

"You met at the festival?"

"Of course," Louise said, as though it was obvious.

"That's great! See you when you get back."

"Your three o'clock confirmed and will be here any minute."

The office phone began to ring, and Foster leaned over Louise's desk to answer it,

"Dr. Foster. Can I help you?" He glanced at caller ID which read, 'Out of Area.' "Dr. Foster," he repeated, when there was no response other than the sound of breathing. "Hello?" Still no response.

Years ago, in the days before Caller ID, Foster had had one memorable harassing phone call against which he measured all others. The phone rang in the middle of the night. When he picked up the receiver, he was still half-asleep, but managed a gravelly "Hello?" He heard only silence, and then, breathing. It angered him that someone would seek pleasure at his expense. Being the young, hotshot psychologist he thought he was, he decided to play the spoilsport. He returned the caller's breathing with his own, only louder. His competitive spirit was engaged.

Foster could hear the caller changing position. "Getting agitated," he thought as the contest continued. Both breathers picked up the pace. Each exhalation was met with one more powerful. As he approached hyperventilation, Foster stopped abruptly, and there followed a deafening silence. Then, over the line, he heard an adolescent female's voice, "Say something, you jerk!"

To his continued silence, Foster finally heard a muttered, "Son of a bitch," and the slamming down of a receiver.

"Gotcha!" Foster had whispered and pulled Joyce to him with a sigh.

Now, Foster was playing the game of silence again with his out-of-area caller. His first thought was that it could be Vinson, a Vinson who was losing patience.

"Is that you, Eddie?" he thought, or had he said it aloud?

Foster could hear someone entering the clinic as the caller hung up. He was alone. His stomach was taking on a life of its own. "Butterflies" was not an adequate description; vultures gnawing away was more like it!

"Hello? Is anyone here?" a tremulous voice called from the back door of his office.

Strange! "I'll be right there." Foster called. *Could the caller have been Vinson? Gotta call Cook and Doonan.*

Foster reached for his cell phone and pressed 'redial.'

Cook growled, "Yeah? What's up, Doc?"

"Look, Tim. It's probably nothing, but I just had a hang-up call. Breathing. I had a feeling it might be Vinson, but it was an 'out-of-area' call, so I don't know."

"Hit star six-nine, John."

"Yeah, right. I forgot. Look, I'll hang up and try it. If I get something, I'll call you right back. Let Doonan know."

"Right-o," Cook said tersely.

Foster, spooked now, punched the star-six-nine buttons on Louise's desk phone with a trembling forefinger. A polite message stated that the Call Return feature had been blocked by the caller.

"You can't stay one step ahead all the time, Vinson," Foster muttered as he redialed Cook. "No luck, Tim. Call back was blocked."

"No sweat, buddy, we're on you. I called Doonan. We're almost there."

"Thanks, Tim."

"Don't worry if you don't see us right away. We'll be watching and circling for a few minutes, just in case."

"OK, but swing by the back door, and Louise will bring your food to you. You must be hungry! Now all I have to do is pull my act together for my next client."

"Who is it?"

"I don't know, actually, a new patient."

"Are you packing, John?"

"Oh, yeah. I've got it strapped to my calf. I figured it wouldn't be mentally healthy to wear a shoulder holster while I deliver mental health messages."

Cook cracked up! "That's it! Keep your sense of humor, John. You're going to need it before all is said and done."

Bringing a loaded weapon into a therapy session was usually a non sequitur, and Foster had never done so before now. The same could not be said of his clients, and he suspected more patients had been armed than he cared to think about.

Foster remembered one long-ago client, in particular, a distraught woman whose husband left her, and she wasn't coping well with the loss. Foster had believed they were making progress, and that the woman was adjusting satisfactorily. On the morning of her third appointment, however, he felt less sure. The woman seated herself beside his desk, but didn't speak for the first few minutes. He, too, sat quietly, waiting for her to initiate conversation.

The woman positioned a black leather handbag on her lap, which she held in place with her elbows as she wrung her hands. Suddenly, she launched into a description of a phone call the previous night from her estranged husband. He had advised that she would soon be receiving legal documents because he was moving forward with divorce so he could marry her childhood best friend. Intense sobbing distorted the woman's face and speech so that Foster could barely understand her. There was no confusion about how she felt, however, and some of her words were clearly understood. For example, "I can't go on…I'm afraid…I want to kill myself."

As she spoke, Foster watched the woman unzip the bag she carried and reach slowly inside. He assumed that she was searching for tissues, although there was a Kleenex box on the corner of his desk. What happened next was as clear to him now as the moment it happened.

She withdrew her right hand, and in it, she was holding a walnut-handled .357 magnum.

Before Foster could say anything, she lifted the pistol. Time froze. Foster's thoughts raced through options and possible outcomes, all catastrophic.

"Dr. John," she whimpered, "would you please take this gun and keep it for me? I'm afraid I might hurt myself." Slowly, she placed the gun on his desk and slid it toward him.

Light-headed, Foster picked up the weapon and removed the bullets with a calm he did not feel. "Thank you so much. I just don't trust myself right now."

"Thank you for trusting me. I will lock the gun in my office safe until it's time to return it to you,"

"Live and learn," Foster thought as he turned his attention from past to present, and the needs of his next patient.

CHAPTER THIRTY-EIGHT

Foster checked the day's schedule before walking into the waiting room where an elderly man sat, head down, one hand on an aluminum walker. He was coughing so hard that his hand slipped from the center support bar. He wore flesh-colored elastic gloves, probably to control arthritic pain. He looked up at Foster's greeting.

"Hello, I'm John Foster. You are Don Devines?"

"Yes, that's me," the old man replied, his soft, raspy voice that of a long-time smoker. "Don I. Devines, actually. But, you can call me Devine."

Foster supposed that the man was making a joke to break the ice, and his smile seemed to communicate that, indeed, such was the case.

"And I would suppose that your favorite sweet is Divinity?"

Mr. Divine huffed and cleared his throat.

"All right. Please come back. You need some help?"

"No, I can make it OK." There was a hint of the south in the old gent's voice.

Foster turned and walked slowly to his office doorway so that he didn't rush Mr. Devines. His steps were baby steps, and the soles of his brogans made a "scrape and swish" sound on the tightly-woven carpet as he moved the walker forward then let his feet catch up. Devines leaned heavily on the walker, and his arms trembled as they took his upper body weight. He grunted with each exertion.

"I'm sorry, Doctor, for taking so long."

"No problem, we're in no hurry," Foster assured. He could see Louise coming into the courtyard and heard the clinic door open.

Mr. Devines turned to his left as Louise entered. "Hello, young lady," he grinned and his eyes glinted merrily. He was pale, but not sickly looking. He had a full gray beard that obscured many of his facial features. His salt and pepper hair was long and flowing, and darker than his beard. Watery gray eyes were evident despite thick lenses in bold, black frames. His teeth were stained from smoking, or, perhaps, from medication. His dress was eccentric and tattered, and Foster suspected that he shopped at a thrift store. It was difficult to estimate his height because his knees were bent and his back, twisted. There could be no doubt that every courageous step caused him intense pain. *Talk about true grit.*

Standing in his office doorway, Foster's cell phone vibrated. It was Joyce. He stepped into his office. "Hey, hon. What's up?"

"John? Are you OK?" Joyce had tried to reach him several times already, but the phone had been busy or she had gotten voice mail.

"Yeah, Joyce, I'm fine, but about to start a session with a new client. Can I call you back in an hour or so?"

"I understand; it's OK," Joyce murmured, "I love you."

"Me, too."

As Foster disconnected, Mr. Devines was finally entering his office. "My wife," he said, snapping the phone shut.

"Ah…you know, it's hard to move through pain, Doctor Foster. It's like a dream where I'm stuck in molasses and the bad guys are coming on fast. The harder I try to escape, the more the sticky stuff clings. I get mad, but the more angry I become, the greater the hold on me. That's pain, my son. That's pain." He lowered himself slowly into the chair beside Foster's desk. He was panting from the exertion.

Foster sat, elbows on his desk, and nodded soberly as he looked over steepled fingers. "How can I help you, Mr. Devines?"

"I don't know if you can help me. I've never been to your kind of doctor before.

"I've been so miserable…. Not just because of what you can see, but because of what I'm thinking and feeling."

"Tell me," Foster said gently.

"First, I'd like to ask a few questions about you. Would that be OK? I got your name from the telephone book."

"Of course, you can ask anything that will help you decide if you're in the right place." Foster settled back into his chair and relaxed. Such Q&A wasn't unusual, and he found that it often accelerated the development of rapport, and consequently, therapeutic progress.

"Are you a Christian, Doctor?" Mr. Devines asked. "I mean, do you believe that Jesus Christ is our Lord and Savior?"

"Mr. Devines, I am a Protestant, raised in a strong Lutheran family. I do not, however, use a faith-based orientation in my psychotherapy as some counselors do. I am a behavioral scientist, and I select my therapeutic methods based on what I believe will provide my clients with the best possible outcome for them during a reasonable treatment time." Foster paused to give Mr. Devines time to assimilate his answer. "Is there anything else you would like to know about me?"

"No, Doc. That'll do. You seem pretty forthright to me. Don't pull many punches, do you?"

"No," Foster smiled. "In most cases, I try not to. Therapy is no place for dissembling and half-truths. I try to give my clients benefit of the doubt and work with them accordingly. Some might consider that kind of trust a professional weakness, but I find that, in the long run, it affords me knowledge about the individual that allows me to guide them to a resolution of their difficulty. I'm not suspicious by nature, so this feels comfortable for me, as well." He picked up his pen and aligned his legal pad. "Now, Mr. Devines, what brings you here?"

Foster wondered idly whether Louise had checked to see if Mr. Devines had insurance coverage, not that it mattered, because he had accepted him as a patient. "When did you call for your appointment, Mr. Devines?"

"Oh, only yesterday," he said, coughing through his response. "I couldn't believe that you could see me so quickly, you having such a reputation and all, but I'm glad."

That's odd; he said he picked my name from the telephone book....

"Well, I've been out of town for a bit so my schedule was more open than usual. As for my reputation, you didn't get that from the Yellow Pages, Mr. Devines."

"No. I asked around. You come highly recommended.... What's that?" Devines had focused above and behind Foster's head.

"What?"

"That picture behind you."

Foster didn't need to look. It, too, was a frequent question when clients wanted to avoid difficult subject matter. "It's dolphins surfing in the bow waves of a large ship. Dolphins are playful that way."

"Playful. That's good. Playful, like taking a free ride, I guess."

"That assumes motive, or rather, intent. Mr. Devines."

"Of course, no one can know what's in the mind of the dolphin."

"What's your intent, Mr. Devines? Why did you call for an appointment?"

With a shrug of his bowed shoulders, Mr. Devines launched into a diatribe of festering grievances, betrayals, and losses that went back some twenty years. It was as though a boil had been lanced and the poison spewed forth. His wife was the offending party. As he rambled, Mr. Devines gestured dramatically. His voice was tremulous, sometimes loud and, sometimes, barely above a whisper.

"You said she ran off with your family doctor?"

"Yeah, Dr. Ertsof, the bastard! Not a name I'm apt to forget."

"*Your* doctor?" Foster repeated.

"You know, at first I thought it was a joke. I read her *Dear John* letter and said to myself, 'Real good, Yvonne. Way to go!' but then I realized that it was no joke."

From across his desk, Foster had encountered dozens of individuals who couldn't let go. It seemed that their life's purpose was to live and relive an injustice. In so doing, they justified their own hurt and anger, while also losing quality of life, personal growth, and any sense of satisfaction. "It's a paradox," Foster said, shaking his head.

"A what?"

"A paradox, Mr. Devines. The more you hold on to your wife's injustice, the more you lose over time."

"Are you saying I've caused my own misery?"

"Well, not exactly, but you've had a part in the process because you haven't been able to let go and move on."

"Uh, huh." Devines' expression suggested considerable skepticism. He shifted uncomfortably to his right buttock and winced. "Damn, but that hurts," he said.

"How did you get hurt, Mr. Devines?"

Devines looked at Foster's office window and cleared his throat. He made a "hub, hub, hub," sound that seemed to do the trick. "I fell; well...not fell...actually, I jumped. Well, actually I walked."

"You walked?"

"Uh, huh. After the bitch's letter sunk in, I went to the roof of our apartment building and walked right off. I didn't stop at the edge. I just kept walking. I fell three stories, about thirty-three feet they told me later.

"I beat the odds, you know."

"Yes, I'd say you did."

"Statistics indicate that for falls from twenty feet, fifty percent are fatal. I survived a thirty-three foot fall.

"Have you heard that when you fall, time slows down?"

Foster nodded.

"Well, that's total bullshit. The fall was over before I realized what I had done. I landed on my feet, but, of course, one leg snapped at the knee, and both hips fractured. Wham, I was flat on my back. I also fractured my back at L3-4. They did all the repairs they could, miraculous work really, but as you see, it wasn't enough. I endured a full body cast for about nine months."

"Nine months would seem like..."

"What? What were you going to say?" Devines snapped. He was becoming agitated.

"I was about to say that nine months can seem like a lifetime," Foster grimaced.

"I'm sorry, Doctor Foster. I didn't mean to be abrupt. It's just that when I think about that rat-bastard who stole my wife, I lose my composure."

"That is certainly understandable, given your circumstances," Foster agreed.

"I've tried to get it out of my head, but I just can't let it go. I've never been to a psychologist before, so I don't know what to expect from you; still it's so hard to talk about...."

"I think I understand. Take your time, and when you're ready, I'll just listen. Why don't you get it over with...get it all out."

"Sure," Devines stated, but several minutes passed in silence before he continued. "I've rehearsed it in my mind a thousand times, but never said it aloud to another soul. While Yvonne and the good physician were getting their jollies, I was laid up in that stinking hospital. I was helpless at a time when revenge was all I could think about. I wanted to make them suffer, maybe even kill them. I don't know.

"The nurses kept me abreast, each...just a joke my boy. They kept me up on what was happening, which only made it worse. I suppose they felt sorry for me. After all, I had tried to end my pitiful life over a deceitful woman. Other women can find that attractive, would you believe it?"

"Certainly. In my career, I've come to believe that all things are possible. If you can imagine it, it can happen."

"That's right, Doc! Hey, you're not so bad. Very smart, it seems to me."

"Please continue, Mr. Devines."

"OK. Go on...yes. Put it behind me."

Foster waited while Devines seemed to collect himself. A glance at the clock, a simple gold and silver disc, told him it was 3:17. *We're moving much too fast.* "One moment, Mr. Devines. I think we should take a break before we move on. Can I offer you some water...coffee or tea, some Earl Grey?"

"Sure, my boy. I've got to pee, anyway." He rose slowly and tottered across the floor; the accompanying groans and grunts would have been comical, but Foster's experience with chronic pain patients told him it was unlikely that Devines was exaggerating his distress.

Foster gazed out his office window while he waited for Mr. Devines' return. He was uneasy, still preoccupied with the unknown phone caller. He had requested that Louise bring two cups of tea, and they appeared on his desk so quickly that he suspected she had been brewing a pot for herself.

"No sweat," he said to himself, "Doonan and Cook are out there. I'll be alright."

"What's that, Doc? I'll be all right, you said?"

"Yes, you will be all right, Mr. Devines, as soon as we get a handle on your fixation with the past."

"Fixation, huh? Is that what I have? A fixation? If it's only a fixation, then by God, you can fix it, eh? How does one 'fix' a fixation?" he asked sarcastically.

Foster bit down hard on his back teeth. Devines might look like a kindly old gentleman, but he had a mouth on him, and a mean streak. His little asides were moving from humorous to passive-aggressive. He had only been in the office about twenty-five minutes, but Foster would gladly have ended the session. He suspected that Devines might be shopping for a therapist who would see things his way, and Foster knew that he was not going to be that individual. Mr. Devines did not want to make changes; he was seeking a Band-Aid and some sympathy.

As a therapist, Foster was well aware that he could not meet the needs of all clients, all of the time. A good therapeutic "fit" was essential for counseling to be effective, and he had no difficulty referring a client to another provider if rapport did not emerge by the end of the first or second session.

One of the random statistics that rolled around in his brain was that one of every fifty clients or so could be a potential victim of their therapist were it not for intensive professional training and personal discipline. Even then, sometimes, clients were victimized. Borderline Personalities were near the top of the list of possible victims. These individuals, in particular, were at the mercy of their distorted perceptions of the world, and yet, they sought to preserve these distortions in the face of therapeutic guidance. It was another of those clinical paradoxes that ensured he would always have work.

"Well, Mr. Devines, to 'fix' a fixation, as you put it, one first must break it. You can't fix something that isn't broken, now can you?"

Foster's answer was apparently unexpected, given Mr. Devines' look of surprise. He also seemed aware that Foster was subtly setting limits. "You are a smart fellow, aren't you, Doctor?"

"Smart enough, Don, for the moment. Tell me why you seem so angry."

"I'm not angry; I'm hostile. I hate everyone. Even you, and we've only just met."

"Well, that does bring us back to why you came here today, doesn't it? Your hostility and how it consumes you?"

"Yes, yes, it does...eat me up, I mean. Somehow, though, it feels like the right thing for me. When my wife left, it was like I left, too. She left; I'm gone. Does that make sense, Doc?"

"Possibly."

"Maybe?"

"Maybe you put too much of yourself into the relationship."

"Too much? How much should I have put into a marriage that was to last forever?"

There it is again, the challenge. Put the shrink on the defensive, and you can remain as you are—miserable.

"A safe amount, like a good investment portfolio, so that if the relationship ends, you still have some of yourself left."

"You've never lost anyone, have you?" Devines queried, his eyes narrowing and his chin coming up pugnaciously.

"Look, Mr. Devines. I don't think this is working out."

"What?"

"This line of counseling. I think we should consider a different approach."

"And that would be...?"

"I have a colleague who specializes in medication that moderates the problems you've described."

"Oh?"

"It's seems that you might be suffering a chronic, low-grade depression. It's called dysthymia, technically. I recommend that before we even begin to process these issues through counseling, you try a regimen of antidepressant medication."

"Doctor Foster?"

"Yes?"

"You haven't taken a history yet."

"No, but...." His ears were suddenly warm.

"I've been on all of them. Medications don't help. You name them...I've taken 'em. Go ahead, name them."

"That won't be necessary, Mr. Devines.

"Look, let's schedule an appointment for a comprehensive social and medical history. Once I have the full history, I'll be prepared to make recommendations that should afford you some relief. However, I'd also like you to reconsider the medication. There are several newer meds; any one of them might be effective for you."

"No, I don't think so. I don't feel comfortable with you, John. It's like you have something on your mind...like I'm not the focus for you. There's something else that's more important than me, and you're not giving me your full attention."

"You are right, Mr. Devines. I sincerely apologize. I do have something on my mind, and obviously, I am not at my best."

"Hey, no sweat, Doc. I'm never in my groove. I'll be back, I suppose. You're a good conversationalist." Just then, Devines went into a coughing frenzy. As the spasms shook him, his face and ears turned from pale to red to reddish-blue.

Foster sat quietly while Devines struggled to regain his composure. "It's hard to see you struggling this way."

"I'll be OK. I'm used to it. Gotta go."

"Right," Foster said, rising. "I'll walk you out."

"No, don't bother.

"Where do I make another appointment?"

"Just ask...."

"Louise?"

"Yes, Louise."

Foster was surprised that Devines knew Louise's name, but said nothing since it was possible she told him her name when he made his appointment. He could hear the shuffling of an uneven gait down his hallway for a good thirty seconds. He turned to look at his clock and shrugged.

Only forty minutes had passed since the phone call that had rattled him to such an extent that a new patient had become cognizant of his distraction.

"Don't lose your nerve," Foster chided himself as he made his way to the front office. Louise was sitting there, pale and still.

"Something wrong, kid?" Foster asked. "Looks like you've seen a ghost!"

Louise dropped her eyes and didn't reply. When she looked up, she said, "It was him."

"Him? Who him?"

"You know…Vinson."

"Vinson? Where? Where did you see Vinson?"

"Devines. Vinson is Mr. Devines."

"Come on, Louise, he was a sad, but argumentative, old man. Not Vinson."

"Dr. John, he said almost the same thing to me that Mr. Vinson said, and in the same voice. This time he said, 'Hope you've *had* a good life,' and then he winked at me and walked out. He left that behind." She pointed to the abandoned walker.

"Damn! Damn! Damn!" Foster bolted for his office and was speaking before the speed dial had completed its connection. "Doonan, Cook where are you?"

"Wha…?" Cook sounded befuddled.

"Tim, he was here."

"Who? You've got to be...? Vinson?"

"Of course, Vinson."

"Are you positive?"

"Louise recognized him. I sat across the damn desk from him for thirty minutes and never tumbled. How stupid! So much for my powers of observation."

"How would Louise recognize him, John? Louise, and not you? "

"When Vinson came for his first appointment, Tim, he said something that freaked Louise out. He used almost the very same words to her again as he was leaving today. He was telling her blatantly that he was just shovin' our noses in it; worse, today I think he threatened her."

"Oh, man. That's just great," Cook said, clenching his fists 'til his knuckles blanched. "He came at you from the blind side. I thought the plan to snare him was flawless. How did he know?"

"Dammit! Damn him, he sees me as gullible and he's using it…and laughing at me.

"Cool it, guy. We're just outside. We're coming in." Within seconds, Cook and Doonan were walking through the clinic's back door. Cook was dressed in camouflage fatigues, and Doonan had on sloppy jeans and a sweat-shirt that was living up to its name. Foster could smell the sweet wash of vodka.

"Doonan, you been hitting the bottle?"

"No, man, just one hit. Not a lot of hits." Doonan dropped to the nearest chair in the waiting room while Cook paced back and forth.

"Shit," Cook said breaking the silence; then he looked guiltily at Louise.

"I'm sorry, Louise, but this is bad, real bad. Caught with our pants snarled around our knees, all three of us."

"Two over-the-hill Feebies and a washed-out Marine!" Doonan muttered.

Louise watched as the three men sat there, each looking at the others, nothing to say.

Cook was reminded of the helplessness that followed Sonya's death at Vinson's hand. Doonan was calculating the number of minutes 'til he could take a belt of vodka from the flask in his pocket. Foster's thoughts were…a total mind-blank. He felt violated, and if Louise was correct, and he could see now that she was, Vinson had evaded all their careful plans, looked him in the eye, challenged him, insulted him, and walked away clean. Vinson could have taken him out easy, any way he chose. For what-ever reason or reasons, he had not, but the gauntlet had been thrown, and the sting of shame on Foster's cheeks would have been no more disconcerting had it resulted from the slap of a leather glove.

As Foster began to marshal his wits and pull himself together, he realized that, for Vinson, this afternoon's cha-rade had been an appetizer, an overture or a prologue, foreplay...call it what you will, his intent had been to define the game, delineate the playing field, and taunt his opponent. Score one for the lion; the gladiator never saw his opponent enter the arena. The unanswered question: Who would initiate the next encounter?

"Tim?"

"Yeah, John?"

"This is bad, true, but surely we've learned something about Vinson."

"Like what?"

"I don't know, but it must be right here in front of us. We just don't see it."

"What did he look like?" Doonan asked, finally entering the conversation.

"Just a sick old man. The alterations to his appearance were first rate, professional quality. I did not recognize him; even when he began to toy with me, it didn't register. He put me on the defensive from the get-go, and I saw only what he wanted me to see. As a member of my profession, I should be drawn and quartered."

"Stow it, Doc; you're not the only one flummoxed by his actions. Vinson got by all of us."

"Tell us more about his appearance."

"Much of his complexion was concealed by facial hair. His clothes were mismatched, tattered, but clean, like the elderly who live alone. He wore thick glasses; now I know why. He also wore heavy elastic gloves, ostensibly because of severe arthritis pain, but most assuredly it was to hide his younger skin and muscle tone. His limp was realistic; his balance adjusted for the awkward locomotion." Foster seemed to run down; he sat staring at his own hands. He responded with a nod when Louise said goodnight and left by the back door. Cook, however, jumped up and watched until Louise was safely locked in her car and had pulled out into the flow of evening traffic.

"So...should we abandon our strategy and go looking for Vinson?" Cook floated the question they were all considering.

The trio looked at one another, and, in unison, their response was a resounding, "No."

As they continued to talk, collectively they came to the conclusion that Vinson was trying to flush them out in the open, much as they had intended to do to him. By drawing them into his territory, he would seize control.

"Cagey bastard," Cook grumbled.

Doonan wondered aloud whether it might not be a good time to call in the authorities.

"Why should they have all the fun, Jerry?" Cook asked, eyeing the pewter flask Doonan liberated from his pocket.

"Care for a hit, old soap?"

"Thanks, I don't mind," said Cook, taking three long draughts before returning the flask to Doonan who took another hit. His face lit up like a jack o'lantern.

"Damn, that's good."

Foster grabbed for the flask, took a solid hit himself, and returned it to Doonan without a fuss. He went to the doors and checked that they were locked. "Stay the course? Is that what I'm hearing?"

"Right," said Doonan.

"Yeah," said Cook.

"OK, then. Let's tighten up our act. Clearly there isn't any safe haven, not if Vinson can walk in my front door."

A tap on the glass of the front door showed Louise standing there.

"Well damn," muttered Foster, going to let her in. "Did you forget something?"

"Nuh-huh. Came back to ask why you didn't offer me a nip. Besides...I need to know what I can do to help." She grinned as all three men were shaking their heads like bobble-head dolls. "Where would you be without me this afternoon? Vinson got past all of you, but not past me.

"What am I supposed to do? Sit here knitting socks for all of you? Vinson has been toying with me, too; at least I think he's been toying with me. I wouldn't say he has threatened me 'though he surely gives me the creeps. I've been thinking I'd do good as the one person who knows where you three are at all times, here at the command center so to speak; I can facilitate communication and movements even if I'm not *in command*."

Foster grinned and rolled his eyes at Cook and Doonan. "So much for thinking I was sheltering her from the realities of life! OK, Kid, you're in. Want a hit?"

Doonan passed the flask to Louise who drained it. Despite their careful scrutiny, not one of the men saw her eyes water!

"I didn't know you had it in you! Maybe it's time to rethink your job description," Foster put one arm around Louise's shoulders drawing her to him.

"I didn't either, Dr. John." she ducked gracefully and giggled, sounding like the young woman he knew her to be.

"All right, here it is, folks. Vinson is playing us...me, probably just me, but he'll hurt anyone he has to, to get to me. We know he's killed at least four, perhaps, as many as seven times already; if we are correct, three of the seven deaths appear to have resulted from a chance encounter. The four planned deaths we're sure of are the bartender, the woman found in the dumpster, his boss at the ambulance service where he moonlighted, and, of course, Sonya. If we use Vinson's logic for killing his employer, then it's conceivable that Louise could be at risk, as well as his partner, Jenny, at First Alert.

"At my urging, Jenny has taken a vacation to places unknown, and to be honest, Louise, I think you should do the same. Yes, you would be valuable here keeping us all straight and in touch, but I couldn't live with myself if something were to happen to you."

Cook shuffled his feet and Doonan cleared his throat, looking at Cook, who nodded, then at John. "We agree with you, John. Vinson has shown how danged unpredictable he can be, and he has shown a familiarity toward Louise that, to my mind at least, says she is at risk.

"That's it, then. Louise, you have to go. Get lost, with pay."

"Lost?"

"Yeah, lost! Would you like to join Joyce in Vermont?"

"But...."

"No buts! She and Vi would love to have you, and if you play your cards right, you can be pampered and fussed over 'til you can't take it another minute!"

When he could see a refusal was imminent, John dropped his voice and drew Louise to him in a hug. "Please?" he said quietly. "I'm going to need you when this is all over. I won't be able to stay focused if I'm worrying about you."

Louise's shoulders dropped in resignation, and she nodded. "I'll be all right, Kiddo. Go have some down-time with my other two girls. I suspect it'll cost me another raise for you, but they'll teach you things about shopping you never dreamed of!"

"'Scuse me, guys, I'm going to walk Louise back to her car.

"Arrange a flight for yourself as early as possible tomorrow. Put it on the office expense card, and travel under your sister's name. Don't tell anyone where you're going, even your new boyfriend. Is there anyone in your new apartment building who might ask questions or be alarmed by your absence? No? If someone should ask, make up a creative lie. Keep your cell phone with you and keep it charged while you're traveling. Would you feel better if Cook or Doonan went with you to the airport?"

"You're babbling, Dr. John. I'll be fine. You will call Joyce to tell her I'm coming? Tell her I'll be on the Albany flight that arrives closest to noon. I think I can work that, and if I run into problems, I'll call her cell."

"Good deal, Kiddo; stay aware and be safe, OK?" John winked and locked her door as he closed her in. He waved as she merged into traffic.

Cook pounced as soon as John came through the door. "OK, Doc, what about us?"

"No sweat, guys. We're not changing a thing. He's trying to make us doubt ourselves and play into his hands. He's doing a fine job of it, but we won't let it happen. We'll play dumb, do a NIGYSOB."

"A what?"

"NIGYSOB. Yeah," Foster said confidently, "It's an old psychology acronym, police and military too, I think; it stands for 'Now I Got You, Son Of a Bitch.'

"When I was at the state hospital, I found that psychosis and playing word games, using acronyms or anagrams, were frequent correlates. I had a paranoid schizophrenic patient once who named his self-made church, doGmA. He believed he was God, and doGmA backward was 'AmGod.' See?"

"Right. So, what did psycho Vinson call himself today?" Cook asked.

Foster was momentarily stunned by the question, "Uh, it was Don I. Devines. He was very specific, said it more than once, too."

"Don I. Devines, huh?" Doonan grabbed a pencil. Spelling the name aloud, he wrote the letters in a random order, then began reordering them and crossing letters out as he used them. "Well...shit, man. What do you know! E-d-d-i-e V-i-n-s-o-n."

"Ok, take it a step further. Devines, er uh, Vinson, complained repeatedly about a doctor who, in his words, robbed him of his life," Foster said pensively.

"And the doctor's name?" Doonan asked.

"Ertsof."

"E-r-t-s-o-f?"

"Yeah, that's the way I spelled it anyway."

"Too easy, Doc. It's not even a challenge. Ertsof. Ertsof is Foster, Doc. He's accused you of robbing him of life."

Even though they'd already established that Devines was Vinson, this new information caused the blood to drain from Foster's brain; his vision narrowed. Reflexively, he drew a deep breath, and his vision cleared.

"Vinson may be a bastard and a cold-blooded killer, but he's got a brain and he's not afraid to use it." Doonan scratched the bristles on his chin as he examined the new pieces of the puzzle that was Eddie Vinson.

"He's got a sense of humor, too, macabre though it may be," Cook put in.

Foster and Doonan looked at Cook as if he'd lost some marbles; then they began to laugh. Doonan's bulk slid bonelessly down the wall to the floor, and still he laughed. Cook's belly laughs were punctuated by hiccups, and he grasped his middle as though losing the battle to hold himself together. Foster's laughter rolled out of him, as did the tears. Just when he thought he was gaining control, Doonan's snort or Cook's hiccups would set him off again.

"You know what the good...doctor says," Foster whooped. "Laughter is...the very... best...medicine! I pronounce us...all...cured!"

Foster was the first to wind down while Doonan and Cook continued to yuck it up. Cook had had one too many sips from the flask, and Doonan, probably, one too few. As if on cue, they both looked at John, and their laughter ceased as suddenly as it had begun.

"OK, then, to reiterate," Doonan huffed. "We stick to our plan. We play dumb; we don't see or hear or speak the evil that is Eddie Vinson. He should be expecting us to freak out, change our plans, scatter our resources, and mount some dumb retaliation. We won't; it'll be hard to wait, but we must let him come to us again."

"Nigysob, John?" Cook asked.

"Yeah. Now I gotcha, ya sonuva bitch!"

"Amen!" added Doonan solemnly, and if you didn't look carefully, you would have missed the laughter lurking in his eyes.

CHAPTER THIRTY-NINE

Creating a new identity is not difficult, but it is a pain in the ass. Vinson didn't like this part of the game; to obtain the necessary documents required paper pushing, nothing more. It was boring and annoying, but essential. It took time away from what he did best, which was to fuck with people. Nevertheless, if he couldn't walk away, if he got caught, it would be because he had been careless. So, he planned and paid attention to details.

Vinson had over forty thousand dollars in cash stashed in hidey-holes throughout the city. Cans of money and the pieces of jewelry he'd stolen from dead accident victims, a ring here, a bracelet there. He wasn't greedy. Once, he'd found a wad of hundreds wrapped in plain brown paper in a man's backpack. He'd guessed the man, his head split wide open, had been a gambler or, worse, a mobster. Ordinary Joes didn't carry around sixty two hundred dollars. It had been his biggest cash take. He also found a large diamond ring on the amputated hand of an elderly woman who died at the scene. Because police seldom do extensive searches for valuables amidst the gore of accident scenes, Vinson was never suspected. Now, the cash and jewelry he had acquired over time would finance his next metamorphosis.

The Don Devines ruse had been a lark! Maybe Foster wasn't so smart after all. The dimwit never caught on, but his saucy little secretary would educate the good doctor! Vinson had donned a messy beard, shopped at a thrift store for his clothes, shoes, glasses and wig, and the battered walker. He put marbles in his shoe; he'd seen that on late-night television, and it hurt like hell. The limp had been very real! Vinson preferred "low-tech" wherever possible. It was simpler that way. Besides, people saw what they expected to see. Foster had been a perfect example; despite his professional training and years of experience, the bleeding heart doctor had seen only an old man with a limp and a battered walker. What a hoot!

In keeping with his low-tech orientation, Vinson now relied on cabs and the occasional bus or subway to get around; he missed his Corvette, which he had moved twice more since stashing it at the impound lot. The car was memorable and could be traced to him so it had to remain under wraps for the time being, but it was a small price to pay for freedom of movement and not calling attention to himself. As for the spoof he'd pulled off this afternoon, he'd bet his beloved wheels that Foster was seething. Oh ya! The shrink had been bested on his own turf, and he would be embarrassed, but good!

Vinson's euphoria had erupted once he disappeared behind the apartment complex across from Foster's office. "Got you, gotyou, gotyou!" he chanted. He'd entered and pissed all over Foster's territory, marked it but good with his own scent, and got away clean. How much better could it get? Plenty! He would make it better! And the kill? That day was coming....

"I could have killed you today, Doc," Vinson grinned and slugged down two fingers of Charter from a half-pint. Around the corner from Foster's office, he had stashed the disposable pieces of his disguise in a dumpster and rid himself of the tattered outer layer of clothing. When he looked like himself again, he hailed a cab, which pulled over immediately. His good karma was holding.

Tonight, he wasn't holed up in some flophouse. No, he'd pulled a couple thou from his stash, and was living it up at the Marriott. He had needed a pleasant atmosphere to celebrate and to plan his next move. He was approaching another incarnation, and it was going to be a good one. He was tired of being a working stiff. Next go-round, he would live the high life! *Have to order me up a tuxedo or three. Armani and Versace, and aw hell! There has to be another one out there. Need a new name, too. Somethin' with class, worthy of my elevated social standing.*

Maybe it's time to move on; have you thought about that?

"Wait! Wait! That's gotta be the booze talkin'. I say when it's time to move on, and now is not the time. Vinson dies; I don't. I'm on to bigger and better; I'm steppin' up, and it's goin' to be right here. I've done pretty good up to now, don't you think?

"You? You who? Who'm I talking' to?"

Vinson found himself standing naked in the hotel's spacious bathroom, staring into the full-length mirror on the back of the door. He moved closer to the mirror 'til his nose, penis, and knees all touched the glass. The recessed lights were over his left shoulder, and they cast the right side of his face in shadow. He looked deep into his reflection. He could see himself in his pupils, reflection within reflection within reflection, until he lost sight of his smallest self. In its place, he sensed another, familiar somehow, but no less frightening in its familiarity. It was himself, his innocent self, the child lost to him.

The recognition jolted him, and Vinson stumbled backward. He whacked his elbow on a towel bar and dropped heavily to one knee. Pain exploded, fogging his senses, and, for the moment, wiping out all thought. He lowered himself to the floor. The cold tiles on his ass registered dimly in some far corner of his brain.

When, at last, he gathered his feet under him and stood, Vinson leaned on the sink for support and tested his weight on the injured knee. He turned his back on the damn mirror; he wanted no reminders of what just happened because he'd marshaled enough clarity to understand that he had momentarily lost touch with reality.

As his mind began to reorganize and assimilate, Vinson searched for a reasonable explanation. He supposed that mental health professionals would call it a psychotic break, and his gut told him that Foster was somehow responsible, but in that moment, he could not say how, only why...to turn the tables on him, to negate the success of this afternoon's con.

Vinson stumbled from the bathroom and fell into a stiff and unyielding Victorian chair. An unopened pint of Charter was at his elbow on a walnut library table. Ignoring the glass, he twisted and removed the cap, put the bottle to his lips and swigged. His eyes watered, and he flashed on the three guys he'd shot in the parking garage. He remembered pulling the trigger; the kills had been dictated by the situation, not voluntary, but necessary, self-defense. The victims had come to him, after all. As the whiskey flooded his forebrain, Vinson smiled and warmed to the certainty of his justification, if not outright innocence. He took another hit of the Charter.

Vinson drank steadily while his thoughts meandered through images of his escape from the parking garage before honing in on Foster. He was beginning to think of "Foster" and "Asshole" interchangeably. Foster wasn't much of a poker player, or maybe he was just a bona fide liberal, a touchy-feelly kinda guy after all. His *professional concern* (Ha!) had been evident from the very first appointment as he listened solemnly to the garbage Vinson spewed for his benefit.

It was Sonya's fault. She started it all by tattling to Foster; she had ratted on him, her husband, for Christ's sake. She had no right. He'd showed her; that was for sure! And Dr. Asshole, he hadn't been content to be Sonya's confessor; no, he had to become her trusted advisor, too. Sonya wouldn't have left him of her own accord. Foster never should have interfered.

Another hit of Charter polished it off. Vinson remained sprawled in the uncomfortable chair, his arms hanging loose at his sides. The bottle slipped from his fingers when he passed out.

At 7:00 a.m., Vinson awoke in bed and wondered how he got there. He glanced around the hotel room, remembering bits and pieces of the previous day. He felt good lying there, quiet, not driven as he had been during the past few days. It was a pleasant change, and unusual considering the empty whiskey bottle that lay on the floor. No hangover.

Vinson stretched languorously. Then, as though his very thought gave them life, little men with hammers set up a fearsome rhythm as they swung away at his whiskey-polluted brain cells. He fell back against the pillows, covered his eyes with his hands, and went back to blessed sleep.

The phone rang, sounding like the opening stanzas of Beethoven's Fifth. "God damn," he muttered reaching for the phone.

"Yeah?"

"Mr. Edwards?"

"Yes?" Vinson said.

"Will you be extending your stay with us, Sir? Checkout time has passed." The hotel desk clerk was soft-spoken, polite in the extreme.

"It has? What time is it?"

"Sir, it's one thirty. If you're not remaining, we'll have to admit the cleaning staff within the hour."

"No, no, I'm staying. I don't think I could leave. I fell last night and injured my knee. Didn't think it was serious, but now, I am unable to put my weight on it, and it is quite swollen and painful."

"I am very sorry, Sir. Is there anything we can do? We have a physician on staff, Mr. Edwards. I would be happy to have her come to you for an examination. Shall I page her, Sir?"

"Yes, I think that would be wise, considering. Thank you for your assistance."

Vinson threw back the sheets and glanced at his knee. It was discolored, hot to the touch, and swollen to about twice its normal size. He poked at it, then wished he hadn't. Pain throbbed from his pickled brain to his battered knee and everywhere between. He needed a drink, but the Charter was all gone, and the damn mini bottles in the stocked bar were only good for a swallow or two, and a very pricey swallow at that. He closed his eyes. *Sleep is always good.*

Vinson was again awakened by the telephone. The ornate bedside clock told him three hours had elapsed.

"Yeah? Vin...Edwards here."

"Sir, the doctor is here."

"Send him up," Vinson said, groggy and disoriented. He scrubbed shaking hands over his face. Even his fingernails hurt.

To the brisk rap on his door, Vinson barked, "Come in." A single second knock elicited a groan as he realized the security bar prevented entry.

"Hold on, I'll be right there." Vinson wrapped the sheet around him and shuffled across the room. He opened the door, leaning heavily on the frame. Before him stood a stunning woman in her mid-thirties, black physician's bag in hand.

"Mr. Edwards?" she said.

"Yeah, that's me. Come in."

"I'm Dr. Ellis. I understand you fell last night?"

"I'd say," Vinson muffled a groan as he turned toward the bed. Dr. Ellis stepped forward and offered a surprising muscular forearm for his support. She held his weight easily as he lowered himself to the mattress.

Vinson looked down at the sheet. "Sorry I'm not dressed. I wasn't expecting a woman doctor."

"No problem, Mr. Edwards, I'm used to it." Her quick sweep of the surroundings passed over the empty Charter bottle lying on its side by the chair.

"Let's take a look, Mr. Edwards. Ah…you did a bang-up job on the knee, so to speak! You have an abrasion and sizeable goose egg on your forehead, too. Did you lose consciousness?"

"No, ma'am, not from the bump. From the whiskey…I passed out." He ducked his head, wouldn't look at her, feigned discomfiture.

Dr. Ellis circled the swelling above his eye, prodding gently. Then she dropped to her knees and gave the swollen knee a thorough once-over. "A severe sprain," she said finally, "painful, I'm sure, but not serious. If you'll give it a week's rest by staying off your feet, you should have no problems."

Vinson's "problem" at the moment was not his knee. It was the lovely doctor's fragrance and the bounteous cleavage revealed by the deep V of her silk blouse. A quick glance showed that she did not wear rings on either hand; her nails were unpainted, trimmed, and clean.

"What is your perfume?" he asked.

"Tabu, my favorite."

"Tabu, huh? Appropriate."

"How so?"

"Well, you know, lady doctor, and a gorgeous one at that…taboo."

Dr. Ellis moved away as she realized her patient seemed to be hitting on her. "Mr. Edwards, let's keep my presence here in its proper context. I'll wrap this knee and clean the abrasion above your eye. I'll give you some pain medicine and arrange for x-rays at the nearest hospital."

"All right, Doc. You're just not what I expected. I guess I got my wires crossed."

As Dr. Ellis tended to his injuries, Vinson took her in with all of his senses. Her skin was a creamy, flawless peach, unusual with her green eyes and cropped red hair. She was not your typical redhead. She was only about 5'2", but she wore three-inch heels so she appeared to be of average height. The heels altered her posture slightly, and, thus, called attention to her heart-shaped ass. He breathed her in as she applied a topical antibiotic to the cut on his forehead.

"No stitches will be needed; just keep it clean. You might have a shiner, but I don't think so."

"That's good news," Vinson replied lackadaisically. *Already knew that, Doc*. "Would you hold off on wrapping the knee? I really need to clean up."

"Sure. Can you handle an ace bandage? Don't be over-zealous when you wrap it.

"Here's my card; I wrote the name of the hospital where you can be X-rated, I mean x-rayed, and there won't be any charges for my exam or the x-rays. The hotel will assume all costs."

"Oh, that's great," Vinson said, smiling at her slip of the tongue and the accompanying flush.

"Take one of these every four to six hours, as needed. Don't drive, because…"

"Doc, I'm not driving."

"All right then, if there's nothing else…?"

"There is one thing, Doc. Would you have dinner with me downstairs?" His request seemed to catch her off guard, but she considered for the moment, smiled and nodded.

"That would be very nice, Mr. Edwards. I think I would enjoy dining with you, but downstairs is out of the questions with your knee. You really must stay off it for at least several days or you risk further injury."

"Room service then? With all the trimmings!" Vinson had played a hunch; the cleavage, the absence of a wedding ring, her body language, and the Freudian slip all suggested to him that she was as aware of a volatile chemistry between them as he was. He had nothing to lose by asking, and now he had lots to gain.

"I have one more hotel guest to see, Mr. Edwards. Would an hour from now…?"

"Perfect. Gives me time to make the arrangements and clean up."

"A bath, Mr. Edwards, not a shower. Bad for the knee, and you could fall."

"A bath?" he asked plaintively. "I don't do baths, Doc!"

"Then, perhaps, you should wait until I return, in case you need assistance?"

Vinson glowered at her, then shrugged and grinned. It was an opening he couldn't refuse. "Me naked, and you outside the door? That's the best offer I've had all day, Doc!"

"I am not amused, Vincent." Dr. Ellis gave him an icy glance, but there was fire in her eyes that belied her statement, as did her use of his first name. "I'll be back in an hour, no more," she said and stepped out into the corridor.

"Perfect," Vinson mused aloud. "You could come in handy."

How did she know my first name?

"Must have got it from the desk clerk," he reasoned. "Hotels require guests' full names." He would have been identified to her as Vincent Edwards when she was called to request her medical services. "That would explain it."

Vinson registered the sudden urge to flee. He probably would have bolted if it weren't for the bum knee. He made his way slowly into the bathroom and swallowed a Percocet. Lowering himself into the dry tub was a real bitch and would have been impossible without the bars required by ADA regulations. He adjusted the water temperature to 104 and turned it on full force. The sudden intense cold of the shower spray took his breath, but the water warmed almost immediately. He let the water rain down upon him, and then, inspired, he closed the drain so the shower would fill the tub. The pain reliever was kicking in, and the hot water soothed both his head and his knee. He knew he needed to get his act together since he suspected that the curvaceous Dr. Ellis would be a demanding dinner partner. He turned off the shower and lay back, closing his eyes and giving in to the narcotic. Maybe Dr. Ellis wouldn't be gone an hour.

Just when the fantasy was getting good, the *other* doctor in his life intruded. Foster, the sonofabitch, always sticking his educated nose in where he didn't belong. Vinson's relaxation evaporated in a spurt of molten anger. He was faced with having to put the chase on hold for at least seventy-two hours because of his knee. That alone was a source of frustration, but if he were honest, it was because he was not sure what to do about Foster that he remained so unsettled. Sure, he knew the eventual outcome of their match; there was only one acceptable resolution. It was the *how to* that Vinson couldn't get a handle on; he couldn't visualize Foster's death, and that had never happened before, not since he had planned his first victim's demise at twelve.

What is there about Foster as foe that is so disconcerting? Maybe it comes back to intent. He's dedicated his life to doing good. Maybe I'm mistaking kindness or concern for weakness, guile for gullibility. I've fooled him more than he knows, or have I? Do I still have the upper hand?

The water in Vinson's bath had cooled to the point of discomfort. He had friggin' goose bumps on his goose bumps, and he'd lost track of time. Why couldn't designers make a decent tub that retained the heat of its bath water? How long did he have before Dr. Ellis returned?

Too quickly, Vinson pulled himself up out of the water. The pain was wrenching and bone-deep, and he could swear he heard his knee screaming. Gripping the sink, he lowered himself to the edge of the tub. Arctic-cold porcelain on his ass counteracted the Charter-flavored nausea that erupted. *Great! Puking my guts out will certainly endear me as a dinner companion to the luscious lady physician. How much more miserable can I get?*

It was all he could do to reach the bed and swallow two more Percocets. Was there anything in the closet suitable for an intimate dinner for two? Damned if he could remember what he'd packed for this little celebratory jaunt at the Marriott. He lay back against the pillows and closed his eyes, willing the pain and the nausea to be gone.

Vinson wove his way through the congestion of psychic traffic in his brain and surrendered to sleep. His last coherent thought was whether or not death would be pleasant. He was dreaming that he was able to come and go unseen when a soft, but persistent, knocking roused him. Eleven p.m. He had slept more than four hours. What's more, he had slept through his dinner date with the doctor. He reached beneath the extra pillow for his gun, wondering idly if....

"Mr. Edwards? It's Dr. Ellis, can you hear me?"

"Hold on, I'm not dressed."

"I'll wait; don't push the knee.

"I just thought I'd check on you. I suspect, I hope, you fell asleep, and that was, by far, the best thing for you. We can share dinner another evening."

"Just another minute." His voice was deep from sleep.

By the time Vinson opened the door, he was perspiring profusely. The effects of too much alcohol last night, the pain, and the Percocet-induced deep sleep were all ganging up on him, and he was really woozy. *Some Casanova I'm gonna be tonight.*

Dr. Ellis slipped by him, but not without brushing across him from shoulder to thigh. He swallowed, and when she had passed, he swiped hastily at the sweat on his upper lip and forehead.

"I'm going to order something to drink from the hotel bar. What can I get for you?"

From an over-sized leather briefcase, Dr. Ellis pulled a bottle of Old Charter. "I have this right, don't I Vincent?" she smiled.

Vinson looked from the bit of black satin that accompanied the liquor bottle from the briefcase to the half-gallon of Old Charter now cradled in Dr. Ellis's arm, and he nodded. Unless he missed his guess, he was in the presence of a woman with plans for her late evening, and despite his less than sterling physical condition, he had the feeling he could rise to the occasion.

"Pour me three fingers, Doc...hair of the dog!" Vinson limped to the edge of the bed and sat gingerly. He didn't resort to any of the false modesty that would have had him tugging at the towel around his waist. No reason why Dr. Ellis shouldn't see what she was getting.

As she turned from the wet bar with his drink, her glance dropped to the teasing gap of the towel. Dr. Ellis closed the distance between them, her eyes never leaving his crotch. As he leaned forward to accept the Charter on the rocks, Vinson opened his legs slightly. The lady's sharp inhalation was a much-needed stroke to his ego.

"Doc, are you all right?"

"No, not really."

"Oh?"

"I couldn't get you off my mind. I know it's late, but I had to see you again." Her hand moved slowly to the pearls at her throat, then dropped to the top button of her blouse. One by one, the buttons slipped to freedom, yet the blouse remained modestly in place. The only testament to her growing arousal was the hardening of nipples, like pencil erasers, that disturbed the drape of creamy silk. With an almost imperceptible shimmy, the blouse slithered off her shoulders and down pale arms to be caught at her wrists.

"I think you should know my first name. Don't you? It's Maria. I'm no longer on duty, Vincent."

"Maria." Vinson extended his hand as though in greeting. The hand that met his was small and soft, delicate-boned, but the grasp was surprisingly strong. With a gentle tug, he drew her to the bed beside him. She placed several pillows against the headboard, and then supported his knee as he settled himself against them. Her left hand cleverly snagged the towel so that when he slid back, he divested himself of its cover.

"Oops!" Her eyes, now a deep gray-green, were snapping with a naughty glee. She came up onto her knees and straddled his thighs. "May I lead, Sir?" she asked as she settled over him. An ivory full slip concealed the fact that she wore no panties. Moist heat slid up his thighs until his erection halted her. Maria extended her arms and entwined her fingers with his. With her eyes locked on his, she rose to her knees, took him into her body.

Vinson would have said that he knew all there was to know about sex. The next few hours would prove that he had been mistaken. Maria showed him things about her body, and his own, which prolonged their lovemaking and intensified his responses beyond anything he had ever experienced. As dawn bathed the room in a muted rose, Vinson lay with his head on Maria's shoulder. Weary, replete, he asked the only coherent question that floated through his brain. "Would these be the benefits of a medical education?"

He could feel Maria's smile as she buried her face in his hair. "No," she murmured, "these are the benefits of a young woman's introduction to pleasure by a cosmopolitan older gentleman who had traveled the world."

"You are a beautiful woman, Maria, beautiful, learned, and sensual, 'though the words don't do you justice. I have to say that the pleasure we've shared is a far more effective 'medication' than any pills you could prescribe. That must mean that the pleasure center of the brain is more dominant than the pain center. Is that true, physiologically speaking?"

"I don't know, Vincent. My medical training goes on hiatus when sexual pleasure is the goal.

"Would you excuse me for a few moments?" Maria slid gracefully from the bed. At the door of the bathroom, she turned and winked at him, then disappeared.

Vinson levered himself onto his elbows and surveyed the room. His towel lay on the floor beside the bed. Maria's clothes, now a silky heap, remained where she had stepped out of them. The nearly full bottle of Old Charter sat on the bedside table just out of reach, and he felt a fleeting thirst. His eyes moved on to the collection of Styrofoam take-out containers that had been delivered after midnight from a hole-in-the-wall Bohemian restaurant down the way. They had shared the eastern European fare, Pirogues and liver dumpling soup (*yeech!*), succulent roast pork, dumplings, and sauerkraut, a very heavy meal considering the hour and the activities of the evening. Consequently, they had eaten sparingly, but with full enjoyment.

By the time their food had arrived, they had already made love twice. It seemed that the elegant Maria could be an animal! By way of explanation, when it seemed that she couldn't get enough of him, she admitted that overwork and the fickleness of a former partner had left her in a sexual desert for almost a year. Not that she couldn't come...hell, she was multi-orgasmic! To Vinson, it seemed that the more she got, the more she wanted, and the more she wanted to try. *Sort of like doing crack*!

With that thought, Vinson's eyes returned to the Charter; its allure was more compelling, but he was distracted by Maria's return to the bed. She smelled fresh and clean with a hint of Tabu, which suggested to him that he should be a courteous lover and take a shower.

"No shower, not with your knee." Maria was reading his thoughts. "I could give you a sponge bath. That might be fun!"

"God forbid! I'd have to be prostrate at death's door to submit to one of those!" He rolled over onto her, waggling his eyebrows and leering at her. He nudged her with an erection he wouldn't have believed possible after the night just passed. "Or...we could screw again, then you'll smell like me."

"Now there's a plan! However, you're an invalid, and, like the witch that I am, I vowed to do no harm. You should sleep." She lay down beside him, flat on her stomach. She trailed a finger lazily over his belly and lower; she stroked him gently. "Still, it seems a shame...." She yawned.

"Let's nap first, huh?" Vinson brushed a damp copper curl behind her ear. Dr. Maria Ellis was a natural redhead, he had been pleased to learn. At that thought, his penis bobbed up eagerly. *Down boy!* "There's always later." He smiled to see that her eyes were already closed. He followed suit.

How long had he slept? Vinson surfaced; but for the erection, he felt relaxed and lazy. *When was the last time you lolled around in bed past noon?* He rolled to the edge of the bed and put his feet on the floor. Gradually he increased the weight on his knee, and there was little pain. *Intensive sex as therapy for pain.... In my next life, I'll submit a treatise for JAMA.*

Vinson inhaled and rose from the bed. Favoring his knee only a bit, he limped to a chair, taking the bottle of Charter with him. From where he sat, Maria's perfect ass was the bull's eye in his line of vision. *Sweet, succulent Maria...what a magnificent piece of work!*

The Charter bathed his throat and spread its radiant warmth. His hand dropped to his penis. It felt cold. *Charter's coming!* His hand wrapped around his dick, and he began a slow, rhythmic massage. There was some soreness from the excesses of last night and this morning, but Maria's Penthouse pose was too worthy to ignore. He continued a lazy stroking, squeezing, and pulling of penis and scrotum; his thoughts evaporated.

Maria rolled to her back, destroying the fantasy. He felt an incendiary flash of anger.

"Vince?"

"Yeah, baby?" Vinson continued to masturbate.

"What are you doing, Vince?"

"What does it look like?"

"Please share," Maria smiled, turning to face him and propping herself on her elbow. When Vinson's rhythm didn't falter, she bent her knee and touched herself. "Is this what you want?" she asked, joining his party.

Vinson loved her show. Apparently so did Maria. Soft moans became whimpers; she never took her eyes off him, and their sexual connection seemed even stronger than at any time last night. Vinson felt the sensations of imminent ejaculation and reflexively jerked his head up and back. That momentary break in eye contact appeared to turn Maria on even more. She knew he was approaching orgasm, and she seemed determined to accompany him. Vinson stopped stroking abruptly and nodded to her. Maria's eyes lost focus, and she crested with a rush of panted praise for his anatomy and his skills as a lover. Her legs clamped down on her hand; that and one more stroke were all Vinson needed.

He was aware that Maria continued to watch him. When he had caught his breath, he followed her nod to the splashes of cum across his chest and belly. *Four times in twelve hours. I could repopulate the world! With Maria, I feel no inhibitions. We've done everything we learned from previous lovers; we've done more than some life-long lovers dare.*

Vinson swallowed the last of the Charter.

"I've got to go, Vince."

"Why?"

"I have patients this afternoon. I'm sorry."

Vinson flashed on Foster, and the glow vanished.

Maria began gathering her clothing, shaking out wrinkles, and laying her blouse and skirt over a chair. Vinson tracked her every move. Feeling awkward as the silence grew, he said the first thing that came into his head.

"*Doctor* Maria Ellis...it's got class, has a nice ring to it."

"Well, speaking of bells, you certainly rang mine... every time, Vince! I'm glowing, from the inside out."

"You mean you liked my clapper inside your bell, that it?"

"I hope you don't have the clap," she said, laughing.

"No, but if we'd had an audience, I'm sure the applause would have been thunderous!"

Maria dissolved in giggles. "Do you hear that, Vince? I sound like some impressionable teenager! I'm a mature woman, for Pete's sake, a respected professional. I don't giggle. What have you done to me?"

"Like you said, just rang your bell a few times! You told me it had been a while."

"You're really something, Vince, an accomplished and considerate, but humble, lover. How did I get so lucky?" She ran her fingers through his hair and her hand across his shoulders, then stepped away to tuck in her blouse. "I don't want to leave you."

"I'll keep, don't worry. Say, do you suppose you could arrange for me to get my hands on some crutches? Once you leave, I'll go batty if I don't get out of this room."

"Sure. Consider it done. My nurse will see that they're delivered to you ASAP," she said, walking toward him. She kissed the top of his head. "I missed this spot last night."

"Thanks." Vinson tipped his head back, asking for her lips.

"I had a great time, Mr. Edwards." She winked and backed toward the door to the hallway.

"See you soon?"

"I'll call you when I finish this afternoon. OK?"

"I'll be here."

CHAPTER FORTY

Before the door latched quietly behind her, Vinson was mourning Maria's loss. Because he could, he considered for the moment whether Maria might simply become a part of his transition, or, perhaps, his future. But no.... As Sonya had done, her presence would weigh him down, hamper his ability to read and react to any eventuality, and, therefore, compromise a clean escape. She would require too many explanations, and, despite her free spirit, Vinson suspected that, at her core, Dr. Maria Ellis was a straight shooter.

So, he had a bum knee to thank for his memorable interlude with a gorgeous woman, but it was time to move forward. Without Maria for distraction, Vinson felt mighty edgy. John Foster, Ph.D. should have been history by now, another cadaver for the county morgue.

Vinson took another shower on the floor of the tub and swore it would be the last. He shaved and selected the clothing he would wear. Because the promised crutches still hadn't arrived, he snapped up the telephone and dialed the hotel concierge. "This is Edwards, 114."

"Yes, sir. How are you feeling?"

"I'm fine, but...."

"Yes, sir. You're calling about the crutches, I presume? Dr. Ellis made the arrangements. Shall I send them up?"

"Yes, now if you could."

No more than three minutes elapsed before there was one firm knock on the door. Vinson opened the door just wide enough for the crutches to be handed to him. *No tip needed. They're still wondering if I'm gonna sue. A tip could alter my leverage with hotel management. They haven't even asked how much longer I'm staying. If my luck holds, they'll cancel my bill, too, as a goodwill gesture.*

Vinson's knee was only slightly better. There was less swelling, however, and while he'd been up moving around, he'd been able to put weight on it without as much pain. The crutches would hide the improvement while making him look pitiful to hotel staff! He grinned.

Vinson dressed in gray flannel slacks with razor-sharp pleats and one-inch cuffs. He hated the no-cuff look; it was sloppy. He slipped on a lightweight cashmere black sweater, black socks and loafers. He'd let his hair dry naturally, and now he ran his fingers through it to give it some body and lift. The crutches were adjusted perfectly for his height and arm length. Was he flattering himself to think that Maria had cared enough to order just the right size?

From the elevator, it was a short walk to the concierge's desk. *Were all the hotel service staff of the mild-mannered variety? He doubted that the man who greeted him politely had a backbone, much less a dick! Jeez!*

"Can I be of service, Sir?"

"Well, I'll tell you. I was planning to stay in your wonderful establishment for one night only," Vinson said, exaggerating his enunciation and mocking the pasty concierge.

"Yes?"

"Then, I fell in your well appointed bathroom, and sustained a complex sprain of the knee."

"Yes, Sir. We are aware of your situation. We are very sorry for your mishap. I have been directed to make any arrangements you require, and, of course, you will not be billed for your stay with us."

Vinson feigned surprise and dropped his eyes, hoping to pass for humble. "Thank you. Please relay my appreciation to management.

"By chance, would it be possible for you to secure an item for me? I need a Polaroid camera, you know, the instant kind? Oh, and a selection of postcards, not picture post cards, blank ones from a stationer or post office. As you know, my travel plans have been altered because of the injury, and I must cancel arrangements for some of my planned destinations."

"It will be my pleasure, Mr. Edwards, to provide you with anything you need."

"Well then, add four bottles of Old Charter to that list," Vinson said with a smirk. As he turned away from the desk, he saw annoyance in the man's eyes. *Maybe the fellow has a bit of spine, after all!*

"Will there be anything else, Sir?" the concierge called out.

Without turning to address him, Vinson replied, "No, that will be all...for now." A Cheshire cat grin appeared, then faded.

Vinson made a production of settling himself on a green chenille love seat in the hotel lobby. He picked a place where his back was to the wall, and he propped his crutches against a table. The late afternoon sun was rippling through a row of small art glass windows creating a pleasing kaleidoscope effect. As he watched the comings and goings of the well-heeled, his stomach growled loudly. A bellboy who was walking past turned to looked him.

"Say, young fella, do you suppose you could bring a BLT and a Coke so I can feed this roaring beast?"

"Yes, Sir, what is your room num...? Oh, Mr. Edwards," he said noticing the crutches, "Room 114, right?"

"Yes. Nice of you to remember, Julio."

"You're easy to remember."

The comment tweaked Vinson uncomfortably. "How's that?" he asked, thinking the kid might be trying to dis him somehow.

"Ah, well, it's my birthday, November 4. Get it? 11/4?"

"Yes, I see...makes it easy. OK, the BLT?"

"Coming right up."

Vinson dozed, thereby abandoning his usual vigilance when out in public. *Must be the activities of the night, little food, little sleep, and a whole hell of a lot of sex.* His awakening floated on the delicate fragrance of crisp bacon.

"Mr. Edwards, your BLT, Sir." Julio placed the sandwich and drink on the coffee table in front of the sofa.

"Thanks a lot," Vinson replied, clearing his throat. He reached into his pocket and handed over one of several twenties he had put there. He didn't feel right about stiffin' the kid twice. Now that his room charges had been waived, he could afford a little generosity.

"For you, kid." At the bellman's wide eyes, however, he realized that he had overplayed his hand and called more attention to himself. Julio would remember him now, and that was risky. He fought the urge to grab for the twenty, but that would only compound the problem. *Stupid!*

Vinson's leg had stiffened while he sat, and Julio noted that he was having trouble reaching the sandwich. "Here, Sir. I'm sorry. I didn't realize," he said, placing the plate on the lamp table at Vinson's elbow.

"Thanks, kid, I'll remember you, too."

The taste of the bacon reminded Vinson of his mother's cooking. Before her death, she used to labor in the small kitchen of their mobile home. She fried bacon to perfection, or, at least, to his liking. She'd serve it and watch to see if it was crisp, just the way he liked it. If not, it went back in the skillet. He didn't have to say a word. Vinson had learned extortion and blackmail under the tutelage of his unsuspecting mother. To his way of thinking, it was the price she paid for the sexual abuse. At the tender age of seven, demanding crisp bacon had been his revenge. His demands had escalated since then.

Vinson had finished the sandwich when Julio returned to check on him. He delivered a cardboard box filled with the things Vinson had requested. When he removed the empty plate and glass, Vinson asked if he would return in a few minutes, and the young man agreed.

Vinson opened the flaps of the box and removed the Polaroid camera. It was sealed in one of those rigid plastic packages that were such a bitch to open, and impossible without a knife or sharp scissors. Before closing the box, he absently caressed one of the bottles of Charter. It was cool to the touch, and he was thirsty.

"Do me a favor, Julio?"

"What?"

"I need you to take my picture. Do you have something sharp that will open this darn packaging? Don't you hate these things? It's not like somebody is going to put Cyanide in the package like they did with Tylenol years ago. Extra Strength, I think." *Anthrax, maybe, but not cyanide.*

"No, sir. It's not," Julio replied dubiously. The look in his eyes told Vinson he didn't have a clue what the Tylenol incident had been.

"You want me to take your picture, Sir?"

"Yeah, several, in fact, but not here. Over there." He pointed to the central lobby where traffic was heavy and people were milling about, suitcases in tow.

"I was supposed to be on an extended trip, to visit a number of friends across the country, but the injury has forced me to delay my travels. I need to let people know, and want to send photos with my explanation about why I have to postpone."

"OK then. Ready, Mr. Edwards?"

"No, wait. Let me get rid of these crutches.

"Now, I'm ready, Julio. Shoot away." Vinson altered his stance and his facial expressions from photo to photo to create some variety.

"I've taken six. Shall I stop, Sir?"

"No, keep going. Run it out. There are ten in all." The flashes continued. When the pack of photos was empty, Julio gathered the Polaroids and handed them to Vinson.

"Do you have the postcards I'm sending?"

"Yes, Sir. I put them on the table where you were sitting."

"Would you get them for me? I'm running out of steam. Also, please get the box and take it to my room." Julio headed for the elevator. Vinson sat to rest his leg, wondering idly whether Julio might serve some other purpose.

CHAPTER FORTY-ONE

Foster and his entourage were getting antsy. There hadn't been one single indication that Vinson was interested in a showdown, that he was interested in Foster, period. "It's been damn expensive for me, too," Foster complained to Doonan who was bitching about a lack of funds. Since Doonan wasn't working regularly, his expensive taste in Russian and Polish vodkas had put a big dent in his federal pension checks, and he had little savings to fall back on while he was in Chicago.

"Not to sweat it guys, we're on the right track," Cook cajoled, looking at the two sourpusses before him. "Hey! We've got a plan; we just need to stick tight. Waiting is always the hardest part."

Cook's cheerfulness brought a smile to Foster's face, but Doonan was getting downright surly. Sobriety was not his preferred state, and only for John would he be on the wagon.

"All right, Tim, we can keep our eye on the goal, but where the hell is Vinson anyway?" Foster stood and stretched. He began to pace in front of Louise's desk.

"You're the one who figured it, John. He has to come to us. We're trying to force him to break cover, and since he's not used to working out in the open—except on his own terms—he'll plan his moves to the nth degree. All we can do is wait. Let's not forget what we know."

"Louise, what...?" Foster began as she came through the office door. "I thought you were going to join Joyce in Vermont?"

Louise surveyed the remains of a fifteen-piece spicy chicken bucket with extra rice and fries that littered the waiting room floor, tabletops, and empty chairs, and she shook her head. "I couldn't make a mess like this if I worked at it for a week. I could smell grease from the parking lot! You aren't trying to remain incognito or whatever they call it, are you?"

"Naw, we're just going batty with the waiting's all." Doonan lay sprawled across two waiting room chairs, oblivious to the fact that his fly was open. Neither Cook nor Foster had noticed 'til suddenly there was a woman present. Cook turned his back to Louise and pantomimed zipping up. Doonan stared at him quizzically, his forehead wrinkling.

To hide her grin, Louise turned and walked to the front door. They were like three little boys! After what she hoped was a suitable pause, she walked to her desk. She fished in her purse and found her keys. When her desk was unlocked and she had taken the phone off the answering service, she looked at each man in turn. Doonan's pants were zipped, and his face and ears were crimson. "Well, gentlemen? Where do things stand?"

"Louise?"

"I'm sorry, Dr. John, I told you I would leave, but I just can't. You need me."

"Look, Kiddo, I know things would run smoother with you here, but we're dealing with unknowns, and Vinson has shown us he is both unpredictable and dangerous. Worrying about you will distract me, and it could compromise my ability to stay one step ahead of him. Louise, he's made it clear he'll hurt anyone who gets in his way."

"I had every intention of leaving, Dr. John; it's just that I want to do more, and you really do need me."

"Look, we've been together three years, right?" Foster said.

"Three years, eight months, and twenty-three days."

"Twenty-three days?"

"I have a calendar on my computer that keeps a running total. It lasts ten years, and I started it my first day of work." Foster noted she was now more sheepish than irate.

"John, you all right?" Doonan's interest had been captured by their exchange.

"Fine, Jerry. Louise is concerned about us and wants to help."

"I'm sorry. It's just that, for a few weeks, things have been so out of kilter, you know; it's strange, and now, Mr. Vinson is back."

"Look kid, I'm not going to tell you that you have to go, but for your safety, and ours, it would be best if you did."

"But, I'll worry about you."

Foster was touched. "You'll be in good company. You and Joyce can worry together, and Vi will keep feeding you. Take my advice and add a daily walk to your routine while you're there! Think of this as a bonus paid vacation, or if your conscience hurts, think of it as a sabbatical. You've said you want to learn to do psych testing. Take the WISC and the Woodcock; learn them while you have the time. Joyce and Vi can be your guinea pigs. I have no doubt you would really enjoy working with children. You're a natural!"

"You called it a what?"

"A sabbatical." Foster looked away so as not to laugh. "You take time off—with pay— to study in your field, do research, learn something new. Academicians take sabbaticals, for example; professionals do it so they can study with a mentor, expand their knowledge or skills."

"I thought sabbaticals were forced on you when you burned out."

Foster laughed. "That, too, can sometimes be the case…a burned-out professional who is suddenly short on coping abilities. Public school teachers, for example, earn one of the highest statistical rankings. The employer sends them off so they can get their act together! A sabbatical can also be used when someone has prolonged medical problems. Then it becomes a way of keeping a valuable employee who simply needs some time away from the job—for whatever reason."

"OK, Dr. John, enough of the lecture; I'll go. And I will learn the WISC and the Woodcock Johnson while I'm away. If I stay busy, I won't worry so much…or eat so much!"

Louise turned toward the door as the day's mail fell through the slot. She added it to the growing pile on the corner of her desk, then thought better of it. She pulled the accumulation toward her and began opening and sorting. She stopped when she came to a postcard with a photo of a man wearing sunglasses. She swallowed hard, her throat suddenly bone-dry. "Dr. John?"

"What?" Foster asked.

"This photo...look!"

Foster reached for the picture. Staring back at him was a smiling Eddie Vinson, dressed to the nines, hands in his pockets as though he had not a care in the world. Only the dark glasses suggested that he had something to hide. Foster's reaction was instant and visceral. His stomach clenched and a spurt of fear raced from his tailbone up the spine. He stiffened and nearly lost his balance.

Seeing his reaction, both Doonan and Cook stepped forward. Jerry plucked the photo from Foster's fingers and showed it to Tim so that they were seeing it together. "Vinson. Cocky little bugger, ain't he?"

Cook took the photo and turned it over. Thus, he was the one who found the text of Vinson's message written in tiny letters on the back. "Here's looking at you."

"Here's looking at you," Cook repeated, showing Doonan.

"Let me see it again," Foster asked. He was recalling an FBI case he'd worked. For months, the serial killer had tormented police with riddles. Vinson's taunt reminded him of that case. "Here's looking at you...a Bogart thing... Casablanca...looking at you; looking at you...," he paused, "I'm looking at him, where he is. Is he challenging me to come to him? Surely he knows we're trying to lure him into revealing himself on our turf. Maybe he wants to change the rules."

"But where is he? Is this some kinda clue?" Doonan asked.

"Doonan," Foster asked, "Remember how you found that guy who photographed his victims with their eyes open? In some cases, he'd tacked their eyes open with neat little stitches. It was as if he wanted them still to be alive. The eyes, remember?"

"Sh...yeah," Doonan said, recalling, too, his haunting dreams during that case. "That was a terrible one."

"Well, anyway, remember how you broke it?"

"Ya! We blew up the photo...the image in her eyes... and there he was," Doonan muttered to himself. "It was all in the eyes. The eyes have it, don't they?"

"Doonan! Focus, will you?" Foster's voice was stern, commanding.

"What, already?" Doonan snapped. The grief was as fresh as it had been so long ago.

"Look closely, Jerry, there's something on the glass of the window behind him."

"What?"

"I don't know, but it's there. Think back to the case; it was1973. Remember?"

"I know, John. I'm already there. Right there."

"Doonan, c'mon man! We need a photo lab that can blow this up. I think we might be able to pinpoint his location."

"OK. I'm on it."

"You mean where he wants us to think he is," said Cook. "Isn't that more likely?"

"That's a point," Foster mused. "He plays his game, always sees three or four steps ahead. Like any good chess player."

"OK, OK, but let's just take this next step. Listen to the old man, here! I'm the voice of reason. We'll decide what to do *after* we get the blow up. Doonan...photo lab about a mile from here. Out the driveway, turn north; same side of the street." Cook pitched him the car keys as Doonan walked by.

"How can I help you, sir?" asked the woman behind the counter.

"Need a photo enlarged. Really, I just need one part of the picture blown up. Can you do that?"

"Depends."

"Oh? On what, Ms. Deshotel?" asked Doonan, reading her nametag.

Annie Deshotel had been an employee of the Fast Track Photo Lab for about six weeks. She'd studied photography in high school, but didn't have the expertise that Doonan needed to answer his questions. "We're just a photo developer; we specialize in fast, but the owner is a photographer, and he can probably do what you need."

"OK, then, let's talk to the owner. This is important, and time is critical."

Ms. Deshotel hit redial on the counter telephone. She gave the necessary introduction then passed the phone to Doonan.

Mr. Greg, as he called himself, answered Doonan's questions. "As Annie explained to you, the photo lab where you are now is very basic, not capable of doing what you need. If you will come to my studio, however, I have the necessary equipment to enlarge the specific details that you require."

"Sure, OK. What's the address?" Doonan asked. "Uh, huh. OK. I can find you. When should I come over?"

"Right away, if you want."

"Sure, I'll be about fifteen minutes." Using the directions he'd been given, Doonan drove straight to the studio. His impression from talking to the man was that he knew his business, so Doonan hoped he wasn't gonna be sold a red herring. Mr. Greg lived in a two-story bungalow with a full basement that looked to be circa the 1930's. Solid construction, dark brown brick, the steps and front porch were concrete. The front door was old and beautiful with stained glass surrounded by beveled panes. Looking through the glass, Doonan could see someone inside, but images were distorted. Before he could ring the doorbell, the door opened with a loud creak, "Mr. Doonan?"

"Yes, that's me," Doonan said.

Mr. Greg was a tall, lanky fellow with a prominent Adam's apple. His nose was rounded at the end with enlarged pores. His eyes were a washed out green that clashed with gaunt red cheeks. His overall appearance was that of a caricature, as it seemed that Mr. Greg had been blessed with every ugly facial feature Doonan could think of. He was dressed in tan slacks and a T-shirt bearing the logo of his photography studio. Dark brown sandals matched a stylish, handcrafted leather belt. Rather than shake Doonan's hand, Mr. Greg bent forward at the waist in a bow that would have done a sixteenth century courtier proud.

"Did you have trouble finding me?"

"Oh, no. Your directions were letter perfect. I stopped by my office to tell them where I was going, you know, just in case." Doonan lied.

"In case?"

"In case they needed to know where to reach me. I gave them your number. Cell phone is kaput. I stepped on it this morning." Doonan kept up the patter as he followed Mr. Greg down the stairs to the basement photo lab. He could smell the mix of chemicals, and, upon reaching the bottom of the stairs, he saw an elaborate array of computers and equipment.

"Show me what you want blown up."

"Sure," Doonan said, reaching into his coat pocket, pulling out the photo of Vinson, which he placed under a task light.

"Precisely what is it you want to see?"

"The writing on the window behind the man wearing sunglasses," Doonan pointed.

The photographer looked at Doonan, then back at the photo. "Uh, uh," he muttered, pulling the photo close to his face, then reaching for a magnifying glass. He studied the photo for all of a minute. "I see, well...," he said, clearing his throat. "This won't be easy."

"I know, I know. How much?" Doonan grumbled.

Without blinking, Mr. Greg said, "A hundred dollars."

Doonan didn't hesitate. "OK, go ahead."

"Fine, I'll begin immediately."

"How long?" Doonan asked.

"Well, that depends, Mr. Doonan, but if you'd like to stay while I work, maybe talk, have a coffee or something...?" His voice had suddenly become low and suggestive.

"Thank you, but no." Doonan smiled politely, hoping his smile didn't reach his eyes. *Never been hit on by a man before. Wonder what that says about me.*

"Very well. I'd say maybe one to two hours...that should do it."

"All right, I'll come back about one."

"Right," Mr. Greg said, winking his left eye. "Just ring the bell and come in; I'm not expecting anyone else."

"I'll see myself out." Doonan could swear he was blushing.

Back at the clinic, Cook was saying he would feel better if Foster were to stay at some out-of-the-way motel or hotel, just until they had a better fix on what Vinson was up to.

"Naw," Foster quipped, "If he was coming now, he never would have sent the post card. He wants us to simmer and stew for a while longer. His ego strength dictates that we should be trembling in our boots. So, to my way of thinking, this is exactly the time for us to get in a little R & R. We let the good times roll, and don't have to look over our shoulders."

Just then, Cook reached for the cell phone vibrating at his waist. "Yeah," he snapped. He listened for several moments. "That's so cool. Right. Oh, shit, that's funny! I didn't know you had it in you."

"What's that, Tim?"

"Yeah, OK." He punched three buttons before he got the disconnect.

"Doonan'll have a blowup in about two hours. Give or take. The guy doing it tried to put a hit on him."

"A hit?" Foster sputtered, thinking threat.

"No, I mean a *hit*. The guy's gay."

"Oh lord!" Foster chuckled.

"That's what I thought, too," Cook said as he dissolved in laughter. "Leave it to Doonan; only he could get himself into such a situation," he chortled, wiping at tears.

Foster, too, was guffawing. He slumped against the wall and slid 'til his butt hit the floor. Even after he gained a modicum of control, his shoulders shook every time he thought of Jerry being propositioned. He and Cook pledged to worm out of Doonan every juicy detail of the libidinous photographer's come-on.

"That's the second roaring-good belly laugh we've had," Cook wheezed, mopping his face with his sleeve. "Damn that was fun!"

When the hilarity had passed, Foster and Cook continued to slump on the waiting room floor. Foster felt drained, and he suspected Tim did too. The intensity of their laughter left a hollowness in its wake. A quick glance at Cook confirmed that he looked drawn, worn out. *The death of a child will do that to you.*

Cook had put his grief on hold and let his anger guide him while he worked with Doonan and Foster to bring Vinson down, but grief would have its day, and the longer it was delayed, the more likely it was to catch Tim before he was ready. Foster was hesitant to put on his therapist cloak with Tim, but maybe, if he were cagey, he could pitch him a few pearls of wisdom that might help. If their friendship was as strong as Foster perceived it to be, Tim might come to him, as a friend, when he felt the need, and then again, he might not. It could go either way—all for the same reasons.

While they waited for Doonan's return, Foster wandered into his office. He felt unfocused, at loose ends. Looking at the telephone on his desk, he was overwhelmed with longing for Joyce. He had expected their separation to last a few days, not weeks, and he was not a happy bachelor.

Foster dialed quickly, hoping that his energetic wife was not out hiking or shopping. When Joyce answered, relief poured through him like a fine old brandy. She was smiling; he could hear it in her voice. Over the next twenty minutes, he gave her the details of Louise's travel plans, and admitted he had browbeaten her to leave the city. When she asked, he told Joyce he was doing well, but sensed she knew he was struggling. They continued to talk about little that was important, but everything necessary was communicated. That the bond between them could be reinforced with a few loving words, a sigh, and silence was something he had never understood, but never taken for granted either. Despite the breadth of his psychological training and his understanding of human nature, there were still miracles, even for him.

With two hours to kill, and needing some down time, Doonan drove past three or four bars before he caved. The Jonesing was impossible to ignore, and he hated it.

The walls were closing in on him. He spotted a neighborhood tavern down the block and knew he was going in. *I'll have just one…take the edge off; that's all. Uh huh, and I got land to sell in Florida, too!*

The bar was like any other in the morning hours, and would be unrecognizable if one returned for happy hour. It smelled of Pine Sol, which never quite managed to mask the odors of spilled drinks, urine, vomit…all the leftovers when the booze genie was loosed from the bottle.

Doonan almost turned and fled; the operative term being *almost*. He knew the damn genie had no magic; it was all a con, and he'd fallen for it more times than he could count. Thus, he had stopped counting…until John had thrown a net over him, hauled him up, and suckered him into sobriety under the guise of needing him. What a crock!

"Genie, meet John; John, meet Genie. Face off, you two; the winner gets my weary, pickled soul."

The bartender was inventorying bottles when Doonan settled his butt on the barstool. Without turning around, he asked the patron in the mirror, "What'll you have?"

"Vodka, a double."

"Stoli?"

"Polish…Chopin or Belvedere? Biala Dama?" Doonan asked hopefully as the bartender pulled shot glasses from a deep stainless steel sink and arranged them on a clean cotton towel.

"You know the price?"

"Yes."

"Neat or ice?"

"Neat," Doonan said.

Without looking, the bartender selected a bottle from high among the hundred or more that lined mirrored shelves. From shoulder height, he poured the precious vodka into a small frosted cylinder that had been nestled in a bowl of ice, his aim, perfect.

"Still got it!" the barkeep grinned at Doonan in the mirror.

"You're a connoisseur," Doonan observed, tilting the small vodka glass toward him in thanks.

"Thought I recognized a fellow aficionado. Not many ask for the best."

The bartender poured a second shot of Biala Dama. He mirrored Doonan's gesture with his glass and drank. Then, on what signal Doonan didn't know, the bartender poured a double Jameson and slid it down the slick walnut bar to the only other patron. The glass stopped directly in front of the man; he had only to open his hand to raise the glass for a sip.

"How many times you s'pose you've done that?" Doonan asked.

"Too many to count. My dad left me this bar when I was twenty-four. I'm sixty-two now, so that makes it…?"

"Thirty-eight," Doonan said.

"Right, thirty-eight years. Then multiply that by 365."

"Thirteen thousand, eight hundred seventy days," Doonan supplied.

"How'd you do that?" The barkeep was shaking his head.

"Just something I've done ever since I was a kid. Numbers move through my head like I've been programmed."

While Doonan was taking another appreciative sip, the barkeep was punching numbers on his calculator. "Son of a bitch if you aren't right! Name's Billy. Billy Ryan."

"Doonan, Jerry Doonan."

"Well, I'll be! A brother Irishman."

"Looks to be," Doonan said, setting his empty glass down with a slight tremor of the hand. "I'll have another."

"Sure. Another. Say, I haven't seen you around here before. Visiting?"

"No, I've got some business down the way with a photographer. I'm just waiting on him."

"Say, you oughtta watch out for that fellow…he's a little…."

"I know. I've already been hit on," Doonan sniggered.

"What do you do, Doonan?"

"Do? I guess that's hard to explain. Right now, I'm a bodyguard of sorts."

"No shit? That sounds interesting."

"More like...frustrating," Doonan said, watching Ryan pour vodka into another frosted cylinder.

"Why do you say that?" asked Ryan.

"It's long on wait and short on action," Doonan said. "Of course, we're always hopin' there won't be any action. Sometimes, though, like now, we're looking for someone *before* he gets a chance to hit our man."

"So you follow a trail...or what? You set him up?

"Can you do that? Isn't that entrapment? Is it legal?" asked Ryan.

"You watch too much TV," Doonan joked, trying to divert Ryan; then, he thought better of it. "There's lots that goes on in this life that has to be done, and it's not all legal. If we take a guy out *before* he kills the President...that's OK? Now suppose the intended victim is only John Q. Average American? Is it still OK? What's justifiable? Is it a matter of value, the worth of the individual? And who the hell decides?"

Ryan poured himself another vodka, and one for Doonan. He slid another Jameson down the bar, then raised his glass. "Here's to you, Doonan, and to asking the hard questions."

"And to you, Ryan." Three heads tilted back to swallow. Silence followed.

Doonan watched Ryan wipe the bar from end to end. He sliced lemons and limes, fished cherries, olives and cocktail onions out of large jars; he tuned in WGN on the overhead television in the corner. Doonan placed three $20s on the bar and slid from the stool. An old clock above the bar struck a sonorous one o'clock. Doonan saluted Ryan and pushed through the door to the sidewalk. He couldn't tell Ryan he'd be back, because he wouldn't.

I've had only three, three of the very best, by god! Not too much damage done if I go now. The wagon's outside, right where I fell off. I'll climb back on; I can do that for John.

Doonan's vision blurred as bright sunlight attacked his retinas. It was the sun, not the vodka. He decided to walk back to the photography studio. The walk would allow him to shake off the boozy haze.

Mr. Greg greeted Doonan at the door before he could

knock. "Mr. Doonan, I think I've got something of interest for you. It was a bit difficult; I had to use filters and computer enhancement, but the resulting image is clear." He handed Doonan a manila envelope. "I don't know what it means, but hopefully, it's of value to you."

Doonan removed the 8" x 10" color enlargement. Behind a smiling Vinson was an ornately etched ceiling-to-floor window that looked out over a busy four-lane street. Doonan suspected that anyone who knew the area would be able to identify the street based on details from the photo. Because he was not familiar with the greater Chicago area, he needed a bit more to help him make an identification. However, the enlargement gave him all he needed to know!

"Well! Well! The Marriott Hotel…I'll be damned!" Doonan pummeled the photographer's slender shoulders. "I do know this place!"

"That's good then, Sir? Does it help?"

"Good, my man? It's downright terrific! You're a genius!"

Mr. Greg blushed a becoming shade of rose and shuffled from foot to foot.

"Here's your hundred, Mr. Greg, and well worth it, too! Thanks a lot for your time and your expertise." Doonan passed the photographer Foster's $100 and bolted for the front door.

Back at the clinic, Cook and Foster were chewing nails and spitting battleships! About the time Foster was ready to give voice to his fear that Jerry was warming a barstool somewhere, Doonan plowed through the door, grinning from ear to ear.

"We got him, the bastard," Doonan crowed. "He's at the Marriott in Downers Grove. I know the place, stayed there once with a bunch of Marine buddies who got together after Nam. Look at this picture, John. The name is on the window behind Vinson. It's just too perfect!"

"The Marriott," Foster mused, taking the photo from Doonan. Cook reached for the photo, but Foster shook his head and moved away.

"Let me see, John," Cook pleaded. Foster had seen

enough and handed the enlargement over. "What do you want to do, John? It's your call."

"My call? It's our call. This involves all of us, now." Foster stood with his back to Doonan and Cook. "Jerry, you may have hit the nail on the head. It *is* too perfect. Would Vinson miss something like this, or is it deliberate? We've gotta decide if this is a set up. Do you think Vinson's this calculating, that he's still trying to draw us in?

"We've been figuring there is an advantage if we can get him to come to us, on our terms, on our turf. Is he seeking that same advantage?" Foster was thinking out loud.

Doonan and Cook both shrugged their shoulders. Their euphoria had been short-lived.

"Why would he want us to come to him?" Cook asked again as he paced the perimeter of the waiting room. "Why would the hunter want the prey to come to him?"

"Because he can't go to the prey?" Doonan conjectured. "Or...because he doesn't feel like it?"

"Oh, no. He feels like it. Something's happened and he can't come to us, maybe."

"What could have happened, John?"

"Hell, I don't know. But what else explains the photo, 'Here's looking at you,' and a shit-eating grin on the guy who was alone with me in my office, and I never even recognized him. He could have gutted me and walked out clean. Why not come back for a spectacular finish, unless he can't come back?"

"You could be right, John. He's a calculating sonofabitch. Everything he does, he does for a reason," Doonan said, putting his hand on Foster's tension-rigid shoulder, "but hold on, Buddy; if it is a trap, we've got to go in undercover. Can't just tumble in there like the Keystone Cops. Stealth is what we need...to glide in, to slide like a glass down a well-worn bar, coming to a stop right in front of him. His inclination will be to open his hand, take the drink. That's what we want. 'Your cup of hemlock, Mr. Vinson. Drink up!'"

Cook looked at Foster with a quizzical expression on his

face. "Pardon for asking the obvious, Jerry, but have you been drinking?"

"Me? No, why? It was only a metaphor, Tim. John taught me all about metaphors one god-awful, frigid night on stakeout. Never forgot it. Useful tools, metaphors."

"Never mind," Foster said with a sudden swipe of his left arm, "I think you've got it wrong…all wrong. True, for some reason Vinson can't come to us right now, so he's taunting us just to keep the pressure on. But look, maybe what he's done is make a mistake. Without realizing it, he's given us information we didn't have, and now we can track him to his lair."

"Well, Boys, what say we go get the asshole? We hunt him down, verify his location, call the cops. We aren't vigilantes after all." Cook grinned facetiously.

"Vigilantes, that's just what we are! What the hell! The police haven't done their job since Branan was hospitalized." Doonan clapped his ham hands.

"Gentlemen, I hear impatience and frustration talking. One, or the other, or both, can get us killed. How do we prevent that from happening?" Foster looked from Cook to Doonan, then he made another circuit of the waiting room. *I'm getting real tired of this room.*

CHAPTER FORTY-TWO

Vinson was getting paranoid. He'd been in one place too long and he was feeling vulnerable. His instincts were insisting that he relocate, but his knee was uncooperative. After Maria's sex therapy, the knee hadn't gotten much better that he could see. Ambulation was still possible only with the crutches, which made him stand out like a sore whatever, so he had remained in his room.

He wondered if his nemesis, the shrink, had received his photo. Had the ploy to taunt Foster been too subtle... not subtle enough? If it weren't for the lousy timing and his boredom.... Foster and his cohorts were out there beating the bushes for him. Well, otherwise, he was in high cotton; he had sumptuous lodgings, a masterful hotel chef and unlimited menu, a dutiful physician and accomplished lover who were one and the same, and a bellboy who had fallen under the spell of Vinson's wallet. What more could he ask for? A couple girlie mags and another half-gallon of Charter came to mind.

Vinson hopped over to the chair and side table where he usually made the Old Charter vanish. He recalled the scene from Scent of a Woman in which a blind Al Pacino holds a glass of Gentleman Jack while he interviews the prep school kid who is to accompany him to NYC over Thanksgiving. Due to an editing faux pas, however, as the scene unfolds and Pacino is sipping at the Jack Daniels, the level of liquor in the glass is rising rather than falling. *Wouldn't that be nice...the ever-full libation of your choice? If only!*

Maria's card was under the telephone. He had not seen or heard from her since she left his bed. He was a little surprised, but glad that she was no clinging vine. *Lots to be said for a strong, independent woman; have to remember that.* Vinson dialed Maria's office number; no answer. He waited, then pressed redial. Where was her answering service? He scanned the business card again; he'd overlooked a pager number. Within three minutes of his page, the phone rang.

"This is Dr. Ellis. I believe you paged me? How can I help?"

"Maria, it's me, Vince."

"Yes, I know, Mr. Edwards. Excuse me, but I'm in the middle of a consult."

"OK, Baby, I gotcha. Can you call me ASAP? I hate to ask, but I need a favor."

"Tell me what you need, Mr. Edwards. I'll be through here in about ten minutes."

"I can wait ten minutes to talk to you, Maria. Call me back."

"OK, but give me the bare bones."

"I just received a call from an associate who believes I'm being targeted again over a long-standing grudge. I've gotta change my immediate location, but I prefer to stay on here. Keep your enemies close and all that, right?"

"What can I do?"

"When you're finished there…can you come over to the hotel?"

"It may be an hour, give or take, as I have one more examination before I'm finished."

"That'll work. When you get here, go to the desk and ask for a room for the night; you have an early meeting tomorrow or something. Try to get Room 116 without being too obvious. It adjoins mine and it's empty right now. See if you can arrange it, OK?"

"Sure, but Vi…Mr. Edwards, never mind; I'll do as you ask."

"Good. Just be sure to call me before you leave your office. The situation's fluid; I may want you to alter the plan. Then, when you get here, and the coast is clear, knock four times on my door. I'll know it's you. Four for the four times we did it.

"Are you blushing, my lovely Maria? I'll be waiting." He dropped his voice. "We can make it five… and six. I need you."

Vinson gathered his few things together. He would be ready to move to 116 when Maria arrived. He paced; he took a leak. About three-thirty p.m., fours sharp raps ended his hunt for the remote. Vinson opened the door.

Maria stepped in and kicked the door closed behind her. She set a small overnight case on the floor, and parted the lightweight London Fog she was wearing. Nude and blushing, she stood on tiptoe to kiss him. "Care to make it five?"

Vinson needed no further invitation. He stalked her as she backed toward the bed; with his gentle push, she tumbled, spread-eagle, onto the tapestry coverlet. Number five was fast and furious, and served only to set the stage for number six. Room 116 could wait.

CHAPTER FORTY-THREE

Foster was still trying to figure out how he'd let these two clowns talk him into the need for a disguise. It was like being back on Uncle Sam's payroll. He suspected that Cook was a frustrated spy who had the FBI confused with the spooks at the CIA. Doonan...no telling what Doonan was thinking. Foster wondered if he was just trying to deflect attention from his morning detour into the local pub.

Resigned, Foster slathered on one of those instant tanning lotions and put it on thick. From a cedar chest in the guestroom, he'd unearthed a ratty black wig from a long-ago FBI sting, counterfeit videotapes or designer jeans, some such thing. A pair of scratched Foster Grants left behind in his waiting room, a flak jacket and baggy jeans, steel-toed work boots, and he was set. An aggressive five o'clock shadow would add to the camouflage; in fact, with a couple more days' of growth, he could be a bum until his beard began to itch, which it always did.

Cook opted for his Marine fatigues and added an SP armband, which allowed him to wear his sidearm. He accepted Foster's offer of a retainer to alter the shape of his lower face and mouth, some makeup to broaden his nose, and color for his hair and brows. The results of these alterations were startling, but how long they would fool Cook's former son-in-law was anybody's guess.

Doonan decided that he didn't need a disguise because Vinson had never laid eyes on him. He opted to pose as a street person so he would "blend in" on the streets. Cook suggested slyly that he just wanted a reason to tote a brown paper bag with his bottle in it. Doonan flushed scarlet, but he didn't argue.

When no one appeared to be looking, Doonan slipped out of the office. Foster wondered if they had overplayed their hand and sent Doonan running to the nearest tavern for the second time that day. In fact, Doonan was shopping at the nearby Goodwill Store for a tattered and too-big corduroy shirt in a bilious shade of pea-green, an orange Beatles T-shirt, and khaki cargo pants with enough pockets to carry all his worldly possessions. He was back in about forty minutes.

"I couldn't find a hat, and they were fresh out of brown paper bags." His glance at Foster was challenging, but his heart wasn't in it. It was probably as close as he would come to an admission of his lapse.

Foster burrowed in the office "lost and found" for a moment, and came up with a battered old Cubbies cap that he offered with a flourish. Doonan plopped it on his head backward, and he was finished.

Foster surveyed his bodyguards. "Oh, lord, please let's get this over with!" he muttered.

"Now, guys, come on." Cook was again trying to put a positive spin on their plans. "We'll go in separate cars to the Marriott, park on adjacent streets, opposite sides of the street, whatever. Good thing you thought to drive Joyce's car today, John. That antique of yours would be a dead giveaway!

"Doonan, you take up position in a likely looking doorway so if Vinson should be out of the hotel when we get there, you can alert us to his arrival; John, you park yourself in the lobby and make like a piece of the furniture. I'll go to the front desk and see what I can learn about the rat bastard. Are we ready?"

"Hell yes, Timmy, me boy!" Doonan cuffed him good-naturedly. "I was ready ten minutes ago. Let's get this show on the road."

Cook received a leer and a cheeky salute when he passed Doonan lolling in the recessed doorway of an abandoned furniture store. He jaywalked across the street, and stopped to read the marquis that listed several conventions currently in progress at the Marriott. Dentists, county commissioners from across the state, social workers, and morticians were gathered in the windy city for… what did they call it? Professional development? Continuing education? Just feel-good terms to justify the drinking and carousing that went on at someone else's expense!

Doonan's ass was numb already from sitting on the concrete step where he had hunkered down for what he imagined would be a long wait. There was absolutely nothing going on, and in another minute or two, he was going to be bored outta his skull. He had definitely drawn the short straw in this gig. Good thing he brought along a pint so he could take a wee nip or two. Reaching into one of the pockets of his cargo pants, he broke the seal and took a swig of the Stoli. "Might as well get into character." He wiped his mouth with his sleeve, and returned the bottle to his pocket just as Foster came around the corner.

"Let the games begin, ole buddy," he snickered as Foster passed.

"Hope so," Foster answered without looking Doonan's way.

Cook was standing at the registration desk when Foster picked up an abandoned Tribune and seated himself where he could track anyone coming or going. His scruffy getup earned him a frown from the concierge, but his right to be there wasn't challenged.

After a heated exchange with one of the hotel management types, Cook walked toward him and took a seat to Foster's left. "No Vinson," Cook muttered. "Could be using an alias."

"Did you try Bobby Burton or maybe…something… Edwards?"

"Jeez, no! Didn't think to. You'll have to do it. Look funny coming from me now. Besides, I ticked the guy off. I challenged sacred hotel policy!"

"How do you do that?" Foster asked from behind the newspaper.

"Do what?"

"Talk without moving your lips!"

"I used to do it for Sonya when she was little…and then Dottie. I would make their stuffed animals talk."

"You have talents I never dreamed of, Mr. Cook!

"Well, guess I'll mosey on over and see if the Honorable Mr. Burton or Mr. Edwards are in residence. Should be fun; the concierge already gave me dirty looks. Obviously my attire is not *de rigueur* for this posh establishment.

"Looks like the man you talked to is gone. Don't want to get him again. The names are too similar, and he'd surely catch on."

The lone clerk at the desk bore a remarkable likeness to Homer Simpson. Once he had that thought, it was all Foster could do to keep a straight face. Although there were no other guests at the counter, the clerk took his sweet time before he acknowledged Foster. He was shuffling through invoices, and didn't seem to be in any hurry.

Finally, without looking at Foster, the clerk asked officiously, "May I help you?"

"Yes, Sir, you *can* help me. I'm here to meet friends, and I would appreciate it if you would notify them that I am here. Their names are Robert Burton, or Bobby Burton, and his colleague, a Mr. Edwards."

The clerk still hadn't looked at Foster, and he failed to pick up on the correction of his grammar. "We're not allowed to give the names or room numbers of our guests, Sir."

"I didn't ask you for the names or room numbers of your patrons. I asked you to notify my friends that I am here. I believe you can do that, can't you? My other friend and I would be ever so grateful."

"Your other friend?" the clerk asked, turning for the first time to look at Foster.

"Yes, my friend, Ben Franklin," Foster said smiling and sliding a hundred dollar bill onto the counter.

"I see your friend. Do you have two friends?"

Greedy bastard! Foster pulled another hundred from his pocket and placed it next to the first. The clerk reached for the money as Foster put his left hand casually over the Franklin twins. The clerk flushed and withdrew his hand.

"You say the names are Robert or Bobby Burton and a Mr. Edwards?" the clerk asked.

"Yes."

"Well, let's have a look, shall we?" The clerk approached a computer and entered the name.

"Ah yes, Sir. I don't find a Mr. Burton, but you and your friends will be pleased to know...Mr. Edwards checked in about a week ago. I'm sure he's the gentleman who injured his knee and has been under the care of the hotel's consulting physician. Pretty much confined to his room unfortunately, so, under the circumstances, I think I can justify giving you his room number. It's 114."

Foster lifted his hand from the two hundreds. "Thank you."

When the bills had disappeared into his vest pocket, the clerk cleared his throat. "Uh, Sir? You're not *really* looking for a friend, are you? You're a cop, right?"

"No." *Let him read that any way he wants.*

Foster walked back to the chair where he had been seated, and picked up the newspaper.

"He's here. Room 114, registered as Vincent Edwards. Homer Simpson over there became quite chatty when he made the acquaintance of the Franklin brothers. Seems our Mr. Edwards hurt his knee and has been confined to his room. He is under a doctor's care."

"Poor fellow! That would certainly explain his recent absence."

"Tim, I'd be willing to bet my best shirt there's a little asterisk by our Mr. Edwards' name. I worked one summer for a big hotel chain. The asterisks meant special guests, as in *problem* guests, as in possible legal proceedings. The usual instructions were 'No charge and give them everything they want,' and I do mean everything!"

"You got all that in three minutes?" Cook asked, incredulously.

"Three minutes and two hundred bucks. Money talks every time."

"Well goddamn, we've nailed him! Let's let Doonan know."

CHAPTER FORTY-FOUR

Vinson was lazing in the post-coital indolence of a two-hour sexual bout with his treating physician. Now settled in Room 116, the room registered to Maria, Vinson felt secure in his new lair. If Foster or the cops were coming for him, he'd be able to evade them.

"You're great, Vince," Maria murmured, her fingers sifting through his chest hair.

"Thanks, Baby. Just wait 'til I'm in good form again. Pain and your wonder drugs are cramping my style."

"Maybe I won't be able to handle you when you're at your peak."

"You're being modest. We're terrific together, and you know it."

Maria rolled gracefully to the edge of the bed. She pulled Vinson's shirt from the floor and slipped one arm into it; as she approached the ornate full-length mirror in the bathroom, however, the shirt slipped from her arm and landed on the floor, again. She studied herself in the glass. Her hair was a tumble of curls around her face. A sexual flush still tinted her breasts, and there was dried semen on her upper thigh.

"I'm a well-loved woman," she told Vinson's reflection as he limped to stand behind her. He bit the moist skin beneath her ear and inhaled deeply.

"Share a shower with me?"

"Vince, who are the guys who are looking for you?" Maria asked.

Vinson hadn't conjured up a story yet, but told her that they were sore losers in a high stakes poker game who accused him of cheating.

"Did you cheat, Vince?"

"Of course I did. I don't rely on luck in cards. Knowing the game isn't enough, either. I say use whatever tools are at my disposal. They didn't see me cheat; they assumed it because of the way they lost. Each of them had a great hand that I had generously dealt them, but I had the best hand. They were stunned! It was a respectable gambling parlor on the north side. Ten grand to get in. By the time I walked out—with forty-two grand—they didn't know what hit them."

"You're a professional gambler, Vince?"

"You could say that. Life is a gamble. When the cards aren't receptive, there's always a bluff."

"I had no idea," Maria said, looking concerned. "I thought you were a salesman or something."

"Salesman? Shit, girl, I'm much more than that, although salesmanship is part and parcel of being a successful gambler."

"Oh," Maria replied, standing naked a few inches from Vinson who was admiring her backside.

"Does what I tell you scare you, Maria?"

"No, not really. It's just unexpected. It's also exciting. I like it, really. I've never met anybody quite like you."

"Not likely you'll meet another like me either," Vinson said, reaching for the delectable Dr. Ellis and pulling her back onto the bed. "I'm hungry," Vinson announced as though his hunger were newsworthy. "Why don't you go to the hotel deli and bring us back a couple of Reubens, a six pack of dark beer, and, oh yeah, extra kosher dills and a side order of coleslaw."

"Sure." Maria sighed, looking down at her breasts cradled in Vince's hands.

"I'll be here when you get back," Vinson said, laving each nipple. "Little Vince will be here, too," he said, placing her hand over his semi-erect penis.

"Dessert, hmmm?"

"If you can handle the calories," Vinson waggled his eyebrows.

"I'm on a diet, but I might make an exception," Maria kipped herself into a standing position off the bed.

"Nice move, Kid."

"Sophomore high school gymnastics," Maria grinned. Looking around at the pieces of clothing they had discarded on their way to the bed, she found her slacks and the White Sox sweatshirt Vince had been wearing.

"You mind?" she asked before pulling it over her head. "No undies, see? Think about that and I'll be back before you know it!"

CHAPTER FORTY-FIVE

Doonan, Cook, and Foster were seated at a round metal table littered with the remains of their meal of *man foods*, meaning the kind of high fat, high salt fare that was never permitted at home. Foster's gaze was snagged by a beautiful redhead entering the deli, and they made eye contact briefly before she looked away. "We just can't crash into his room," Doonan was saying. "Besides, if we can't take him down, hold him for the police to make an arrest…if he makes a break for it, and we have to take him out…. What we're talking about? We don't have that authority."

"Fer cryin' out loud! Spit it out, Man. We're talking illegal, yes?" Cook was exasperated with Doonan's pussy footing.

"What's illegal about killing a dead man?" Foster asked sarcastically.

Doonan didn't even blink. "Look, the police are going on the assumption Vinson's alive now that they have the DNA evidence obtained from the exhumation. There's a case here, if only that deadhead detective who took over for Branan would do his job."

"So?" Foster asked.

"So, let's figure out a way to flush him out of the hotel, get him alone, some place we can take him down without endangering civilians…."

"Need I remind you?" Cook groused. "*We* are civilians, Good Buddy, and Vinson will have no scruples about shooting at us. John, you're not listening. Where's your head?"

"The redhead," Doonan nodded at the woman who could be heard ordering two reubens and a six-pack of dark ale to go. "She's gorgeous."

"So what?" Cook snapped.

"There's something about her…looks familiar."

"It's just that no-bra look you've always favored," Doonan elbowed Foster. "She's either got a boyfriend stashed close by or she has a voracious appetite."

"Yes, but there's something…reminds me of Vinson."

"Vinson?" Doonan queried. "Come on, John, we've got him. Let's focus here…decide what to do…preferably something that doesn't end with us doing life without parole."

While Cook and Doonan batted around possible scenarios, Foster continued to observe the woman: Red hair, combed in a hurry judging by the uneven part; no earrings, but pierced ears; no makeup, but hell, she didn't need it; sandals, tight jeans, White Sox sweatshirt…too large, a man's size, maybe?

When the redhead turned to leave with her order, she paused at the realization that Foster continued to stare at her. The glare she gave him would probably bend steel at twenty paces!

"What is it about her?" Foster muttered. "What's wrong with this picture?"

Doonan had seen Foster fixated like this before on federal cases they had worked together. When he realized that John would not stop until he had resolved the questions related to the woman's appearance at this time and place, Doonan signaled Cook for silence. Several moments passed before Foster bolted to his feet and ran from the deli, leaving Cook and Doonan staring at each other in confusion.

Foster could not see the redhead in the corridor leading from the deli, but as he turned a corner into the lobby, he could see her beyond the concierge's desk where she turned another corner and disappeared. He sprinted across the lobby, earning a frown from the starched bell captain for his lack of decorum. When he reached the head of the corridor, he saw her enter a door about halfway down on the left. Keeping his eyes fixed on the door, he approached. The number on the door read "116."

Adjoining rooms, huh? Smart, Eddie. Really smart.

Foster was psyched! There was no doubt in his mind that Vinson was keeping company in Room 116. "Float like a butterfly, sting like a bee," he chanted a la Mohammed Ali as he bobbed and weaved back to the reception desk. Doonan and Cook had just entered the lobby from the deli. With a nod of his head toward the revolving doors, Foster indicated that they should follow him from the hotel.

When Cook and Doonan joined him in front of the Marriott, Foster was grinning like a loon. He held up his hand to stave off their questions about his behavior. "I told you guys there was something familiar about that woman! She's with Vinson."

"How do you know, John?" asked Doonan.

"Because she was wearing his Sox sweatshirt, the same one he wore to my office for his second or third appointment. I forget which...."

"You're like a dog with a bone. When you sink your teeth into something, you don't let go, do ya?" Cook was shaking his head.

Doonan clapped Foster on the shoulders enthusiastically. "You're the best, John, always were; guess you still are! Details just don't get past you!"

"Never mind. That's enough smoke up my butt! Let's get our plans solidified. My guess is that Mr. Vincent Edwards, a.k.a. Eddie Vinson, has created a nice little diversion in Room 114, on the outside chance that we should be better than he gives us credit for. He's brought in a stooge, albeit a rather beautiful one, and is hiding in 116. It's perfect!

"The guy's good, really good, but if he's been forced to hole-up for what...four, five days, because of some injury, the inability to take his show on the road is probably driving him nuts, if you'll pardon the lay terminology."

"He never relaxes," mused Doonan, as he unscrewed his flask and waved it under his nose.

"Hold up on that, Jerry. This is the real deal, now, and we've got to be sharp."

"When I titrate my old friend, Stoli, I'm as sharp as I get, John."

Foster didn't respond, but reasoned that Doonan was probably right.

"Let's go back to the deli," Cook said.

"I don't think so; our scent is there, so to speak. Let's go to the pizzeria two doors down. The smell is tantalizing, and we're too full to eat again, so…no danger of incurring calories!"

"OK," Cook said, stepping off the curb.

"Oh, I dunno," Doonan burped and grinned. "I maybe could eat a slice or two."

CHAPTER FORTY-SIX

Vinson was sinking his teeth into the Rueben when he noticed Ellis staring at the blank TV screen. "What's wrong, Maria?"

"Nothing...not really," she said flatly.

"Sure there is. I'm the face reader, remember?"

"It's probably nothing."

"Nothing?" Vinson asked.

"There were these three weird-looking guys who were paying me a lot of attention at the deli. At least one of them...he was staring."

"What did these guys look like?" Vinson asked, all senses on alert.

"That's just it. They didn't belong here; even in the deli they were out of place. One was a Marine M.P., only it said "SP" on his armband, and he had a gun at his hip, except he was old, too old to be on active duty; one looked like an Ernest Hemingway type, or a survivalist who'd been in the sun too long; and the third looked like he'd wandered away from his cardboard box."

"What did you make of them?" Vinson asked.

"Could they be the guys, Vince? The ones looking for you?

"If it wasn't so strange, it would be funny really. What I don't understand is why they seemed so interested in me. They can't connect me to you, can they?"

"Doubtful," Vinson mused. "We haven't been together outside of this room. Three of 'em, huh?"

"Yeah," Maria bit her lip. "I'm scared."

"It's OK. They didn't follow you did they?"

"No. I looked behind me a couple of times; no one was there. No one."

Vinson noted that Maria had ignored her sandwich and the ale he poured for her. She had lost her sensual glow. When he pulled his pistol from the back of his waistband, she paled even more; her features became pinched and her eyes, haunted. He felt a stab of disappointment. He had thought she was made of sterner stuff.

"Look, Maria," Vince said, polishing a smudge from the barrel of his gun. "Nothing's going to happen to you. There's no way they know exactly where I am; I haven't been out of my room for two days. Hotel staff isn't allowed to give names or room numbers…and even if someone accepted a bribe to give out information about me, they don't know I've moved into the room registered to you.

"Even if everything should go wrong, it's me they're after. You're going to be leaving in a few minutes. We won't take any chances with you. Then, if they find me, my 9mm will do the rest. I can defend myself."

Maria removed Vince's sweatshirt and began gathering her things. She was not reassured by Vince's words, and his ease with the gun was frightening. She put on her blouse, and ran a comb through her hair. She was beginning to believe that she might be in over her head. She enjoyed risky adventures, but gambling and mobsters and guns were a bit more than she had anticipated. Up to this point, she thought she was the one pulling the strings, but as she looked at Vince, there was a steely control about him that was unnerving. Not only was he not frightened that three goons appeared to have tracked him down, he was alert and, perhaps, even eager for a confrontation.

"Look, Vince. You're right. I'm in your way, and I don't want to distract you. I'm on call in the ER this evening anyway. I know you're just passing through, and we have no future, but that doesn't mean I don't wish it could be otherwise. We're good together and…."

"Can't you call in sick or something?" Vince interrupted, suddenly not ready to let her go.

"No, I can't. There's no one to cover for me. I'll be on until 7:00 a.m."

"OK, Kid. If that's the way it has to be."

Tears threatened, but Maria refused to give in to them. She had little information upon which to base an assessment of danger, but the relief that washed over her as she closed the door to 116 behind her screamed that she was getting off lucky. Better that she didn't know getting off lucky from what!

The desk clerk saw her leaving and asked if she still planned to stay the night.

"I don't think so; my plans have changed. Bill me for the room, OK?" Maria smiled. Only she knew it would be a miracle if her legs carried her to the exit and out to the street.

"Sure, Dr. Ellis, it's my pleasure," the manger smirked and winked at a trio of bellhops who were enjoying the sway of her hips. Mr. Edwards hadn't been the doctor's first extended care at the Marriott; her dedicated *services* were common knowledge among the hotel staff.

By 6:30 p.m., Vinson was settling into the soothing embrace of his third Charter when someone knocked on 116. He couldn't summon any worry. He had difficulty getting up from the chair, and limped slowly to the door. A glance through the security glass revealed a middle-aged cleaning lady and her supply cart. Must be a mistake he thought, noting that he had not put the security chain in place after Maria left. *Too late now*.

Several additional knocks and a rattling of keys indicated that he was about to be discovered. Vinson decided to brazen it through, and pulled the door open just as the lady turned her key and pushed. He bit the inside of his lip to stifle a grin, and reached out to support the woman until she regained her balance.

"Maid Service," she squeaked. She was blushing from the top of her ears to the deep V of her uniform.

Vinson shrugged, puzzled. "I didn't call for cleaning services."

"This Dr. Maria's room?"

"Yes, I know. I was...."

"The lady...she check out; say her plans change suddenly. I am sent to clean so room is open for tonight. We have many requests for rooms. I am sorry, sir. I am just the lady what cleans rooms."

"Oh, I see. She checked out? She must have tried to call while I was out." Vinson smiled. "I'll just pop back into my own room then, get out of your way."

"Si, it says so right on my assignment sheet. Check out at 3:00."

"Just give me one moment," Vinson said, turning his back to the woman, and scanning the room. There was only his glass and the almost empty bottle of Charter, which he fumbled as he collected them.

Shit! The bitch had her fill and bailed on me. I'm forced back into 114 with no cover. Just like Sonya, all over again...only now, it's likely Foster knows where I am; he's waitin' and he's in the catbird's seat. Think, think.

Stunned and reeling, Vinson realized that the cleaning woman had a clear view of the pistol that was still tucked in his waistband at the small of his back. Since there was nothing he could do except look guilty as hell, he offered no explanation. He crossed to the door of his adjoining room. As he reached for the doorknob, the phone began to ring behind him. He turned to look at the phone, then at the cleaning lady. With a shrug, he stepped into 114, closed the door and locked it.

Immediately the phone in his room began to trill. Vinson was rattled, but he schooled himself to speak slowly and remove all traces of rage from his voice. *It's probably Ellis.*

"Maria?" No answer.

"Maria, that you, Sweetheart?" Still no answer.

"Damn it, Maria, you checked out without telling..."

"No, not Maria, Eddie. It's me, your old nemesis, Dr. Ertsof. Remember? The doctor who stole your wife."

"Foster? How...?"

"Did I find you?" Foster finished Vinson's sentence. "The grass...the grass, Eddie, it just isn't tall enough; you don't blend in and you can't hide any longer."

"Grass? Tall grass? Hide? What the fuck are you talking about?"

"Oh, you'll find out soon enough," Foster let his voice trail off; then he hung up.

"We got him, boys. He's back in room 114 and he's reeling for sure," Foster declared to his two cohorts who were polishing off the pizza they'd sworn they couldn't eat.

"What do you think he'll do, John?" asked Doonan.

"Just as we predicted. He'll run. He's been flushed into the open, no cover, and he senses he's become the prey. He realizes we have the upper hand. His reaction, not response now, reaction, will be directed by fear and impulse. All we have to do is follow where he leads.

"I'll call Branan at home and let him know we've located Vinson. He's still on convalescent leave, but maybe he could make a call, get Pellegrino to give us some backup; maybe the police can grab him before he runs."

"So, the hunter's now the prey," Cook said pensively to Doonan, while Foster dialed Branan's number.

"Branan here."

"Branan, it's Foster. We've found Vinson. He's holed up at the Downers Grove Marriott. I'm here now with Cook and Doonan. Vinson knows we're onto him, and it's likely he'll try to bolt. It will be difficult to capture him here, too many innocent bystanders; if we force him into a corner, he'll fight, and he won't care who gets hurt, so it would be best if we let him leave the hotel. We'll stay on him, but it would help if you could request some uniforms to back us up."

"You got it, Doc. I knew you wouldn't let it drop. I'll see if a team is available to back you up, a couple of uniforms and a sharpshooter. The firepower might be needed to take Vinson down. We both know he's not going to surrender."

"Tim, Jerry, Branan is in the loop and is sending backup with added firepower. The best we can hope for is that Vinson leaves the hotel so that no civilians become involved. We'll follow where he leads; we'll have to be ready for anything and think on our feet. Leave you cell phone lines open."

"It's not likely he can shake all three of us." Doonan dropped the last crust of pizza with a groan. "He may not suspect that we have police backup until it's too late."

"OK, let's take up positions around the hotel; we'll give him room to flee, and flee he will," Foster said.

"John, I think I should stick with Tim; I don't know my way around here all that well. He can drive and I can track Vinson. Otherwise...if I get lost, I'll be absolutely no help to you."

"That's wise, Jerry; I wasn't thinking. I have no doubt Vinson will go to ground, try to disappear. If he runs us through the maze of city streets, and Jenny told me he knows them better than anyone, we'll be hard-pressed to follow. You would be at a definite disadvantage. Hell, we all will be, but at least this way, we have a chance. What we have going for us, and it's a big plus…Vinson is feeling pressure. He's no longer the aggressor, and his behavior will become increasingly erratic and disorganized, so stay sharp. The waiting is over."

CHAPTER FORTY-SEVEN

Vinson was trying to figure out how to get out of the hotel without being seen by Foster and his henchmen. A call to the front desk and a request for Julio's assistance would do for starters.

When Julio reached 114, he entered an empty room through the door that Vinson had propped open. "Mr. Edwards? Are you in here, Sir? It's Julio."

Vinson emerged from the bathroom and closed the door with a sharp snap.

"Oh, Mr. Edwards, you scared me."

"No sweat, Kid. I've decided to check out, and I would appreciate some help packing. There's a twenty in it for you."

"Sure, Mr. Edwards, I'll be glad to help." Julio surveyed the room, which was now littered with take-out cartons and two empty liquor bottles. "What would you have me do?" he asked turning to look at Vinson. A look of puzzlement had reached Julio's eyes by the time the butt of Vinson's 9mm connected with his temple, cracking his skull and sending lethal shards of bone hurtling into the brain. Gravity did the rest.

Vinson placed a towel around Julio's head and struck him twice more to finish the job. "Sorry, Kid, but I need your uniform." He stripped off the boy's jacket and pants, careful not to transfer blood onto the fabric. The jacket fit reasonably well although the pants were too long. One roll of the waistband was all that was required to adjust the length.

Vinson dragged the body into the bathroom and rolled it into the tub as he recited the seven deadly sins. "Greed, Julio, it'll get you every time," Vinson grinned.

Vinson had wrapped his knee tightly with the ace bandage Maria left for him. Since a bellboy on crutches would attract attention, Vinson needed to walk out of the hotel under his own steam. He was taking nothing with him; there was no longer anything to hide. He needed only speed and cunning to make his escape.

Vinson reached the lobby and walked past the concierge's desk without incident. He approached the nearest of the front doors and stepped out. On the curb, he scanned both directions, looking for Foster's Porsche or for cars that were occupied by drivers who could be providing surveillance.

A Yellow Cab pulled up to the hotel to drop off guests, and when a quick glance told him no one was waiting for the taxi, Vinson seized the moment and signaled to the driver. He limped across the sidewalk to the cab, braced himself as he opened the door, and landed awkwardly on the back seat. The exertion of the past forty minutes was causing his knee to burn with each step. "Give me just a moment," he gasped to the driver.

CHAPTER FORTY-EIGHT

A bellboy with a limp leaving the hotel at peak registration time in a Yellow Cab? What's wrong with this picture? Foster had been watching people enter and exit the hotel from his location in the recessed doorway of a flower shop adjacent to the hotel. Joyce's Mercedes was parked directly in front of him, partially hidden by a boxy panel truck. He stepped out of the doorway and moved behind the truck so that he could approach the cab from the left rear while using the truck for cover.

Suddenly, the taxi driver turned on his directional signal to indicate that he was waiting for an opening to enter traffic. Nevertheless, one look at the cab's passenger, *the bellboy*, was all Foster needed to identify Vinson. As he retreated to his car, he speed dialed Doonan and got a busy signal. He started his engine and jockeyed for position so that he could pull quickly out of the parking space as soon as the cab merged into traffic. While he waited, he turned on his headlights so that he couldn't be seen as clearly if Vinson should look to see if he had a tail.

Foster wasn't sure of the hour, but it was approaching dusk. Personally, he preferred surveillance under cover of darkness, but following a vehicle at night could be tricky. A minute or two passed before the taxi finally pulled into traffic; Foster tucked himself behind it and allowed two vehicle lengths to open between them. He punched redial, and this time, Doonan answered.

"Yeah?"

"I'm following Vinson in a Yellow Cab. No cops here yet. I'm going east on...I don't know, give me a moment to give you some landmarks. Vinson came out of the hotel dressed in a bellboy's uniform. He was limping. I'm pretty sure he didn't see me. Where are the two of you?"

Foster was already about a mile from the hotel, following the cab now from two cars back. He'd done a quick replay of the mandatory surveillance training courses from his FBI days, but he had had no opportunity to use such skills thanks to the thousands of hours he logged at a desk.

He was having difficulty navigating in heavy traffic and following the cab. He was sweating profusely, and his alarm was growing by the second. Without Cook and Doonan's backup, Foster feared he could blow their advantage at having found Vinson.

"Where are you, John?" Cook raised his voice so he could be heard on Doonan's cell.

"I'm headed north on Palmer. I still got him, but it's getting so damn dark and there's a whole shit-load of cabs around me."

"Get the number off the back of the cab. Concentrate on the number; not the vehicle, that way you can remain focused on the right one," Cook yelled.

"OK, OK," Foster muttered. "How far behind are you?"

"We'll catch you," Cook said, "We've got balls to the wall and we're not stopping for lights. Just hang on, John. We'll be there for you...just a few more minutes."

Foster was concentrating on numbers, 427, Yellow Cab 427. Suddenly the cab slowed and pulled to the curb. *Maybe my luck is changing, law of statistical regression… it's bound to go right eventually. It always comes down to math.*

Foster pulled to the curb behind a monster pickup. Hoping he wasn't making a big mistake, he got out of his car and moved to the side of the truck so he could see the cab and any move that Vinson might make. He watched and wondered as Vinson exited the right rear door and crossed behind the vehicle so that he approached the cabbie's door. A dead streetlight above and the flicker of oncoming headlights cast eerie shadows. It seemed to Foster that the cab was rocking, moving erratically, and then it stopped.

For Vinson, the cheap, flexible belt to Julio's uniform served as a garrote with which to strangle the puny, unsuspecting cabbie. He had uttered one word, "Dio," and struggled only briefly before he surrendered to the inevitable. Opening the driver's door, Vinson elbowed the cabbie's slender frame toward the split between the front bucket seats, and tumbled his body into the rear of the cab. He was again in the driver's seat.

A glance in the side mirror showed Vinson a fortuitous break in traffic. He turned off the cab's lights and pulled onto the highway. He didn't know if he was being followed, but assumed that he was. Vinson accelerated to 50 in a 35 mph zone; seeing a one-way street on his right, he turned abruptly although it put him going the wrong way. If he was being followed, his pursuer would also have to go against any oncoming traffic. He slowed and turned his lights back on in self-defense. A yellow cab was impossible to hide, lights or no lights.

Foster reached for his cell phone to let Cook and Doonan know his location. In the moments that it took him to return to his vehicle, the cab had suddenly peeled into traffic.

"Shit!" Foster slid behind the wheel, but traffic conspired to keep him at the curb for about twenty seconds before he could give chase. In those crucial moments, he debated whether Vinson remained a passenger or had overcome the cabbie and taken control of the vehicle. If he were a betting man, and he was, he would go with his instinct, which told him Vinson was now driving.

Momentarily, the glare of headlights in his rearview mirror confirmed for Vinson that he was being followed. "Dr. Ertsof, I presume!" He pounded the steering wheel with the heel of his hand, and gave in to the urge to shout. "Whooah! I gotcha now! Eat my dust, you dumb desk jockey!"

As he accelerated, Vinson glanced about, trying to get his bearings. He knew he'd been in this area before, but couldn't recall the exact layout of the decaying neighborhood. What he did know was that he was gonna take Foster on the ride of his life, a ride that would end in death, Foster's death. Vinson began to drive erratically; he turned left and right at will, often the wrong way on one-way streets as it suited him. Foster might conclude, mistakenly, that he was rattled, which would give Vinson further advantage as he drew the good doctor toward the evening's finale, the swan song of one John Foster, Ph.D.

CHAPTER FORTY-NINE

Cook and Doonan were waging a dogged pursuit when Foster called again. "Where are you? I turned right off Palmer. Now I'm going bass-ackwards on a one-way in some little abandoned neighborhood," Foster yelled into the phone. "It's a miracle no one's been killed, but there's nobody on the streets. I'm on Justin past Fairfield, I think.... The streets are narrow, not much more than alleys, and most of the houses look empty. Tail lights showed the cab made a brief stop just after it turned in here, and now I see only one person—the driver. I suspect Vinson overpowered or ejected the cabbie. The way he's driving, he knows I'm following."

"Shit!" Doonan muttered, "I've gotta tell Cook, John. Just hang on."

Neither Doonan nor Cook knew this part of Chicago so when they passed up Justin, it was no surprise. They traveled a half-mile before they could turn around on the dark, narrow pavement, and, by then, Foster himself was so lost he couldn't direct them to pick up his trail.

"There's not a street light that hasn't been busted out...kids with rocks, gangs practicing their marksmanship. I don't know if Vinson is ahead of me or behind me now. He could be breathin' down my neck or crawling up my backside and I wouldn't know." Foster brushed at the sweat that was searing his eyeballs. "You're on your own, guys; I'm so disoriented I don't know what to tell you. What I wouldn't give for one of those GPS gizmos like we had in the Bureau! You might just tuck tail and listen for the fireworks.... They're sure to come. Vinson thinks I'm alone; he might get cocky and do somethin' stupid. Of course, I am alone! I could lay on the horn, make enough noise to raise the dead. He knows I'm here anyway...and maybe you can get a fix on me.

"God, it's scary! I'm too old, too soft; I've lost my edge. What was I thinking? Vinson is moving in a world he knows well. Me, I feel like I'm in a foreign country."

"But some things you never lose, John. You were always one of the Bureau's best; let it come back to you. Quit second-guessing yourself. Vinson may know these streets, but you *know* Vinson. Let the knowledge guide you. That's *your* advantage."

Foster expelled a gusty sigh that both Doonan and Cook could hear through the cell phone. "Thanks for the pep talk, Jerry. I'll settle down." He slowed to a crawl as he came to a four-way intersection. A battered and rusting sign with an arrow pointed straight ahead to Br ther Manufacturing."

In the all-pervasive darkness, Foster caught the red pulse of what he believed to be the taillights of the cab. If that was the case, Vinson had turned right and stopped once he'd cleared the intersection. *The cat waiting for the poor blind mouse?*

"Jerry, Tim. I passed a sign for Brothers Manufacturing. Looks to be an abandoned industrial complex. It isn't much, but...Vinson is about a half block ahead. I spotted his taillights for just a second. Could be an ambush."

"We're moving, John. If Vinson engages you, do like you said, lay on your horn. We'll find you."

"Keep your powder dry, good buddy. Goes without saying, you should be careful!"

"I'll try. Thanks, Tim, Jerry. My cell battery's getting low...signing off."

No lights. No people. A god-forsaken place. Wonder what it was like here twenty-thirty years ago?

Foster took a right, drove one block over and one up. When he turned the next corner, he would be facing Vinson in the cab, if that's where he remained. Perhaps Vinson was on foot by now...reconnoitering, leading Foster where he would have him go, because if Foster was sure of anything, it was that Vinson still saw himself as the hunter and Foster, the prey. *So where does that leave me? Surely Vinson doesn't expect me to walk right up and tweak his whiskers? Now there's a thought!*

Foster used the butt of his gun to smash the overhead courtesy light. Then, he slithered from the car and pasted himself to its side, moving slowly, taking what cover the vehicle offered. No sooner did he grant himself a full breath than Vinson flashed the cab's headlights on and off. Still in the cab then, at least for the moment, and the lights would have compromised his night vision.

Again Vinson turned on his headlights, and this time he left them pointing menacingly at the corner where Foster watched and waited. He wanted to swipe at the icy sweat rolling merrily down his temples, but was afraid to do more than draw breath. In a momentary panic, he wondered if he cast a shadow in the beam of the headlights, but reasoned that since there was no light behind him, it was unlikely.

"How ya doin', Doc? We're gettin' right down to it now. Do you feel it, the fear that gums up your brain and turns your bowels to liquid? I can smell your fear; I know you're here. Want to play some more?" Vinson shoved the cab into reverse and gunned the engine. He backed into the street and executed a deft turn that put him on a course parallel to Foster and one block over.

Foster was surprised by Vinson's sudden maneuver; he wasn't so stupid as to perceive that Vinson had retreated. No, Vinson was confidently drawing him to his Waterloo, Wellington to Foster's Napoleon.

No one had ever accused Foster of lacking imagination, and he could imagine a bullet streaking for his forehead with stark clarity. He stood and stretched, then returned to the driver's seat. He propped the door open with his foot and searched his pockets for a handkerchief to mop up sweat. Then, he sat quietly, slowing his breathing and running through options that might allow him to do the one thing that Vinson would least expect. His brain sorted and circled, but kept coming back to Doonan's words, "You *know* Vinson. Let that knowledge guide you."

Five minutes elapsed, maybe more, before Foster started the engine and followed Vinson. He drove slowly and looked to the left and right as he passed through each intersection, but the wide stance and ponderous weight of the cab had drawn clear tracks in the dirt and cinders that coated the abandoned streets, thus indicating that Vinson was no longer using the maze of narrow streets to confound him. He had changed tactics.

When Foster reached a railroad spur that ran parallel to a ten-foot security fence, his assurance wobbled momentarily. Left or right? While he debated, a reflection of the cab's brake lights to his right again gave him his answer. Foster swung right and slowed to a crawl. He knew Vinson was making it easy, but not too easy, for him to follow. It probably didn't occur to him that Foster would do anything else. He turned right again as Vinson had done and could see the cab waiting for him to catch up.

Gimme a little credit, Eddie, I'm not that weak an adversary.

Foster followed meekly when Vinson began to move forward. When he passed the next one-way to the right, Foster stomped on the accelerator, closing the distance and climbing right up Vinson's back bumper. When it was too late for Vinson to make the turn at the next intersection, Foster cut a hard right and continued to accelerate. "Eat my dust for awhile now; I'm done following," Foster challenged, watching in his rear view mirror as Vinson backed up and made the turn. He was banking on Vinson's refusal to switch roles without a fight.

"What are you up to, Doc?" Vinson growled. "Getting too big for your pinstriped britches?"

Foster was traveling about 40 mph straight down the center of the narrow street. True to character, Vinson wove left and right, obviously looking for room to make a move. He could have veered off as Foster had done, but he remained glued to Foster's ass looking for his opening.

Foster reasoned that Vinson would stay to the end if he continued to up the ante. "Let's see if I'm right, Eddie." he said aloud as he passed a bullet-pocked sign that read "Hope Street."

Apropos! Foster thought seeing the sign. A sense of rightness washed over him, and confidence returned. He was in the lead and ready to take Vinson for a ride! He headed back in the general direction of the abandoned manufacturing complex.

Vinson was experiencing a controlled, burning rage, a state he likened to the functioning of a nuclear reactor. His energy, harnessed or contained, could drive him indefinitely, allow him to do whatever he wanted or needed. Let loose, however, he could, and would, destroy whatever was in his path. Right now, that was Foster.

Vinson was aware that his control was slipping, but, for the moment, the rage was euphoric. "Fun, fun, fun, Doc, even if you don't stand a chance," he jeered.

Foster's mood was far from giddy. Resignation and a sense of purpose were the two things he could identify. A profound weariness hovered on the fringes of awareness, needing only the cessation of conflict or a loss of focus, whichever came first, and it would swoop down like some hell-bent buzzard and snatch him.

Foster summoned the focus that would get him through the coming minutes. He began to increase his speed slowly, hoping that Vinson would not notice right off. Forty-five miles per hour on these narrow, empty streets was tricky, but not dangerous.

"Let's try fifty, Eddie." Foster accelerated. He reasoned that the faster he went, the more control he exerted over Vinson, an obsessive-compulsive influence of sorts. The more Vinson needed to wrest control of their contest, the more he would be compelled to remain fixed on his goal. Control was Vinson's thing; he knew how to operate only from the captain's chair!

Foster flashed on an old cartoon of a psychologist dropping pellets into a cage wired so that when the laboratory rat pressed a lever, the psychologist produced the desired food. The cartoon caption read, "*Who's controlling whom?*" This wasn't much different, Foster thought wryly. He might be wearing the white coat, but Vinson and his pathology were not without considerable influence, and he damn well mustn't lose sight of that fact.

"Let's try fifty-five, Eddie," Foster shouted over the clamoring engine and slapping tires on night-chilled pavement. In the rear view mirror, the cab's headlights flickered, suddenly smaller.

"Can't take it, hey, Eddie?" Foster hooted and backed off the accelerator. "Fifty is your limit, Scumbag?"

Foster clamped down on emotion that could still get him killed. He focused. "OK, let's tinker with the rules of this game," Foster said to himself. He shot a quick look over his shoulder to gauge distance, then slammed on his brakes. The Mercedes came to a gut-wrenching stop. He noted a VFW Hall to his left and, on his right, an empty drunk of a house that listed precipitously on sagging block piers.

"What the fuck are you doing now, Doc?" Vinson stomped on the brake pedal and the yellow behemoth rocked and knocked before complying. The smell of rubber charred his sinuses, reminding him of his drag racing days when he had come to love Corvettes. Right about now, he missed his cherry beauty!

When silence fell, Vinson estimated that he was only two to three feet behind Foster's vehicle. He placed his hands on the steering wheel, mimicking Foster, who remained equally as still. From the tilt of Foster's head, Vinson judged that he was focused on the rearview mirror, yet there was no acknowledgement of their sudden proximity…or what would come next.

Is this surreal, or what? Who blinks…?

Wisps of smoke from the cab's tires floated on the currents of night air. Foster wondered idly if Vinson could hear his heart beating. He sat, unmoving, for a count of sixty. He imagined them as two gunfighters in a spaghetti western, eyes fixed, waiting for the signal to go for the six-shooter. A twitch of a finger, the blink of an eye...in the code of the West, the good guy never jumped the gun; ergo, Vinson, knowing deep down that he wasn't the guy in the white hat, would make the first move. No sooner did the thought take shape than....

"OK, Doc, let's see what you've got." With that, Vinson floored it, ramming Foster's Mercedes with the cab's dominating bulk, but with little force. Lacking room to accelerate, neither car sustained more than the crumpling of bumpers; however, when Vinson tried to back up, he discovered that his front bumper had locked with Foster's rear bumper. Since both vehicles sported heavy-duty steel, the tangle was a solid one.

Foster realized what had happened when he felt a tug from the cab as Vinson tried to back up. Instinctively, he pushed the gas pedal to the floor. Equally instinctive, Vinson, still in reverse, also hit the accelerator.

Foster's rear wheels screeched and smoked as he fought the inexorable pull of the stolid, lumbering cab. The only possible outcome…the Mercedes would eventually surrender to the mauling of the cab because Vinson wouldn't quit. Because they were now locked together, Foster could not continue the feinting and parrying with which he sought to taunt Vinson. Neither could he see a way to regain his advantage. Vinson had nothing to lose and everything to win, and Foster was no fool. They both knew…one of them would not survive this night.

Without warning, the cab broke loose, sending Vinson a good thirty feet back before he could react. The Mercedes, severed from the cab's restraining weight, shot forward toward the end of the block.

Then…silence.

Vinson was the first to see a lone man standing outside the VFW. Foster caught sight of him in his side mirror. He wondered how long the old gent had been there, the only audience to their battle royal.

The flash of a muzzle and the pop of an anemic firecracker were the only warning. Their witness folded at the knees and tumbled into the street, all seemingly in slow motion. Foster's mouth and throat worked to give voice to his horror, but he made no sound. Only in his brain did his thoughts ricochet with ferocious agony. "You bastard; you cowardly bastard!"

Foster was stunned by Vinson's needless assault on the old man. He realized it was imperative that he draw

Vinson to a location where there would be no chance for further loss of innocent life. The abandoned industrial park seemed the closest place. There might be a crackhead or two hunkered down inside the rusting hulk of the plant or its outbuildings, but it was unlikely that anyone would be in the streets at this time of night, especially after the screech and roar of the two cars locked together in combat.

Slowly Foster traveled forward. Vinson trailed him at a distance of some thirty to forty feet; he occasionally jerked the cab's steering wheel so that it rocked back and forth as if to say, "I'm still here."

"Here's looking back at you, Vinson," Foster thought. He was relieved to see one side of the industrial park directly ahead...new territory. The complex was rimmed with rusted barbed wire fencing that had been sliced here and there. Large metal gates barred what appeared to have been the entrance to the main factory. Foster figured he could continue wandering about like a fart in a mitten, or he could commit to the here and now. Considering, he saw only one move to make.

While Vinson watched, the Mercedes accelerated and plowed through the gates without flinching. "Whoa!" he cheered, surprised by Foster's bold move. "Shit, I wish I had done that!"

Foster stopped in front of the largest building where rusted doors hung askew and another pitted green and white sign identified "Brothers Manufacturing." He counted seven other metal buildings of varying sizes, separated by a central drive about forty feet wide. The array of buildings stretched for one full block. Beyond was a rail spur and three boxcars that could only be approached through a sprawling blacktopped parking lot. Doing some rapid calculations, he estimated that the parking area would once have accommodated several hundred employee vehicles. Brothers must have been a prodigious enterprise in its heyday, he thought, but for now....

Foster crossed the empty lot and tucked his car behind a stand-alone pump house of some sort that was only a few steps from the railroad tracks and ten yards from the closest boxcar. He turned off the engine, satisfied that he was buried deep in the darkness. He couldn't see Vinson approaching, but he could hear debris being crushed by the cab's tires and smell diesel fuel and burned rubber. Vinson was near, but moving away, he thought.

"This is the perfect place to play, Eddie. Come and get me; the final curtain's going up."

Vinson, too, was studying the heart of the abandoned complex. Instinctively he knew this was where it would end, for one or both of them. He saw Foster cut his lights and accelerate into the shadows of the parking lot. The Mercedes evaporated.

Vinson doused his headlights as well; remembering the overhead courtesy light, he smashed it with the butt of his gun. Then he followed to the point where he thought Foster had disappeared. A visual sweep of the shadowed parking lot came up empty. He rolled down his window, but there were only damp night sounds.

Vinson flashed back to the teen-aged gang member he'd hurtled from the roof during the riots. He was surprised to feel a sexual rush, but shook it off. He would recall it later in celebration. He had traversed the parking lot from front to back. He considered a cement block bunker-like building, but judged it too small to hide Foster's car.

Because his window remained down so he could listen, Vinson heard the trill of Foster's cell phone, which appeared to be coming from somewhere in front of him. He stopped and opened the cab door so he could orient toward the sound, but the phone did not ring again. It appeared that he had erred by dismissing the block building. Foster's car might not be there, but Foster was.

Foster knew Vinson had heard his cell phone because the cab stopped within seconds of the single ring tone. How could he have failed to put the damn thing on vibrate? It was a costly mistake.

"John? It's Cook. Where are you?"

"In hell, I think," whispered Foster. "I'm at the back of the abandoned industrial park, south off Fairfield, that's all I know. Vinson shot an old man standing outside the VFW

Hall just before the entrance to the plant. Wrong place, wrong time, that's all it was.

"If you find the VFW, you'll find the factory…eventually."

Just then, Foster saw a familiar flash of light and that damnable cracking sound. He knew Vinson was taking pot shots at him. He felt the Mercedes lurch down and right, and figured Vinson had just taken out his right rear tire.

"John, John!" Cook pleaded. "Answer me! What's going on?"

"Gotta go, Timmy, or he'll have me in his sights," Foster whispered and disconnected. He left the cell phone on the front seat and headed out on foot. Foster reasoned that Vinson must have left the cab and approached from behind the boxcars, the only angle that would have allowed him to see the Mercedes. Foster duck-walked around front of his car, almost landing on his ass in the wet weeds. He regained his footing and moved away from Vinson's line of sight. If Vinson was firing from behind the first freight car….

Foster jogged across the corner of the parking lot, then cut to his left when he came to the second boxcar. The sliding doors to the first and second cars were ajar, two to three feet maybe, no more. The door to the third car was closed, and a padlock glinted ridiculously against the rust.

The freight cars seemed to offer as good a place as any to hole up, and Foster's choices appeared to be Door #1 or Door #2. Within the coal-black interior of the car, with a corner at his back, Foster would face Vinson head on, and what little ambient light there was would silhouette Vinson if he exposed himself. Not much of an advantage, but better than none.

Foster decided on Door #1. The opening was narrower, and he could only enter by turning shoulders and hips sideways to slip through. Thus, the limited access would slow Vinson's entry and put him momentarily at a disadvantage. In addition, Vinson would probably expect him to skirt the first car since he was right outside. What Vinson expected was exactly what he would not do.

Foster crawled, feeling his way into the bowels of the rail car. He tried not to think of the things his fingers had identified, like Braille, on the floor of the boxcar. Fresh cat shit was one; his nose was very definite about that. He wedged his backside into the corner to the right of the door, placed a cocked .45 on his knee, and waited. The only sounds were of his own making, the lub-dub of his heart and his harsh breathing, which he struggled to subdue.

The dank interior of the rail car oozed another pungent odor with which Foster was all too familiar. During one absence from Perdido Key, a broken seal from the toilet in the unit above had allowed water to seep down between walls of their condo and produce a healthy colony of glutinous black mold, the kind that gives one Technicolor nightmares. Suddenly, he found himself hoping that Vinson would not tarry.

Vinson had no idea whether Foster was hiding or prowling, but figured he would be close. He had clearly underestimated the esteemed doctor, and could admit to a growing admiration. No one else had ever come this close.

"Where are you, Doc? Are you hiding? You've got me out in the open. Isn't that where you wanted me?"

Vinson crouched where he could see the back of the listing Mercedes. "Good shot!" He applauded his marksmanship despite the difficult trajectory. Before he could think better of it, he stooped and skittered through the weeds to approach the car from the driver's side. The door was unlatched and partly open. Foster's cell lay on the front seat. Vinson palmed the sleek little phone. It took him a moment, but he finally found and pressed the "Send" button twice to dial the last number called. While the connection was being made, he slipped down against the door. He heard one ring, then the unmistakable bark of his former father-in-law.

"John, man? Where are you? We're coming as fast as we can, good buddy. Just hold on."

Vinson screamed into the phone, "Ahhhhhhh" as loud as his voice would allow.

Aghast, Cook's first thought was that Vinson had taken Foster down. Struggling for control, he responded, "Eddie, I know it's you, pussy, my daughter's killer. Think you can do me as easy? C'mon! I'm waiting, but you won't fight someone who'll fight back, will ya? You're nothing but a chicken-shit coward to kill a defenseless woman. Couldn't shoot yourself out of a paper bag with an M-16 all locked and loaded and handed to you."

Cook's immediate recognition rattled Vinson, and his tirade was all the more powerful for the venom sluicing from every word.

"Cook," Vinson acknowledged.

"I'm here, Eddie," Cook responded just as the cell phone battery indicator blinked. Before Vinson could have his say, the phone went dead.

"You'll get yours, you dried-up old jarhead," Vinson hurled his impotent threat into the night. He dropped to his belly and slithered through the weeds until he was only four feet from the tracks. He crouched and moved to the narrow end of the first freight car before he stood. His back was to the cement-block building, and he was exposed, but he knew Foster wasn't behind him. He wondered, in passing, if Foster might have him in his sights. The prospect was more intriguing than frightening.

Unconsciously, Vinson emptied his mind, closed his eyes, and listened. Every cell was on alert. He raised his head and scented the night air. He smelled mold.

Sorting through the possibilities, Vinson decided that, were he in Foster's shoes, he would burrow into a corner of one of the boxcars and protect himself on three sides. Given that Foster had to know he was firing from behind the first boxcar, he would probably bypass that one rather than risk being heard crawling around inside. On, then, to the second and third cars. "Here I come, ready or not."

Vinson slipped along the track; he noted that the door opening of the second car was wide enough to allow entry. The sliding door of the third car was closed and padlocked. *If that don't beat all!* He stepped between the second and third cars, and looked back down the line. He held his breath, and, again, he waited. Distant headlights on Fairfield and a flickering street light a half block away distracted him. His impulse was to shoot out the friggin street light, but, of course, he could not.

Vinson climbed up and over the massive coupling between the two cars and scanned the area between the rail and the fence. He climbed back down and crouched to look beneath the cars, but could see nothing in the darkness. His only discovery was a pile of shit, human; no, not human, crackhead, lower than animals. He turned away abruptly, and only some fancy footwork saved him from stepping in what had once been someone's dinner. How had he missed that smell?

The hypodermic needle at his feet was the last damn straw. Vinson moved. He approached the open door of the middle rail car, stopped, and listened. Though the second car appeared the more likely as Foster's hideout, the first car remained an alternative. When the lights of a 737 entering the flight path to O'Hare Airport passed directly above the first boxcar, Vinson thought, "Well, why not? It's as good an indicator as anything else I've got."

Again, he approached the first boxcar, but the narrow opening caused him to reconsider whether Foster could have wormed his way inside. He was vacillating, now, uneasy. He couldn't make a decision, and he couldn't afford to make the wrong decision. Vinson stepped to the narrow aperture and looked right, then left. All he could see was pitch black. There was a moldy scent to the place...and something more. Perspiration, he thought, the smell of fear. His hunt was over. Foster was inside.

Foster had neither heard, nor seen, Vinson's approach. Suddenly, muzzle flashes lit up the boxcar like a strobe light on a dance floor as shots bounced from wall to wall and ceiling to floor. Foster caught sight of Vinson's hand firing randomly through the doorway. He was not shooting *at* Foster; he was *just* shooting!

Foster had expected more finesse from Vinson, not this hail-Mary barrage that sent bullets ricocheting through the boxcar like some psychotic pinball game run amok. Crude though it might be, there was no denying it could be just as lethal.

Then, there was nothing.

Foster sat petrified and hyperventilating in his corner; he shook his head to quit the buzzing of an imminent faint. A cursory inventory of random body parts yielded no wounds, mortal or otherwise. He tried to analyze the implications of the oppressive silence in the wake of the metallic din he had just endured. Had Vinson simply emptied his clip, and was he, even now, preparing for a second salvo? Could Foster's luck survive a second salvo?

Foster marshaled his senses and rocked up onto knees that he doubted would support him. Slowly, he willed himself to stand. He wove like a drunken sailor with each step forward, but he remained upright and on course, his back to the wall. When, at last, he reached the door of the freight car, he stole a quick glance outside. What he saw robbed him of all thought.

Eddie Vinson lay spread-eagled not five feet from the rail car. Blood oozed from a gaping neck wound and seeped into dirt and cinders. Foster stepped into the narrow doorway with his .45 still cocked and aimed. Vinson's eyes were wide open, his gaze fixed squarely on Foster.

Foster leaned against the rusted metal door and dropped his head to his forearm, wiping sweat from his eyes and pulling himself together. When he finally pushed against the door of the boxcar, it screeched like a banshee as it yielded another measly foot, although Vinson didn't seem to notice. Foster jumped down; his knees buckled on impact, but he planted his palms in the dirt to keep from pitching forward and landing on his face. Making his movements look deliberate rather than feeble, he rose and kicked Vinson's pistol out of reach. Vinson tracked his every move.

Trusting his legs to support him, Foster squatted next to Vinson. He removed a sweat-soaked handkerchief from his pocket and pressed it against the wound though he knew it was futile. He debated the wisdom of doing so, but allowed his concern to reflect in his eyes. "Are you in pain, Eddie?"

"Naw, no pain, Doc."

"Must be some truth to what they say: 'What goes around, comes around.' Kind of appropriate, isn't it, Eddie?"

Vinson didn't respond, but his frown clearly asked for clarification.

"You know," Foster continued. "You, here, lying next to another rail car…just like the last time you died…by the EL. Must be your destiny."

As Foster watched, Vinson's breathing became shallow and rapid. The blood loss was slowing, but shock was setting in. He was fighting it, but the wildness in his eyes gave him away. He was a paramedic; he knew what came next, and he was scared.

"Why did you do all this, Eddie? To what end?"

"No end…only because I could," Vinson whispered. Then louder and more assertively, "Because I could, Doc."

Foster glanced down Vinson's body. His limbs were lifeless and his bladder had emptied, unmistakable signs that the bullet had damaged the spine. As he had said, he probably didn't feel any pain; the injury was too severe.

Choking, Vinson struggled to ask, "What did you mean, when you said the grass wasn't tall enough?"

Foster figured Vinson was due an explanation. He reached for compassion through the adrenaline-laced fear and anger that had spawned his cruel words about Eddie's destiny. "I profiled you as the consummate hunter, Eddie, like the lion on the African plain, tucked into the dry grasses to wait patiently for unsuspecting prey; then, at your will, to attack without conscience or mercy."

"Me, Doc? A lion?" Vinson smiled, seemingly pleased by Foster's metaphor.

"Yes, Eddie, once I drew that analogy, I had only to flush you out of the tall grass and into the open. I knew you'd follow me, and you did…to a place of my choosing, to a place where you couldn't blend in."

Vinson's eyes drifted shut, but the smile remained on his face.

Foster raised Vinson's arm to place his hand awkwardly over the handkerchief at his neck. He strode quickly to the Mercedes for his cell phone. It was no longer on the front seat. Hurriedly he searched the trampled weeds and brush around the car, and located it by the left rear tire. Foster ran back to Vinson as he dialed 911 to request police and ambulance, but the phone was dead.

When Foster returned to sit by Vinson, his eyes were open, but glazed.

"Great shot, Doc! Didn't know you had it in you."

"It wasn't me, Eddie."

"What do you mean?" Vinson turned his head, and his eyes locked with Foster's.

"It was your own bullet, Eddie. I never fired a shot."

Several moments passed in silence. Foster was reaching to take Vinson's pulse when he was startled by a sudden chuckle.

"My bullet? That's rich, Doc."

Vinson closed his eyes. Then, in a voice growing weak with effort, he said, "You know. I've always blended in, since I was a kid, wherever I went, Doc."

"Would I be right to conclude that you never felt you could be your own person, stand on your own, be seen for who you are, Eddie? Be *valued* for who you are?"

"Right, Doc. I always understood if people could know me as I know myself, they would see the void, the emptiness inside me."

Over the years, Foster had heard similar admissions from severely damaged individuals, and, like now, he was always moved to sorrow for the needless waste of so much potential.

Vinson's eyes opened once more and he stared up at the empty boxcar. Foster followed his gaze and wondered if Vinson saw more than the blackness of the car's interior, a space devoid of light, as most of his life had been.

Foster remained silent, sensing that Eddie had more to say.

"What do you think is inside me, Doc? You know, now, at the very end?"

"I know you probably think there's nothing, Eddie, but it's not that you're empty or devoid of goodness. It's simply that whatever goodness you had at one time was lost to you with each malevolent act, with each of the lives you dispatched. Your first murder was...?"

"I was twelve, Doc. I killed a man when I was...I was just a stupid kid...."

"It was spiritual suicide for you, Eddie, that first murder. Whatever inherent goodness was in you became irretrievable. You closed the circle of abuse begun by the adults in your life. It was your choice to close the circle...and to step inside. You isolated yourself, condemned yourself to a lonely life of blending in so that no one would, or could, come to know you.

"If we had had more time together, I would have tried to help you understand that the young Eddie, the innocent child, had three choices: to find the way to live a productive life in society with family and friends of your choosing, to be a survivor; or to remain a victim, passive and at the mercy of each new abuser who entered your life; or, lastly, to become a perpetrator who reenacted the abuse time and again as the aggressor, which you have done, and at a very high level of proficiency.

"What you never realized was that each time you embraced the role of perpetrator, you committed an act of violence against yourself, and with each act, the goodness you once possessed moved further beyond your grasp until you no longer recognized it. You have lived the cycle of violence, Eddie, but, for you, it ends here, tonight."

"That's good, Doc. I really like that. It's too bad, though."

"What, Eddie? What's too bad?"

"Me, Doc. Me." Vinson's eyes closed.

Foster hesitated, then reached out and grasped Vinson's hand. "Yes, Eddie, it is too bad." He watched Eddie's breathing slow to a few breaths each minute. Then, with one last, deep breath, he was gone. It had taken almost twenty minutes for Eddie Vinson to die. Foster wondered what he had seen in his last moments. A hint of a smile remained, and an arrogant jut of the chin that did not match the bewilderment in Eddie's eyes.

Foster could hear the approaching sirens of emergency personnel. When he raised his gaze from the body of Eddie Vinson, he saw Cook and Doonan standing a respectful distance away. Their eyes told him clearly that they, too, had witnessed Eddie's passing.

When the first police car pulled to the edge of the parking lot, Cook and Doonan stepped forward to help Foster to his feet. Neither man acknowledged the tears in his eyes.

"Lieutenant Branan? Tim Cook here. Vinson died a few minutes ago. Uniforms and medics are arriving now. John was with him when he died. Doonan and I were here, too. From what we heard of their conversation, it appears the bullet that killed Vinson was a ricochet from his own gun. John turned over his weapon, and your officer confirms that it has not been fired.

"There were three other victims tonight, Sir. An elderly man was shot by Vinson as he stood outside the VFW Hall on...I don't know what street. I'm starting to unravel. The others were a bellboy at the Marriott and the driver of the cab that picked Vinson up at the hotel.

"Want to know what's ironic, Lieutenant? The ambulance dispatched to the scene? It's a First Alert team. They'll be taking all four victims to Cook County before this night is over, and this time, Vinson will stay dead.

"Oh, John asked me to tell you we'll all come to you in the morning for a full debriefing...any time you say. Are you up to it?"

Branan rumbled, "I'll meet you at the precinct, 11:00 a.m., even if I have to beg my wife."

EPILOGUE

Four bodies were delivered after midnight to Cook County Morgue. Clothes were removed; each corpse was transferred to a stainless steel table and covered hastily with a crisp white sheet. The coroner, all but dead on his splayed and swollen feet, had performed eight autopsies during a seventeen-hour day. One by one, he flipped down the sheets to peruse the faces belonging to the names that would be on tomorrow's schedule. Three of the victims were unknown to him. The fourth victim, he most definitely recognized; it was the bastard who had stolen his key. He flipped the sheet back over Vinson, but failed to cover him completely, leaving the eyes and forehead exposed. He left the body as it was. It would still be there in the morning.

By dawn, rigor mortis had set in. As is sometimes the case during rigor, Vinson's right arm had risen by increments, gradually pulling the sheet up to conceal his face. There in the dark cold and darker silence, he did what Eddie Vinson had always done, he hid in plain sight.

THE END